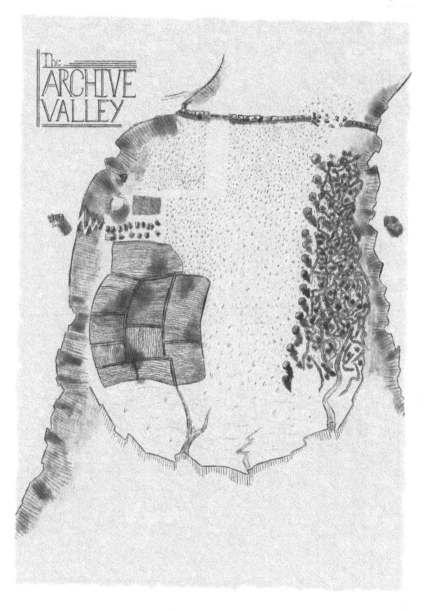

The ARCHIVE VALLEY

THE ARCHIVE

First edition. December 4, 2020.

Written by Dan Fitzgerald.

Chapter:
One

Carl watched Dunil run his pupils through their paces in Islish. Some of them were older than Dunil, but there was no doubt who was in charge.

"*Repeat: One, two, three, four, five...No, five, fiiive, not fa-eve, six, seven, eight, nine, yes niiine, ten...*"

Karul and the council had decided that all Maer children would learn Islish, and the adults were encouraged to as well, though that was more complicated. The children were making great progress under Dunil's tutelage, and occasionally one of the bolder ones would try to engage with Carl in a 'Hello, how are you?' dialogue. He was not great with kids, but he respected the courage it must have taken for them to try, so he gave them what little time he could spare.

"He seems to be a born teacher," Fabaris said, sidling up next to Carl. "How is his Islish?"

"Amazing," Carl said. "Better than my Maer, for sure."

"You speak Maer better than any human I've ever met," Fabaris said with a smile.

"*And how is your Islish coming?*" Carl asked.

"*I am not speak of this.*" Fabaris chuckled, then switched back to Maer. "Perhaps I just need a little private tutoring from Ujenn."

"We have an expression in Islish: Need is the mother of...how do I say it?"

"Invention," Fabaris said, nodding. "Necessity is the mother of invention. We have this expression as well."

"It makes you wonder if the two languages came from the same source," Carl mused.

"I am certain of it," Fabaris agreed, "as I am certain that our people are one and the same, if you go far enough back in history."

"And with any luck, if you go far enough into the future it will be true again." Carl thought of his nights with Ujenn, and his awkward couplings with Grisol under Ujenn's guidance. She had not recently spoken of the need for another ritual, but he could tell it was on her mind. He was working hard to keep it out of his.

"Gods willing," Fabaris said. "I look forward to Finn and Sinnie's return, for we surely need more Islish speakers around." He paused, twirling one of the little braids on his chin, his eyes thoughtful. "You know, it is said there was a full set of Maer-Islish word scrolls in the Archive."

Carl's ears perked up. He had heard Fabaris mention the Archive before, with a kind of scholarly reverence. "Do you think it still exists?"

Fabaris shook his head, widening his eyes. "No one knows for sure," he said, "but I believe it is still intact. It was designed to withstand millennia. As you know, the Maer are a very far-thinking people."

"That you are," Carl agreed, and the two of them stood quietly, half-watching Dunil's lesson. Carl appreciated the thoughtful, deliberative way the Maer managed their resources and planned for the future, and the decision to teach Islish was just another part of that. Castle Maer was more a place of living and growing than a military stronghold. To be sure, they took their defense seriously, but they valued the raising of children and the nurturing of their culture even more. Carl wished the Realm took such an approach.

"So if the Archive is still intact, where could it be?" Carl turned to Fabaris, who screwed up his face and shrugged.

"Like I said, no one knows for sure, but it is bound to be in the mountains somewhere, toward the south, perhaps near the Great Tooth, since according to Maer legend that is where we came from. It would be a fitting place to house the Archive." He paused, toying with his braids again. "There are surely those who know more than I, but..." He shook his head, his eyes distant. "Much was lost after the Great Betrayal," he said, "and not all of it can be regained."

Carl nodded thoughtfully, trying not to feel personally attacked by the term. The Maer occasionally made reference to it, and he had mostly puzzled it out. After the Great Treaty between the humans and the Maer, the humans had supposedly conducted a series of midnight raids to decimate the Maer's defenses, then scattered them across the Silver Hills, pushing them to the brink of extinction. Carl imagined them gravitating toward the Great Tooth, the tallest mountain on the continent, which he had seen on an old map Elder Gummache showed the children during their studies back in Brocland.

The map showed the Isle and the northern half of the continent in great detail: cities, towns, rivers, lakes, mountains, and roads, all drawn and labeled with care. But the Silver Hills, beyond the ones visible from the north, were represented as a series of more or less equal and nameless carets, with one exception: the Great Tooth, which was five times their size, located near the southern end of the Silver Hills, at the center of the continent. The mapmaker had drawn a great dragon curled around the base of the mountain, smoke oozing from its nostrils. In their childhood games, the village children had plotted explorations to the Great Tooth, and whoever could defeat the dragon would find a hoard of treasure so vast it would take a lifetime just to transport it.

"*Do you like mushrooms, Kyol?*" Dunil was asking a boy in the class.

"*Yes, I love mushrooms!*" Kyol answered with gusto. "*And you, Dunil? Do you like mushrooms?*"

"*Oh yes,*" Dunil said, rubbing his stomach. "*Mushrooms are my favorite foods.*"

"*Food,*" Carl said to himself, smiling.

"What was that?" Fabaris asked.

"Nothing," Carl said. "Dunil made a little mistake, but it doesn't matter. He's really doing a great job."

"He relishes the authority," Fabaris commented. "I think it helps him cope with..." He eyed Carl almost apologetically.

"His father." Carl touched Fabaris on the shoulder. "Sometimes I forget." Though it was Sinnie's arrow that had felled Roubay, it could just as easily have been Carl who killed him. Everything had happened so fast, and the six Maer they had slain after being ambushed had seemed like monsters at the time. No one in the castle ever mentioned what had happened on Hollow Road, not even Ujenn. Ever since the Parzek had cleared Carl and his friends, the subject seemed to have become taboo, and as a result, Carl sometimes went an entire day or more without thinking about it. But he was living and working every day alongside friends and family members of those he and Sinnie had killed, and he was sure that in the eyes of some he was a murderer.

"*Hello Carl!*" Dunil called from inside the room. "*Come to speak in the class!*"

"Well, I'll leave you to it." Fabaris touched Carl lightly on the back. "I have some research to do. I'll see you at dinner."

"Indeed," Carl said, then walked into the little room and switched to Islish. "*Okay, Dunil, but just for a moment. What are we learning about today?*"

"*Mushrooms!*" called one of the girls, no more than five years old. "*Carl, do you like mushrooms?*"

Chapter:
Two

F abaris listened outside the classroom for a minute as Carl engaged with the children in Islish. He only understood a few words, which as a scholar was embarrassing, but he would find time, he assured himself. If only he could get his hands on some written texts, he was sure he could make more progress. When Carl had shown up with his wagonload of goods for the castle, Fabaris had been crestfallen to see there were no written documents among the supplies, but Carl had brought him a blank ledger, which Fabaris treasured so much he had not allowed himself to write a single word in it. He had decided to use the ledger to keep a record of their modern occupation of Castle Maer, but had not yet begun. He needed to be unshakably certain this was the best use he could make of it, since there was no telling if he would ever be able to get another. Rarely in his life had he come across paper, and then only scraps, maps, and scrolls, yellowed with age. Now that he had an actual book full of blank paper, ninety-six pages of pure untapped potential, he was terrified of wasting one line.

Fabaris skirted the edge of the bailey and made for the roost, the crumbled remains of a watchtower where they kept their pigeons. It was one of the few places in the castle where he could be truly alone, as no one other than himself and Jundum ever went there. The pigeons cooed in their wooden cage as he made his way up the uneven stone steps, and he retrieved a few seeds from his pocket and tossed them into the cage. The birds fell upon the seeds in a flurry of wings and beaks, then strutted around, looking for any stray seeds that might have fallen in the corners of the cage. Stromus, the undisputed cock of the roost, poked his orange beak out of the cage, and Fabaris tweaked it playfully with his fingers, then stroked Stromus' black head. Some of the other pigeons cozied up, hoping for a few more seeds, but Fabaris had to disappoint them. He stepped past the cage, leaned against the spot between the two remaining battlements, and looked down onto the valley below.

He casually scanned the edge of the forest that lined the river, which they had named the Free River, despite Fabaris' objections. He felt strongly that natural features should be named for their location or physical nature, but Karul had sipped of the Great Council's sickly-sweet verbiage and wanted to make his mark in their world. Only time would tell if his gesture would yield any returns, but it irritated Fabaris every time he looked at the river or the woods it ran through. He shook his head and focused, watching the forest edge for any signs of movement. Carl had said he didn't think there was any imminent danger of an attack by the Realm, but the patrols had found tracks in the forest, and they had spotted two humans from a distance. One was a robed figure carrying a staff, the other an armored man with a sword and a bow, and they surely weren't out to visit their sick grandmother.

Fabaris saw nothing of note, and his mind soon wandered. His talk with Carl had brought the Archive creeping back into his thoughts. He had pictured it in his mind a thousand times, a huge vault full of marble shelves lined with rows upon rows of books, scrolls, and maps, but more precious still, untold numbers of original bronze cylinders, ready to reproduce the sum of all knowledge of the ancient Maer civilization on command. Only a few of the cylinders were still in circulation, and the rest were presumed buried in the

Archive. Karul had been granted three map cylinders by the Great Council, one for each of the territories along what the humans called Hollow Road and the Snake River. Now that was a name for a river, he thought; it could be the serpentine track of the river, or the creatures that lived along it, or both. It satisfied reason while leaving room for the imagination. But no matter the name, it belonged to the Maer, as the cylinder maps attested, and Karul was free to do with the cylinders, and the maps they produced, as he saw fit.

Fabaris struggled to imagine the difficult decisions made by the Maer leaders of old, as they saw their empire, even their very existence, hurtling toward the void. Which cylinders to keep, which to lock away forever, and how far to throw away the key. Or hide it in such a way no one could find it. No *one*, he mused. No *one* Maer could be trusted with the key to their entire civilization, but neither would they let the knowledge become lost forever. Or so he hoped.

But it wasn't just the wonder of the Archive's contents that kept it constantly in the back of Fabaris' mind. The Archive, if it still existed, would give concrete benefits. It would contain documents vital for the Maer's claim of dominion over many territories now controlled by humans. It might even contain proof of the Great Treaty which, according to Maer lore, the humans signed, then reneged on, attacking the Maer at their most vulnerable after promising peace. They had broken the bulk of the Maer army and spent the next decade hunting down any remaining pockets they could find in the mountains. The few Maer who survived the purge had fled farther away from human civilization, scratching out a bitter existence in the rocky heights of the Silver Hills, biding their time until they could once again lay claim to their rightful territory.

Whether or not the legends were true, the time was nowhere near right for any kind of drastic action. The Maer were on a century clock, hoping to rebuild slowly, far from the reach of the Realm's military, until their numbers were sufficient to make their move. Except that Roubay and his band had screwed it all up, awakening the *Kalar* and trying to claim Brocland when they had no means to hold it, and bringing scrutiny to the Maer in the process. Fabaris doubted the Maer's apology to the citizens of Brocland and their promise of compensation held much weight, but it could open the door for diplomacy, and with Carl in their camp, they might just stand a chance.

Fabaris turned to look behind him, across the mountains to the southeast, where the Great Tooth pierced the clouds somewhere far beyond the reach of his eyes. He imagined himself flying like an eagle, soaring between icy mountaintops and over misty valleys toward the Tooth's towering white peak, then gliding down the side of the mountain, through the clouds and into a wooden glen, to a door cleverly hidden in the side of a boulder or in a crevice at the base of a cliff. At the touch of his beak, the door would slide open, and the wonders of the ancient world would be spread out before him, treatises on law, science, history, and religion alongside untold reams of poems, longstories, and songs. The few songs he knew from that era were of such richness and beauty that they had clearly come from a culture overflowing with music, only a tiny fraction of which had survived in the minds and on the tongues of those privy to such learning.

He turned to look back down over the forest, and found himself humming bits of the Skin Man, the ancient tale of the Maer queen who took a human lover, resulting in great tragedy for all. He had not sung the song for the residents of Castle Maer, for obvious reasons, but its melody haunted him in spare moments, and he sang it low in his throat, his memory unleashing the music with such force it was hard to keep from singing it at the top of his lungs. As he built up to the chorus, he heard another voice humming in tune, and he could not have been more surprised when he turned and saw Karul sticking his fingers in the pigeon cage, humming along to this ancient, little-known song.

When they had finished humming the chorus, Fabaris stopped and smiled at Karul, whose lips turned up ever so slightly in return. "Where did a warrior learn such an obscure song?"

Karul stood and walked to the battlements next to Fabaris, looking out over the forest below. "I sought the path of scholarship at the time of my Choosing," Karul said, "but I was not among the wisest, and given my size, the elders saw fit to put me in a warrior slot." He turned to Fabaris, squinting into the setting sun. "It was probably for the best. Reading was always hard for me, though I got better as I worked on it. My voice was an awkward low baritone, but not deep enough for bass, and I fought much better than I sang. And more often." He gave a snort, picking a bit of pebble from the wall and tossing it over the edge.

"If I had known you could sing, I would have called on you to join me in Nightsong from time to time."

"Precisely why I never let on." Karul pulled out the hollow sunflower stalk he used for scanning the forest edge.

"According to Carl, the humans have such devices with crystals in them that somehow make everything look ten times bigger," Fabaris noted.

"Maybe if we catch those spies they will have such a device," Karul said. "For now, this helps me focus on one bit of terrain at a time, so it's better than nothing." Fabaris had noticed Karul's distance vision was not the best.

"Didn't Carl advise against engaging with the spies directly?" Fabaris tried to give Karul a stern look but could not catch his eye.

"He did. And he might be right. But if we catch them, think of what we might learn." Karul lowered the stalk and turned back to Fabaris. "I have no intention of harming them unless absolutely necessary, but they cannot be allowed to spy on us with impunity. This territory," he said, waving his arm toward the forest below, "is not under Realm jurisdiction. It belongs to us."

"They may not see it that way," Fabaris cautioned. Karul was a shrewd leader, but he was stubborn, and left to his own devices he might push things too far.

"They may see it as they please," Karul replied. "For my part, I intend to capture their spies, treat them with the utmost consideration, and send them back with a message." He stood up, indicated Castle Maer, the mountains behind it, and the valley below. "If what Carl says is true, by their own law they control only territories north of what they call Hawthorne Mountain. Anything south of that is not their concern."

Fabaris twirled his braids between his fingers. "I was speaking with Carl earlier about the Archive, and it got me thinking—"

"You told Carl about the Archive?" Karul spat. "You are a trusting fool."

"Carl is on our side. He would never—"

"You have no idea what he would never do. For all we know, he could be a spy, and this whole thing could be a setup."

"Ujenn would have sniffed that out a thousand times over," Fabaris said. "But that's not my point. They say the Archive holds the original cylinder of the Great Treaty. If we could find it, imagine—"

"Yes, imagine how the humans could find a way to betray us again. The Archive is a pipe dream, Fabaris. I'm not convinced it even still exists."

"And I'm not convinced it doesn't," Fabaris replied. "I don't yet have the status to be given such knowledge, but I believe there are those who know. And perhaps, given our relative success thus far, there might be someone willing to share this knowledge. I was thinking of sending a pigeon, with an encoded message, to see if I can get any traction." Karul scratched his ear thoughtfully, and Fabaris added, "With your permission, of course."

"This should be discussed in council," Karul replied. "I'd like to hear Ujenn and Luez's take. In the meantime, I have some spies to catch."

"Do tread lightly," Fabaris urged. "If they feel we are a threat, they will take what steps they deem necessary," Fabaris said.

"And if they see us as weak, they will take those steps sooner," Karul answered, lifting the stalk to his eye and turning back to his search. "You probably won't have to worry anyway," he said. "It seems they have a mage with them. I doubt we'll be able to catch them. But it doesn't mean we aren't going to try."

Chapter:
Three

Karul sat on the edge of his bed and tightened his sandals, wishing he had boots like the ones Carl wore. The forest was filled with sharp and prickly things, and though he would never let on to anyone, his feet were very sensitive. He picked up his spear, fingering the ancient bronze tip, which was still frighteningly sharp, though he hadn't attended to it in a while. Carl had brought them a few steel swords, and Ivlana, Melka's replacement, had abandoned her spear for the shiny metal. He could see the look in her eyes when she handled the blade, but he preferred the reach and penetrating power of the spear. Plus, the weapon had been a gift from the High Council, one of the few ancient weapons still in service, and he carried it with pride.

"I signaled the patrol at dawn using the new code, as you asked," Ivlana said, peering around the door frame. "They will be expecting us."

"I'm almost ready. Where's Grisol?"

"She went to check in with Dunil." Ivlana paused, a hint of judgment in her voice. She had little patience for children getting in the way of security operations. "She'll meet us at the gate. The others are already there." She lingered in the doorway, and Karul nodded, waving her away.

He cast a wistful glance at his bed, feeling ashamed that he would be missing it as he slept in the forest. Command had made him weak, too dependent on his creature comforts. He needed to get free from the castle walls, out into the world, lest he lose a step. Patrolling the forest for invisible spies was not going to scratch the itch he was feeling deep down, but it was a start. He took a pull from his bottle of mushroom wine, savored its bitter, earthy bite for a moment, then stalked out to meet the patrol by the gate.

Ivlana stood talking to Grisol, who wore her new bow over her shoulder like she'd been doing it all her life. She'd trained with Sinnie, and they seemed to have taken a shine to each other. Maybe she had a knack for it, or maybe Sinnie was a great teacher, but Grisol had quickly become their best archer by far. Karul had granted her one of the two bows Carl had brought back, which were sleek and stout, easily twice as powerful as the Maer's bows. She had asked for a spot on patrol, and it had been an easy decision for Karul, who could see what Sinnie saw in her, and much more. He had always been jealous of Roubay, and now that he was gone and the mourning period over, Karul had hoped maybe something might happen between him and Grisol. Though he knew of her arrangement with Ujenn and Carl, as far as he knew it wasn't anything romantic, and it wouldn't last forever. He wasn't sure if she had any interest in him, but he didn't hate the idea of spending a whole day in her presence.

Goi, the boy with the fastest feet in the castle, and Dren, a quiet, unflappable warrior, rounded out the patrol. They normally went out in groups of four, but when Karul told Ivlana he was going out, she had insisted on accompanying him, and he could not well refuse. Her slumping posture and round belly belied her explosive strength and quickness, and there were few in the castle who could best her in a fight, fewer still with more common sense. He missed Melka, but he had to admit, Ivlana was an improvement.

They met the returning patrol just inside the woods a half-mile upstream from the castle trail, which they traveled less frequently now that human spies had been seen. They used an irregular rotation of meetup spots, communicated by the hooded lantern Carl had brought them. Communication only worked one way, from the Castle to the patrol, but it made it easier to be unpredictable, which was the goal. Being unpredictable meant keeping the spies on their toes and on the move, thus increasing their chances of being seen. Meanwhile, the Maer had been hunting for traces of the spies' camp, as well as monitoring likely water access points.

"What news?" Karul asked Goreg, the returning patrol leader.

"We found traces of a fire behind a rock that would have shielded it from castle view," Goreg replied, adjusting the heavy load of wood strapped to his back. "Just past the second bend, on the west side of the river. We left the spot undisturbed."

Karul nodded. "Good. We will investigate, and await the signal at dawn tomorrow."

"Sir," said Goreg, nodding with his arms stiff at his sides, then gesturing to his patrol to follow him through the forest toward the castle path.

?

Karul led his patrol across the skinny rapids, which were tame enough, as it hadn't rained in a week. They worked their way along the game trail on the other side, Karul leading the group, scanning the ground in vain for boot prints. When they passed the second bend, Karul brought Grisol with him and motioned the others to stay back. Ivlana stood anxiously squeezing her sword handle over and over, while Dren remained impassive, his spear lowered, his shoulders relaxed. Goi slunk near the back of the group, looking nervously at the trees around him. Grisol followed Karul past the open patch of riverbank to the rock-studded forest beyond, where they quickly found the rock with burn marks Goreg had mentioned, set in a space between trees just big enough for two to make a rough camp. Grisol motioned with her eyes, but Karul shook his head.

"We will keep our distance. If they return, we will be waiting for them. If we get too close, they will see our footprints and we lose the element of surprise."

Grisol smiled and nodded without a word, which Karul appreciated. He wasn't sure what had lit the fire in her to join in the castle defense, but she was a natural. They returned to the group, and Karul laid out the situation, clearing a swath of pine needles and drawing a map in the dirt beneath. They had some water and a bite of jerky and took up their positions, hoping to catch the spies as they returned at dusk. Grisol was posted with her bow on the other side of the narrow river, along with Goi, who was too young to be much of a fighter, but if things went south, his swift feet would carry news to the castle. Karul and Ivlana hid behind two entwined trees near the clearing. They were just out of sight of the game trail leading along the river, where the humans were almost sure to travel, though from which direction there was no way to guess. Dren set up on the other side of the encampment, crouching under a holly bush that looked plenty prickly, but Dren was too stoic to complain.

When at last they heard light footsteps coming from the game trail downstream, everyone made eye contact for a moment, then faded back into their surroundings. There wasn't much daylight left, and Karul hoped the humans would light a fire, to make them better targets. He also hoped they would hurry up, as he had a sudden, distracting urge to pee, which he suppressed at some cost to his attention. The two humans spoke in low tones as they approached, slowing as they neared their camp and scanning the darkening forest in all directions. If they saw any of the Maer they did not let on, and when they arrived at the clearing, they lay down their packs and sat on a log, still talking too low for Karul to hear, not that he would have understood much with his rudimentary Islish.

One of them had a sword and bow and wore some kind of armor, and he lay his bow down to spark a fire into life with remarkable speed. He must have been using some kind of pre-made firestarter, like the sawdust and tallow cubes Karul and his tribe had been given when they first set out for Castle Maer. The other wore a robe and carried a staff as his only weapon, no doubt a mage, as the first report had suggested. Ujenn had warned Karul they needed to put an arrow in him or a body on him from the very beginning or they would lose the fight in an instant, and he had instructed Ivlana and Grisol to go for the mage first, while he and Dren would double up on the fighter. The plan was to force surrender or at worst subdue them, but Karul had given strict orders not to kill the spies, with menacing but unspecified consequences for anyone who did so, even by accident.

Karul waited until the fire grew steady. The humans had wisely kept it small and shielded by the rock, so it would not be visible very far across the river, and certainly not from the castle. The two seemed to relax a bit by the fire, though not as much as Karul had hoped; they clearly knew what they were doing, and they would not be caught completely unaware. When at last the robed one laid down on a fur and pulled a blanket over himself, the warrior stood up and scanned the forest all around, sword in hand. After an hour, the man showed no signs of relaxing his guard, and Karul's bladder wasn't getting any emptier. He decided it was as good a time as any, so he caught Dren's eye, nodded to Ivlana, and moved at a fast walk to the edge of the firelight, at which point Dren emerged. The human barked at his companion, scurrying back to shake him awake as Karul and Ivlana advanced from one side and Dren from the other. Grisol surely had her bow drawn and an arrow pointed at the mage.

"Surrender, and we will not harm you," Karul shouted, hoping his Islish was good enough to be understood. The mage struggled to his feet, helped by the warrior, and they whispered to each other.

"Surrender now!" Karul yelled as he and Ivlana moved to within ten feet. The warrior held up his left hand as he crouched to place his sword on the ground, and at just that moment the mage stood up tall, raised his staff, and said a word, the end of which was swallowed by a thunderous boom, and an invisible force blew Karul and his companions off their feet. Karul lay on the ground, his head spinning in a silent whirlwind of throbbing pain. Ivlana lay next to him, clutching her head as she curled into a ball. Karul fought through the pain to raise his head enough to see Dren in a similar position, and the humans fleeing along the game trail downstream, the mage limping and leaning on the warrior for support.

"Grisol!" he tried to shout, but the effort stuck in his throat as his stomach bucked and released its contents onto the ground beside him. He scooted away from the puddle, the pain throbbing less intensely. Sounds began to filter in, as if heard from a long way away. His name, perhaps, and splashing, then footsteps. Grisol's face appeared, hovering above his, her brow wrinkled in concern. Karul sat up, shaking his head and fighting off another round of nausea. He took the hand she offered and tried to stand, but had to drop back down before he got halfway up. He sat until the vertigo slowly waned and he was finally able to push himself up on his own. Ivlana and Dren were making their way back to standing as well, with pained expressions on their faces. Dren had a thick gob of blood streaked from his nose to his mouth, which he wiped with the back of his hand.

"Fucking mages," Karul said. "You can't give them an inch."

"I gave him a couple inches of arrow to remember us by," said Grisol, grinning. "In the leg, just like you said."

"Good," Karul said, stepping to Grisol and putting a hand on her shoulder. "Good!" She beamed up at him with a glint of pride in her eye that reminded him a bit of Roubay when he was hot on the trail of a kill.

"They won't be back any time soon," Ivlana said. "But when they do return, I bet it won't just be the two of them."

"Let them come," Karul said. "We sent our message, and we didn't kill anyone. I don't think they'll send an army. They'll send a messenger, maybe a diplomat, if we're lucky."

"And if we're not lucky?" Grisol asked.

"Then we'll find out how good a job we did fortifying the old castle," Karul replied, a smile creeping onto his lips, despite the lingering headache. It was good to be back in action again.

Chapter:
Four

Grisol dropped her load of wood, which she'd made sure was as big as Karul's, onto the pile. She had to prove her toughness to show Karul she belonged on patrol, but the searing pain in her back told her she would pay for it later. She wasn't weak, but she was no Ivlana, not that she aspired to be. She would much rather have been like Sinnie, strong all over without looking like a brute. One way or another, she needed to work on her strength, and carrying the extra wood had seemed like a simple way to start. She only hoped it didn't make the evening's ritual any more difficult than usual. Carl was gentle and respectful, and she had even grown to like him, but it took a lot out of her, more mentally than physically. She had agreed to be Carl and Ujenn's surrogate, and she did enjoy the part of the ritual after Carl left, but the whole thing left her feeling out of sorts. Karul's obvious crush on her was an added annoyance, but she had no mental energy left to worry about that, with everything else going on.

She had to push it all down when she saw Dunil, who was bubbling with energy and questions as usual.

"Did you shoot the mage? I heard you shot the mage!" Dunil said.

"Yes," she replied in Maer, "and I'm sorry I'm too tired to speak Islish right now."

"That's exactly when you need to try harder!" Dunil's voice rose with joy at the end of the sentence.

"Tomorrow," she promised. "We will have breakfast and we will speak Islish. Or you will, at any rate. I'm not sure what I speak counts."

"Nonsense, Mao-tay!" Dunil said. "Your Islish is very good. Better than Karul's anyway. But what about the mage? Tell me about how you shot the mage!"

Grisol closed her eyes and forced a smile. She was desperate for a hot trickle-bath, and she had earned one after patrol. She opened her eyes again, summoning all her energy to bring her face and her voice to life.

"Karul, Ivlana, and Dren had the human spies surrounded in their little camp by the river. I was on the other side of the river with Goi, my bow at the ready. Karul shouted '*Surrender!*' in Islish, though his accent is so bad they might not have understood him." Dunil giggled, and she chucked him under the chin. "Just as the warrior went to set down his sword, the mage sprang up, barked a word, and Boom! This invisible wave of energy flattened Karul and the others, but Goi and I didn't get it as bad, since we were farther away. The two humans grabbed their belongings and were about to flee when I got off a shot and hit the mage in the leg, just like Karul told me to. We were under strict orders not to kill them, and you would be wise to remember that as well: never kill a human, unless to save your own life or that of another."

"Mao-tay! I would never! Can't you see I'm not a warrior like Dad was, or like Carl. When my Choosing comes, I want to be a scholar like Fabaris, or like Elder Gummache, with a long, flowing beard, which I would stroke and stroke as I thought deep thoughts."

"Gummache is a good sort," Grisol agreed. If it weren't for the human priest, who had stood up for them against the aggrieved villagers, they might never have made it back to Castle Maer. "He is careful, and fair. Fabaris too. If you promise to be careful and fair, just like them, I will support you. You could be our foremost linguist. Of course, you'd have to learn Southish too, at the very least."

"Oh I'm working on it," Dunil said. "I got Finn to teach me a little before he left, and Carl knows a bit, and I bug Luez once in a while, but she always looks like she's thinking about how she would kill me, even as she's wishing me a good day in Southish."

"She never kills children," Grisol assured him. "After all, she was the one who decided to spare Spore."

"Oh, can I see him? Can I please? I won't get too close, I promise, I—"

"That's a firm *no*," she said, pulling him in by the back of the neck. "Not until Ujenn says it's safe. Only trained adults get to interact with Spore. And even for them, it's dangerous. Remember what happened to Tuomo? He's lucky he can still walk."

"Okay. I can wait. Besides, the longer I wait, the bigger he'll be, and that will be so amazing!" His smile faded and his face grew thoughtful, and he took hold of her arms, which were still locked around his neck. "I have to go get ready for class," he said, giving her a hug and a kiss. "You stink Mao-tay. Don't you get a trickle-bath after patrol?"

?

The water that trickled down from the crevice was scalding hot, so she could only stand under it for a few seconds at a time, but she let it burn the dirt and sweat off her body, then rubbed a few drops of herbal oil on her privates, chest, and armpits. She felt the need to be clean and fresh before the ritual, though it was afterward that she most longed for a trickle-bath. She wrung out her hair, retied it, and got dressed, hating the fact that she had to put stinking, dirty clothes on her clean body. She made her way down the tunnel toward the forge, carrying her sandals while her feet dried, watching her step by the dim light of the candle. The floor was littered with tiny stones, which stuck to the soles of her feet and had to be removed every few steps.

The forge room was hot and smoky, and the fire from the forge cast a dim orange light on the chamber walls. Tuomo was pouring what looked like liquid fire into a mold, and Spore crouched on the floor next to him, watching the proceedings intently. Spore had grown since the last time she had seen him, and was now wider than Tuomo, and probably at least as tall if he stood up straight, which he never did.

"There we go, there we go...Gods be cursed and damned for all eternity!" Tuomo shouted as the mold cracked and the metal oozed out in a blob, slowly dimming as he struggled to coax it back into the little cup with a stone spoon. "Come on, you *mashtorul* bastard, get that reed and hurry back over to the forge. The reed, the reed!"

Spore picked up a thick, hollow reed, which had a clay piece attached to one end, and followed Tuomo back to the forge, sticking the reed end in its mouth and the clay end in the hole in the side of the forge.

"Blow, damn you! Blow! That's it, that's it. Good Spore, good Spore." Tuomo set the cup down in the indentation in the top of the forge, stirring it with the skinny end of the spoon until it began glowing again. He stood up, stretched backward, then straightened when he saw Grisol.

"Down for your trickle bath?" Tuomo wiped his hands on his apron and ran them through his hair.

"I needed it after patrol. How are the spearheads coming?"

"Terribly. The molds break half the time, since we don't have the right kind of clay, so I spend most of my time dealing with that, when I'm not smelting, which is a whole other issue. This—" he gestured toward a tattered book propped on a pile of rubble, "is written in Southish, which I can hardly read, and the artist was not the most accurate. I'm bumbling my way through. No, Spore, no, back!"

Grisol put out her hands to stop Spore from jumping up on her, and he nuzzled her hands, legs, and privates, almost knocking her over, before bounding back to pick up the reed and fit it in his mouth again. He blew air into Tuomo's face, tilting his head back in what looked like silent laughter as Tuomo slapped him on the head with his glove.

"Blow, accursed beast! Blow!" Spore put the tube back and began blowing.

"I heard you shot their mage," Tuomo said, his face lighting up. Grisol knew he had a thing for her, but she had resolved to ignore it.

"It's true," Grisol said. "Thankfully I was far enough away I didn't get knocked out by his spell. The humans have powerful magics." She paused, staring at the glowing liquid in the cup. "How do you know when it's ready?"

"I just swirl it around a little and see if it's the right texture. Like this." He dipped the end of the stone spoon in and moved it in a gentle circle. "It's just about ready. Want to try?" He stepped to the side, and Grisol moved beside him and gently took hold of the spoon, which was hot to the touch. "Nice and slow," Tuomo said. The heat radiating up from the cup was so intense it singed the hairs on her hand, but she gritted her teeth and gave the liquid a slow stir, then slid her fingers to the side so he could take the spoon back.

"All right, now stand back," he said, putting his glove back on. He picked up the cup by its handle and moved it in slow motion back to the slab where his molds were set up. He squinted as he poured the molten metal into the clay mold, which was sunk into a bowl of sand. He poured in a few drops at first, then the rest, setting the cup down and tossing the glove to the side. The mold hissed but did not crack, and he beamed at Grisol.

"That's my second one today. Not a bad day's work, I have to say."

"And how about the arrowheads?" she asked. They had a hundred steel-pointed arrows Carl had brought back, but Karul insisted on equipping his warriors with Maer-forged weapons to the extent possible.

"I can do a dozen or so a day, if I focus on it," Tuomo said, "but Karul wants the spearheads first, so—" he gestured toward the mold. "Let's see how we did." He brushed the sand aside and gently tapped with the spoon on the clay mold, which crumbled off quite easily. He picked up the spearhead with his glove and dunked it in a bowl of water, which hissed and steamed for a moment. He pulled it out and held it up like a mother holding a newborn. Like most mothers, he seemed oblivious to how ugly his baby was. Though it did have the general shape of a spearhead, its edges were uneven and it bent slightly in one direction.

"Well I've got my work cut out for me now," he said, examining it in the light of the forge.

"I'll leave you to it then," Grisol said, wanting to linger, not because she particularly liked Tuomo's company, but because she was fascinated by the power he wielded to shape hunks of mixed metals dug out of solid rock into deadly weapons. In theory, at least; it was clear he didn't know much about forging, but apparently he was the best the Great Council could spare, which was not encouraging.

?

"That was a long trickle-bath," Dunil said when she returned, sniffing as she walked by. "You smell like smoke. You've been to the forge! You've seen Spore!"

"No one ever accused you of not being observant," she replied. "I was watching Tuomo make a spearhead."

"How does he do it?" Dunil asked.

"It's complicated, and you know Carl and Ujenn are coming over, so I'll tell you about it tomorrow. You'll have to go stay with Sabna tonight. You can tell stories to Anbol and Anti."

Dunil nodded, his brow furrowed. He made as if to open his mouth, then stopped.

"What is it, Duny-Dune?" She almost never called him that anymore.

"Mao-tay, if Carl gives you a baby, will that make him my father?"

Grisol sighed and forced a smile. "More like an uncle. The baby would live with them, but we would still be family."

"And the baby would be my cousin?"

"Something like that. Look, sweetie, it'll all be fine. You'll get to see Carl and Ujenn more often, and you'll have a new cousin to play with."

"I doubt I'll be doing much playing by the time he gets big enough to play."

"Nonsense. You're never too old to play."

Dunil's eyes brightened. "So will you play castle with me tomorrow at breakfast?"

"In Islish, no less," she said, touching his cheek, then dropping her hand as she heard footsteps outside the room.

"Go let Carl and Ujenn in." Grisol pushed Dunil toward the doorway. Dunil nodded, gave her an inscrutable look, and pulled aside the curtain.

"*Good evening, Carl,*" said Dunil in Islish. "Good evening, Ujenn," he said in Maer.

"*It's good to see of you,*" Ujenn replied, pulling Dunil in for a human-style hug.

"*How are your classes going?*" Carl asked, studiously avoiding looking at Grisol.

"*Great!*" Dunil replied, then switched back to Maer. "Anbol shows a lot of promise, and the others too. Speaking of which, I have to go tell her and Anti some bedtime stories. Good night!" He ran over to kiss Grisol on the cheek, then darted awkwardly between Carl and Ujenn and through the doorway, pulling the curtain shut behind him. Grisol worked to unclench her jaw into a smile as Ujenn led Carl into the room.

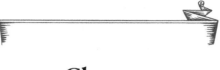

Chapter:
Five

Carl picked up his cup and drained the bitter brew at the same time as Ujenn and Grisol. He smiled awkwardly at Grisol, and she smiled back, wiping her lips delicately. Ujenn beamed at both of them, crossing her legs and putting her hands on the little table.

"So," she said, her bright eyes fixed on Grisol, "You're the talk of the castle today. You must be a quick study with the bow."

"Sinnie is a good teacher," Grisol said.

"She's the best with a bow I've ever seen," Carl offered, flushing as he realized that Sinnie's arrows had killed five Maer, including Grisol's husband Roubay. "She used to shoot for a...*traveling show.*" He switched to Islish for a moment, then back to Maer. "It's a kind of theater, with acrobatic feats. I saw her shoot a tiny apple from the top of a puppy's head."

"Why would anyone want to do that?" Ujenn asked with a bewildered smile.

"Entertainment," Carl said, shrugging his shoulders. "Kind of like Nightsong."

"And if she missed?" Grisol asked.

Carl shrugged again. "It never happened. Like I said, she's the best. Although maybe soon you'll be able to challenge her for the title."

Grisol giggled, a sign that Ujenn's brew was taking effect. "A mage's leg is a lot bigger than a tiny apple."

"But in the dark, with your heart racing, with sweat running down your armpits..." Carl laughed, and Grisol flashed a warm smile. The brew was definitely kicking in.

"So tell me about this mage's spell," Ujenn said. "Karul said there was a loud noise and then everyone was knocked flat in an instant. It sounds quite powerful."

Grisol nodded, stifling a giggle. "It was. Karul, Ivlana, and Dren were only ten or fifteen feet away, and they were knocked on their backs. Goi and I were across the river, which is narrow at that point, maybe forty or fifty feet away, and it was like we got hit with the strongest gust of wind you ever felt. Goi fell over, and I stumbled back but kept my feet. And then, as the humans quickly gathered their things and made to leave, I shot the mage in the leg, like Karul told me to do."

"And just like that, you're a hero," Ujenn said, leaning over and putting a hand on Grisol's knee. Carl's stomach leapt a little and he could feel his heart beating harder, but somehow slower. Grisol's mouth formed an odd smile as she slid her hand on top of Ujenn's, and Carl's loins stirred as he watched Ujenn put her other hand on Grisol's shoulder, running it up and down her arm, across her chest, and up her neck. Carl had become accustomed to Ujenn's body hair to the point that he almost didn't see it, but with Grisol he was acutely aware of it, though it bothered him less and less with each ritual.

"Shall we begin?" Ujenn looked them both in the eyes, taking each of their hands. Carl took Grisol's hand, and when she looked up at him, he recalled for a moment the wild intensity of her eyes when they had first met in the valley below Brocland. They had been monsters to each other then, but with time and the repeated rituals, he now saw her as a person, a partner, and as strange as it felt given his relationship with Ujenn, a lover.

"We are here, united in a common purpose." Ujenn's voice resonated, low and calm, in the small chamber. "The making of one life, out of three. We all come to this ritual from different places, with different feelings, which we cannot ignore." Grisol squeezed Carl's fingers, and he tightened his grip on both of their hands as his head began to spin. "With such closeness, such intimacy, may come emotions we do not expect. Whatever they may be, however we may feel, I ask that we let our feelings flow and accept them without judgment, or jealousy, or regret."

Grisol's hairy knee touched Carl's, and he let his leg relax against hers. He did not feel about her the way he felt toward Ujenn, but her touch moved him in ways that were not purely physical.

"Grisol, do you agree to your part in this surrogacy, to accept the life that springs from the three of us, to grow and nurture it within you, to be part of our family, in whatever role your heart may wish to play?"

"I do." Grisol's voice was steady, and she looked to Ujenn, then to Carl, with eyes both bright and deep.

"Carl, do you agree to your role in this surrogacy, to give a part of your life, to join it with mine, and Grisol's, to form a new life, and to nurture this life and the family that forms from it, in whatever shape that may take?"

Carl gripped Ujenn's and Grisol's hands tightly. "I do."

Ujenn blinked slowly, sliding her fingers up Carl's wrist and holding him fast. "I, Ujenn, agree to my part in this surrogacy, to give of my life, to join it with Carl's, and Grisol's. I pledge to nurture and cherish this life we create together, and the family we will soon become, as individuals and as a whole, and never to let my own feelings stand in the way of the health and happiness of all." She paused, and the silence that followed was broken only by the sizzle of the candles. "Now, close your eyes."

Through the darkness behind his eyelids, Carl saw shapes of shining gold and silver, swirling around and coalescing into forms like letters in an ancient script, pulsing with the sound of Ujenn's voice, which he heard in his mind, though she did not speak aloud. The sound and the shapes merged into a pool like molten bronze, spreading through him, roaring into his heart and down to his loins, which stirred with a deep, otherworldly tingling that soon penetrated his limbs, fingers, toes, even to his ears and the tip of his nose. By the time Ujenn let go of his hand, his body was filled with a vibration like the groan of rock shifting before an earthquake.

He opened his eyes and sat silently as Ujenn stood Grisol up, removed Grisol's tunic, then her own, pulling it over her head and tossing it carelessly to Carl as she put both hands on Grisol's face and kissed her long and slow. Grisol's arms rested delicately on Ujenn's shoulders, eventually sliding down her back to rest on Ujenn's ample hips. Carl shifted in his seat as the two embraced, Ujenn pulling Grisol in tight as Grisol's hands moved more freely across Ujenn's curves. Ujenn walked Grisol over to the bed and slowly pushed her down, turning her head to Carl and summoning him with her eyes.

Carl shed his clothes and walked over to the bed where Grisol lay. Her thin, muscular body was very different from Ujenn's, and as he looked down at her he was pulled by something more than duty or desire. Ujenn turned to him, pulled his face in close, and kissed him deeply. He sank into her kiss, enveloped in her aura, and wrapped his arms around her, running his fingernails through the fine hairs on her back. She worked his body over with her hands until he was short of breath, then she pulled him over to the bed and sat down next to Grisol. She kept one hand on Carl and let the other roam over Grisol, whose breath came in short huffs as Ujenn ran her hands up and down her thighs and between her legs. Without warning, Ujenn let go of Carl, grabbed Grisol by the hips, and flipped her on her stomach, pushing her legs wide.

Chapter:

Six

Ujenn stepped behind Carl, pressing her body into his back and putting her fingers on his temples, her lips on his ear as she whispered: "Take her as you would take me." She slid her hands down and held onto his hips as she pushed him down toward Grisol, who leaned up into him, turning her face up toward Carl, then locking eyes with Ujenn as she reached her hand back to guide Carl inside her.

Ujenn straddled Carl's leg, leaning into him as he pushed into Grisol, slowly at first, tentative, almost hesitant. Ujenn clung tight to Carl, grinding against his hip bone, and his breath grew hoarse as he thrust with increasing intensity. She reached around Carl to pull Grisol's hips back, and Grisol twisted her neck to look over her shoulder for a moment, her eyes wide and hot. Ujenn thrust with all her weight onto Carl as she pulled Grisol's hips back harder, and Grisol's torso fell forward, her arms stretching out in front of her as her breath grew short. When Ujenn closed her eyes, she could feel what Carl felt, his conflicting desires, the residual shame of having feelings for more than one person, slowly vanishing as he gave in to the moment. Ujenn slid one hand around to stimulate Grisol, and Grisol's feelings flooded into her, the lingering sense of guilt at being with someone besides Roubay, the shock of Carl's bare skin against her hair, the sudden, urgent pleasure of Ujenn's touch. Three moved together as one, until Ujenn could hardly tell if it was her own pleasure she was feeling or that of her partners.

In the end she lay panting atop Carl and Grisol, her forehead resting on Carl's neck as their breathing slowed together. She slid down to the side, one hand in the small of Carl's back, holding him in place, while the other hand touched Grisol's forehead and face, and Ujenn whispered into Grisol's ear: "Thank you, thank you, thank you."

When at last she released her hand from Carl's back, he rose to his knees, and Ujenn slid over and blanketed half of Grisol's body with hers, snuggling her face into Grisol's neck. She smiled up at Carl as she stroked Grisol's back, rear, and thighs.

"You know you're welcome to stay," Ujenn said, then she turned her back on him, rolling Grisol over on her side to face her. Grisol's eyes looked toward Carl for a moment, then closed as Ujenn kissed her, running her hand over the curve of Grisol's hip and pulling their bodies closer together. Ujenn heard Carl pull on his clothes and slip through the curtains, and she smiled as she took Grisol's ear between her teeth. Part of her wished he would stick around for the last part of the ritual, but his residual sense of shame was too great. Perhaps with time he would get over it.

Ujenn's breath caught as Grisol's fingers slid between her legs, and she looked into Grisol's eyes, which showed none of the confusion and guilt of their earlier rituals. Ujenn pressed into her touch for a moment, then raised herself to all fours above her. She spread Grisol's legs wide and slid her body down, pinning Grisol's arms to her sides as she kissed her way back up, finding Grisol's eager mouth as their beards tangled together. She tasted Grisol for some time, then lifted her lips just out of reach and looked into Grisol's eyes as she let her weight sink down, increasing the pressure and heat.

"My heart to your heart. My womb to your womb," Ujenn said, closing her eyes and conjuring the ancient words of the spell, which echoed in her mind as the energy flowed between them, dissolving the separation of their bodies and minds until they were one in stillness. She could feel Grisol's heart beating along with hers, and a spark grew inside her chest, like a fire blown into life by a gust of wind, until it filled her mind and body, which felt light and heavy all at once. She slid a hand up Grisol's neck, clasping the back of her head as the energy flooded out of her body and into Grisol, who gasped, her eyes wild and probing, her hands clutching at Ujenn's neck. Ujenn felt a great lightness within herself as she realized that this time, at long last, the ritual had succeeded. She laid a soft kiss on Grisol's lips, then shifted over to straddle Grisol's leg as she walked her fingers down Grisol's body, gently scratching, teasing, squeezing. Grisol's face tensed as Ujenn's fingers found their mark and began moving in delicate circles, and she angled toward Ujenn, hardening the muscles in her leg as Ujenn pressed down with all her strength. Their bodies moved together with slowly building urgency as the candle on the table beside them melted and oozed down onto the wood.

?

Ujenn left Grisol half-asleep, rinsed her hands and face, and slipped on her tunic. She made her way through the warren of the keep's sleeping quarters to the council meeting place, which was open to the cool night sky. Karul, Luez, Ivlana, and Fabaris sat in a tight circle around a fire that was smaller than usual, since most of the wood was being diverted for the forge. Carl had not been invited to the meeting, though he was usually a fixture at all council gatherings. Ujenn wondered if it was a mistake, but she had left the matter in Karul's hands.

"It's good of you to join us," Karul said, giving her a gruff look, the copper-tipped rod dangling from his hand.

"I had some family obligations to attend to. I'm sure you understand." Ujenn knew Karul was jealous of her arrangement with Grisol, but they were not exclusive, not strictly speaking. If Grisol had rejected his advances, he would either need to step up his game or get over it.

"May the gods be bountiful to you," Fabaris said, standing and taking the rod from Karul, "and to us all." Everyone nodded, and Fabaris stood silent for a moment, the shiny ball of bronze atop the rod reflecting a blob of yellow light on his otherwise shadowed cheek.

"I have convened this meeting," he continued at last, "to take up a subject we have discussed before, but which I believe has new urgency, in light of recent events." He paused for dramatic effect, as he often did, and Ujenn covered her mouth with her hand to hide a smile. Everyone knew what they were here to discuss, and everyone was going to be in agreement, but Fabaris did enjoy his theatrics. "You all know the stories of the Archive, the repository of all knowledge, literature, and wisdom of the Maer civilization from before the great war. That it once existed, that it contained countless cylinder scrolls, books, maps, and other treasures, is not in doubt. Whether it survived the tragic events following the Great Betrayal, whether it still exists, and where it may be, no one knows. And yet..." He paused again, walking in a circle around the fire. Ujenn's smile faded as she fell under the spell of his words, and of the idea the Archive represented.

"And yet, I do not believe that all knowledge of the Archive is lost. We know our ancestors were very wise when it came to protecting our heritage. They chose to keep the cylinder maps and to ensure that they ended up in the hands of those with the birthright to possess them. They chose to leave certain documents relevant to law and governance, as well as some of our most important songs, poems, and longstories, in the hands of the scholars. They left some words of power in the hands of the mages. But they surely left much other knowledge in the Archive itself, as the reach of the humans grew too far and our numbers too few to safely protect this legacy. But they would not have let all clues to the Archive's whereabouts vanish into oblivion. Of that we can be sure." Karul gestured for the rod, and Fabaris put out a hand to hold him off for another moment.

"I believe," Fabaris continued, "that the knowledge of the Archive's location and entrance has been compartmentalized, to protect against loss or misuse. I believe that a piece of it lies with the mages, a piece with the scholars, and a piece with the leadership. I believe that if we can reach out to trustworthy Maer in each camp, we may be able to cobble together enough information to find the Archive, to the benefit of us all." He walked silently toward Karul and handed him the rod. Ujenn's stomach turned as she saw the hunger and impatience in Karul's face, and she suddenly realized what it meant. He would not wait for spring, even though undertaking this mission with winter approaching was obvious folly.

"Thank you, Fabaris, for your thoughtful explanation," Karul said. "I hope what you say is true, for I now believe the key to the success, even the survival, of the Maer, lies in finding the Archive and making use of its power. After seeing the skills of the human spies, in particular the mage, it is obvious that the humans are decades, if not centuries ahead of us, and that without the knowledge of our ancestors, the Maer are at an impossible disadvantage. If we are to make our case to the humans that our claim to sovereignty over certain territories is legitimate, we will need documents that may only exist within the Archive, if at all. And even if we have all the documents, including the treaty which they disregarded in the Great Betrayal, there is no guarantee they will accept such ancient claims. And in that case, we will need the Archive to rebuild our technical knowledge, for even if our numbers were sufficient to defend ourselves, which they are not, our metallurgy and smithing capacity are sadly lacking." A great unease grew inside Ujenn as Karul's urgency increased.

"To me, the case is clear: we must find the Archive if the Maer are to survive and thrive. But," he continued, waving off Fabaris' outstretched hand, "there are those in Great Council who feel this is a fool's errand, a waste of resources. So it may fall upon us to undertake this task without their help or approval. I know of at least one member of the council I can trust, a woman named Saru, who was always skeptical of the military ambitions of some of our leaders. I hope Fabaris, Ujenn, and Luez have similar contacts. I propose that we send word to a small number of Maer, asking for any information they may have about the Archive, and see if we can find out enough to pursue this vital errand." He handed the rod to Fabaris, who stood again.

"I agree with the proposal, and I am certain most of the scholars would share my view, as the Archive would contain not only documents of legal and practical value, but also literature, poetry, and song, which are of equal importance if we are to rebuild the great Maer civilization of old. Not to mention wordbooks for Southish and Islish, which would be of immeasurable help in our dealings with the humans. I can send word to my old master Nara, whose knowledge of literature and history is second to none, and who can surely be trusted." Ujenn held out her hand for the rod, and Fabaris handed it to her.

"I agree, to a point." She took a deep breath, hoping to slow the impetuous momentum of the males. "The Archive no doubt contains magics that no living Maer knows. But we must proceed with caution, as some may be dangerous in the wrong hands. Like the Great Council, the *Sabrit* has some who would seek to use those magics to awaken the *Ka-lar*. We know from Roubay's mistake that the *Ka-lar*, if awakened improperly or prematurely, will wreak havoc on human and Maer alike." She remembered the feeling when she first reached into Carl's mind, the hollowness, the hunger for violence the Kalar's bite had inflicted on him. "If, as the *Sabrit* believe, the Archive contains a cylinder scroll with the secret to awakening and controlling them, and if this scroll gets into the hands of mages bent on destruction, they will start a war that we cannot win, and which may result in the final annihilation of all Maer. For as powerful as the *Ka-lar* are, I have no doubt that the humans have magics far more destructive, which they would unleash to wipe us from the continent." She paused, her spirit sinking as she realized she was feeding into Karul's argument.

"I know that Stuock, who is currently training Finn, opposes the *Sabrit*'s position, despite his penchant for magic of destruction. We have spoken at length on the topic, and he shares my concern. I can send him a message in mage script, so that only a mage of sufficient training can read it. I know the scholars have some knowledge of the ancient Maer language, so Fabaris' message would have similar protection. In either case there is some risk, for if the messages were intercepted, they could fall into the wrong hands, but that is a risk we will have to take. My biggest concern is for Karul's message, which would presumably have to be written in standard script, which anyone could read. In that case—" Luez held out a finger, and Ujenn stopped and handed her the rod. Luez spoke rarely at council, so it had to be important.

"There is a kind of coded script known only to a few in...special positions, like myself," said Luez. "If Saru got Karul's message in this script, she would know of someone who could read it. Though to be frank, none of these protections means much. If anyone is snooping on pigeon messages and sees something written in any kind of code, they can find someone to interpret it if they have connections. This kind of communication is best done the old-fashioned way, mouth to ear, to limit exposure. But I can confirm several details of Fabaris' theory. The general location of the Archive is known. It lies in one of the valleys surrounding the Great Tooth, and its entrance is sure to be well hidden, either by ancient magic or by clever design, or both.

There is a map of sorts, which I have seen, and I could recreate it from memory, with a fair degree of accuracy. The secret to entry is said to be hidden in one of the great poems, though no one knows which one."

Everyone turned to Fabaris, who nodded his head softly, his eyes unfocused, his lips moving as if mumbling words. "I'll work on it," he said, waving away the rod Luez held toward him, "and I'll share what I find as soon as I have anything."

"Anything at all," Karul said, his eye stern.

"And I can send a pigeon to Stuock," Ujenn said. "It's two roosts away, but Stromus is trained to bypass the first roost, and Stuock is the only one who touches the roost in his tower. It's as low a risk as we can get. I'll tell him if he knows something to send it back with Finn and Sinnie."

Karul's brow raised almost to his hairline. "You put much faith in the humans," he said. "Not that they've given us any particular cause to doubt their motives, but..." He stood up and took a few long steps in Ujenn's direction, crouching down to her eye level. "Are there not some things best kept between Maer?"

"Like the *mashtorul*?" Ujenn spoke quietly, but her words rang clear. Carl had nearly lost his life helping them rid the mines of the creatures, and there was no question where his loyalty lay.

Karul waved her off, standing up and turning away. "Your point is made," he grumbled. "And right now we need them, so we will use them. But I want everyone to be aware of the possibility, however remote, that they may not be entirely on our side." He swiveled to face the others, then turned his head back to Ujenn. "Can I count on you?"

Ujenn pushed her anger down as she stood up. Karul glared down at her, and she looked up at him and stuck her index finger on his chest. "You can count on them," she said, nodding to the group before swirling out through the doorway.

?

The roost was quiet, but Ujenn heard some rustling and muted cooing as she approached the cage with her taper, which she had to cup with her hands to keep the wind from blowing it out. She nestled the taper in a chink of the parapet shielded from the wind while she prepared her little wooden tray. It contained a bowl of seeds, a bowl of water, a length of thin goatskin cord, and the note, which she had rolled and tucked inside an oak leaf, for some protection against the elements. She opened the door to the cage, stuck in her arm, and scooped up Stromus, who pecked gently at her finger as she pulled him out and closed the cage. She set him on the tray, and he immediately began working on the seeds, giving her a chance to tie the cord onto his leg. She had to start over a couple of times, as everything was so small and the light so poor, but she finally got the leaf tightly rolled and securely fastened. She stroked the back of Stromus' head as he finished the seeds in the bowl, then pecked around the tray for the few that had fallen to the side. When he had finished, Stromus dipped his beak into the water, bobbed his head three times, then hopped up onto her arm. She always found that endearing; he could have just taken flight off the tray, as he knew exactly what was happening and where he was going, but he never strayed from his routine.

Ujenn chucked him under the chin a couple of times and put her nose right up against his beak. He gave her a soft peck on the nose, then she held her arm out over the battlements.

"Take this to Stuock," she whispered. "I'll have another nice bowl of seeds for you when you get back." She shook her arm and Stromus took off into the darkness, his wings squeaking in the distance, fainter and fainter, until at last all she could hear was the low hum of the wind and the sound of a child crying somewhere off in the keep.

Chapter:
Seven

Stuock cocked his head sideways as he heard the pigeon wheel into the roost above, but he couldn't tell from which direction it had come. Was it a message from Castle Maer, or from the Great Council, or maybe news of another relative's death? His head snapped back as he heard the *crack* of the rock Finn had split in half. Finn was on his fifth out of ten, and sweat was starting to bead on his forehead and roll down into his eyes, with nothing but a pair of inadequate eyebrows to slow its progress. Stuock marveled at the bizarre diversity of human and Maer physiology, and wondered if it was really true that they were merely different tribes of the same race.

"Keep it up," Stuock said in Southish, glad to have someone to practice with. Finn nodded, pushed his hands forward in claw shape, and brought them together, shaking, until the sixth rock burst into a dozen pieces, sending a cloud of dust into the air. Stuock had moved Finn more than ten feet away from his targets, but the distance did not seem to affect him. Before long, his range would be as far as Stuock's.

"Good. Keep going, and have a drink when you finish the tenth," Stuock said over his shoulder as he turned to head up the spiral staircase. "I need to see to the pigeons."

"I bet that's a message from Castle Maer," Finn said, breathing heavily as he brought his hands back up for the next rock.

"I bet you slop duty it isn't," said Stuock, chuckling. He was prepared to lose the bet; the risk was worth it for a chance to give the human a little comeuppance, lest he think his skill with magic made him better than anyone else. Which, to be fair, it kind of did, but he could still empty a bucket of shit like anyone else.

"Son of a mixed-breed bastard!" Stuock muttered as he saw Ujenn's sigil on the outside of the leaf. He suddenly remembered the particularly unpleasant odor of Finn's shit, and the smug expression Finn got whenever he won a bet. Stuock recognized the pigeon, Stromus, who was big and strong enough to deal with any wind the mountains could throw at him. He dropped a handful of seeds in front of Stromus, unrolled the note, and smiled. "Mage script," he mumbled to himself. "What a delightful distraction." He hadn't read mage script in years, but it pulled him in with its thicket of entangled letters and symbols, half of them meaningless. There were only a dozen or so Maer who could read it, and Stromus always flew directly from Castle Maer, without stopping at the Gray Tower. Ujenn would have known this, so she was counting on utmost secrecy. That meant this had to be good.

?

Stuock sat at his makeshift desk in the courtyard, where Finn was resting in one of his odd poses, seated with his right leg straight out and his left tucked under him. It looked painful, but Finn's face was serene, his brow had dried, and his breathing was slow and steady. Stuock had never seen a bodily control mage up close, and he hoped to learn some of what Finn could do, once he finished his training.

"I finished the ten, and I made this," Finn said, picking up a perfectly round stone the size of his fist.

"Very good," said Stuock, snapping his fingers and crushing the ball to powder. "Now put it back together."

Finn dusted off his hands, cupped them around the pile of dust that had recently been a ball of stone, and squeezed it together into a ball again, wincing and straining the muscles in his neck as he did so.

"Now put the rest of them together. But from where you are." He knew Finn could do it, but he needed practice, and Stuock needed time to decipher Ujenn's message. The sound of Finn struggling to re-form the rocks, the grunts and groans interspersed with the *crack* of rock fragments locking back together, formed a soothing background for Stuock's endeavor. By the time Finn had remade the last rock and slumped back against the wall, Stuock had read and re-checked the message, but he still read it one more time to be sure.

"You were right," he said, looking around to make sure the guards had not returned from their training with Sinnie, though neither of the guards spoke Southish, unless they were spies, and damned good ones. "I'm on slop duty. But you, it would seem, have been summoned."

"Back to Castle Maer?" Finn's voice mixed hope and disappointment. He had been putting every ounce of his focus into his training with a hunger like few pupils Stuock had encountered. He had quickly mastered most of the basic feats of breaking and remaking, and was on the verge of moving to some of the more challenging feats.

"You will leave in the morning," Stuock said, "once I have composed my message and dug out a few things for you to take. But before you go, there is one more lesson I'd like you to try. If you are up for it, of course."

"I'm ready," Finn said with such earnestness Stuock had to stifle a laugh.

"Good. While I write, I want you to catch a mouse and bring it here."

"A mouse? How am I—"

Stuock pulled his quill from his pocket and pointed it at Finn. "If you can't figure that bit out, I don't see how I can help you with the important part."

Finn rolled his tongue inside his cheek, gave a tight smile, and stood up. "Yes Master Stuock," he said, bowing in an awkward imitation of the Southern way. He had clearly learned a few cultural tidbits along with his makeshift Southish, but his movements were all wrong.

"Run along now." Stuock smoothed out a line of birch bark and weighted it with stones on either end. "We don't have more than a couple more hours of light. And you might want to let Sinnie know if you get a chance."

?

We seek that which has been lost. Send what you know with Finn.

Ujenn's note could only have been referring to the Archive. They had discussed it at length when her group stopped at his tower on the way to Castle Maer, but Stuock had kept his secret even from her. He had not revealed it to anyone, figuring he would know if the time were ever right, and he would entrust it to someone else if he sensed his days drawing to a close. But his old master had passed the year before, so he might be the only one to know this particular secret: the shape of the entrance to the Archive. The shape of the soul.

The Great Council would know of its general location, but even the *Sabrit* would not know the shape of the entrance, so they would not be able to find it. Even if they did, they would need a scholar who was complicit with their plans, for the key to opening the Archive was said to lie in one of the great poems, which only the scholars knew. The Maer of old had seen fit to create a balance of knowledge, to keep the Archive safe until their society had reached a point where consensus was possible, either through a flourishing system of culture and governance or through dire need for the preservation of all Maer.

The Maer were surviving, even expanding, but they were far from flourishing.

Since Ujenn was asking, she had to believe the threat of the *Sabrit* moving on the Archive was real. Castle Maer had come under scrutiny from the Realm, and this fact would not have escaped the *Sabrit*. Stuock knew all too well that if the human threat were perceived as imminent, the *Sabrit* might vote to go all out in search of the Archive, to secure the secret to controlling the *Ka-lar*. They would send the *Shoza*, with their warriors and assassins and mages of destruction. They would not stop until they found what they were looking for, eliminating anyone who got in their way. And if the *Shoza* found the *Ka-lar* scroll, the *Sabrit* might seize control of the Great Council itself, and use the *Ka-lar* as weapons to start a war against the humans. It was a war they could never win, but the hubris of the *Sabrit* knew no bounds. The humans would hunt down the Maer, to the last female and child huddling in their mountain hideouts, and the second age of Maer civilization would never come to be.

Stuock selected a fine piece of gray obsidian he had been saving, cupped it in his hands, and closed his eyes to conjure the image he had been gifted. A huge gray rock, covered in mosses, flowers, and even a couple of small bushes, sat at the foot of a deep valley leading down from the Great Tooth. Its shape was distinctive but forgettable, with the bottom rectangular and the top pentagonal, the kind of thing one could see many times without noticing, but there were very few rocks with this exact shape. Stuock had been looking ever since the image had been first burned into his mind, and he had seen a few that were close, but none shaped quite like it. He molded the obsidian with light touches of his fingers until it held the precise shape of the rock from his vision, polishing the sides so it glowed in the fading light. Finn returned, cupping his hands together, as Stuock was admiring his handiwork, and he quickly dropped the rock into his pocket.

"I have the mouse," Finn said, holding his cupped hands up. "Now what?"

"Put it in here," Stuock said, pulling out a small wooden cage he used when he needed to isolate a sick bird. Finn slipped the mouse into the opening and shut the door. The mouse ran around for a few seconds, then crouched in a corner, its nose twitching furiously. "Now step back, a little more, that's it. Very good." He set the cage on the ground about ten feet from Finn. "Now, remember what you did to those rocks? Do it to him." He pointed at the mouse, and Finn's eyes sank.

"But I can't just—he didn't—it's not right."

"No, it's not. But this is why you came to me, is it not? Surely you aren't here to learn how to break rocks and put them back together."

Finn shook his head, set his jaw, and stared hard at the mouse. He held out his hand in a claw, squinted, and the mouse vanished in a cloud of fur and a spray of blood. Finn let out a high-pitched scream, falling to his knees and clutching his head in both hands.

"It doesn't get much easier," Stuock said, walking to Finn, who sat down hard, his breath coming in ragged bursts. "If you're expecting it you can brace yourself a little, but I thought you should know what you're getting yourself into."

Finn shook his head and scrambled to his feet, his head cocked sideways, the veins on his forehead popping out. "That's the worst pain I've ever felt."

"And that was just a mouse," Stuock said. "Try that on a Maer and it might kill you, or at least make you wish it had. I think the pain was built into the spell by the old masters, to prevent its being used lightly."

"Mission accomplished," Finn said, shaking his head again.

"Speaking of missions, let's have some roast marmot and talk about tomorrow."

Chapter:
Eight

Finn examined the little parcel Stuock had given him, and was hard-pressed to see what message the rock would convey. It was a piece of smooth obsidian wrapped in a little roll of birch paper with some elaborate writing on it that looked like a version of the mage code he had learned about in study. Stuock also sent them with a bag of nuts and two balls of the chewy, twiggy substance that passed for bread in the tower. Sinnie would surely be able to shoot something along the way, but it was good to have insurance, and Finn knew what precious gifts these were.

"I do not have the words to express my thanks," Finn said to Stuock as they stood in the cold gray morning light. "I will return, to repay your teachings with some of my own, as promised."

"I should think a bottle of mushroom wine would also go a long way to showing your gratitude," Stuock replied, grasping his shoulders in a gesture Finn had seen the Maer do many times, but it was the first time he had been the recipient himself.

"You shall have it, or better if I get back to Brocland before I see you next," Finn promised. Sinnie hugged the two guards, who had trained her in knife fighting while she taught them how to shoot. They accepted her embrace with obvious awkwardness, as the Maer did not do hugs, except with their children. She reached out to hug

Stuock, who insisted on the Maer shoulder clasp, which made Sinnie giggle a little.

"Thank you," she said in Maer. "We will deliver your message."

Stuock raised his hand in a slow wave as Finn and Sinnie turned and tramped off into the mist.

?

It would be a week's journey to Castle Maer, and the only roof between Stuock's tower and the castle was another crumbling edifice known as the Gray Tower, which served as a roost for pigeons flying to and from the castle. Stuock had given them strict orders to avoid contact with the tower or with anyone else they might come across, however unlikely that was, so they would have to spend an extra day and a half to skirt around it to avoid being seen by its two guards. A cold drizzle, occasionally interspersed with wet snow, fell all the first day and into the second. Thankfully, Sinnie had insisted on sleeping curled up against him, so only Finn's feet had gotten cold, but between the damp and the hunger and the constant gray it was a dismal trip.

"I'm looking forward to a decent night's sleep back in the castle," Sinnie said as they walked through the cold drizzle. "Stuock's hospitality was as good as it could be, but it was so cold and drafty, and the beds at the castle are sooo much better."

"I wouldn't mind a bowl of hot mushroom stew," Finn said. "Not that I have anything against marmot, roots, and dried berries per se, but I miss Ty's cooking. It's actually better than my mom's."

"Oh, don't get me started on home cooking. I would give my left arm for some roast lamb right about now. I'd even settle for marmot, but they seem to be hunkering down until this crap passes." She held her hand toward the sky, and Finn watched fat snowflakes land on it and melt instantly.

"Just be thankful it's not coming down any harder," Finn said. "Stuock warned me that this time of year you're just as likely to get a rainstorm as a snowstorm, and either one would put a serious dent in our travels. Although on balance, I'd rather—" He stopped as Sinnie held out her hand, crouching and readying her bow. They were following a faint path that crisscrossed a burbling creek through one of the valleys between the peaks, and the path ahead ran between two house-sized boulders before crossing the creek again. That spot of the creek was shallow, with flat stones sticking out of the water, so the crossing looked easy, unlike the upstream and downstream parts, where the water flowed down hard over slippery rocks.

"Behind those boulders," Sinnie whispered, remaining crouched. "I heard something."

Finn quickly found his center and pushed out a force shell just in case. He looked around for cover, but there was none. They stood watching the boulders for a moment, but there was no movement, and no sound other than water splashing over rocks. He looked over at Sinnie, who mouthed *I don't know* and made her eyes wide.

"I've got a force shell up," he whispered. "I could go ahead and see what it is, and you could cover me."

"Duh," Sinnie whispered with a nervous smirk.

Finn crept toward the boulders, which stood about five feet apart, forming a kind of passageway leading to the creek crossing. As he passed between the boulders, the whole thing started to feel wrong, but he couldn't quite say why. He didn't see or hear anything, but his spine tingled as he approached the water's edge. He readied his energy and continued, walking as slowly and silently as he could without using a feat, which would have been wasted anyway, since whatever it was already knew he was there. As he got to within ten feet of the stream, he noticed something in the water, like a piece of rope wrapped around one of the stepping stones. He scanned the others and could see there was rope, or perhaps some kind of rough net, lining the creek crossing. He turned toward Sinnie, pointed at the creek, and held up his palm. The boulders ended just short of the edge of the water, and as he got close, he heard a muted sound, like gravel grinding under someone's heel. He took a deep breath and swung his staff out past the edge of the boulders.

His staff was immediately whacked by two spears, and he fumbled to keep hold of it as the front end was knocked to the ground. Two Maer appeared in the opening, dressed in rough furs, their spears pointing at him.

"Finn, look out!" Sinnie called, and he heard the twang of her bow, then a yelp, followed by a growl. He backpedaled away from the Maer, looking over his shoulder to see a brown-furred creature the size of a small bear rounding the corner of the boulder, its claws skidding on the gravel as it thrashed at the arrow stuck in its side. It shook its whole body, crouched, and bounded toward him.

Finn's legs gave a jolt as he rammed his energy down, propelling his body up and onto one of the boulders, where he stumbled but kept his feet, startling another Maer with a spear, who was rearing back to throw it at Sinnie. Finn took a wide swing with his staff and caught the surprised Maer on the side of the head, sending him tumbling awkwardly off the edge, bouncing off the other boulder before landing in the passage between with a sickening crunch.

"*Enough!*" Finn called in Maer, peeking over the edge of the boulder to see the two Maer crouched over their fallen companion, the furry creature sniffing and growling, turning its toothy jaws up toward Finn, then back to Sinnie. "*We are not your enemy,*" Finn continued, hoping he said it correctly; he spoke Maer well enough, but the panic of the moment made it harder. "*We are friends of the Maer!*"

The two Maer looked at each other, then up at Finn. One of them spoke to the other in what sounded like Maer, but Finn couldn't quite make it out, though the last word sounded like 'dead.' One dropped his head, put his hands on the fallen Maer's eyelids, and closed them. He turned his eyes, red with rage, up toward Finn, and let out a shout as he jumped up on the side of the boulder, found a fingerhold, and began climbing at an alarming speed. He barked out something over his shoulder, and the creature, which was between the size of a dog and a bear, turned toward Sinnie, scratched its claws in the dirt, and bolted off in her direction. It tumbled as Sinnie sunk an arrow into its snout, and it rolled about awkwardly, scraping its head against the ground to try to dislodge the arrow, then shook its head and braced for another charge.

Finn looked down at the climbing Maer, who was almost halfway up the twenty-foot high boulder. He centered his energy and channeled what he'd learned from Stuock to crush the stone the Maer was gripping into powder. The Maer tumbled to the ground, crying out in pain as he clutched his knee. The other Maer called to him, then ducked low and went to help his companion. The bear-like creature bounded back to them, then snarled and turned to face Sinnie, who had another arrow nocked and ready. The standing Maer helped the injured one up to one foot, supporting him with his shoulder. The injured Maer looked up at Finn and shouted what must have been a stream of curses, and they limped off across the creek, with the creature following behind them. Finn watched them climb up a narrow path around the edge of a rock formation and out of sight. He looked down at the long drop, closed his eyes for a moment, and jumped down, sending just enough force to his legs to cushion the blow and save his knees.

"They're gone?" Sinnie approached and put a hand on Finn's bicep.

Finn nodded, leaning a bit on Sinnie to catch his breath. The new magic took it out of him more than the bodily control, which was coming more and more easily to him.

"Do you think those were the Wild Maer we've heard about?" Sinnie stared off in the direction they had gone, then down at the dead Maer on the ground between them.

"Well they certainly weren't very civilized." Finn knelt by the body, whose neck was twisted at an unnatural angle. It was a male, perhaps Finn's age, wearing furs that might have been from creatures like the one they had been traveling with. His hair was bound in intricate braids, and his features, in death, were no different to Finn's eyes from any other Maer. A bone dagger was strapped to his waist, attached to a hide belt, decorated with patterns of dots and circles. Perhaps they weren't as wild as their name suggested.

"Well, we'd better get moving." Sinnie touched Finn's back as he stood up with difficulty, and she turned toward the creek.

"I could do with a breather first, if that's all right." He leaned on his knees, then slowly stood up all the way as his breath returned to normal.

"Sure, give them time to go get their buddies, come back, and find us well-rested and ready to do battle again, but against gods know how many more."

Finn nodded, closing his eyes. "You're right. Shit, you're right. Let's get a move on." He wouldn't have more than one feat in him if they ran into any trouble soon, but they needed to get some distance between themselves and the Wild Maer.

Finn followed Sinnie across the creek, looking down at the crude net hidden under the water. "With any luck, they'll have to come back for their dead and attend to his body, which should buy us some time. Let's get a couple more hours in, then we can have a rest." She clapped Finn on the shoulder, rather harder than he thought was necessary, and started off down the path away from the site of their encounter, and the dead Maer lying between the two boulders.

?

They saw no more of the Wild Maer that day or the next, when the mix of drizzle, snow, and sleet cleared, leaving a cold, clear stretch that lasted for three days, by which time they were within a day of Castle Maer. The sun brought some warmth when they were not walking in the mountains' shadows, which unfortunately was most of the time. Finn went to bed with cold feet each night, but he and Sinnie had worked out a way to best share their blankets and body heat, and he woke up every morning warm, but hungry. The only thing Sinnie had managed to shoot was some kind of hawk, which had a leather string tied around one of its legs with several wooden beads on it. Finn had never heard of falconry among the Maer, but the strap and beads did not look like a human's handiwork either. Perhaps there were more of the Wild Maer in the area than they thought.

Sinnie felt bad about killing the hawk, but it had been just enough to keep them going, along with the last of the nuts and the doughy tower bread. By the time they reached the castle the following afternoon, their hunger had them both in a sullen funk, but when Carl greeted them with a stick of goat jerky in each hand, they giggled like children opening birthday gifts.

"Ujenn asked you to come see her straightaway," Carl said to Finn. "And you will both be expected at the council meeting tonight."

Sinnie raised her eyebrows at Finn, smiling as she sucked on the tough jerky, then threw her arms around Carl, spinning him around twice before letting go.

Chapter:

Nine

S innie followed Carl through the bailey, stopping off at their lean-to, which had been turned into a proper little cabin, with a slant-ed wooden roof, log walls, and a thin window just wide enough to shoot an arrow through.

"You really thought of everything," she said, punching Carl in the arm. Her stomach lurched as Carl doubled over in pain. "Oh gods I'm so sorry, I forgot—" When she saw him come up laughing and realized it was his other arm that was hurt, she punched him twice as hard.

"I deserved that," Carl said, rubbing his arm. "The other arm is fine, by the way." He circled it over his head, turned it sideways, and made a muscle. "Ninety-five percent. At least fifty of which is thanks to you, Finn." He grabbed Finn and pulled him in for a hug. For once it was Finn who looked taken aback by Carl's affection and not the other way around.

"Well you did kind of take one for the team with the *Ka-lar*," Finn said.

"Let's not forget about the *mashtorul*," Sinnie added.

"I guess we're even then," Carl said. "And we're expected. Ujenn will want to hear all about the new magic you learned. And I wouldn't mind hearing a bit about it myself, if you don't mind letting a few whispers slip through the veil of secrecy."

Sinnie saw Grisol shooting a bale of hay across the bailey, and she waved goodbye to her companions and went running over behind where Grisol stood.

"*You want to sink your hips down just a bit,*" Sinnie said, then switched to Maer when she saw Grisol looking confused. "Like this." Sinnie put her hands on Grisol's hips and shifted her right one back and down an inch or so. "Feel that muscle there? It needs to be going this way to give you the best...not-movement?"

Grisol looked up at her, a playful smile on her face. "Stability, I think is the word you're looking for." She turned back to her target. Sinnie took a few steps back and watched. Grisol's form was very good, but a little more strength wouldn't hurt. Grisol released, and the arrow wobbled its way toward the target, hitting close to the mark despite the wobble.

"There's something wrong with your arrow I think," Sinnie said, running up to pull the arrow out of the hay. The tip was of rough bronze, its surface pocked and uneven, its tip bent ever so slightly. "Is this one of Tuomo's tips?" she asked.

Grisol nodded, grinning. "He's still figuring it out," she said.

"Well he's got a long way to go." Sinnie pulled out one of the bronze-tipped arrows Mr. Massey had made and held it out. Its edges were clean, the surface was smooth, and it was as sharp as any steel arrowhead she had seen. "Mr. Massey made ten of these in a night, and he was out of...he hadn't done it in a while. Tuomo is going to need some help."

"Shoot for me," Grisol said, holding out her bow. "I want to see how it's done again."

Sinnie nodded, took the bow, and nocked one of her regular steel-tipped arrows. She focused on her posture, making sure to get her form just right, aimed, and pegged an arrow right in the center of the target, just like in Hertle's show. Grisol clapped, and a couple of the children came running over from the playground and started clapping too.

"Sinnie!" said a chipper voice. *"Did you hear my mom shot the mage?"* Dunil said in Islish as he ran up, out of breath, looking at Sinnie expectantly. She obliged him with a big hug. The Maer were not big huggers as a rule, but some of the children were quite receptive to the gesture.

"What mage? There was a mage? It wasn't Finn, was it? Because I was just with him, and—"

"No, silly, the mage who was also a spy, in the woods down by the Free River. They were on patrol, and they found the mage and this warrior man, and they had them circled by their campfire, and then the mage holds up his staff and says a word and BOOM! He lets out this giant wave of boom, and everybody hits the ground, except not my mom, because she's across the little river, and then she shoots him on the leg, just like this!" He shot an imaginary arrow, his fingers splaying out after the release, then grabbing his leg as if hit.

"Is that right, Grisol?" Sinnie said in Islish, touching Grisol on the shoulder.

"It was easy, really," Grisol answered in Maer, glancing sheepishly at Dunil as she did so. "I had a few seconds to aim while they were getting their things together, and he was lit up by the fire, and I just..." She made a small shooting gesture, then shrugged.

"And now she's the hero of Castle Maer. Anbol! You play the mage, and I'll play my mother, and..." Dunil ran off toward the other kids without a backwards glance.

"He seems good," Sinnie said, giving the bow back to Grisol, who leaned it against a rack and sat down on a stump.

"Yeah, he's doing great, really, when you consider..." Grisol's smile fell for a moment, and her eyes pleaded for an escape.

"How's his teaching going?" Sinnie asked, her eyes wet as she pictured the look on Roubay's face as her arrow sunk into his heart, though she had only seen him as a monster at the time: The surprise, the anger, the disbelief, fading to blankness as his body crumpled and the *Ka-lar* sword clattered onto the gravel. She had replayed the scene in her head so many times she wasn't sure how much of it was memory and how much was her imagination. Grisol was talking, but Sinnie couldn't focus on what she was saying. She had killed Grisol's husband, and Dunil's father, and her chest felt ready to explode whenever she thought of it.

"...and he seems to love it, so, yeah." Grisol squeezed Sinnie's hand. "And how was your trip to the tower? Such dreadful weather you must have had on the way back though!"

"It wasn't so bad. I had Finn to keep me warm." She saw Grisol grinning, and pushed her back gently. "Not like that, just, well, it's nice to have another body to keep you from freezing to death. I guess there's a lot of that going on up here too." She tried to keep a straight face. Grisol's arrangement with Ujenn and Carl was the talk of the castle.

"There's a lot of stuff that goes on behind closed curtains," Grisol agreed, turning her face down.

"I'm sorry, I didn't mean..." Sinnie touched Grisol on the arm. "It's just...I think is great, that you would do that for Ujenn and Carl. It must be pretty...strange though."

"You're right." Grisol picked up the bow again and notched an arrow. "It has been cold up here, and everyone does what they can to ensure the survival of us all. But the light is getting low. I need to get in a little more practice before dark. You should go get a trickle bath; there's nothing like it after a spell out in the elements."

Sinnie smiled, a little ashamed to have pried, and squeezed Grisol's shoulder. "You read my...head? Mind?" Grisol nodded, her smile returning. Maer was coming more easily to Sinnie, but she had a long way to go. "I should get cleaned up anyway, since Finn and I have to give a...talk at the council meeting tonight. But listen, I was thinking, tomorrow morning, would you like to go...run with me?"

Grisol nodded. "Sure. Where are we going?"

"I don't know, just down into the valley a little. I need to...move my legs after all that walking."

Grisol's expression was puzzled, but she smiled again. "Okay. I'm supposed to do some archery training with the older kids, but I can put it off until the afternoon."

"Great. I can help with the training if you like. How about a little after breakfast? That will give our food time to..." She made a gesture with her hands, pushing down on her stomach.

"Settle, yes. See you then," Grisol said, raising the bow and lining up for another shot. Sinnie noticed her lowering her hips, perhaps a little too much, but she would figure it out.

?

Sinnie, Finn, and Carl sat together facing Fabaris, Luez, and Ujenn around the fire in the open-air council meeting place, where a few flakes of wet snow drifted down. They made small talk as they waited for Karul and Ivlana. Sinnie mostly listened, but she could understand the bulk of what was said. Winter was approaching, and their stock of fungus was recovering from the *mashtorul* invasion, but their dried meat supply had been declining. Luez said they had been over-hunting the forest along the Free River, though she didn't have any easy solution. They had tried to make up for it by increasing their fishing catch, but the waters were cooling fast and that too was becoming more challenging. They had some vegetables in storage, along with some foraged roots, dried fruits, and nuts, but it was going to be a long and hungry winter. Everyone stopped talking at the same time when Karul and Ivlana entered.

"I'm sorry for keeping you for waiting," Karul said, taking his seat and picking up the rod with the bronze ball atop it. Ivlana stood silently behind him, looking watchful and protective of Karul as ever, even in the most secure location imaginable. Sinnie wondered if Ivlana didn't have a thing for him. "We have much to discuss and too little time, so let us begin," Karul said, standing up. "First, I must tell you," at which point he looked at Finn, Carl, and Sinnie, "that we believe the Archive, which you have no doubt heard of, is real, is intact, and contains materials and artifacts crucial to the survival of the Maer. And we intend to find it, and use it for our betterment, and protect it from those who would use it for their own gains. This is why we have sent for you, to bring back word from Stuock regarding the Archive, and I gather this was not in vain. Finn, please show the council what you showed me."

Finn stood and pulled out something wrapped in a leaf, and held it out to Karul, who waved him over to Ujenn. Sinnie craned her neck to see, as Finn had been cagey about what Stuock had given him. Ujenn took the parcel and unwrapped it, smiling as she read a note written on birch paper between the leaf and a smooth, gray stone with an odd shape.

"Find this, and you are there," she said, dropping the note into the fire, where it flared for a moment as it was incinerated. She held up the rock, examining it from all angles, then passed it to Karul, who looked it over and gave it to Fabaris, who studied it before passing it to Luez.

Luez held it on the flat palm of her hand, a smile creeping across her thin lips. "Clever little man," she said, tossing the rock back to Fabaris, who fumbled but caught it. He turned it over in his fingers, his eyes transfixed, then he shot Luez a quizzical look.

"This is the door," she said. "Or the shape of the door. Find a big rock with this exact shape, and you have found the Archive."

"Doesn't look much like a door," Karul said, laying down the rod and taking the stone back from Fabaris. Sinnie's fingers twitched; she wished she could have a turn examining it.

"Perhaps the door is concealed in such a rock," Fabaris suggested.

"Or maybe the rock *is* the Archive," Ujenn said. "If it's a big enough rock, that is. Maybe everything is inside."

Fabaris shook his head vigorously. "The Archive is a great underground structure," he said. "This much we know. The rock could be the entrance, or mark the entrance somehow."

"Well we'll figure that out when we find it," Karul said. "And with winter fast approaching, we have little time to spare. It must be three weeks travel to the Great Tooth, if we can even find the way." Sinnie's stomach began turning as he spoke. She had never been invited to a council meeting before, and it was starting to dawn on her why she was here. She nudged Finn, who put a hand on her knee, his eyes fixed on the proceedings.

"I can find it," Luez said. "I have seen many maps, and I keep them all in here." She tapped on her forehead. "But once we find the Tooth, we still must scour every valley for a rock that looks like this. In the icy rain and snow, with limited food. It would be wiser to wait for spring," she added in a defeated tone.

"It has been decided." Karul dropped the rock in his pocket. "We leave in two days. This gives us just enough time to square away a few things here and prepare for our journey. Which brings me to my next point." He picked the rod back up and turned toward Carl, Finn, and Sinnie.

Sinnie found herself standing up and reaching for the rod. Karul smiled in surprise and let her take it. She glanced over at Finn and Carl, who both nodded, Finn with a little smile, Carl with a frown.

"We're in," she said, suddenly half out of breath. "I mean, I'm sure Carl's in, and Finn and I won't want to stay behind if Carl's going, so we're in, if you will have us, that is." She glanced at Finn and Carl, who both smiled, then she handed the rod back to Karul and sat down, her legs trembling with nervous excitement. As unpleasant as a long trip through the mountain cold sounded, the mystery of the

Archive, and the thrill of this unknown adventure, had lit a sudden fire in her.

"Very good," Karul said. "Then all that remains are the details, which can be worked out tomorrow. In the meantime, we would hear of your encounter with the Wild Maer during your return trip."

Sinnie motioned to Finn with her chin, as she was feeling spent after her little outburst. Finn stood, awkwardly accepted the rod, and gave a blow-by-blow account of the encounter. The Maer all listened intently, and it seemed that Fabaris took a particularly keen interest, asking for clarification on several details. Finn's Maer wasn't perfect, but it was better than Sinnie's, and the Maer seemed satisfied.

"They call themselves the Free Maer," Fabaris said to Sinnie and her friends once he had taken the rod. "They do not align themselves with the Great Council, but to individual clans, which occasionally fight, but more often help each other in times of need. And the beast you described, it must be a *Frasti*, a kind of over-sized badger that is native to these mountains but seldom seen. The Free Maer are known to be especially good at taming beasts of all kinds, and each clan specializes, if you will, in one beast, or a family of beasts. It would not surprise me to hear that the Free Maer you encountered might make use of weasels, badgers, or even bear."

"And if as you say, oh, excuse me." Sinnie paused to take the rod, which Fabaris extended with a kind smile. "If as you say these clans each have one type of beast, could that mean this, which we took off the...foot of a...*hawk*, sorry I don't know the Maer word, a hunting bird, that I shot, might come from a different clan?" She handed the beaded cord to Fabaris, who inspected it, nodded, then passed it to Ujenn, who looked at it for a long time.

"This is from the Wild Maer, for sure," Ujenn said. "The knowledge of falconry has been lost to us since the Great Betrayal, but it is said there are Wild Maer who control hawks and other birds, crows, pigeons, eagles, even, it is said..." Ujenn glanced at Fabaris, who nodded. "If they have a mage with enough knowledge and power, they could even control dragons."

The very word sent Sinnie's mind spinning into a universe of tangents, and the rush of words shared between the Maer and her companions flew by her like sparks from the campfire, fading too fast for the eye to catch. She pictured her father, a younger man then, his shoulders still broad and his chin held high, venturing out alone into these very mountains, with nothing but his wits and his long knife. He had told her of seeing a baby dragon, the size of a pony, curled up on itself like a boulder, with perfect camouflage, down to scales that looked like lichen and moss. Tales told of dragons many times that size, slithering, climbing, and leaping among the mountain peaks, and there was a painting in the Brocland chapel of a dragon slithering its way down a long, sinuous valley from a mountaintop shrouded in mist.

These visions stayed with her that night, following her into her dreams, where she chased a dragon through a dark forest, its feathery tail slipping behind one tree, then the next as it forever eluded her, crashing through the underbrush as she followed in its wake, a fierce grin on her face and fire in her legs.

Chapter:
Ten

Grisol stood awkwardly outside the humans' lean-to. She had seen Carl consulting with Luez, and Finn was standing in the yellowed stalks of the garden doing his ritual poses, dressed only in a light tunic despite the cold. She knew Sinnie was a sound sleeper, but breakfast time had come and gone, and Sinnie still had not emerged. Grisol decided there was no point in waiting; with the big expedition coming up tomorrow there was plenty of work to do, and she could ill afford to go running about the countryside. But the idea of it, of running just to run, with no destination, free of walls and chores and responsibilities—she could not put it out of her mind. She stepped up to the lean-to and knocked on the door.

"*I'm awake,*" said Sinnie in Islish, sounding very much the opposite. "Come on in," she said in Maer, and Grisol moved the door aside and entered the dark, drafty little space the humans called home. Sinnie sat on the edge of her bed, rubbing her eyes and shivering. "Good," she said. "I love to run when it's cold."

"Your Maer is much improved," Grisol said.

"Well, the guards in Stuock's tower didn't speak Islish, so I had a lot of time to practice."

"And did they teach you a thing or two about knife fighting?" Grisol eyed Sinnie's long steel knife, which sat on the stump by her bed.

"They did," Sinnie said, pulling on her wool coat with the black leather shoulders and sliding the knife into its scabbard, which was fitted onto the coat's built-in belt. What the humans could do with clothing was a marvel. "And I taught them about shooting, though we had to make them a bow, and not a very good one I'm afraid. It's not really my...*specialty*, my thing; I mostly just shoot them and let the bow maker do his job."

"Your specialty," Grisol said. "Humans seem so specialized." She had noticed so many little details, from the buttons on Sinnie's coat to the craftsmanship of her knife, not to speak of her boots, all of which suggested a culture where people mastered a single trade to such a level they couldn't well have done much else.

"A lot of people are, yes," Sinnie admitted as she tightened her belt, then drained a cup of water. "Like me. Before I came here, before my...adventure with Carl and Finn, I was...I shot...things with my bow in a *traveling show*, to give people a bit of fun."

"And that's all you did? Just shoot your bow for people's entertainment?"

"Well, I helped with the show, I did a bit of acting, a bit of singing, some...*acrobatics*, jumping and tumbling, but the bow was my main thing. My *job*, if you will." Grisol looked at Sinnie, perplexed by the Islish word, which she did not recognize. "It's what I was paid to do."

"You were paid, in coins, tiny metal discs, in exchange for services, yes? Copper, silver, and the like?"

Sinnie nodded. "Stamped with the Realm's symbol, good anywhere in the Realm, and beyond. Here, let me show you." She reached into her bag, pulled out a small leather pouch, and tossed it to Grisol.

It was heavier than it looked, and when Grisol loosened the string she found it half full of shiny metal discs. Sinnie gestured her approval, and Grisol pulled out one of the coins, which was silver in color like Sinnie's knife, but duller, and had the image of a five-pointed star stamped into its surface. "Your word is *coins*, yes?" Sinnie nodded, smiling. "And you can give them to people in exchange for other things? Like, a knife, or a coat? Our stories from the old days mention this kind of trade, but we haven't used coins for a long time."

"It's kind of strange now that you mention it," Sinnie said. "Something about the shiny metal, I guess. People kill for it." Her voice went soft, and Grisol wondered for a moment if the coin in her hand had been payment for Sinnie to kill Roubay. It was ridiculous, of course; Roubay and the others had attacked the humans, but still she wondered if Sinnie hadn't been paid these very coins to go down the road that led her to that fatal encounter.

"I brought you some jerky and a couple figs," Grisol said, shaking her head and blinking away the thought. She held out her offering to Sinnie, who took it with a smile.

"Just right before a run," Sinnie said, tearing into the jerky with her teeth. "Something to keep me going, but not enough to slow me down. You've eaten?" Grisol nodded. "Drink some water, more than you think you need, and meet me at the gate in a bit. You don't think anyone will...be bothered, do you?"

Grisol closed her eyes and shook her head. "It will be fine," she said, though it was not entirely true. The guards wouldn't stop them from leaving, but there would be questions to answer on their return, responsibilities she would have to make up for. And that was a price she was willing to pay.

?

The air was cold and sharp in Grisol's lungs, and she struggled to keep up with Sinnie as they made their way down the mountain at a slow jog. Once they reached the valley, they stopped for a breather, though it didn't look like Sinnie needed it. Sinnie leaned into a rock and stretched her legs out, and Grisol followed her lead. She had seen a few soldiers stretch, before or after training, but she hadn't done it much herself.

"If you don't mind, I'd like to run this way, along what we call *Valleys Road*. Just so I can feel a little closer to Brocland."

"Sure," Grisol said. "I'm ready. Just not too fast; what we've done this far is about as much as I've ever had to run without stopping."

Grisol felt her face sink as a childhood memory rose in her mind. Her family had been forced to run from a group of Wild Maer, who had surprised them on their way back from foraging. The Wild Maer had two wolves, one of which had pulled down her little brother as they fled toward the relative safety of the village, where the Wild Maer wouldn't follow them. Her father had scooped up her brother and kept the wolves at bay with his spear, but whenever she ran fast, the image came to her.

Sinnie squinted toward the path ahead. "Shall we?" Grisol nodded and followed Sinnie, who kept a steady but slower pace, her strong legs light and nimble over the rutted path. After a time, Sinnie slowed a bit and began running next to her.

"I'm sorry if I was rude yesterday, about the situation with Carl and Ujenn," Grisol said, struggling to keep her breath as she ran.

"Oh gods no, please, *I* am sorry. You're right, it's private, and I was rude to ask."

"No, it's fine, it's...you're right. It is strange, it makes me feel weird, but it's...gotten better, and Carl is very...respectful." She found it hard to say that she had feelings for Carl. "I just...well, I don't know your and Carl's history, so I figured it was best not to—"

Sinnie started laughing, and finally slowed to a walk, then stopped, putting her hands on her knees as the laughter subsided. "There's no...history, there never was, and there never will be. I'm not interested, at all."

"What, is he not...attractive? He does have fine muscles, and his face, well, I don't know how to judge. The whole skin thing has taken a little getting used to. No offense," she said, and Sinnie waved her off with a smile. "I imagine it must have been weird for him too, though being with Ujenn, he would have grown accustomed to the hair."

Sinnie giggled, a bit nervously, Grisol thought. "He's fine, he's good-looking enough I suppose. There's nothing wrong with him. I'm just...not into that. At all." She made a definitive gesture with her hands.

"So you prefer women then?" Grisol asked, hoping it wasn't inappropriate, as she didn't know the humans' sexual customs.

"No, well, I do prefer being around women, but mostly because men are such...*pigs*, such animals, or a lot of them anyway. But not all of them, and not Carl, and not Finn. No, it's just...sex isn't something that ever...interested me." Sinnie turned again toward the direction they had been heading, her face flushed, and not just from the run.

"It does add some unnecessary complications, that's for sure," Grisol said. Sinnie turned and flashed her a warm smile. "So how much farther are we running, anyway?"

"How about we make for that big rock there, then head back?" Sinnie bounced up and down a few times, huffing her breath in and out. Grisol nodded, looking at the rock, which must have been a half-mile ahead. She forced her weary legs to lift and fall, lift and fall, in rhythm with Sinnie's frustratingly easy stride.

As they came around a bend in the path, they both stopped cold. Before them, several hundred yards away, stood a large tent of the richest red Grisol had ever seen, with red flags bearing the same five-pointed star as the coins, in a silver color that glinted in the sun. A group of horses grazed beside the pavilion, and a handful of humans milled about.

"*The Realm*," Sinnie said in Islish, her voice distant. "They're here."

"The who?" Grisol's heart raced, and not just from the running.

"The...soldiers of the king."

"The Realm? That doesn't sound good." Grisol looked up at Sinnie, whose face showed no fear.

"Well I guess if it were really bad, they would have come with an army." Sinnie scanned the group. "This looks like an...*invitation* to talk." Grisol cocked her head as she tried to puzzle out the word Sinnie was trying to say. Sinnie waved her hands about. "Like they want us to talk. And if I didn't know any better..." she trailed off, shielding her eyes to get a better look, then turned to Grisol. "I think I know that man. I think...that's Gerald Leavitt."

"Who's he?" Grisol asked, bewildered by the spectacle, the sudden appearance of such flamboyant luxury, which did not seem to bother Sinnie at all.

"Come with me and I'll introduce you," Sinnie said with a smile, taking Grisol's hand and pulling her forward. Grisol held her ground for a moment, but the look in Sinnie's eyes said there was nothing to fear. As they got to within about fifty yards of the tent, Grisol could see that in addition to the old man, there were four soldiers, plus a female figure she could not see well, and a couple more perhaps behind the tent with a cart and horses. Two of the soldiers began walking toward them, wearing shiny silver armor with red scarves, and red plumes on their helmets. They carried shields of similar brilliance with a silver star inside a red circle, and their swords gleamed in the sunlight. The older man, who wore a long fur coat, called after them, stopping them in their tracks. He spoke with them for a moment, then strode onto the path, walking toward Sinnie and Grisol with his arms open wide. The two soldiers followed about ten feet behind.

"Sinnie!" he called as he got closer. "*It is good to see you...*" He continued, but Grisol missed most of it, as her Islish was still a work in progress. It was clear that his words came from a place of genuine warmth, whatever he was saying, and whatever motives might lie beneath.

"Mr. Leavitt," Sinnie said, stepping forward and offering her hand, which he took, trying to pull her in for a hug, but she held her ground, so he put a hand on her shoulder. Grisol felt a nervous giggle bubble up inside but managed to quash it. *"What brings you to the Maer..."* Grisol ground her teeth as she struggled to follow the conversation.

"Well I was...to speak with Karul, if it's not...." Grisol missed half of what he said, but he spoke with more delicacy than Grisol would have expected for a man of such obvious importance. *"But there is no... Please, come, sit! Have a glass of wine and some..."* He gestured toward a table, on which were laid out several silvery covered platters, presumably filled with whatever he had said. *"Does she...?"* The man gestured toward Grisol, who bowed slightly.

"She speaks a little Islish, but I can speak Maer, more or less, so I'll..." Sinnie finished whatever she was saying, then turned to Grisol and spoke in Maer. "Grisol, I'd like you to meet Gerald Leavitt. He's the father of a friend, and a very important man." Mr. Leavitt squinted at them, as if that would help him understand better. "Mr. Leavitt, meet Grisol, a good friend of mine, and Finn's, and Carl's."

"It is," Leavitt said in badly pronounced, recited Maer, "an honor to meet you, Grisol." He held out his hand, and she shook it as best she could, the gesture being foreign to her. His hand was warm and incredibly soft, like the hand of a baby, untouched by the rigors of life.

"The pleasure is mine," Grisol responded, her head spinning with the weirdness of it all. "I will relay your request to Karul." She glanced at Sinnie, who translated, and Leavitt nodded.

"We can't stay for a drink, Mr. Leavitt. We must go...Karul..." Sinnie continued in Islish, and Grisol missed the rest. Sinnie and Leavitt exchanged a quick look Grisol could not decipher, but she sensed there was something the two of them were hiding, and it filled her

with a sudden rage. She tried to keep it inside as they said their good-byes and turned back toward the castle.

Grisol took out her frustration by walking away as fast as she could once they got moving, then breaking into a run, quickly slowing to a trot as her breath failed her, and Sinnie caught up.

"It's good that they sent him," Sinnie said. "He is...he feels...good things about the Maer."

"How do you know?" Grisol asked, huffing as she tried to keep up the most basic trot.

"He comes from Brocland," Sinnie said. "But I didn't know him very well back in the village. I knew his son Theo a bit, but not well. But...when Carl and Finn and I...when we went back to Brocland, when we..." *When you killed my husband,* Grisol thought, her teeth grinding. "We were taking Theo's body back to Brocland to be...put in the ground, when we were attacked." Sinnie's eyes kept drifting toward the path moving beneath their feet, then back up to Grisol's.

"And how do you know how he feels about the Maer?" Grisol managed, nearly at the end of her breath. "You said no one had ever seen a Maer before your...encounter with..." She tried to keep a tremor from creeping into her voice.

"I know it from Carl," Sinnie said, looking away, then back. "You know all those tools and weapons he brought back?"

Grisol stopped, rested her hands on her knees, and caught her breath before looking up at Sinnie.

"Were those from Leavitt?" Grisol's chest heaved for breath, her brain trying to puzzle out why this human who had never seen a Maer would want to contribute to their cause.

"The money was," Sinnie said, straightening up and stretching backward. "I doubt he told Carl to buy them, but Carl didn't have that much money of his own."

Grisol closed her eyes and nodded. "Okay," she said, opening her eyes and locking them on Sinnie's. "I didn't mean to be suspicious of you. I just can't help feeling like this is a setup somehow."

"Well, you can let Karul and the council decide that," Sinnie said. "And the sooner we get back, the sooner you can tell him all your doubts and fears. If you don't...fall down from tired first."

Grisol let a smile bloom on her face. "Okay. Okay. Let's just take it slow and steady. I can do this." Though she wasn't sure if she could at first, after a few minutes she fell into a rhythm, and the aches in her legs and feet and back dulled as her heart opened, and she even forgot, for a moment, where she was running, and why. It wasn't until they had entered the bailey that the morning's exertion hit her with its full force, and she crumped against the wall.

"Get Karul," Grisol managed as she accepted a waterskin from one of the guards. "The humans have come."

Chapter:
Eleven

KARUL HELPED GRISOL to her feet, and she stood in a half-slump for a moment before straightening up. She was bathed in sweat, despite the cool morning air, and her fatigue showed in her face, but her eyes were sharp, and she looked more appealing than ever.

"Tell me about the humans," Karul said, even as Luez and Ivlana rushed around, making sure every Maer had a weapon in hand. "How many? How far?"

"Just a few, and they have not come for battle." Grisol counted off on her fingers as she spoke. "There were only four soldiers, an old man named Leavitt, whom Sinnie seemed to know, and a woman, but I didn't get a good look at her. Some kind of warrior, I think. And one or two others, taking care of their horses. You can tell everyone to stand down. They have set up a big red tent, just around the north bend, with flags and tables covered in food and drink."

"It sounds like a trick." Karul found himself almost disappointed that the humans had not come for battle. Though Carl had warned him the Maer were no match for the Realm in terms of sheer numbers and armaments, he thought Carl might just be underestimating the Maer's strength, and he hoped the Realm would as well. "We will remain on high alert. I will send out extra patrols, one in the woods and the other in the mountains, to make sure this isn't a diversion."

"I'll help get the archers set up." Grisol's eyes were hungry for approval. She clearly wanted to move up in the ranks, and she was doing what it took to get there. As to whether she would be open to advance more than just her position in Castle Maer, that was a question for another day.

"Very good. I will leave Ivlana in charge of the infantry, and you will be in charge of the archers. Get Sinnie to help if you can."

Grisol conveyed the orders to Ivlana, who looked disappointed not to be joining him in his foray to meet the humans, but she was the only one he could trust with the castle defense. Karul summoned Luez, Fabaris, Carl, and four of his better warriors.

"We ride out to meet the humans the Realm has sent," he said. "We do not expect battle, but if it should come, we will be ready." The warriors puffed up as he said this, and Luez smirked. Karul shot her a scorching glance, which had little effect. She let the smirk fade from her lips, but he could swear it was still present in her eyes.

"Carl," Karul said, "I assume Sinnie has informed you of what she saw. What counsel would you offer?" He did not like relying on the humans, but there was no denying their usefulness. They had proven their loyalty on more than one occasion, but he had a hard time trusting them completely.

"I know Mr. Leavitt," Carl said, his eyes unreadable. "It was he who hired us for the errand on which we encountered the...Roubay and the others. As you may recall, we were transporting a body back to Brocland for burial. The body was that of Theo, Gerald Leavitt's son, who, I should mention, was also a mage like Finn. Leavitt is fascinated by the Maer, and I believe him to be sympathetic to your cause, though he may have hidden agendas I am not aware of."

"Good, we can use your familiarity with him to our advantage" Karul said. "When we—"

Carl held up a finger to interrupt him, which Karul would not have tolerated from one of the Maer, but he held his tongue. "I should tell you," said Carl, looking uncomfortable, "about an arrangement I have with Leavitt. You remember all the tools and weapons I brought back with me when I returned?" Karul nodded, his jaw clenching. "It was Leavitt who gave me the money to buy them. Or rather, he gave me the money, and I chose to spend it to help you out. Our agreement was that I would return in one year's time, and would share information with him, but only what I chose to share. And—"

"I knew it was too good to be true," Karul spat. "To think that we believed your gifts were pure generosity. But no, I am learning that you humans have a most subtle way of operating. You give with one hand, but with the other—"

"Karul." Luez spoke softly. "Take a breath." Karul glared at her, and at Carl, and Fabaris for good measure, then took a moment to regain his composure. Luez continued. "If Carl had ulterior motives, why would he be telling us all of this? Why would he have risked his life against the *mashtorul*? Why would he be training us in sword-play, and in Islish, and putting in as much work as any Maer in the day to day maintenance of Castle Maer and its security? And yet..." Luez turned toward Carl, her voice taking a turn lower. "I would like to hear the rest of what he was trying to say."

Carl nodded, glancing up at Luez, then at Karul. "Thank you. I made it clear to Leavitt that I would not be giving any information detrimental to Maer security, and he agreed to give me information in return, answers to my questions. Gerald Leavitt has many connections among the Realm's power brokers, being one of their number himself. Think of the value of having access to that kind of insider information, just think—"

Karul silenced him by raising his hand. He breathed deeply, hoping to keep at bay the tremble of rage he felt creeping into his limbs. "And when exactly were you planning on telling me about this, arrangement, as you call it?"

Carl looked down, then back up. "I didn't know if it would pan out, what information he would offer. But you're right. I was wrong to keep it from you, and I apologize. I understand if that means you don't want me to join you, if you don't—"

"Bah!" Karul said, putting a hand on Carl's shoulder as his anger subsided. He had a soft spot for people who admitted when they were wrong, and at any rate Carl's inside knowledge was irreplaceable. "We need you, Carl. And we need to trust you. You have given us much, and we have much yet to ask of you." He kept his hand on Carl's shoulder, at a loss for what to say next. "I choose to believe you for now. Let us go and see what this Mister Leavitt has to say."

?

The pavilion was impressive, blazing red in the sun that filtered between the clouds. Red flags with silvery stars billowed in the breeze. A long table under the pavilion was laid out with shiny covered dishes, and a man tended some kind of carcass stretched over a fire. The aroma of roasted meat filled the air, something Karul did not recognize, which set his stomach growling. Behind the tent were a number of horses, as well as an arrangement of what looked like equipment and provisions. An older human male draped in a heavy fur coat approached. A female walked at his side, wearing mesh armor similar to Carl's, with purple accents, and two short swords in leather scabbards at her belt. Four warriors in shiny armor with red plumage on their helmets flanked them, their shields painted red and emblazoned with the same silver star as the flags. The opulence of the humans was almost unimaginable.

"Greetings," the old man said in Maer, though his accent was terrible. He switched to Islish and continued. "*Thank you for...*" he said, but Karul didn't catch the rest of it.

"He says thank you for accepting his invitation," Carl said.

"*You are welcome,*" Karul managed, nearly exhausting his knowledge of Islish. "I am Karul," he said in Maer, "and I represent Castle Maer. I welcome you to our land." He spread his arms toward the mountains above and the forest below as Carl translated.

The old man nodded, his expression kind, while the woman's face remained stern, her eyes alert, her bearing proud and unflinching. Karul took an instant liking to her.

"*I am Gerald Leavitt...*" the old man said in Islish, going on at some length. Karul heard the words 'Maer' and '*men,*' but not much else. He then gestured to the woman and said a name, Christel, and a few more words. She gave a curt nod at the mention of her name.

Carl turned toward Karul as he translated. "Leavitt says he is an ambassador, here to assure you of the Realm's peaceful intentions toward the Maer. I should add that I have never known him to be an ambassador, but rather a..." He gestured as he looked for the word, shaking his head. "He puts together armies and sends them to war, but he was never a warrior. It's complicated. Anyway, he says the woman with him is Christel of the house of Aguen, who I believe is the niece of King Rodolf, the Realm's ruler. If that's true, she's a potential heir to the throne."

"Tell Mister Leavitt we hope their spies have recovered from their injuries." Karul waved down Luez's disapproving look. "Insist that we only responded to their aggression, and that we did not shoot to kill." Carl looked him in the eyes for a moment, then blinked and translated. Leavitt nodded, smiled, and almost gave a chuckle. Christel did not visibly react, but she was scrutinizing the faces of each of the Maer, and seemed to spend the most time studying Luez.

Leavitt spoke at some length, but Karul hardly caught a word of it. Carl answered in Islish, and Karul shot Luez a glance, which she deflected. They did not want the humans to know she understood Islish.

"He says their scouts are fine," Carl reported, "and he thanks you for asking. He says they showed poor...I don't know the word in Maer, but it's what spies do to collect information and stay hidden."

"Tradecraft," Karul, said with a chuckle.

"They showed poor tradecraft," Carl repeated, stumbling a bit on the new word. "He insists they were only there to make sure the...you...were not massing forces for an attack. He says they needed to know if what happened near Brocland was an isolated incident. He seems satisfied on that count, though the presence of the king's niece shows they are taking you seriously."

"Ask him how he got here so fast," Karul said. "We flushed out their spies less than two weeks ago. It hardly seems time enough to organize a diplomatic mission like this."

"The humans have falcon messengers, just like your pigeons, but faster," Carl said. "Shall I ask anyway?"

Karul waved him off. "Ask him..." Karul was at a loss. "Ask him why he's here. What does he want? I think we've had enough pleas-antries."

Carl said in Islish, "*Karul wants...*" Leavitt nodded, closed his eyes, and gestured toward a man in the tent. The man tugged the leash on one of the horses, which trudged forward, pulling a cart with five barrels of various sizes on it. The humans with their horses, Karul mused, were a lot like the Wild Maer. The service of such beasts would be a huge advantage, and he made a mental note to ask Carl to teach him to ride. Carl had brought his own horse, which he rode on occasion, but Sinnie and Finn had come on foot, having rid-den borrowed mounts as far as Brocland, from what he could gather. Leavitt spoke, gesturing toward the barrels, which had words burned into them.

"He says he has come to bring gifts, as a show of good faith," Carl said. "He hopes you will accept them, and that this will be the begin-ning of a long friendship between our...between men and Maer."

"Well this is awkward. I haven't brought him anything," Karul muttered. "What's the protocol here?" He looked to Fabaris, who held his hands wide and shrugged his shoulders.

"I think you accept the gifts, and next time, you reciprocate."

Karul nodded, then turned to Leavitt. "We thank you for your kind offering. What gifts have you brought?"

Leavitt smiled as he listened to Carl's translation, then said a few words to the man, who must have been a warrior in his day. The man heaved the barrels down from the wagon with ease, lined them up, and pried them open with a small piece of metal.

"Flour," Carl said, apparently reading the words on the barrels. "Honey, dried fish, wine, and salt."

"Which one is salt?" Karul asked. Carl pointed to a barrel the size of a pumpkin. "Such a gift," Karul murmured. Leavitt lifted the lid from each barrel and showed the contents, saying a few words about each one.

"He says the five barrels represent the five regions of the Realm," Carl explained. "Fish from the Isle, flour from the plains, salt from the north coast, honey from Gheil, and wine from the east. Those regions are what the points on the star represent as well."

"A most well-thought-out gift," Fabaris commented. "We shall have to think long and hard about how best to return the favor."

"And we must think long and hard on the true motives behind all of this," Karul said. "Carl, what is your take?"

Carl shook his head, squinting. "I can't put my finger on it, but it is not how I would expect the Realm to approach the situation. They are not known for diplomacy. I expect Leavitt used his influence to get appointed ambassador, and the princess is here to keep an eye on him."

"And an ear on us," Luez whispered, her glance flickering from Karul to Christel. "I think she can understand us."

Karul mouthed *How?* Luez shook her head. Karul wondered if Christel had sussed out that Luez understood Islish as well.

"*Thank you, Mister Leavitt,*" Karul said. "We receive these gifts in friendship," he continued in Maer, "and we look forward to being able to return the favor at our next meeting."

Leavitt beamed with pleasure as he heard the translation, and he began babbling excitedly in Islish, pointing toward the table.

"He says—" Carl began, but Karul stopped him.

"I get the gist," he said. "It's time to eat. And I, for one, am eager to taste whatever is cooking over that spit."

Chapter:
Twelve

Luez waited while the leaders served themselves, heaping their plates with unreserved gusto. She noticed Christel standing to the side, observing the festivities while sneaking sidelong glances at her. Christel stood straight and strong, like Sinnie, but with a warrior's muscles. If she was put off by the presence of the Maer, she hid it well. Luez sidled over to her, determined to break the ice.

"Nice swords," Luez said in Southish. Christel's green eyes flashed for a moment, then cooled. Luez had struck her mark.

"Thank you," Christel responded in perfect Southish. "My father gave them to me as a gift on my fourteenth birthday." She pulled out one of the blades and handed it to Luez hilt first. Luez smiled as she took the blade, hefted it, took a step back, and swung it a few times. It was not unlike the Southish blade Luez carried, though more ornate. Flawless steel, perfect balance, sharp as the break of day, though she couldn't imagine how Christel could wield two swords with any efficacy. She handed it back, then offered her own sword, which brought a smile to Christel's lips.

"You've spent some time in the South," Christel observed.

"Have you not?" Luez asked.

Christel shook her head and looked Luez in the eyes. Her gaze was both flat and piercing, giving away little while seeking what Luez was trained not to reveal. "I have studied the language, among others," she said, "but I have not yet had the opportunity to travel as widely as I might like."

"I'm surprised they let you come this far." Luez relished the flush Christel was not able to keep from her cheeks. For all her skills and her swagger, she was a protected princess, and that obviously bothered her. "You should visit the South. It's lovely. One feels free there, and the food is spectacular. If you like it spicy."

"I do," Christel said. "I'll see if I can get permission to visit one of these days." Her eyes sparked with something that felt like respect. "Tell me, are there a lot of Maer in the South?" Her tone was so smooth Luez almost dropped her guard.

"More than in the Realm."

"Touché." Christel seemed to be enjoying their interaction just as much as Luez was. "Well, it appears the men have left us a little something to eat if you're hungry. Oh, but look at the poor soldiers standing there with hands on their hilts like little boys waiting to be told what to do." Christel barked at the soldiers in Islish to put aside their weapons, sit down, and have some food, her eyes flickering back to Luez as she spoke.

Luez did her best to pretend she didn't understand, but she was pretty sure Christel had figured it out, just as Luez was certain Christel understood at least some Maer. Luez told her warriors to follow suit, gesturing to them to sit opposite where Christel's men were gathering. Luez and Christel watched the men stare at each other and at the food until finally one of the Maer warriors stuck a tong in a piece of roasted meat and dropped the meat on one of the humans' plates. The human took the tong and did the same for him. Within moments, the warriors had all served each other, and Christel moved to the platter and picked up the tong.

"It's kind of sweet, actually, how civilized they can be when they don't know what the hell is going on," Luez said.

"I doubt if anyone here really does." Christel served herself a thick slice of steak with a bone in it, a helping of dripping greens, and a slab of bread, which she smeared with butter. Luez almost melted at the sight; as good a cook as Ty was, the Maer did not have proper bread, or butter. It had been years since she had eaten it, when she was in study in the borderlands, and then only on special occasions. It was said to be commonplace among humans, especially on the Isle. She watched Christel dig in, then served herself, not as much as she wanted, but more than she needed.

"Is this beef?" Luez asked, her taste buds flooded with the unusually rich meat. She'd never had the chance to try it, but now she understood why humans were always talking about it.

"It is," Christel said, smiling and wincing as the sun came out from behind a cloud. "The finest steak in the Isle. Mr. Leavitt insisted on it."

"He's a very generous man," Luez said. "A suspicious person might wonder what he wants in return for this show of goodwill."

Christel pointed at Luez with a piece of steak on her knife. "A less suspicious person might wonder why you would want to ruin a perfectly good steak by quibbling about politics."

Luez raised her palms, then picked up her knife and fork and went to work as best she could. She had seen humans eat with a fork, but she had never actually used one before. She managed well enough, and she worked her way through the steak and most of the bread and greens before she took a breather. Normally she didn't eat much at ceremonial dinners, as she was too busy looking out for all the ways things could go wrong. In this case, maybe it was the butter, but she felt at ease, and she was enjoying trying to interpret Christel's smallest gesture. Was she listening in on the conversations between the Maer leadership? And how much could she understand?

"You seem very gifted with languages," Luez offered.

"*I was about to say the same about you*," Christel whispered in Islish. "Which is why I can't figure out why you insist on speaking Southish with me," she continued in Southish. "Not that I mind the practice; it's been almost a year since I had a regular conversation partner."

"And who was your conversation partner when you learned Maer?" Luez said in a low voice in Maer.

Christel's weak smile showed she understood, but not everything. "It must have been a different dialect," she said in Southish.

The Wild Maer, Luez thought. The Realm might have captured one, kept them as a prisoner, and forced them to teach her the language. They probably had no idea there was a difference between the Maer and the Wild Maer. "Could be," Luez said, making a show of furrowing her brow. "Even I have a hard time understanding some of the Maer from the east."

Luez waved away the wine brought by a human boy, who seemed to be some kind of servant. He carried a tray with two silver cups on it, and Christel took both cups when Luez refused, placing one in front of each of them.

"I can see you're not a drinker, but you simply must try this wine. It's been sitting in a cask for thirty years, waiting for this moment. You won't regret it."

Luez lifted the glass along with Christel and took a sip. She had to work hard to hide her pleasure in the elixir. She flashed what she hoped was a wan smile and put her cup back down.

"It's a sight better than our mushroom wine," Luez admitted.

"Mushroom what?" Christel covered her mouth.

"We don't have grapes," Luez said. "At least not anymore." Some of Fabaris' boring old poems spoke of wine from grapes, but that was another age.

"We could bring you some. A...a vine, a rootstock, whatever they call it. As, you know, a sign of goodwill. I'm sure my father—" Christel stopped, wincing. Luez could tell she didn't like relying on her privilege. "I'm sure we can work something out."

"Our gardener would be thrilled," Luez said, noticing the Maer and human warriors getting chummy and pouring another sloppy round, though none of them could understand a word the others said. "Oh, but look, the men are downing entire cups of this wine in...what looks like a drinking contest. With thirty-year-old wine."

"I wouldn't worry about that. The warriors will have been given the younger stuff. Mr. Leavitt's generosity does have its limits."

Christel cut off her warriors soon thereafter, and things seemed to be winding down. Leavitt stood talking to Karul and Fabaris, with Carl interpreting. Luez stood in time with Christel, and they made their way toward the conversation.

"*I like your offer*," Leavitt was saying, "*and I will pass it on, and send the Realm's response via messenger. And please, if it's not too much to ask, don't shoot him.*"

When he heard Carl's translation, Karul threw back his head in laughter, which Luez could tell was for show, since that was not one of his usual gestures. "We don't shoot messengers," Karul responded. "Only spies." Leavitt forced his own laugh when he heard it in Islish.

"*Look for a response in a few weeks' time*," Leavitt said, shaking hands with each of the Maer, even the warriors, who did a poor job of hiding their discomfort with the gesture. Leavitt's face wore the same amazed smile as when they had first ridden up. It appeared Carl had spoken the truth. For whatever reason, Leavitt was a friend to the Maer. But the Realm might well take a different view.

"I look forward to meeting you again," Karul said.

"And next time, we will supply the lunch," Fabaris added.

?

They made their way back to Castle Maer with their cart full of gifts, and the horse that came with it. Karul and Carl became locked in a deep conversation, and Fabaris slowed to fall in step with Luez.

He looked eager to talk, but he said nothing for a while, longer than usual.

"I noticed you talking with the woman, Christel, who is...some kind of princess?"

"Some kind, yes," Luez said. "But not the kind I've ever heard of." The Maer no longer had royalty, but tales of the old days often had princesses waiting to be manipulated for the good of their fathers. None of the princesses in the stories carried a sword, let alone two.

"And you spoke in Southish, I presume?" Fabaris said.

Luez nodded. "She speaks it like a native, but she said she has never been to the South. She also understands some Maer, but not very well. I think the Realm must have captured a Wild Maer and forced them to teach her their language."

Fabaris' face twitched for a moment before returning to its usual placid state. "The two of you seem to have a lot in common," was all he said, but Luez sensed something was bothering him.

"Indeed," Luez replied. "I like her. But if the Realm sent her along with Leavitt, she must be in intelligence too. She figured out that I understand Islish, and there's no telling what else she sussed out from our meeting. No doubt more than we'd like."

Fabaris stroked his chin braids. "We will have a lot to digest in council tonight," he said.

Luez nodded. "As will they, no doubt."

Chapter:
Thirteen

Fabaris left Luez to her preferred silence for the remainder of the trip back to the castle, mostly because he thought she had noticed his hesitation at the term Wild Maer. Ujenn was the only one he had told of his background, but he was afraid Luez might puzzle it out, at which point he would have to tell Karul. He should have said something before, but Karul's disdain for the term Free Maer had kept Fabaris' lips sealed. He tried to play the impartial arbiter whenever the subject came up, but in reality he was sickened by the way people talked, as if the Free Maer were primitive just because they chose not to ally themselves with the Great Council. It was true that the Free Maer had been known to attack and kill Maer who unknowingly stumbled into their territory, but it was also true that the Maer would kill or imprison the Free Maer whenever they got the chance. Though it had been more than thirty years ago, he still retained the memory of his own abduction.

He had been sent on a fishing trip with two older boys, along with an otter, an old one they called Vistreef, with a white stripe on his forehead. They would set their net in the shallow end of a pool in a mountain stream, and Vistreef would dive into the deep end of the pool and chase the fish through a narrow opening in the net, which they would close, then collect the fish. They would give Vistreef the biggest one, then toss the rest into a leather sack and head upstream.

They worked every third pool, marking the ones they had fished with a little pyramid of rocks, so they would remember next time which one to skip. They weren't allowed to return until their sack was full, which took the better part of a day. As they approached their village near dusk, they could see the smoke from over the next hill, and they dropped their sack full of silvers and broke into a run.

The older boys had pulled ahead of Fabaris, and when he came around the edge of the big round rock at the village entrance, his legs were swept from beneath him. His face slammed into the ground, and he tasted dust and blood. A sack was pulled over his head and his arms were bound. He heard a lot of shouting in a language he did not quite understand, but also the cries of the older boys, who sounded like they had put up a fight, or as much as two boys could against grown Maer. He never saw his captors during the days-long march; the sack was pulled up above his mouth to allow him to eat and drink, but his eyes remained covered. He could tell that his captors were Maer by the hair on their arms, but more than that he could not determine. He tripped and fell countless times and was dragged to his feet by the cursing soldiers. The curse words, at least, were mostly the same, and after a time he began to pick up a few other words, like drink, eat, stop, get up, idiot child.

Every time they stopped, the soldiers would spin him around and around until he got dizzy and fell to the ground, so there was no way to tell what direction they were traveling. After a week or more of marching up and down and through icy creeks and hot valleys and windy passes they arrived in a village, much larger than his by the sound of the voices, which he was starting to understand a little better. He had heard the speech of other tribes of Free Maer, which he could mostly understand, but this was another dialect altogether. He realized at last this could only be the tongue of the Old Maer, as they were called in his tribe's stories. To hear their language was said to be the kiss of death.

According to legend, the Old Maer had gone deep underground after the Great Betrayal, hiding away from humans and developing dark magics and secret rituals. They were thieves, plunderers, kidnappers, murderers, soul eaters. They would kill the adults in a village and take the children away as slaves, or worse. To be captured by the Old Maer was to live a short, miserable life of pain, hunger, and thankless toil, if one were lucky. Those who were not so fortunate were kept underground in dank caves, their souls extracted drop by drop by the mages, who used them to work spells of unspeakable evil. Fabaris mentally prepared himself, as best an eight-year-old boy could, for a fate beyond imagining.

When at last his hood was removed, he stood in a thatched hut, not unlike his home back in the village, facing two female Maer with kindly faces and beautifully decorated fur robes. One of them walked up and released his bonds, while the other held out a wooden bowl of some kind of stew. The one who had freed his arms gestured toward a carved wooden chair more elaborate than anything he had ever seen. She put the bowl down on a strange table made up of a slab of wood supported by four sturdy sticks, all worked smooth like the chair. She said something, and the only word he understood was 'eat.' He eyed the two of them, then turned back to face his captors, who had vanished. He looked through the doorway into an open space between huts, and he saw dozens of Maer dressed like the two women who had greeted him: males, females, and children, walking, talking, carrying, laughing.

He had waited for this moment, when he would be free of his bonds and his hood and could make a break for his freedom. He was fast for his age—everyone told him so—but he was tired, and he was hungry, and the stew smelled so good. And besides, where would he go? He had no idea where he was, or how to get back. He was alone, and there was no way to escape for now. So he eased into the chair, held the bowl up to his nose, and hid his tears by taking a big drink of the broth. It was rich, pungent, and earthy, with bits of meat and something it took him a moment to identify—some kind of mushroom he had never tasted before.

Living in Castle Maer, the taste of the sacred mushroom was a daily reminder of what he had lost, of what he was, and what he wasn't. And it was something he had never been able to share, not even with Ujenn, though she knew of his origins. But as much sadness as the memory brought him, it also fed his hunger to know the history of the Maer, and to plan for their future. The Old Maer and the Free Maer had once been the same people, just as, perhaps, Maer and humans came from the same source. He found tidbits in the old poems and songs that supported his theory, though even among scholars this idea was considered sacrilege. But deep down he was sure of it, and his dream was to present incontrovertible evidence to the *Glernedan*, the Maer council of scholars. Evidence, he believed with every fiber of his being, he would find in the Archive.

?

When they were safely inside the bailey, Fabaris took advantage of the crowd awaiting the group's return to slip away to the roost, where the pigeons cooed at his approach. His pockets were empty, and he apologized to the birds, who eventually sulked off to a corner of their cage and huddled together against the cold wind. The rhythmic purring of the pigeons brought to his mind the Ballad of the Place Below, the dirge-like recital of the Maer's suffering as they fled human persecution, the cold and hunger of the caves where they hid, and the memory of what they had left behind. He imagined the poet crafting the lines in the frigid dark, desperate to keep the spark of their culture alive in the Place Below. It took some time for the words to return to the surface, as he had not heard it sung in a long time; the chorus came to him first, then the verses, a line or two at a time, and after an hour or so the whole song had come back to him. He sang it as low as he could, and the pigeons sidled toward him as he sang, their orange beaks sticking out between the sticks of the cage, their heads bobbing in rhythm with the song. As he sang it a second time, he felt chills up his neck and arms when he got to the second verse.

And they buried their songs and their deeds
In the place where the ancestors dwell
Neath a rock with no door and no key
In a shape only Sabra can tell...

He gripped the stone ramparts as he looked out over the valley, barely able to contain his joy. The songs and deeds had to be the Archive; there was no question about it. *The place where the ancestors dwell* could refer to one of the ancient Maer burial mounds scattered throughout the Silver Hills. The only way to know which one was by the shape of the rock at its entrance. It was as he had thought: the ancients had hidden the secret to the Archive and divided the clues between the scholars, the mages, and the leaders. The verse in the song would be noticed only by the scholars, and the shape of the rock was known only to mages like Stuock, and the leaders would have the maps, as Luez had attested. As for the lack of door and key, that would take further contemplation, but the pieces were falling into place. He had some old scrolls written in Ancient Maer that he hoped he might be able to look at with fresh eyes now.

As he made his way through the bailey, he saw Finn doing one of his odd poses in a corner of the garden, his shoulders and feet on the ground and his body arched upwards. He watched as Finn held the position for an incredibly long time, his lean muscles taut and steady. He had vaguely admired Finn's body before, from a purely scholarly perspective, but something stirred in him as he stood watching. Maybe it was the excitement of his recent discovery, or perhaps the staleness of Castle Maer's sexual prospects, but he felt an urge stronger than he had in quite some time. Finn released to the ground, lay still for a moment, then sprang up, stretching his arms towards the sky, then lowered them to point forward, his hands cupped in front of him, as if he were pushing an unseen force out among the cornstalks. Fabaris felt his face flush and his loins rise; there was something about the absurdly hairless man's posture, his focus, that suddenly struck him as irresistible.

He had sensed from the way Finn interacted with Sinnie that he was not interested in her, not physically at any rate. Though Fabaris was no judge of human beauty standards, he had noticed Carl looking at Sinnie in an interested, if deferential, way, so she must have been attractive, but Finn never looked at her like that. Sinnie, for her part, showed no signs of any attraction toward either of them. Humans seemed more reserved about their sexuality than the Maer, but what he had observed of Finn gave him some small reason to hope. If he showed no interest in an attractive female, he might well gravitate toward males. And if Carl could be in love with Ujenn, and mate with Grisol under Ujenn's persuasive guidance, surely it was not out of the question for Finn to find Fabaris attractive, in the right circumstances? He fiddled with his chin braids for a moment, then made for his room, lest he be caught spying. His heart leapt when he heard Finn call out his name.

Chapter:
Fourteen

Finn straightened up and tried to even out his breath as Fabaris made his way through the wilting remains of the garden toward him. Fabaris had been watching him as he went through his routines, and Finn sensed that his interest was more than just a scholar's curiosity. Fabaris was tall and solidly built, fit for his age, which Finn put around forty, though with the Maer, it was hard to tell. At any rate, Fabaris walked with more confidence than was typical among human scholars.

"I apologize if my observation distracted you," Fabaris said, doing a poor job of hiding his embarrassment. "As you might imagine, the ways of human mages are of great interest to me. But I understand the secrecy required in such circles, and again I apologize for my intrusion."

"There are no secrets about the physical side," Finn said. "Anyone can keep their body and mind focused with enough practice. It's not all that different from some of what I've seen your warriors do with their weapons drills."

"Indeed," Fabaris said. "Even our scholars must train in self-defense, and a few of the movements are similar."

"Well you're welcome to join me next time if you like," Finn offered.

"I may just," Fabaris said. "I would be interested to see the similarities and differences between our practices. Cultural comparison is somewhat of a passion of mine." There was a catch in Fabaris' voice as he spoke, and Finn wondered if Fabaris was coming on to him.

"I've been learning quite a bit about that myself," Finn said. "What's most..." he struggled to find the word. "Hitting? Painful?"

"Striking?" Fabaris suggested.

"Yes, what's most striking is how similar everything is," Finn said. "Even what I learned from Stuock was...familiar, somehow."

"Well, I expect he told you about the origin of his discipline?" Fabaris showed extraordinary delicacy regarding the secrecy of magic, more so even than Finn himself.

"Yes," Finn said, unsure how much he should reveal. Stuock said he had learned from Southish mages, but that the magic had Maer sources at its base, which had been lost during the diaspora. "He said it was a mix of Southish and Maer tradition, but that he had learned it in the South."

"Much of what we know about our history and tradition comes from the South these days," Fabaris said with a sigh. "It is my hope, through study, to help stitch together the missing pieces, to better understand where we came from, what we have been through, so we might know where to go."

"I guess that's why finding the Archive is so important to you," Finn said, catching Fabaris in a briefly surprised expression. Finn had agreed to go on the search for the Archive, but he knew little about it, as it was always discussed under a veil of mystery.

"Yes," Fabaris said. "Among other reasons." He twirled his chin braids, staring at the ground before raising his eyes to meet Finn's. "I have small fragments of text, transcribed from some form of Ancient Maer, and I have been dying to get my hands on more. I can recognize some of the letters and a few words, but others are indecipherable. I imagine the same is true of ancient Islish. Have you come across it in your studies?"

Finn laughed. "I've seen it, if that's what you mean, but written language isn't really my thing. All ancient languages look the same to me. I saw one of the ancient...round scrolls once, in study—"

"Cylinder scrolls, you mean?" Fabaris interjected.

"Yes, cylinder scrolls, like you have. To me, it looked the same as the writing on the map Karul gave Carl. And really, almost the same as what was on the *Ka-lar* sword. Elder Gummache—he's the scholar back in our village—said he thought it was a form of Old Southish."

Fabaris twirled one of his chin braids so hard it came undone. "That's..." His eyes lit up, and he seized Finn by the shoulders, then quickly withdrew his hands with an apologetic motion. The Maer were big on the shoulder grab, though it was rare for any of them to do it to Finn. "If you're free, I'd like to show you something in my room. An ancient text. I'd like to see if the script is familiar to you." The expression on his face was both earnest and a little embarrassed.

Finn felt butterflies rise in his stomach. "Sure, why not? Like I said, I'm not much with languages, but I'd love to take a look."

?

Fabaris' room was at the end of a hallway, giving it more privacy than most of the rooms, which were little more than curtained-off squares with broken remnants of walls. His room had two solid stone walls and two made of tightly woven branches, with a reed curtain for a door. One of the stone walls was painted with what looked like a map, though Finn was only able to catch a quick glimpse of it as he followed Fabaris to a table made from a smooth stone slab that lay flat atop two logs. Fabaris had brought a reed taper, which he had lit from the small fire kept at the keep's entrance. He used it to light another taper, positioning them at either end of the table, which provided a dim, smoky light. He opened a case made up of a long sheet of leather with wooden rods at either end, rustled through it for a moment, and brought out a deerskin scroll, which he carefully rolled out, placing smooth black stones on each of the four corners. The writing on the scroll was a flowing script with many dots and lines running above, below, and interwoven among the letters.

"The scroll itself is not ancient," Fabaris said, moving close enough that Finn could feel the heat radiating off his body in the chilly room. "It's a copy, a very careful one, but a copy nonetheless. I think it is an ancient poem, though I cannot be sure. The way the lines are arranged suggests poetry, but..." He shrugged his shoulders. "Does it speak to you?"

Finn traced his fingers over the letters, without actually touching the deerskin, as he had seen the masters do. It didn't make the script any less mysterious, but as he did so, his arm stretched out a bit from his sleeve, showing his tattoo. He was about to pull the sleeve down when Fabaris stopped him, reaching over Finn's shoulder and putting his hairy hand over Finn's arm.

"Wait—look here," Fabaris said, pointing to part of Finn's tattoo with the index finger of his left hand. His fingernails were well-manicured, and his fingertip was soft and warm. "And here," he said, moving his finger up to a point in the text. "These three dots, in this precise arrangement, look the same as these three here, on your wrist. That can't be coincidence." He moved his finger back to Finn's wrist, tracing the lines of the tattoo, which didn't look quite like the letters on the scroll, but there was a kind of resemblance. Finn's skin tingled under Fabaris' touch.

"You're right," Finn said, sliding up his sleeve to the elbow. He covered Fabaris' hand with his own, lay his index finger on top of Fabaris' finger, and moved it up his arm to another place where the three dots recurred. "The masters are very secretive about the tattoos, but I know it's some kind of writing."

"Did it hurt?" Fabaris asked, spreading his fingers across Finn's arm and sliding them softly down to his wrist and back up again, with Finn's hand resting atop his. "The Maer do not do *tattoos*, for obvious reasons." Fabaris made as if to pull his hand away, but Finn held on, leaning his head back to rest against Fabaris' cheek, which was softer than any beard he'd ever touched.

"It hurt like hell." Finn stroked the back of Fabaris' hand with his. Oddly, the hairs on his hand were rougher than those on his face. "But with every prick of the needle I felt the work I had done was finally paying off. I don't know if there's any magic in the symbols themselves, but the experience was...special." He felt Fabaris' erection against his back, and he leaned into it.

Finn turned around to face Fabaris, who stood a few inches taller than him. He slid his arms inside Fabaris' robe, running his fingers through the thick hair on his chest, up onto his shoulders, then up the back of his neck, where the hair was soft like that on his face. Finn closed his eyes as he stretched up to kiss Fabaris on the lips, then opened them again as he pulled back. Fabaris took Finn ever so gently by the shoulders, then leaned in and kissed him back, softly at first, then with more heat as their bodies pressed together.

"I wasn't sure," Fabaris said as Finn undid the rope around his waist.

"Me neither," Finn said, pulling his tunic over his head. "But I figure there's only one way to find out." He stepped closer, running his fingers lightly over Fabaris' shaft as they kissed, devouring each other's lips as the heat grew between them. Finn pulled back, panting. "Do you have anything...*slippery?* I don't know the word in Maer, something to...ease things along?"

Fabaris' eyes fluttered and he blew out a long, slow breath. "I have some herbal oil, on the table. It should do the trick." Fabaris leaned over the table and handed the pot over his shoulder to Finn, craning his head around to give him a long, probing look.

Finn leaned against Fabaris' backside, pressing his chest against Fabaris' back and leaning around to kiss him long and hard. Fabaris closed his eyes, turned his head back around, and gripped the edge of the table as Finn rubbed the oil over Fabaris, then himself. Finn pressed in again, kissing Fabaris' hairy neck and back as his hands reached around to tease him further.

"Be gentle," Fabaris said in a hoarse voice as Finn edged between his buttocks. "It has been far, far too long."

?

Fabaris ran his fingertips gently over Finn's body as they lay on the bed, sweaty despite the chill. His eyes were soft, deep, and his smile was playful and a little amused.

"I'm glad I ran into you in the bailey today," Fabaris said. "To think, I almost kept going. If you hadn't called my name..."

"Well it's been a long time since someone looked at me like that," Finn said, rolling over and grabbing Fabaris' hairy bicep.

"I'm sorry, I didn't mean—"

Finn silenced him by leaning up to kiss him. Fabaris closed his eyes, smiled, then opened them again.

"Well in the interest of cultural comparison, I would be open to trying this again sometime," Fabaris said. "If you like."

"I like," Finn said, running his hand down Fabaris' chest and stomach, then grabbing him between the legs. "But why wait?"

Fabaris closed his eyes and took a deep breath, delicately removing Finn's hand. "I have a council meeting now. And we leave tomorrow morning to find the Archive. Perhaps we can help keep each other warm along the way. It gets bitter cold at night in the mountains this time of year." He stood up, slapped Finn on the thigh, and pulled on his robe.

Finn sighed, sitting up and slipping on his tunic. "Aren't you worried about what people will say?"

Fabaris chuckled. "They may say what they wish, just as they do about Carl, Ujenn, and Grisol. Why should I care? In such difficult times, one must find happiness where one may. I must go now," he said, straightening his hair and retying several of his chin braids that had come undone. "As must you. Good night." He took Finn by the shoulders and gave him a peck on the lips.

Finn followed Fabaris out of the room, feeling his way down the dark passageway toward the bailey as Fabaris veered off toward the council room.

"Master Finn," said one of the guards at the gate as he lifted the bar and helped the other guard open the heavy wooden barricade. Finn thanked him and hurried across the bailey, whose frosty grass crunched underfoot. He moved the thatched door to their lean-to aside as quietly as possible, nodding to Carl, who sat up for a moment as he entered. Sinnie's snoring was as steady as ever. He slipped into his bed, pulled the sheepskin tight around him, and lay awake a long time, visions of his lovemaking with Fabaris dancing through his head, before the stillness of the mountain dark pulled him down into its embrace.

Chapter:
Fifteen

Carl lay awake until the light filtered in through the willow branches of the lean-to enough for him to see Finn cuddled up to Sinnie. He was not quite jealous of their physical closeness, but he did feel a slight pang, a remnant of his longstanding crush. He slipped out while they still slept, then stopped by the garden to pick a stalk of seedweed for Stromus and the others in the roost. As he made his way up the steps, he heard a familiar voice.

"There you go boy, now move along and save some for the others. I have the feeling you guys are going to get some work here pretty soon."

"Grisol," Carl said as he emerged from the staircase. "Sorry to disturb you. I'm not used to finding anyone else up here."

"It's become quite the popular spot for anyone trying to get a little privacy."

Carl grunted a laugh, holding up the seedweed. "Did you already feed them?"

"Just a little," she said. "Enough so they remember me."

Carl moved to look over the battlements at the valley below, gray-blue in the predawn light. They stood in silence long enough for it to feel uncomfortable, then a little bit longer.

"Congratulations on your promotion," Carl said, turning his head toward her.

Grisol waved it away. "Yeah, I'm in charge of, what, a dozen archers, half of whom couldn't hit a Maer standing at thirty feet."

"But half of them could." Carl turned to face her. "That's got to count for something."

Grisol's face fell slack for a moment, then grew serious as he had never seen it before.

"I guess you haven't seen Ujenn this morning." Her tone sent a shiver up his spine.

"What?" He took a step toward her, and she put a hand on his chest, closed her eyes for a moment, and took him by the shoulders.

"You're going to be a father," she said, letting go with one hand to hastily wipe her eyes. "I'm sure Ujenn wanted to be the first to tell you, but here we are."

"Well that's—" Carl stopped, feeling the heat of her body as she held onto his shoulder with one hand and gripped his wrist with the other. "That's incredible. Thank you. For telling me," he mumbled. "And for..."

"Yeah," Grisol said, letting go of him. "It's going to be an adventure." She looked up at him, then turned toward the valley. "Anyway, I just figured you should know before heading off..." She gestured to the mountains, and Carl reached out to touch her arm. She did not move away from his touch, but she did not move into it either.

"How are you?" he said, feeling like an idiot. "With all of this, I mean? I can't even imagine—"

"No, I expect not." She sniffed but smiled. "I can't even imagine, and it's growing inside of me." Carl watched her in silence for a while, then she spoke again, her bright eyes tight on his. "I was supposed to go with you to the Archive. You didn't know it, but I was. Karul said we needed two archers in case we came across some trouble, but Ujenn put her foot down. Said she wasn't going to send her entire family off on a dangerous mission." Carl's throat caught as she said the word family.

She chewed on her thumbnail, then flicked it against her upper front teeth. "She's not wrong, of course. It goes against the Family Code to put a pregnant female in harm's way when the role could be played by someone else. But it's never been enforced, as far as I know, and Karul was ready to ignore it. He said we should not live in our fears, but in our vision for the future. It came out pretty eloquent, like something Fabaris would have said."

"I'm...I'm sorry."

She took Carl by the shoulders again and tiptoed to kiss him gently on the lips. "Be safe," she said. "And please don't die."

"I'll try," he replied. "I guess I have another reason or two to stay alive now. You take care of the castle while we're gone." He wasn't sure what the right gesture would be, so he just gave her a lame little wave and ducked down the stairs, feeling like a coward. A coward who was going to be a father very soon.

?

Carl paced about the bailey a bit, doing some half-hearted sword exercises as he waited for Ujenn. Grisol had already returned to the keep, and he could have gone in before the formal opening; anyone could come and go any time, but this waiting had become a part of the daily schedule, and he found comfort in the routine. Finn emerged from the lean-to as the sun was painting the battlements a pale yellow. He nodded to Carl on his way to the garden, where he began his stretches and poses. A predictable amount of time later, the gate opened and Jundum came out, giving Carl a little wave as he stripped a careful half-handful of seeds off the tip of one of the weeds.

Carl was about to give in to his impatience and go looking for Ujenn when she walked through the gate, her robes in perfect disarray, and came to him, her smile doing a poor job of hiding the deep fatigue of someone who has not slept. She had turned him away the night before, saying she was busy, and he had pretended not to be hurt. He greeted her with a light kiss.

"You have seen Grisol," she said, touching his face. "I had hoped to tell you myself, but now I no longer need to worry about my delivery. We are going to be a family." She tiptoed up and kissed him full and slow, pulling back even more slowly, holding his eyes with hers. "And now you leave us, on a fool's errand. Isn't that just the way of things." Carl's heart sank at her tone.

"Karul is right," he managed. "We need to find the Archive before the *Sabrit* starts getting ideas." He stopped as Ujenn raised one eyebrow only, her smile rising on the opposite side.

"We, are we now?" She put her arms around his waist. "You're going to have to get used to using that pronoun more often." She slid back and held him at arm's length.

"Don't say anything too...*mushy*," Carl said, reverting to Islish as he often did with Ujenn, who had a knack for understanding anything he said. She closed her eyes, and when she opened them, they were clear and bright.

"I wouldn't dream of it. And besides, we're not going to be completely without each other. I have something for you, for us, for the trip."

She pulled out a pair of worked copper rings about a hand's span in diameter, with intertwining leaf patterns of impressive detail. They shone as if new, but they had to be old, as old as his *Ka-lar* sword at least, since the Maer hadn't had that kind of metalsmithing skill since before the Great Betrayal. Carl smiled as the term came to his mind unbidden.

"These must be ancient," he said, examining the pattern on the ring.

"They are, but I have made them new again." Ujenn let out a long sigh. "At much cost to my strength, I'm afraid." He touched her face, and she took hold of his hand, putting it to her chest. "I will recover, don't worry," she said. "In a week's time I will be strong enough to make full use of them. Here, put it on." She put one circle on her head, and he followed suit.

"Now close your eyes and think of me." Carl did as he was told, picturing Ujenn's hands on his face. *I am in you,* he heard in his mind. *Focus on my voice as you hear it with your mind, and try to grab hold of it.*

"I don't..."

Be silent and try.

Carl squeezed his eyes shut, put his hands to his temples, and tried to follow the receding echo of her voice. He struggled to clear his mind, let the echo fill the void. *Follow my voice. Find it. Embrace it.* He channeled all his energy into wrapping his mind around Ujenn's message, like trying to recall a memory that was slipping away. *Yes, that's it.*

"You've got it," Ujenn said, removing the crown and draping herself over him, her body hanging from his shoulders. "Help me sit down." Carl held her as she lowered herself to the frosty grass. She gestured for something to drink, and Carl sprinted to his lean-to and brought back his waterskin. She drank greedily, her breath heaving between gulps, until at last she capped the skin and breathed deeply.

"Even at this short distance it takes its toll," she said. "But in a week's time I will be recovered. On the seventh day, I will call to you at daybreak. Be ready."

"Of course." Carl gripped her hands in his. "But how do I..." He had barely been able to find her voice in his mind, let alone communicate an intelligible response.

"I will ask you yes or no questions. Signal for yes only. If the answer is no, save your strength."

Carl nodded. "How long will you be able to keep it up at that distance, with the mountains?"

"Depending on where you are, the mountains may be an advantage. At any rate not long, maybe three questions. More if you answer fast."

"I will practice," Carl said, knowing how foolish it sounded, but Ujenn nodded.

"Ask Finn for some pointers," she said. "The ring is linked to you. It will not work for anyone else, and I cannot remake the link at distance. But Finn can help you find your focus." She closed her eyes, gripped his forearm, and struggled to her feet. "Here come the troops," she said as Karul, Ivlana, and Luez entered the bailey dressed for travel with full packs and weapons. Finn and Sinnie soon joined them, and Fabaris came last, clutching a book to his chest. It was the blank ledger Carl had brought back from Wells as an afterthought. He had noticed it at a neighboring stall as he was picking out blankets, and had bought it on a whim, along with some ink and quills. Fabaris carried it as if it were a great treasure.

By this time, the majority of the inhabitants of Castle Maer milled about the bailey, giving a little space to those who were traveling. Karul stood up tall and gestured to Carl and the others to form a circle, which they did. Karul's eyes were bright, as though he had been drinking, and the look on his face was fierce. Carl felt a stirring deep inside, even before Karul opened his mouth. Something of great import was about to happen, and he was proud to be a part of it.

Chapter:
Sixteen

Ujenn watched as Karul took Fabaris and Ivlana's hands, and the rest of the group did the same until they were one unbroken circle.

"Today we set out on a historic journey," Karul began, and Ujenn tried to hide her disgust. Not that anyone would have noticed; every set of eyes was fixed on Karul, and his words entered every ear. She hoped some of them were more discriminating than the others. He spoke of the Great Betrayal, of how far the Maer had fallen, and how far they had yet to climb, and though he was not the greatest orator, he was far from the worst, and he fed the hunger inside every Maer: to be part of something higher, to rise above cold and hunger, to feel fortune's sunshine warming their cheeks. To get for themselves what the humans had, what they had taken from the Maer.

Ujenn didn't disagree with the sentiment, or even with the idea of looking for the Archive. The magics it contained could bring the Maer up to par with the humans, who used ancient Maer words in their own magic, though they did not realize it. She had recognized some of the symbols on Finn's tattoo, but he seemed to know nothing about them. But to go after the Archive half-ready, with winter approaching and the humans having just made contact, was madness. It was exactly why Karul would never make a great leader. Unless he managed to find the Archive, of course, in which case he would be seen as a genius, and might be made the next High Counsel. In the meantime, his adventure would leave the castle, and its inhabitants, in a vulnerable position, in a difficult time of year. Not to mention taking away her lover, and the father of her unborn child.

As Karul finished his speech, Fabaris stood up straight, holding the book of empty pages Carl had brought him. Ujenn watched his face grow solemn, and when his eyes opened, he had that look of complete belief in what he was about to say that was the closest the Maer got to true religion.

"We have all heard stories of the great feats of the heroes of old," he began. "We know how Gunatir forged the first of the great swords of the ancients, and how Danuk used it to unite the unruly tribes. We have listened to the story of Hertwi, who defeated the beast with seven heads, and the tale of Girana, the warrior queen who shattered the Stone of Suffering. I could go on, but these great stories have one thing in common: they all happened long, long ago. But what stories will be told of us once we have returned to the rock beneath our feet? When our blood and our sweat have dried into dust and been swept off into the Great River? When the stones that heard the echoes of our voices have been ground down by millennia, what will they tell of Castle Maer and its brave inhabitants? That we survived, for a time? That we did our best to scrabble out a meager living from the rock?"

Fabaris paused, lowered the book, then raised it up high again. Ujenn found herself drawn to his words, despite herself. What he was saying wasn't materially different from what Karul had said, but she could not tune Fabaris out. "The story they will tell has already begun. They will tell how we reclaimed this fortress of old, how we built it back up, how we learned again to forge, to cultivate the sacred mushroom, how we kept the humans at bay. And they will learn, gods willing, of the journey that is about to unfold, the quest to rediscover the great wisdom of the ages. They will hear the tale of the recovery of the Maer Archive, the rebirth of our great civilization, and their children will tell this story, our story, to their grandchildren, who will pass it on throughout untold generations, until it becomes legend." He held the book out, scanning the crowd with his eyes. "Today we write *our* page in history."

Ujenn closed her eyes as the reality of the group's departure sank in. Fabaris' words floated in her mind like ashes on the breeze, while she sank down into the void opening inside her. She could not hear the end of the speech, could not watch her lover and her closest friends march off to certain doom, leaving her in charge of a hundred needy souls. She turned away from the circle, returning a heavy glance from Carl with the best simulacrum of a smile she could muster, then hobbled away through the crowd. She trembled at every step, though with fatigue, rage, or sadness, she could not have said. She felt faint as she emerged from the throng, and might have fallen had a hand not propped her up from under her arm.

"Let me help you back inside," Grisol said. "We've had about enough speeches, no?"

?

The castle was quiet, with only the occasional cry of a baby, quickly shushed, breaking the silence. Ujenn pushed herself up to a seated position, then stood on resentful legs. It had been three days since the group had left, and her head throbbed and her body ached as if she had climbed a very tall mountain. She rubbed her earlobes and closed her eyes, and though she was able to chase away most of the pain, she could not shake the hollow feeling in her spine. Reactivating the copper rings had drained her to a level she had not felt since early in her training, and she was not yet back to half strength. But with Karul, Luez, and Fabaris gone, she was in charge of the castle now. When she stepped through the curtain and out into the hallways, there would be voices calling her name, hands pressed on her arm, quiet questions and loud ones. She slid on her sandals, like slabs of ice beneath her feet, slipped out into the empty hallway, and walked noiselessly toward the bailey.

The humans' lean-to was silent, empty behind its thatched door. She could feel Carl's absence down in her bones, which made them ache all the more. Other than the guards at the gates, the bailey was empty. Or so she thought until she heard a low voice humming a quiet tune. She walked over the frost-covered ground to the garden, where Jundum was futzing with the few plants that still held some green.

"How's the winter cabbage looking?" she asked.

Jundum shot her a wry look. "It'd be better if we had the Coldstock variety, but it'll give us something to bulk up our broth a little. The rutabagas were the real powerhouses this year; we put away enough so you'll get sick of 'em before we run out."

"That won't take long," Ujenn said. "I dream of a day when I don't have to eat rutabagas. No offense."

"I don't much like the taste myself, but you have to admire their ability to store energy. As a mage, you should appreciate that." Jundum pointed a crooked finger at her for emphasis.

"It's a shame we can't plant down in the valley, no?" Ujenn was only partly teasing. Jundum had bugged Karul, and anyone else who would listen, countless times about their need to expand their growing space, but no one ever listened. Maybe it was time to do something about it.

Jundum shook his finger at her. "Joke if you want, but it's the only way forward. We could plant a test crop, something hardy that the critters won't like, and the patrols could weed a little on their way out. But Karul..." He threw up his hands, and she nodded. Karul was always focused on the military end of things.

"Well Karul's not here now, is he? I'll have Pulua scope out a spot." Ujenn smiled as Jundum looked up at her hopefully. Pulua sometimes helped him in the garden, but she had become withdrawn since losing Dasta to Sinnie's arrow, and she needed to get out of the castle, to breathe some free air for a change.

"Tell her to come see me first." He pulled away the browning lower leaf of a head of cabbage. "I've got a few ideas about where it might be. It's never too soon to start thinking of next year's crop."

?

Ujenn spent the morning convincing Dren once again that the need to fortify the insulation on the rooms was greater than the need to patrol for spies. As a warrior, he was understandably prejudiced in favor of weapons-ready action, but he also followed the chain of command, and did as she asked after voicing his objections. He led a large team to cut and collect as much dried rush as possible, hauling it up to the castle with the horse and wagon the humans had gifted them. By the time night fell, they had added insulation to over half of the rooms, plus the humans' lean-to.

The next day saw alternating snow and rain showers, so she tasked Jundum and Pulua to lead a group into the mines to try to seed silver spores in some new areas that seemed to have the right combination of silver or copper veins and water. While they worked, she visited Grisol, who was helping Tuomo perfect the consistency of the clay for his molds. She had apparently come across a purer source of red clay on one of her "runs," which she was doing in imitation of Sinnie. Grisol's eyes lit up with more than the flames of the forge as she poured a dollop of molten brass into a clay mold fixed in a bowl of sand. Judging by Tuomo's victorious cry, Ujenn assumed it had been a success.

"You'll be shooting Maer arrows in no time," Ujenn said, grabbing Grisol by the shoulders. Grisol's hair was matted with sweat, and her smile was as big as Ujenn had ever seen it.

"Well we have twenty-six more spearheads to go before we start on the arrows," Tuomo broke in, "but at this rate we'll run out of good ore before we get that far. We need to build our capacity ten-fold at least if we expect to make any difference."

"I think it makes a difference," Grisol said, glancing at Tuomo before turning back to Ujenn. "This spearhead here, hey we need to douse it—" She tapped off the clay, picked it up with a leather glove, and laid it in a bowl of water, which hissed for a moment. "This spearhead here," she continued, shucking her gloves, "could be the one that lands the decisive blow in our battle against—" Grisol paused, dropping her eyes for a moment. Ujenn touched her on the hand, and Grisol smiled sheepishly. "We must be able to defend our-selves, not just today or tomorrow, but forever."

Ujenn fixed her gaze on Grisol, whose newfound conviction shone like the rising sun. "It must be killing you not to be out there with them." Ujenn put her hand on Grisol's cheek. "Wherever they are."

"I'm enjoying the warmth down here, thank you very much." Grisol stuck her hand into the bowl and pulled out the spearhead, which she tossed in her hands a couple of times before holding it out for inspection. It was straight, and the lines were pretty clean, even almost sharpish looking.

"Progress." Ujenn beamed at Grisol as she gave Tuomo a side-eye. Grisol's clay had more than tripled his efficiency, and the quality of the spearheads was looking better under her touch. And she had on-ly just begun to learn about forging. If Tuomo was the best the Great Council could find, the Maer were in a world of crap.

"We'll have another, what, six? Before dinnertime." Grisol grinned at Tuomo, who shook his head.

"Four, if we're lucky. Maybe five." His face said six, and he was clearly relishing the discussion, and the idea of spending more time with Grisol.

"I bet we could up the production even more if we had one of those skin-bag thingies in that book," Grisol said.

"A bellows? Well, I don't know much about leatherworking, but I think old Spore here is doing just fine, aren't you fella!" Tuomo leaned in to scratch Spore's knobby ears, and Spore made his snout into a cone, expelling a silent coo.

"Ivlana is really good with that kind of stuff but with her being gone..." Grisol scratched her beard. "Maybe Pulua? Her clothes seem to fit better than most. Maybe she could do it. Anyway, I'll ask around."

"I'll leave you to that then." Ujenn gave Grisol a long look, stirring desires that had been tamped down by the stress of recent days. "Come by tonight, if you like." She smiled as she saw Grisol's face brighten. Poor Tuomo was going to be awfully disappointed.

?

Ujenn shared her bed with Grisol for the remainder of the week, though they only made love on the first night. Grisol was eager and able to please, and her lithe body was a treat to caress, but Ujenn was still raw from Carl's absence. Ujenn craved his touch, his powerful body restrained by his boyish timidity, until pushed to the point of desperation, at which point his eyes would grow dark and he would give in to his most reckless impulses. After the first night, she only cuddled with Grisol, who seemed confused at first but did not complain, no doubt happy to have a warm body to press against in the growing cold.

?

On the seventh morning, Ujenn sat cross-legged on her bed with herbal tapers burning on either side of her. She had posted a guard outside the door with orders to shush anyone who approached. She rubbed a finger of crushed soma leaf on her gums, savoring the bittersweet taste as her gums and tongue became tingly, her limbs grew soft, and her mind came into a thorny-sharp focus. She laid the copper ring on her head, closed her eyes, and pictured a flaming orange cord streaking out from her mind, searing through the blackness, with a word at the point:

Carl.

Her neck jolted with pain as she projected his name. Several seconds later, she felt a tug, and her joy all but erased the pain.

Is everyone safe?

This time the pain wracked her shoulders, and her hands seized up like claws. Again, she felt the pulse of Carl's response.

Have you found the Archive?

Ujenn cried out as the strength was sucked out of her body, and she fell sideways onto the bed, the copper thread in her mind thinning, fraying, tensing near the breaking point. There was no response.

I— She tried to push out another message, but it felt like she had walked straight into a stone wall, and she fell down within herself, spinning, whirling out of control, fading beneath the rush of blood flooding her mind.

Chapter:

Seventeen

Carl slumped back against the rock and tore the copper circle from his head, his chest heaving as if he had just fought a great battle. The sweat soaking his forehead was icy cold, and he wiped it with his blanket, blinking hard and taking a few deep, rough breaths. He uncapped his waterskin and drained half of it, then tried to stand up, but his legs were still wobbly.

"Karul," he tried to shout, but it came out as a hoarse whisper. He cleared his throat and repeated, his voice louder but shaky. Karul stepped into the crevice, knelt before Carl, and looked deep into his eyes.

"Did she speak to you?" Karul's face was so close Carl could smell his breath. Carl nodded, closing his eyes. "What did she say?"

"She said my name, and I answered, a pulse to signal yes, which is all I can do. Then, 'Is everyone safe?', and I answered again." Carl took a sip of water before continuing. "Then she asked if we'd found the Archive." He cleared his throat a little and swallowed. "I did not respond. She started to say something else, but..." He stared into his hands. Ujenn had never told him she loved him, not in words. Carl wasn't sure if it was a Maer thing, or whether she was just not like that. But he knew it all the same. And when she said "I—" he knew what the end would be, and he had been readying a response with all his mental strength. But maybe she was going to say something completely different, and he was getting all inside his own head for nothing.

"Well I guess at least we know she's alive, and she knows we are." Karul scowled, turned in a slow circle, then stood as if unsure what to do with his hands, which he finally threw into the air and let fall to his sides. "I had hoped somehow this magic would be more useful."

"It may yet be." Carl took Karul's outstretched hand and let Karul pull him up to standing. "In a week's time she'll reach out again, or perhaps sooner, and by then we may have something to share, as might she."

Karul nodded, turning to look toward the ridge opposite them. "Let's hope we make it through the week," he said with a grim chuckle. "That group of *grosti* have been shadowing us since yesterday afternoon. I'm a little surprised they didn't attack us last night."

"They're probably going to wait for us in the pass." Carl chewed on his mustache as he leaned against the rock, then pushed off to stand on his own, his legs having finally stopped shaking. He had already had a run-in with the *grosti*, as the Maer called them, on his first trip to Castle Maer. The giants had hurled rocks at his group, and the range of their throws was fearsome. His eyes turned toward their path to the southwest, where a narrow valley littered with boulders was the easiest way between two mountains. To go around would cost two more days, at the very least, through unforgiving terrain. Luez had been quite insistent there was no other way, but it would be an ugly place to be ambushed by rock-throwing giants.

Carl cleared his throat, and Karul turned back around. "They attacked us from above the last time we encountered them," Carl said. "We were lucky to be able to get out of their range, which is considerable."

"I know. We had to clear out a group of four of them before we could reclaim Castle Maer. We lost six warriors in that fight." Karul's serious eyes belied the pride in his voice. "What would you recommend?"

"We need someone higher up than they are," Carl said. "Finn can move with great stealth, as can Luez. I would send one or both of them atop the ridge to find out where the *grosti* are first, and go from there."

Karul nodded. "Great minds think alike. Normally I would send Luez alone, as her stealth skills are unmatched. But this is the *grosti's* territory, and there is a better than normal chance they might notice her. I'd take her in a fight against one of them, maybe two, but as capable as she is, she wouldn't stand a chance against more than that. But with Finn at her side..." He paused, looking around the edge of the crevice at the group. "Tell me again what he did to the *mashtorul*."

Carl gave a weak laugh. "I was a little busy myself, but from what I saw, the *mashtorul*, the biggest one no less, was charging Finn at full speed, and he held out his arms, and the next thing I knew the creature was lying flat on its back, and Luez had sunk her sword into its armpit. Mages are not very forthcoming about their abilities, but whatever he did stopped that thing cold. I doubt the *grosti* are much bigger than the *mashtorul*. He could hold his own against them."

"Good to hear." Karul clapped him on the shoulder. "And let's not forget whatever he learned with Stuock. I'm glad to have him with us. Sometimes I wish we had a mage like him in the castle. I—I mean," he stammered, "Ujenn's powers have been very useful, but you're a warrior. You understand that when push comes to shove, sometimes you have to fight."

"It's fine." Carl smiled. "Now let's take a better look at that pass, get Finn and Luez in on this, and come up with a plan."

?

"I saw them up on that ridge, just to the left of that little point there," Sinnie said, pointing to the western side of the valley. "At least two of them. As big as they are, they do a good job of staying out of sight."

"Like any good hunter," Karul said, smiling through gritted teeth. He clearly relished the chase, the planning, the fight. Carl was convinced this was half the reason Karul had gone along with Fabaris' plan to go looking for the Archive. "Luez, Finn, make your-selves ready. You'll want to be upwind from them." Luez raised her nose as if sniffing the breeze, while Finn swallowed hard, looking a little pale. "You two are going to slip out and move ahead of our group, heading across the stream to the eastern hills while their eyes are on us. You need to get well past us before you cross, so we will take our time. Once you've gotten far enough ahead, you will cross the pass again, as discretely as possible, then get up onto the west-ern ridge above them. Hopefully they won't move on us before we've gotten to you."

"And once we're in position?" Finn asked, his voice none too sol-id.

"You watch them, stay as close as you can without being seen, and if they make a move, you do too." Karul spread his hands wide, smiling like a merchant closing a deal.

Finn opened his mouth, closed it, then looked at Luez. "We need a signal."

"Listen for their screams," Luez said to Karul, a hint of a smile on her lips. "That will be our signal."

?

The valley, which had been nearly a mile wide a day before, nar-rowed quickly near the base of the mountains into a fifty-yard stretch of brown grasses and shrubs interspersed with boulders of all sizes. The land rose more steeply on their left, where Finn and Luez had disappeared and were presumably far enough ahead that the *grosti* wouldn't be looking for them. Carl hadn't been able to spot them ei-ther, which he hoped was a good sign, but he didn't see as well as Sinnie. She had managed to keep tabs on the *grosti* as they moved along the ridge top to their right, but once the group entered the pass, the *grosti* had vanished into the hillside. There were enough boulders, crevices, and outcroppings to hide an army, and if it weren't for Luez and Finn hopefully moving into position, the *grosti* would have little trouble putting them in a world of danger. Besides Sinnie, the only bow they had was on Ivlana's back, and she looked in no hurry to put down her sword. If they were attacked, they would need Finn and Luez to do some damage and distract the *grosti* long enough for Ivlana, Karul, and him to charge them, and hope for the best.

Before coming to Castle Maer, before Ujenn, Carl would have relished the chance to trade blows with a real enemy. Even now, the *Ka-lar* sword felt good in his hands, but his heart was heavy. He longed to be back in the castle, his face between Ujenn's hairy hands, his mind fuzzy and clear at the same time as he gazed into her eyes. He shook his head and took a few hard breaths of cold air to bring him back to the moment. He had sworn to help Karul find the Archive, and so he would, whatever dangers might lay along the way. Knowing his child grew in Grisol's belly only changed the calculus so much. His child would be raised as a Maer, so the Maer cause was his child's cause, and thus his own.

"Up ahead," Fabaris hissed. "Halfway up on the right, maybe a hundred yards."

"Don't look up and don't stop," Karul barked. "Weapons ready. Keep an eye out at all times for the nearest cover."

Carl spotted a shoulder and the top of a head behind a boulder on the ridge a little ahead to the right, putting them in easy throwing range for the *grosti*. He hefted his shield and did a few slow half-circles with his left shoulder, which was always a little stiff ever since the *mashtorul's* blow. He was the only one in the group with a shield, so he would have to lead the charge.

"There's one in the pass up ahead," Sinnie said, fingering the fletching on her arrow. "Behind the big triangle rock." The rock was less than fifty yards away, in the middle of the pass.

"He's mine," Ivlana said, her lips curling as she gripped her sword.

Carl forced a few more deep breaths as he readied his legs for an uphill sprint. He could hear Karul breathing practically in his ear. As they closed on the triangle rock, Carl spot-checked the hill for cover he could use while charging up. He had lost sight of the *grosti*, but he was pretty sure he knew which rock they were hiding behind. He just hoped to the gods Luez and Finn were in position.

A deep cry of surprise echoed down from the rocks above, followed by a loud roar of pain that ended suddenly. Carl's foot slid on the gravel for a half-step before he got his footing and ran, weaving between two boulders with Karul on his heels. Behind him, the loud crack of rock hitting rock. Ahead of him, a roar of anger and a sickening bashing sound.

Chapter:
Eighteen

Luez planted her foot on the fallen *grosti's* shoulder and yanked out her blade, which had gotten stuck in its back. She tumbled to the side instinctively as a rock the size of her head whizzed past her and careened down the side of the hill. She scrambled toward the nearest boulder, poking her head around to get a bead on where the throw had come from. She heard a roar behind her and peeked over her shoulder to see Finn bracing against the blow of a leg-sized club, which seemed to bounce off the air just inches from his face. The *grosti* wielding the club, who stood two heads taller than Finn, swung it around and struck again, and Finn faltered under the blow but remained standing. Another rock hurtled past Finn, missing him by inches, and Luez saw the *grosti* who had thrown it as it ducked behind a boulder ten yards away, in the same direction the rock thrown at her had come from.

She crawled to the downhill side of the rock she was hiding behind, then sprinted to the edge of the *grosti's* boulder. She crouched tight against the rock, taking a moment to steady her breathing. She heard a roar of surprise and pain from Finn's direction, followed by a great deal of scrambling and rocks skittering down the hillside. From the valley below came a chorus of shouts and roars. She closed her eyes for a moment, trying to block out the more distant sounds and focus on the creature on the other side of the rock from her.

She heard a light scraping noise, which she thought was coming from her left, so she slunk right around the downhill edge of the boulder, grasping a handful of dust in her left hand. She heard careful footfalls behind her, and she pressed her back against the boulder, her muscles tensing as she heard a footstep, then another, then nothing. She guessed the creature was just out of sword range, so she waited, sweat rolling down her brow despite the cold, as the sounds of combat echoed all around her. The *grosti* fighting Finn bellowed, and Finn cried out. Luez seized the moment to spring around the corner, flinging the dust up at the creature who towered over her, its club held high. It shook its head and its club arm wavered long enough for her to dodge the blow and give it a quick jab in the side as she skirted past it.

The creature screamed as it whirled around, swinging its club sideways. Luez was just able to duck under the club, almost losing her footing but recovering in time to hit its club arm with another jab. The creature roared and bashed at her with its other arm, a powerful blow that hit her hip and sent her tumbling over backward. She sprang up, scrambling uphill within diving reach of another boulder, and crouched low, waiting for the *grosti's* next move. Her hip throbbed with the blow and she saw stars in the edges of her vision, but she could still stand, for now.

The *grosti* eyed her for a hot moment, blood flowing from its side and bicep, its eyes wide and rage-red. It rested its club on its shoulder, took one step, then leapt forward, swinging its club overhead as it did. Luez dove at the same time, rolling beneath the creature's legs as the club smashed the ground where she had been standing, and she thrust her sword upward before the creature had time to react. It collapsed to its knees, releasing a desperate howl. Blood pumped from around her sword, lodged between its legs, which quivered as the blood pooled and flowed downhill, picking up bits of dust as it did so. Luez released the hilt, drew her dagger, and stuck it sideways into the creature's neck. The howl subsided to a gurgle, and as the *grosti* slumped before her, its eyes widened with shock, then went blank. She withdrew her dagger, wiped it on the creature's furs, and went to work wrenching her sword out of its underside.

She heard Finn let out a yell, and she stuck her head out over a rock to see him standing over the other *grosti*, which had fallen back against a rock and looked dazed. She pulled her sword free with a yank that threw her shoulder out of whack, then hobbled over in time to see Finn holding his staff in both hands, the tip toward the creature, his eyes hot and his face contorted with pain. He thrust the tip of the staff down toward the helpless *grosti*, laying his full force into the strike and driving the end of his staff deep into the creature's eye. Its body convulsed twice, then lay still. Finn slumped to his knees, turning to Luez with bloodshot eyes. His left arm fell limp to his side, and he closed his eyes for a moment, but a faint smile formed on his lips. Luez heard footsteps hurrying up the hillside and saw Carl and Karul churning their way toward them.

A scream echoed from the pass below, one that did not sound like a *grosti*, and Finn motioned her down the hill with his eyes. "I'll be fine," he breathed. She touched him on the shoulder just as Carl arrived, breathless, his sword poised for battle. She saw Karul sprinting back down the hill toward the sound of the scream. She gestured at Carl to follow Karul, and he nodded, turned, and lumbered down the hill. Luez began making her way down as fast as she could, her hip tweaking with every step, slowing her descent as the pain grew more intense. Down below she could make out a *grosti* sprawled out on the ground, and Ivlana, she thought, facing off against another one, which was hidden from her view by a boulder. Another figure, which could only be Fabaris, writhed on the ground.

Her hip froze, and she sat down hard and watched Karul run around the back side of the boulder where the *grosti* facing Ivlana stood. She saw Ivlana move sideways and heard the sound of something hitting her sword, and Ivlana staggered back for a moment, then a sudden roar sounded from behind the rock. Ivlana charged, and the sound of blades hacking flesh was audible even from this distance, followed by a heavy thud. Silence spread across the valley, almost violent in its suddenness, as the last echoes of battle dissipated into the air.

Luez struggled to her feet as she heard Finn's footsteps behind her, and she accepted the shoulder he offered, though his own left arm hung awkwardly at his side.

"Finn! Come quick!" Carl shouted out, hovering over Fabaris, who rolled about a bit, moaning in pain. Luez let go of Finn's shoulder, breaking into a slow run, despite her pain, with Finn surging ahead of her. Ivlana and Karul emerged from behind the boulder, Ivlana leaning on Karul, favoring her left leg. Both of their weapons were slick with blood, and the grimace on Ivlana's face bordered on a smile, until she saw Fabaris. She shook off Karul's support, limped over, and knelt down near his head.

"His collarbone is broken, probably his shoulder too," Carl said to Finn. "And I wouldn't rule out something worse."

"Nor would I," Fabaris managed, fumbling in one of the pockets of his robe for a pouch. "If you would be so kind," he said, holding the pouch out to Ivlana, who opened it and crushed a wad of soma leaves between her fingers, stuffing them in Fabaris' mouth. Within a minute his moans had eased, and his body lay still.

"Are we all alive?" Fabaris asked, his voice soft, distant.

"Thanks to you," Ivlana said, touching him gently on the chest, then turning her head up to Karul. "He stepped in to take a blow meant for me." She grabbed Finn by the collar. "Can you help him?"

"With time," he said, closing his eyes as he slid his hands inside Fabaris' robe and pressed them against his shoulder. Finn looked close to exhaustion, and Luez wondered how much he had left in him. Finn fell back on his seat, wincing and grabbing his head. "I need to rest before I can be of any use to him."

"He'll live," Karul said, patting Fabaris on the chest harder than Luez liked. "There is a warrior's spirit in this scholar."

"And a scholar's spirit in this warrior," Fabaris said to Karul, lifting his head off the ground for a moment, then letting it fall. "I think I'll sleep now," he mumbled.

?

It took a day and a half for Finn to get Fabaris and the rest of the group in shape to move, which they did more slowly now. But in the growing cold and with limited food, staying put was not an option. Finn spent the bulk of his time with Fabaris, whose spirits improved with his ministrations, though perhaps not entirely for medical reasons. Finn also put a warming touch on Luez's hip, and on Ivlana's leg, which had suffered a terrible bruise, but the bone did not appear to be broken. Luez was able to walk with minimal pain, as fast as Fabaris at least, whose legs were fine but who winced with each step, his arm wrapped tight to his body.

Luez marveled at Finn's gift. He had crushed into powder the rock the *grosti* was aiming at the group below, just by snapping his fingers. He had created an invisible shield that withstood at least three crushing blows from the giant's club, and come out with only a bruised shoulder. He had somehow incapacitated the creature, then had the grit and strength to shove his staff into its eye. And now, after the battle was over, he was healing the wounded. She wondered how many human mages could wield that kind of power. Finn had said he was of lower rank, so it was hard to imagine what his masters would have been capable of. All military questions aside, the Maer would do well to avoid any kind of conflict with the humans. A mere handful of their mages could wreak havoc on Castle Maer. She was glad to have him on their side.

At first she had questioned the humans' motives, for who in their right mind would leave a comfortable life to go live in a primitive castle in the middle of nowhere? But after studying them, she had come to understand them better. Their wealth and comfort level were remarkable, though they would not have seen it that way. Because their lives were so easy, relatively speaking, they actually sought ways to make them more difficult, to feel something, even at great risk. It was like the story of King Egaborth, who grew so bored in his golden castle he threw himself into the sea to see if he could swim across it.

But beyond that, there was a selflessness, among these three at any rate, that Luez could not help but admire. They had been ready to lay down their lives on several occasions, not for personal gain, not for kingdom or family, but for the Maer, whom they had long considered monsters. She wondered how many Maer would have been willing to make such a sacrifice for humans. She doubted if she would, though perhaps for these three, she just might.

"How's your hip?" Ivlana walked with stoic slowness, favoring her left leg quite a lot.

"Better, thanks to Finn, but not great. The *grosti* got me pretty good, and not even with his club. He hit me with his fist and almost broke my hip."

"How many'd you kill? Two?" Ivlana gave her a sly smile, showing her teeth a little. Luez returned the smile but said nothing. "I had to share both of mine, one with Sinnie and the other with Karul. I figure that adds up to one though."

"Well we snuck up on the first one, so he hardly counts," Luez said. "And I had the advantage of cover."

"It's okay. I always thought you were the real badass of the castle. Now I know."

Luez smiled despite herself. She'd always suspected it, but it was good to have confirmation.

Chapter:
Nineteen

Ivlana sat down hard, the cold ground unyielding beneath her weary body. Her leg hurt so badly she wanted to scream, but she had to remind herself she got hit by a giant's club and was lucky to be alive. Which she wouldn't have been if Fabaris hadn't jumped foolishly into the fray as she was recovering from the blow, swinging his staff at the *grosti*, as if that would do any good. But in the time it took the giant to swat Fabaris like an oversized fly, Sinnie had put another arrow into its chest, and it dropped its guard long enough for Ivlana to deal it a mortal thrust up under the ribcage.

She resented Karul for cutting in on her fight with the other one; it was smaller than the first, and not as experienced. She could have taken it. But it did give her satisfaction to sink her sword into it from the front at the same time as Karul skewered it from behind with his spear, their eyes meeting in a moment of blood frenzy that was the closest thing to true intimacy they had ever known. She knew he would never see her as she saw him; she could hear it in the way he talked to her, and see it in the way he did not look at her. Karul was easy to read if he took a liking to a female. Everyone in the castle knew of his interest in Grisol, scrawny little thing though she was. But he had never, not once in a thousand interactions, looked at Ivlana as anything but a warrior. Her only hope of joining him in sweat and heated breath was in battle, so she chose to think of this quest as their pretend honeymoon.

She watched Finn and Fabaris' closeness with a twinge of jealousy. Finn put his hands on Fabaris' shoulder, closed his eyes, and kept his hands in place for a long time. Fabaris noticed Ivlana watching them and flashed her a subtle smile, which she returned before looking away. She doubted Fabaris was in condition for anything more than a little touching, but it was cute the way they hovered around each other. It was also annoying as hell.

"How's your leg?" Sinnie appeared with a cup of tea, which lifted Ivlana's mood considerably.

"I've had worse." Ivlana sipped the tea, which had little flavor but was scalding hot. "But not much." She had taken a spear to the side during a fight with some Wild Maer when she was younger, but it had turned out to be a flesh wound, and she had healed quickly.

"Gods, I can't imagine," Sinnie said, looking down at her own cup of tea. "The size of those things..." She flashed a weak smile. "I guess I was just glad to be fighting from out of reach of their clubs."

"It's a good thing Luez and Finn took care of the ones on the hill, or we would have been sitting ducks for their rocks."

"Yeah, I barely got out of the way of one heading straight for me," Sinnie said, touching her chest with her fingers. "It's starting to sink in a little, how close we came." She was on the verge of tears, but she was holding them in. Ivlana reached out and touched her shoulder, and Sinnie leaned into her. It felt good to have a warm body pressed against hers, and not just for the cold. Life in the castle was a lonely affair, and unless she wanted to accept the fumblings of one of the lesser warriors, she could go days at a time without physically touching anyone, except in combat training. It bothered her more than she let on, not that there was anyone to let on to, except maybe Fabaris, whose counseling style was a little talky for her taste. And she didn't quite feel comfortable letting Ujenn inside her mind, so mostly she just took her frustration out in training, with the hope that someday she would have a worthier target than a *grosti* to direct her attentions to. It wasn't the sex she missed as much as the closeness, the feeling of being part of someone else.

"Thanks." Sinnie pulled back a little, holding onto Ivlana's arm and slurping her tea. "I bet you just take this all in stride, warrior-style," she said.

"Pretty much," Ivlana admitted. The threat of death didn't bother her as much as the threat of ending up old, decrepit, and alone, so she sprang at any chance for action. "But that's what I've trained for every single day of my life. Give yourself some credit. Not everyone has nerves like you, to stand there and deliver while rocks whizz by all around you. I can think of more than a few warriors back in the castle who don't have half your guts."

"They're tied in knots right now." Sinnie's eyes said she wanted something but was building up to asking it. Ivlana patted her hand and stayed quiet. She wasn't sure if it was the right response, but it was what she would have wanted if the roles were reversed. She had always felt that words were overrated, that the air didn't need to be filled with them all the time. When they were ready, they would find their way out, no matter how hard one tried to stop them. Ivlana sipped her tea, saying nothing. Sinnie looked down at her hands, then turned her eyes back up, an embarrassed smile on her face.

"Oh all right, here's the thing." Sinnie set her cup down and crossed her fingers over her knee. "It's really, really cold out here, and, well, when we were on our little mountain journey, Finn always let me sleep next to him, just for warmth, to be clear. But as you can see..." Sinnie shrugged and tilted her head toward Finn and Fabaris, who were snuggled together and talking quietly by the fire.

Ivlana found she didn't mind the idea of sharing a blanket with Sinnie; though she wasn't particularly prone to getting cold, it did make good sense to conserve energy by sharing their bodies' warmth. And it looked like Sinnie really needed it.

"You must get cold with all that...skin," Ivlana said, making a circle in the air to indicate Sinnie's body.

"Well I have to admit I wish I had a built-in layer of fur in this weather. Mind sharing yours for the night?"

Ivlana took Sinnie's shoulders and gave them a tender shake. "Done," she said. Sinnie's sigh of relief turned into a giggle, which would have been contagious if Ivlana were capable of giggling.

Though she was a bit of a snorer, Sinnie was like a furnace when she slept. Ivlana even had to poke her feet out from the blanket in the middle of the night.

?

Ivlana's leg was so stiff in the morning she had to get help to stand up, but Finn came around and laid his hands on her leg for a while, and she was able to walk around with relatively little pain. Fabaris looked to be coming along well too. She watched Finn remove his sling and move his shoulder around a tiny bit, and Fabaris did not scream. The sling went back on, but Fabaris was back to smiling more often than not, which had to be a good sign.

The sky was heavy as they set out, and it smelled like snow. The Great Tooth was no longer visible behind the cloud cover, but Luez estimated they were less than a week away. A vulture wheeled high above them, which was strange given the profusion of recently dead flesh they had left behind them. The vulture should have been drawn to the *grosti* corpses. She pointed it out to Karul, who snarled at the vulture. Even his snarls were adorable.

"Fabaris," Karul barked, pointing at the vulture. "What do you make of this?"

"Perhaps it is an omen." Fabaris shielded his eyes as he looked up. "You know, in ancient times, vultures were thought to be predictors of death to come. It is said that vultures follow those who are about to die, but also those who are about to deal death to others."

"Maybe he saw what happened to the *grosti* and figured where we go, death will follow." Karul's snarl curled into a smile, but a cute, snarly one.

"I was rather hoping to uncover the Archive without any further bloodshed," Fabaris said. "But if it's not an omen, and it isn't circling around a carcass we haven't seen yet, then I would say it's watching us."

"But why?" Karul looked angry at the thought.

"Well, you remember the beads Sinnie found on the hawk she shot?" Karul nodded, and everyone in the group squeezed close to listen in, though they continued walking. "They would have been put there by the...Wild Maer, or the Free Maer, depending on your perspective. There might be a bird clan somewhere nearby."

"How dangerous would they be?" Karul's tone was dismissive on the surface but wary beneath.

Fabaris raised his eyebrows and frowned. "I don't really know. I suppose a raptor could be trained to attack the eyes, or the throat, but it would be vulnerable to weapons. I imagine they wouldn't be as dangerous as the larger mammals, the bears, wolves, and the like. But the Free Maer are cunning, so they might think of something unpleasant to do with a bird of prey." Ivlana noticed he hesitated on what to call them. He was always trying to be fair, about the humans, about the Wild Maer; he had even said a few words over the fallen *grosti* before they left the scene of the battle. "As Ujenn mentioned," Fabaris continued, "a bird mage who is powerful enough might also control dragons. If they really exist, and if they are as closely related to birds as the legends tell."

"That's a lot of ifs," Finn piped in, "but I have to say, if we get to see a dragon at the end of this journey, and if it doesn't kill us, it might be worth it."

"I have always wondered what it would be like to sink my spear into a dragon's heart," Karul mused, his face lighting up, making him more appealing than ever. It was all Ivlana could do not to grab him by the scruff of his neck and lay a devastating kiss on him.

"Dragon feathers, scales, claws, teeth, beaks, and even bones are said to have great potency." Fabaris twirled his chin braids. "Though I would hate to see such a rare creature taken from the earth, if it were to come to pass, the creature's body would be almost as great a treasure as anything found in the Archive."

"You could make a fortune selling it on the Isle," Finn said. "Between the mages desperate for spell components to the super-rich looking for trophies, you would be hard-pressed to carry your reward away without a wagon."

"And what good would human coins do us?" Karul spat. "We have no trade relations, and I can't see why they would welcome us into their territory, no matter how much gold we carried."

"You underestimate the value of money," Carl said. "It can solve many problems."

"And create still more, no doubt," Karul grumbled, though his face showed he was imagining the equipment, weapons, and armor he could acquire with enough of their coins.

"A dragon souvenir would make an excellent offering to Mr. Leavitt at our next meeting," Fabaris said, his voice rising.

Karul grunted, a shrewd smile growing on his face. "Yes, a valuable treasure, and a show of strength. I like this idea."

The clouds thickened as they continued their march, and the vulture kept circling above them until snow began falling around midday. Ivlana had always loved snow, despite the inconveniences it caused. It swept away boredom and made the winter landscape come alive. And as long as snow was falling, it didn't usually get too cold. Sinnie and Finn seemed to delight in the snow as well, tossing the occasional snowball at each other, though near day's end the snow began to pile up, dampening their playful mood. Luez managed to find a pair of large boulders that leaned in toward each other, giving the group partial cover from the snow, and they settled in for the night, everyone huddled close together for warmth. Sinnie nestled in behind Ivlana, keeping her backside toasty, and Ivlana wrapped her arms around her pack, dreaming it was Karul she held in her tight embrace.

Chapter:
Twenty

S innie had to dust snow off her blanket when she got up, but thanks to Ivlana's excellent insulative properties, she was well-rested and warm. Or as warm as she could be while standing in a snowstorm. It would be a little early in the season for this kind of snow in Brocland, and it rarely snowed on the Isle, but this far into the Silver Hills it seemed the seasons were on a different schedule. The snow was past her ankles, but thankfully her boots went close to her knees and had thus far proven waterproof, though not as protective against the cold as she would have liked. The Maer wore fur leggings that came down over their feet, which were shod in sandals. Hairy feet or no, it was bound to be cold, but it didn't seem to bother them much. Karul did tend to stamp his feet more than the others, which made Sinnie smile. Ivlana had confided, with the utmost secrecy, that he had very sensitive feet, and that the one thing he craved more than anything else was a good pair of boots.

They marched on through the snow, which kept up steadily through the morning before dwindling to flurries by midday as an icy wind buffeted them from one side, then the other. As much as she loved snow, Sinnie was most definitely not enjoying it now. The coat her mother had made for her was warm enough, but the wind did cut through from time to time when it blew particularly hard. She didn't regret risking her life to join the Maer on their quest, but she was starting to regret doing so in winter.

They kept a decent pace despite the snow and their injuries, which had been improving at an unbelievable rate as Finn worked with Ivlana, Luez, and especially Fabaris, in the evening and again in the morning. Sinnie watched Finn and Fabaris, fascinated at their interactions. She had seldom had such a front-row seat at this level of intimacy and general cuteness. She had been around sex on plenty of occasions, as neither Hertle's troupe nor the Maer were very inhibited about their couplings. But this closeness, the constant need for touching, their hands brushing against each other in passing, it was just so very, very much.

By afternoon the sun had emerged, and though it offered little warmth, it did brighten Sinnie's spirits a bit. A herd of deer moved across the pass in the distance, stopping to graze in spots where the snow was melting. With any luck, she might be able to hunt in the morning, but the deer kept their distance, so she didn't get her hopes too high. She was a good shot, but she knew little about deer behavior, and they were reputed to be able to smell a hunter's intent long before seeing them. The group stopped when they came to a stream running across the pass, and they spread out to search for a spot narrow enough to cross without getting their feet wet. Luez signaled from the eastern side of the pass, not far from where the creek tumbled down from a rocky crevice. When they got close, she pointed down at half-buried footprints in the snow on either side of a narrow spot in the creek.

"From the look of it, I'd say they crossed here last night." Carl and Karul joined her, crouching next to the prints with serious faces. Sinnie could see prints running along the edge of the stream on both sides, coming from the eastern hills above. A group had come down, crossed the stream, and gone back up the other side. The crevice carrying the stream looked forbidding, so it made sense they would cross here, whoever they were.

"Looks like a small group, three or four at most," Carl said, looking to Luez, who nodded.

"Those are Maer-sized prints," Karul added. "These must be the Wild Maer you were talking about," he said to Fabaris.

"That seems likely, though I do wonder about the vulture. If they have a position on that hill, where the tracks seem to be coming from, why would they need eyes in the sky? Something doesn't quite add up."

"Well, everyone be on the lookout." Karul looked across the pass, squinting against the bright snow. "It looks like we need to set up camp on the western hillside tonight. Luez?"

Luez nodded, hopped over the stream at the narrow point, and trotted back across the pass to the west, snow flinging up behind her feet as she moved. Sinnie had to resist the urge to run after Luez; she was tired of all the walking, and longed to give her legs a good stretch. But Luez had skills she lacked, stealth in particular, so there was no sense pushing the issue. The rest of the group crossed the stream and kept trudging forward, veering toward the western edge of the pass, in case the Wild Maer to the east got any ideas. Karul seemed pretty sure they would not attack such a large and well-armed group, particularly if they knew what had happened to the *grosti*, which were no doubt a feared enemy of the Wild Maer.

About an hour before dark, Luez signaled from the hillside, and they soon found her at the entrance to a cave, well sheltered beneath an outcropping of orange rock. Countless footprints covered the dirt under the overhang, and an odd, pointy statue like a giant tangle of thorns stood just outside the entrance. No one spoke as they stared at the figure, which Sinnie could now see was made up entirely of deer horns. It was shaped vaguely like a person, with two legs and two arms splayed out with innumerable spikes. The bleached skull of something that would have been the size of a moose stared at them with jagged black eyes. The statue was surrounded by a circle of rough quartz pieces, arranged tightly together with no breaks. Inside the quartz circle lay shriveled leaves, carved stick figures, and several wooden bowls. In the darkness beyond the entrance Sinnie could see very little, only what looked like several small mounds of dirt or rock.

Everyone looked to each other, searching for who might have an answer. All eyes eventually fell on Fabaris, who stared at the statue, rapt, his hand dangling a few inches below his beard, his braids untouched. His hand moved in the air as though tracing the outline of the figure, then the circle around it. He closed his eyes, seemed to mumble something, then opened them again, looking around at all the expectant stares.

"Well, what does our scholar have to say about this?" Karul stepped toward Fabaris with outstretched hands. "Do we take shelter here, or take our chances with the elements?"

Fabaris closed his eyes and shook his head. "I don't know. It looks like a burial site, for the Free Maer. A deer clan, I should think."

"Must be the ones whose footprints we saw on the other side," Karul said. There was much nodding of heads and no talking for a good long moment.

"What do your customs say about places of the dead?" Carl asked out of nowhere, snapping Sinnie back to attention.

"They are sacred, of course," Karul said. "But these are Wild Maer..." He paced to the edge of the overhang, turned, and came back, stopping in front of Carl. "I'm not sure we have the time to worry about it."

"We found the time for our brothers who fell against the *mash-torul*," Fabaris said. "And I guarantee you no one will be disturbing their resting place."

"So you would have us freeze to death?" Karul said, stamping his feet a little.

"The overhang will provide us some shelter," Ivlana said, without much conviction.

"Precious little," Karul grumbled, looking around for anyone who would meet his eye. Sinnie did not turn away, but she said nothing. This was Karul's show, and no one doubted that.

Fabaris knelt down, gingerly removed his pack, and pulled out his book, along with a quill and a small block of wood. His movements were awkward, as his left arm was still in a loose sling, but he could move it somewhat. Sinnie watched with fascination as he carefully slid the top of the block to the side, then spit in a hole containing a black powder, stirring the mixture gently with the quill. Though the wind was cold and the light beginning to fade, no one moved as they watched Fabaris carefully wipe the edge of the quill on the wooden block. He opened the book to a blank page, past pages of writing with some drawings, though Sinnie could not see what. He propped the book on his sling, took a deep breath, and began making lines, his fingers moving deftly, dipping the quill every so often into the ink before returning to the page. A drawing of the statue quickly took shape, spare and uneven but haunting in its likeness. Fabaris dipped the quill once more, held it in the air, then wrote a line at the top of the page. He blew on the page, lay the quill on the inkpot, and wiped his fingertips on the hem of his robe. He brushed the page with his pinky, which came up clean, and he gently closed the book and stood up.

"If I could...step inside, carefully, take a look around, I might..." Fabaris put the book and writing supplies back in his bag, which he left leaning against a rock. "Maybe we might learn something valuable?"

Karul grunted impatiently. "In the meantime, we need to look for other options. Luez, you search the high hillside ahead. Sinnie, the hillside behind." Sinnie nodded at Karul, then at Luez. "Ivlana, you search the bottom of the hill ahead, and Carl, you check back that way. The rest of us will stay with Fabaris."

"Finn...your lantern?" Fabaris said.

Finn smiled, unhooked the lantern from his pack, and lit it, with some difficulty, as the wick must have dried out from disuse. Sinnie watched as Finn handed the lantern to Fabaris, leaving his hand resting on Fabaris' arm for a moment. Fabaris blinked slowly, then turned toward the cave. The statue gleamed from the light of the bullseye lantern, which cast huge spiky shadows inside the cave. Sinnie felt a tug on her sleeve, and she took a few steps with Luez while her gaze remained with Fabaris, whose face was solemn, reverent, and not a little terrified.

Chapter:
Twenty-One

Fabaris put down the lantern and knelt to study the offerings around the antler statue. Branches of mountain laurel, still green and shiny, were interspersed with dried elderberries and sprigs of cedar and spruce. Some of the greenery looked fresh enough to have been left within the past couple of days. There were also a number of small figurines, some carved in soft wood, others fashioned from sticks tied together with natural fibers. There were two bowls, one of them containing unshelled nuts, the other what looked like frozen water. The offerings were familiar, comforting; he had a distinct memory of placing a small figurine on the burial mound of his uncle Urnsett, who had broken his leg falling into a crevice and later died from the infection. Fabaris would have been about five at the time, and though he couldn't remember much of his uncle, he could still see his child's hand placing the figure atop Urnsett's mound in the burial cave just outside the village, pushing its legs down into the dirt so it wouldn't fall over.

Fabaris stood up awkwardly, as his left shoulder was still partly bound to his chest. He picked up the lantern, took a deep breath, and walked past the statue. Perhaps it was the rush of standing too quickly, but he felt dizzy as he passed it, as though the statue emanated a faint magical field. He paused in the doorway to the cave, scanning the interior with the lantern. There were five dirt mounds, made fairly recently, about knee height, each adorned with assorted objects. The mounds were spaced evenly around the edges of the chamber, which was no more than ten feet deep and perhaps twice as wide. Each of the mounds had a flat piece of light gray slate leaned against it, with charcoal markings on the slate.

Fabaris stepped toward the closest mound, which had a flint knife with an antler hilt atop it, along with a wooden spoon and a length of worn blue ribbon, most likely a fourth-hand relic from the South. He had never heard of the Free Maer having dealings with humans, but he supposed it was possible. The Old Maer, as the Free Maer called those under the Great Council, had deep ties to the South, so there were any number of ways it could have ended up here, but it fascinated him regardless. The slate leaning against the mound had a rough charcoal drawing of a face, a female with piercing eyes and a strong mouth. He remembered seeing the village elder make such a drawing of his uncle, as his bereaved mother stood watching. Watching the old woman draw, the certain movements of her gnarled hand, the deep furrow in her brow, had been an inspiration for Fabaris. Almost as much as the songs, it was art that had drawn him into scholarship.

He wondered if the Free Maer truly believed in the afterlife, or if they too saw it as a pretty story to tell the children, a comfort, proof that death was not oblivion. He had never thought to question it until his time with the Old Maer, who tended to see religion as a distraction from the business of rebuilding their civilization. The stories that came from the old beliefs still rang powerfully in their culture and language, but he knew of few who truly believed. It saddened him a bit, not because he himself believed, but because he wanted to live in a world in which it was possible to believe in something greater than the grind of everyday survival. Perhaps these mounds, these relics and offerings, were a sign that the Free Maer still lived in such a world. And by visiting their sacred place, so could he, for a fleeting moment.

The next mound had a stone-tipped spear sticking straight out of it, and a set of smooth, colorful rocks lay in a neat circle around the spear. The picture on the slate was of a warrior holding a spear over his head, poised to throw. The next two mounds held weapons, and pictures of warriors adorned their slates, a female with a double-tipped spear and a male with a bow. The last mound was covered with dried flowers, and a pair of wooden figurines sat atop it, dressed in tiny bits of tailored fur. The picture showed the face of a child with wide eyes and a soulful little smile. Fabaris marveled at the craft of the artist, who had managed to make the face look alive, the eyes almost wet, with a few quick, dramatic strokes of charcoal. Fabaris closed his eyes and put his hand to his forehead, holding it there for a moment as he tried to recall the prayer his village elder would say at such times, but the words slipped from his mind like a wet fish flopping down the rocks, disappearing into the dark waters of his memory.

In the back of the cave was a large, flat section of wall, angled slightly toward the floor, with figures traced in charcoal and painted with various colors of ochre. The painting showed three figures, two with spears and one with a bow, fighting a much larger figure, which held a huge club above its head, its eyes red, its mouth filled with jagged teeth. The *grosti*, no doubt. A female huddled behind the three warrior figures, covering a child with her body. At the top of the painting was a line of symbols that had to be some kind of writing, though he had never known the Free Maer to possess written language. He hurried out of the cave, ignoring the expectant looks of his companions, picked up his book, quill, and ink, and returned to the burial chamber.

He opened the book to a fresh page and took his time copying the symbols, which ran in a straight line, without much separation between them. They would be words, he thought, rather than letters, or if they were letters, there was no way to tell where one word ended and another began. He then copied the drawing, unsatisfied with his recreation of the details, but he had to draw in an awkward crouch due to the angle of the stone. He left room at the bottom of the page, and once he had finished, he filled it with a rough drawing of the mounds. He wished he could recreate all the slate drawings, but he had already used up a third of his ink, as well as two pages in his book, which was all he felt he could afford, and it was growing dark outside. He wrote a short description of the scene on the side of the page, then sat in the stillness of the cave as the ink dried. Though he could not summon the words, in his mind he could hear the cadence of the elder's voice as she spoke the funeral blessing, and he hummed a verse from the Ballad of the Place Below. He hoped it would please the spirits of the dead, if they were listening. He heard talking from outside the cave, so he collected his things and made his way out, careful to follow in his own footsteps so as not to further disturb the place.

Sinnie and Luez stood talking to Karul, pointing toward a spot on the hill ahead. Karul winced, then turned to Fabaris, raising his eyebrows hopefully.

"This is the burial place of five of the Free Maer, who I believe were killed by the *grosti*." Fabaris gave slight emphasis to the word 'Free.' "We must sleep elsewhere."

Karul pursed his lips and nodded slowly. "Very well. Luez has found another overhang, with some cover from the wind, but it will be a cold night. We will have to risk a fire again."

"I doubt there will be much risk," Fabaris said. "They will have been watching us, and will most likely know we killed the *grosti*. They will leave us in peace."

"Let us hope it is as you say." Karul's scowl belied his words. "I, for one, have no reason to trust the Wild Maer." He looked Fabaris in the eyes, almost in challenge, as he spoke. "We will set a vigilant watch."

Fabaris maintained eye contact until Karul looked away. Luez stepped toward Fabaris and put her hand on his shoulder. He almost flinched; to his knowledge, Luez had never, in all the time they had been together, touched him, or anyone else, except in combat or training. She gave him the briefest glance, then went to speak with Karul. Fabaris knelt by the antler statue, pulled out his stone knife, and carefully cut one of his beaded braids, laying it among the leaves and berries at the foot of the statue.

"May your journey be filled with light," he murmured.

?

Fabaris awoke as Finn slipped out of their blanket, letting in an icy draft. Fabaris pretended to sleep as he listened to Finn put on his boots, rub his face, and creep out of the overhang, his feet crunching on the snow. The mountains to the east were highlighted by the sun, which had yet to rise above them, and the Great Tooth loomed in the background, looking close enough to reach in a day's walk, though Fabaris knew it was still several days away. His shoulder was stiff from sleeping, so he sat up and rotated it gingerly. It hurt at several points in the rotation, but given the fact that it had been smashed by the *grosti*'s club, its ability to move at all was incredible. Finn had been pouring his energy into healing him and the others, and Fabaris worried that Finn would exhaust himself, but he seemed none the worse for wear. Had Finn not been with them, Fabaris might well have died, and he certainly wouldn't be marching for miles each day.

He struggled to his feet, as it was still difficult to put weight on his left arm, stretched out as best he could, and slipped away quietly. Ivlana and Sinnie lay snuggled together, but everyone else was up. Finn stood off to the side, his arms stretched wide in one of his poses, while Carl, Karul, and Luez stood talking quietly over the map Luez had made, pointing toward the Tooth and down the pass. Karul stamped his feet and jumped up and down a few times, but Carl and Luez remained rooted in place.

"Good morning," Fabaris said. "I trust you all slept well."

"Not as well as some," Karul said with a wry smile. "My feet have been cold since we left the castle. Once the others wake up, I am going to rekindle the fire and stick my toes directly in it."

Fabaris was weighing whether he should suggest Karul and Luez sleep under the same blanket, which was only logical, despite Luez's prickly reputation. It was on the tip of his tongue when he saw the figure marching across the snow toward them.

It was a Free Maer dressed in a long cloak and carrying what looked like a staff over their shoulder. There was nothing hostile in their gait, and surely no lone Maer would be so foolish as to attack such a large group. Karul gestured to Luez, who ran and woke Sinnie and Ivlana. Karul grabbed his spear, gesturing for Carl to follow him. Finn came running, and Sinnie and Ivlana appeared moments later, their eyes bleary from sleep but their weapons at the ready. Fabaris watched the Maer, who was now about a hundred feet away, and chuckled as he saw that the staff over the Maer's shoulder was balancing a bag or parcel of some kind.

"No need," he said, stepping forward and holding his palm toward the group. "They're not here to fight. They're bringing us a gift."

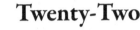

Chapter:
Twenty-Two

Karul shielded his eyes against the rising sun as he watched Fabaris walk out into the snow to meet the Wild Maer walking toward them. Or the Free Maer, as Fabaris seemed determined to call them. Karul didn't like the sound of it; were the residents of Castle Maer, and the thousands of Maer united under the Great Council, not free? It wasn't the first time he had noticed this tic, and it needled him like an ingrown toenail. Fabaris' attitude toward the burial cave had been almost too reverent. Karul accepted that they should not sleep in the cave, that a certain level of respect for the dead, any dead, was appropriate. But he worried that Fabaris' mindset might put them at risk at some point. They would have to talk it out in the coming days.

Fabaris bowing in greeting, and the Wild Maer, who by his attire and bearing must have been some sort of shaman, repeated his gesture. The shaman spoke, and though Karul was too far away to hear clearly, the words sounded strange yet familiar, not quite Maer but not entirely foreign either. Fabaris nodded and spoke, seeming to fumble for words, gesturing heavily. The shaman nodded and spoke some more, and Fabaris gave a one-word response. The shaman unshouldered the staff and held out what looked like a deerskin bag, which Fabaris took, raising it up and bowing again. He gestured awkwardly with the bag in his hand back toward the group, then toward the burial cave, then farther back, and Karul couldn't understand much, between the distance and the language, but he thought he heard the word *grosti*. The shaman bowed three times in rapid succession, then spoke at some length. Fabaris answered, again haltingly, and they bowed and turned away from each other.

Fabaris wore a wide smile on his face as he returned, handing the bag to Karul. It was full of jerky, venison by the look of it. Karul held a piece up to his nose, inhaling deeply, sniffing for anything suspicious, but all he smelled was compellingly smoked deer.

"It's safe," Fabaris said, tearing off a strip and stuffing it in his mouth. "Needs salt though."

"I brought some," Ivlana said, running over to her pack to rummage for it. She held out a little bag to Karul, her eyes eager and bright. Sometimes he suspected she had a thing for him, and on a few occasions he had wondered what it would be like to sleep with her. She was strong and decisive in battle, and though she was not his physical type, there was something appealing about her power and determination. But he was not inclined to jump into bed with his security chief, particularly with so many females in Castle Maer better suited to his tastes.

Karul opened the bag, and Ivlana pulled out a pinch of salt and sprinkled it on a piece of jerky, rubbing it in to permeate all the little crevices. She salted the other side, then held it up to Karul. The look in her eyes made him more than a little uncomfortable. Fortunately, the rest of the group came as robins to worms after rain, breaking up the little moment. They ate standing, tearing off chunks and chewing them with great vigor. The jerky was well cured but not overly dry, and it had a tender consistency he had not known deer jerky could achieve.

"However wild they might be, their curing skills are unmatched." Carl stuffed another piece into his already full mouth. Everyone chewed and nodded in agreement, making an alarming dent in the supply in a matter of minutes.

"If we had a proper pot we could stew this with some potatoes, if we had any, and some dried tomatoes and peas." Sinnie licked her fingers and looked thoughtfully up into the sky as she spoke.

"We should save the rest." Karul licked his lips and eyed the remains of the bag. If they were careful, it could last them close to a week, along with the nuts and travel bread they had brought. "Don't think this puts you off the hook, hunter," he said, pointing to Sinnie with his last piece of jerky.

"No sir." Sinnie fingered her bow, which was engraved with intricate patterns and finished so it shone. Maer bows were things of utility, but this was a work of art, like so many of the everyday items the humans used. Karul pushed down a sudden burst of anger. He wasn't mad at Sinnie, or Carl, or Finn, or any human in particular. In fact, all the humans he had met had treated him with the utmost decency and respect. It was the ease with which they carried their wealth, their complete lack of awareness of their privilege, that left him grinding his teeth whenever he thought about it. Which was exactly why he tried not to think too hard about that, or anything else. These prickly little thoughts always melted away when he was in motion, so he herded the group together as quickly as he could, and they set off down the pass.

The sun warmed enough to melt the snow into a soppy, slushy mess, and by midday Karul's feet were numb, and he had to take a break. He snarled at Ivlana when she asked him what was wrong, and he had to backtrack and apologize. She didn't deserve his anger, nor did anyone, but he couldn't very well keep it inside. He, Karul, leader of Castle Maer, had to stop perhaps the greatest expedition in the modern history of their people, because his feet were cold. It was some small consolation to see Sinnie, Finn, and Carl remove their leather boots and wrap their feet in furs as he did his. They sat for a time, talking very little, and soaked up the remains of the sun's warmth before the clouds crept back in, by which time Karul could just about feel his feet again. They marched onward, and the vulture from the day before, or perhaps it was another, circled above them, coasting in the high winds blowing across the hills. No one spoke of it, but Karul could tell it weighed on everyone's mind.

They camped in a pocket of pine trees growing where a small creek flowed down from the western hillside. They found a snowless spot with a cushion of pine needles for comfort, and the trees broke the wind, so it was better than nothing, though Karul did prefer a good cave. Maybe it was in his blood, a relic of the passage through the Place Below, transmitted through tale and song to each generation. He wondered how his ancestors would see him, how they would judge his actions. They had buried their dearest secrets in the Archive, trusting that some Maer, someday, would have the wisdom and the courage to find it, and use it for the benefit of all. He hoped to prove himself worthy of their trust.

He steeled himself against the cold, as he imagined they must have done for countless centuries. Karul's blanket, while warm, was not quite long enough, and he had to sacrifice the warmth of his shoulders to keep his feet inside the fur. He glanced over at the mound of Sinnie and Ivlana, bundled together and moving with the steady breath of sleep, and wished he had someone to share warmth with. But Fabaris and Finn were already playing house, and it wasn't going to be Carl, and it surely wouldn't be Luez, so he would have to manage on his own. And it was only going to get colder from here.

By noon the next day the snow had melted enough they could walk without getting their feet soaked, and they made good time. Karul sought out Fabaris once they had about an hour of hiking under their belt.

"How far do you think this tribe of Wild Maer's territory extends?" Karul watched Fabaris' face, which remained inscrutable as ever.

"Tribes of Free Maer can be large or small, according to my studies." Fabaris dropped the term as casually as if he were discussing the weather. "I feel like this might be a smaller one, since we never saw any of them except the one who chose to find us. If they had been more numerous, the *grosti* might not have attacked them."

"And their relationship with the deer, is that typical?"

Fabaris raised his eyebrows and shrugged. "Most of what we know about them is third-hand. Free Maer tribes seem to have a special relationship with one type of creature, but as to the nature and diversity of those relationships, your guess is as good as mine."

"I seriously doubt that," Karul said.

"Be that as it may, they obviously pose no threat to us. But that vulture does have me worried."

"You should have asked their shaman about that."

Fabaris shook his head. "I don't really speak their language. I know some words, what I learned in a few weeks studying old books in the South, but not enough to have a full conversation."

"But you could understand him?"

"More or less. I could get the gist anyway. It's not so different from our own language, if you look at the roots of the words. I hope to have the chance to study it someday."

"And how you do envision that happening?" Karul sensed he was getting somewhere, that Fabaris might let something slip.

"I have no idea. Maybe when we pass back this way, we can pay them a visit. Perhaps bring them a gift, to thank them for the jerky."

"And what gift would you have us bring? Should we knock off the tip of the Great Tooth and offer it as a sign of goodwill?"

Fabaris flashed an odd smile. "Something they don't have here. Who knows? Maybe there will be something in the Archive they would like."

"You would give away our heritage to these savages?"

Fabaris kept his smile, but it grew more strained. "To the humans, we are savages. To you, the Free Maer are. To me, savage is as savage does."

"Meaning?"

"Meaning that humans, who possess so much wealth and sophistication, are capable of acts of unimaginable cruelty. The Free Maer, who have so much less even than we, freely gave us a week's worth of food. If that's not civilized, I don't know what is."

"And kidnapping our children and raising them as their own, as the Wild Maer are known to do? How is that civilized?"

"It isn't. But they are not the only Maer guilty of such actions."

"What do you mean?" Karul stopped, squaring his shoulders toward Fabaris, and everyone else stopped as well. It was time to have this out, whatever it was.

"Do you not know that the Old Maer, as they call us, have done the same? That we have raided their villages and kidnapped their children just as often as they have ours?"

"Nonsense." Karul almost spat. "We would never do something like that. It goes against our basic principles."

"*You* would never do that. *I* would never do that. But the Maer have done it, on more than one occasion. This fact is not in dispute."

"I dispute it. Such allegations should not be made lightly. Where is your proof?" He had heard of such practices, but he had always assumed them to be rumor.

Fabaris closed his eyes, tapped his fingers on his thigh, then opened his eyes again. "You are looking at it." He ran his hand from his head down to his legs, straightening his body. "I was born a Free Maer, until my village was attacked and I was captured." He turned to face the others, holding his staff arm out wide. "I was eight years old when I was taken. Eight."

Karul opened his mouth to speak but found he had no words. If Fabaris, the castle's utmost authority on Maer culture, was really a Wild Maer, what did that mean for their mission? What did it mean for their civilization? He stared, as did the others, until Fabaris spoke again.

"I would not change my life for any other, nor my companions." Fabaris scanned the group with fiery eyes. "The Maer, the Old Maer, are my tribe, and you are my family. Let there be no doubt where my allegiance lies, for it lies with all of you, and all those we left at Castle Maer." He looked down, biting his lip, and when he raised his eyes again their heat was tempered, his voice measured.

"But I am part of another tribe as well. We all are. The Maer among us belong to the larger tribe of Maer, Free or Wild or Old or whatever words you care to use. We are all part of the same diaspora, and if we are to rebuild our civilization, it must be for all Maer to freely contribute to and benefit from."

Karul felt his anger being subsumed by the truth in Fabaris' words. He thought of the humans, who had once seen the Maer as monsters, but who now joined them in this sacred quest. He nodded, looking around at the anxious faces of the group, then stepped toward Fabaris and took him by the shoulders.

"You are right," he said, the words shocking him as they spilled out. He touched Fabaris' forehead with his. "And I have been wrong. We have all been wrong, for a very long time now. And I am sorry."

He felt Fabaris' tears on his cheeks, and they merged with his own, the first tears he had shed in longer than he could remember. Ivlana's arms were soon wrapped around both of them, and Luez surprised Karul by joining in. They stood in silence, while the humans stood to the side, Sinnie putting her arm around Finn. Carl stood with his arms crossed, a faint smile on his face.

Chapter:
Twenty-Three

L uez clung to Fabaris, her mind and body flooded with the sensation of contact. She couldn't remember the last time she had hugged anyone. She knew his pain, in a way, from her early days in training. When she had joined the *Shoza*, she had been sent on several missions to abduct Wild Maer children for members of the *Sabrit* wishing to grow their families. She had seen the suffering of the children up close, felt their tiny limbs trying to resist, their voices swallowed by bags over their heads, their bodies soon wilting, becoming trembling and compliant. She had known that it was wrong, that it had nothing to do with the *Shoza's* mission to protect the magical knowledge of the Maer, but questioning orders was unthinkable. She had hardened herself against the guilt, compartmentalized it, telling herself it was a necessary evil. But when she saw Fabaris finally unloading his secret, her shame came flooding back. Holding him tight kept it at bay for a few moments.

No one spoke much during the rest of the day's march, but it felt like the strings uniting the group had been pulled tighter, among the Maer at any rate. Sinnie, Finn, and Carl floated around the periphery, but they too spoke little, perhaps in reaction to the Maer's silence. The Great Tooth dominated the sky, and they stopped in late afternoon to look at the map Luez had made, to figure out if they valley they were approaching was the one they needed to take. The map, which she had drawn from memory, put the Archive in a valley on the northwestern edge of the peak. She was sure what she had drawn was accurate, as cartography and orienteering had been a long and tedious part of her training, but there was no way to know if the original she had studied years ago was correct. Given that it had been made from a cylinder map, she assumed it was. The knowledge of the ancients always seemed more certain, being made during a time when the Maer civilization was at its apogee.

"The Great Tooth is here," Luez said, pointing out the obvious on the map, "and we are about here." Karul and Fabaris leaned in to see, taking up all the space around Luez, so Ivlana had to move around to the other side to follow. "These lines represent the ridges, the legs of the mountain, if you will." The drawing showed six ridges, unevenly spaced, radiating out from the Tooth. "The entrance to the Archive should be on this ridge here, if I've read the map correctly."

"And this space between these two lines would be the valley up ahead?" Karul asked, squinting to see the map. His distance vision was not bad, but Luez had noticed he struggled to see up close.

"I believe so. If I read this right, we head east into the valley ahead, cross over this low ridge here," at which point she touched one of the lines on the map. "Then we head cross this plain to the northwestern ridge at the base of the Tooth, crossing over wherever it looks feasible. And then we start looking for the entrance."

"How do we know the Archive is along this ridge and not one of the others?" Karul grumbled.

"The map had a coded inscription," Luez said. "*The sixth point of the star shines most brightly.* That's what it said." She tapped her finger on the northernmost ridge line, following the others as she counted. "I've thought about it many times. The north is one, two, three, four, five, six." Her finger landed on the northwest ridge.

"It is the kind of mystic clue the ancients liked to leave." Fabaris nodded, toying with his chin braids. "If the map were to fall into enemy hands, they would not be able to read the code, and even if they could, they would have to figure out the true meaning of the inscription. Not to mention finding the Archive's hidden entrance."

"Exactly." Luez studied the map, frowning. "But even with all the clues, we still have a lot of ground to cover."

"The entrance will face the east and a bit south," Fabaris said, "in the direction of the winter solstice sunrise."

"How do you know this?" Karul looked at Fabaris defiantly.

"I believe the entrance is inside an ancient burial mound." He lifted a finger and closed his eyes, nodding a few times, then sang, his voice low and haunting.

And they buried their songs and their deeds
In the place where the ancestors dwell.

Everyone remained silent for a moment until Fabaris opened his eyes, smiling. "It's from the Ballad of the Place Below. You know the song, Karul?" Karul nodded, studying the ground. Luez wondered how a warrior would know an ancient song, since he was notably absent at most Nightsongs. It would seem they were all carrying secrets around on this journey.

Fabaris cleared his throat. "The line refers to a burial mound, beyond a doubt. And they were always built with this orientation, so the first light of the winter solstice could bring hope to the dead."

"But the Tooth would block the sun from that angle." Luez drew a line with her finger from the Tooth to the ridge.

"Not at this curve here." Fabaris put his finger on a spot on the map where the ridge line, which ran northwest off the mountain, curved farther north. "The Archive must be here." He smashed his index finger onto the deerskin, leaving a slight smudge, which he then brushed away.

"Or you could have both misunderstood your ancient songs and inscriptions, and it could be on the southeast side of the Tooth, and it will take us another week to find it." Karul frowned as he stared up at the Tooth, then down at the map again.

"The vulture came from that direction," Ivlana pointed up the valley before them, in the direction of the sixth ridge on the map. "I noticed it this morning when it arrived."

Karul clapped her hard on the shoulder, and Ivlana's eyes shone with pride, and perhaps, Luez thought, something more.

"Finally, some hard evidence! Let's see if we can make it to the valley's edge before dark."

"I can run ahead," Sinnie said, "try to find a good place to sleep. My legs really need a stretch."

"I don't want anyone out here alone," Karul growled.

"I'll join her," Luez said, suddenly excited by the idea. She had been jealous when she heard about Grisol's run with Sinnie. When Luez was in training, they had run twice a day, and she had taken a kind of grim pleasure in it. For whatever reason, her body was suited for distance running, which some of the males had struggled with. Her hip was mostly recovered, and a stretch would do her good.

"If you think you can keep up with her," Karul said. "It's probably a good idea. But keep a sharp eye out."

Luez gave him a long stare. He had a tendency to treat everyone like an idiot child, which irritated her to no end. He waved her off. "I know, I know. Just...just go then."

?

Sinnie kept up a brisk pace, and Luez struggled a bit at first, as she was out of practice, but she soon fell into the rhythm of Sinnie's stride, which was faster than expected. Sinnie fell back to run alongside Luez, but she did not speak until they were nearing the valley's edge.

"What do you think of the question of the Wild Maer, or the Free Maer?" Sinnie asked.

Luez wasn't sure if she could talk while keeping up the pace, but she did her best. "Fabaris is right." She waited a few breaths before continuing. "They are what we were a few hundred years ago."

"After the...Great Betrayal?" Sinnie said the phrase awkwardly.

Luez stopped, putting her hands on her knees to catch her breath. "You know, there are those who call it the Great Mistake instead. In secret, among trusted friends. But you would do well to never utter those words." Luez was surprised to hear herself speaking what she had never said before, but there was something about Sinnie that inspired confidence. Luez had heard the phrase only a couple of times herself, but there was a theory that it was the Maer who had gone back on their word, not the humans, that the Maer had broken the Great Treaty, and doomed their own civilization.

Sinnie nodded, her brow furrowed. "Not to worry. I definitely do not want to bring up old...*hostilities*." She used the Islish word, as she did whenever she was stuck.

"Hostilities," Luez corrected her. "Yes, we have enough of those to go around." She stretched, scanning the valley, which was draped in shadow, as the sun had gone behind the mountains. A stream cut down the center of the valley, which narrowed quickly beyond the pass. It would be difficult terrain for the next day's march. "The southern ridge has a rocky look that favors caves. Let's hurry up and see what we can find."

They found an overhang with a bit of a crevice inside. It was occupied by a group of marmots, which disappeared in a cacophony of squeaks as they entered. The ground was uneven and a bit rocky, with just enough space for the group to squeeze in for cover from the wind, though it wouldn't be the most comfortable sleeping place. They hurried back to the group, who were not as far along as Luez had hoped. By the time they all reached the crevice, they had to set up camp in near darkness. They were able to build a small fire with brush from a grove of spruce, but the feeble warmth the fire provided did little to counteract the heat-sucking cold of the rock. Carl took first watch, his blanket draped over his shoulders at the entrance to the crevice.

Luez watched with envy as she saw first Finn and Fabaris, then Sinnie and Ivlana, huddle together under their blankets, while she and Karul slept separately. She lay shivering, an achy chill penetrating her core, and after a while she stood up abruptly, crept over behind Karul's large frame, and inserted herself under his blanket, overlapping her own blanket with his. She pressed herself against him, and though she could tell he was awake, he did not object. It was cold enough that she easily overcame the awkwardness of the arrangement and settled into a deep sleep.

She awoke when Karul was summoned for his watch, but she had enough residual warmth to fall back asleep for what felt like a moment before Karul woke her for the final watch, a few hours before dawn. She crouched in the entrance, her blanket wrapped around her head and feet so only her face was exposed, and stared out into the near blackness. At one point she thought she heard the muffled wings of an owl, but she saw nothing, and heard nothing else. As the first light of dawn softened the black sky into gray, she woke Carl, who nodded, retrieving the copper ring from his pack and moving down from the crevice to sit leaning against a tree. Ujenn was supposed to contact him, and though he would have little to report, there was hope she might have some information for them.

Chapter:
Twenty-Four

Carl sat leaning against a tree with the copper ring on his head. The morning sun cresting over the ridge blinded him but also brought a little warmth. He focused, using the techniques Finn had tried to teach him. His short time in study had given him some skill in this kind of concentration, but he had lost most of it through the years. He closed his eyes, trying to block out the world, and sought out Ujenn's spark with his mind. He resisted when his thoughts tried to wander, and after a time he felt a great warmth spread throughout his head and heart.

We are all safe. And you?

Carl latched onto the thought and squeezed tight with his mind. He felt sweat beading on his forehead at the effort, and he took a few deep breaths to settle his thoughts, imagining Ujenn doing the same back in Castle Maer.

Have you found the Archive?

Carl sighed, wishing he could send a message of some kind.

Are you close?

Carl squinted and his head trembled at the effort of his response. He did feel they were close, and he tried to send a strong pulse back to Ujenn. He sat for a while, breathing heavily, his head chilling from the sweat. Unsure if the conversation was over. Praying it was not. He leaned his head against the tree, and a thought boomed into his head like the echo of thunder.

I miss you.

Gasping for breath, he gritted his teeth and summoned all his energy to wrap his entire being around the thought and squeeze with all his mental strength. A pain like a lightning bolt shot through his brain, and he shrank against the tree and tore the copper ring from his head, which felt ready to explode. The pain only increased, and he fell over sideways, grasping his head with his hands and letting out a cry that left his throat ragged and his chest heaving. He lay on the ground, tears flowing from his eyes, his body shivering, as Luez and Sinnie hovered about him like seagulls squawking through glass.

"They are safe," he said as his vision inched back toward normal. He closed his eyes and smiled. "She misses me."

"Gods, you look half dead," Sinnie said in Islish, holding his face in her hands. *"Is that it? They are safe, and she misses you?"*

Carl nodded, wincing as another round of pain shot through his head. "She asked if we had reached the Archive," he said in Maer. "Then she said she missed me. It's better than nothing, right?"

"Not by much, but yeah." Sinnie finally switched back to Maer. "Here, drink." She took a waterskin from Karul, who had appeared over him, and gave it to Carl. He drank, shook his head, and drank again.

"Well at least we know it still works," Karul said. "Next time we will have some news to share." He crouched down, helped Carl up to a sitting position, and offered him jerky. Carl took it, but the idea of putting it in his mouth brought on a wave of nausea, which he was barely able to ride out. He tucked the jerky into his pocket and grasped Karul's arm in thanks.

"Give me a moment. I'll be good to go."

"Good. Because I don't plan to carry you, or wait for you," Karul pounded his fist on Carl's shoulder and stood back up.

?

Carl nursed his headache through the morning's march, which led them up a sometimes-slippery path along a rocky stream. They headed uphill for most of the day, stopping to rest more than usual, and by the afternoon they had come to the top of a small ridge. The stream continued up the ridge, but Luez insisted their path was down the other side. As they stood at the top, the Tooth towered before them, impossibly tall and majestic, with snow covering its top half. The clouds in the west whispered of weather headed their way, so they picked their way down the steep hillside with some urgency, following what Luez insisted was a path, though it was hard to make out as they zigzagged down the ridge.

The weather held off until they were near the bottom, then the air began to feel full, and in a matter of minutes the steady patter of sleet pinged off the rocks all around. They managed to get to the bottom, and when he looked back up, Carl noticed a cave less than a hundred yards south from where they had come down. Luez and Sinnie hurried off to check it out, and they returned with serious eyes.

"The good news is, it's a perfect place to sleep," Sinnie said to the expectant faces.

"The bad news is it's been used within the past week," Luez added.

"I like the first part," Karul said. "We'll worry about the second part once we're out of this mess." Flecks of sleet clung to his beard and the hair on his face, giving him an oddly fierce look.

The cave was indeed perfect for sleeping. It even had two piles of straw, plus a circle of rocks with a few usable coals in the middle. By the light of Finn's lantern, they could see marks on a wide, flat section of the wall. Upon closer inspection, they noticed drawings and perhaps even words scratched into the surface, most likely with one of the sharp rocks lying at the foot of the etching. Carl scanned the low plain that lay between their cave and the high, long ridge leading off the Great Tooth like the root of an ancient tree. There wasn't much to see between the sleet and the fading twilight, so he turned his attention back to Fabaris and Luez, who were examining the markings by candlelight.

"There's no overarching artistic or narrative structure," Fabaris said, tracing his fingers along the rough lettering, which ran in slightly crooked lines. "This writing, it does resemble ancient Maer, though some of the letters are different. I think it's mostly names, and I believe these are numbers; maybe dates? A few have what appear to be sentences next to them. Perhaps some kind of informal activity log. If I had my scrolls, and more time, but..." He waved his arms, both of them, though the left still moved less freely. "There are a lot of images of birds though, and this one, I think, might be a dragon." He tapped his finger on a drawing of a bird with its wings spread wide, but its mouth was like that of a lizard and had teeth drawn as a series of short scratches along the edges of the mouth.

"This cave is used regularly by patrols." Luez gestured to the fire and the straw. "Whoever's been watching us from the sky also has feet on the ground."

"That must be a sign we're on the right track." Karul clenched his fists before him. "Maybe these...Bird Maer, for lack of a better name, are positioned around the Archive. They might even be living inside it, for all we know. But surely it can't be a coincidence!"

"It could indeed." Fabaris held up his index finger, his head shaking side to side ever so slightly. "They could be in this place because it offers some resource they need, as we are in Castle Maer. They may know nothing of the Archive."

"These are no primitive people," Luez said. "They write. Even their soldiers write. We surely cannot say the same for ours. If they are near the Archive, they would know it."

"One thing is clear," Karul said, standing up to his full height. "We will have to go through them, or around them, to get to the Archive."

"They have the advantage," Carl said. "Assuming the vulture is theirs. They know where we are. They can follow our every movement. We will need to think carefully about how to approach them."

"True," Karul said. "There is one good thing: if they know where we are, there's no reason not to start a fire."

"Except maybe the sleet covering all the brush," Ivlana said. Karul gave her a sharp look, and she sighed. "All right, I know. Who wants to come help me find firewood?"

Finn stayed behind to keep Fabaris company while Carl ventured out with the rest of the group in the driving sleet to find something to burn. By dark, they had enough brush for a small fire, and they sat, dripping and shivering, as Finn used a bit of lantern oil to get things started. Carl let the heat from the fire sink deep in his bones, as he was the odd man out when it came to sleeping arrangements and would be spending another night struggling to keep himself covered. As much as he missed Ujenn's voice, her touch, the curve of her hip, at this moment he missed her warmth. But at least the fire made the cave a bit less frigid, and when his watch was over, he fell hard asleep and did not wake until the rising sun lit up the wall of the cave.

?

It took them most of the day to cross the plains between them and the ridge, on the other side of which they believed the Archive lay. The vulture continued to haunt them, and as they got within a mile of the ridge, a murder of crows approached, flapping and squawking just over their heads before turning back to fly over the ridge and out of sight. Sinnie pointed at something she saw moving on the top of the ridge, but she couldn't say for sure what it was, and it did not reappear. Any doubt that the group was being watched had vanished, and their faces grew somber as they marched across the soggy brown grass.

Knowing their every move would be scrutinized, Karul had come up with a plan for a diversion. They would make camp at the foot of the ridge, keeping a steady watch, and the group would follow the base of the ridge north for a day or so before crossing over. But Luez would no longer be with them. During the night, she would slip away and climb to the top of the ridge, find a place to hide and sleep while the sun was up, and take a look at what lay on the other side. She would then walk along the ridgeline the following night, with the goal of meeting up with the group the next morning, or the morning after if things took longer than expected. The hope was that the Bird Maer would not notice the group was one member short, that Luez would not be spotted and captured, and that the rest of the group would not be attacked before Luez could return to them.

Despite the many ways it could go wrong, Carl liked Karul's plan. It was the kind of thing Carl had enjoyed about his time in the service, finding creative ways to outmaneuver the enemy. Though as he had learned from the ambush on Hollow Road, if the enemy was clever and capable, they would have thought of it and would sniff it out. But he couldn't think of a better plan, nor could anyone else. Luez's stealth skills were better than anyone he'd ever met, so he liked her chances. As for the rest of the group, he had his doubts. If the Bird Maer determined the group was a threat, which seemed likely, they would surely attack. And given their familiarity with the terrain and their advance knowledge of the group's movements, they would be nearly impossible to defeat. Perhaps a demand of parlay would work, but Karul had bristled at the suggestion. And besides, Carl was pretty sure no one in the group spoke Bird Maer.

As they neared the base of the ridge, Luez pointed out a narrow track that started about a half-mile ahead, zigzagging up to the top. At the bottom, where the path began, was something brightly colored, like a statue or a sign. Karul stood scanning the ridge top for a moment, then waved the group forward, marching straight for the path. As they approached, Carl could see a skeleton strapped to a post, with feathers of many colors running up its length. A large gray bird, the size of a hawk but the shape of a crow, perched atop the skull and watched them as they came closer. Karul stopped about twenty feet from the post, which Carl could now see had writing carved in it. Fabaris stepped forward, waving off Finn, who tried to follow him. He lay down his staff and walked slowly, his right hand out in front of him, palm up, his left arm close to his side. The bird's head swiveled to follow him, its piercing black eyes looking distinctly intelligent.

Fabaris took a knee about ten feet away from the post, his finger in the air as if he were trying to read the writing. It didn't look like human or Maer writing, but it bore an odd similarity to what was on Carl's sword, only less ornate. The bird unleashed a caw that was deep and hollow, as if echoing up out of a mineshaft. Fabaris flinched, then backpedaled toward the group.

"I don't think I'll surprise anyone by saying it's some kind of warning." Fabaris held his hand out, his fingers curling as if he were trying to grasp something. "Something about death, I think, and maybe fire? Or it could be run. It's—" His hand closed into a fist. "Whatever it says, the meaning is clear. They're telling us to stay away."

Karul nodded, his fingers stroking his beard as he looked at the pole, the skeleton, and the oversized gray crow. "I like it." His fingers fluttered as he moved his hand up and down in the direction of the pole. "It's assertive, but then with the feathers, kind of beautiful, no? And the crow, I mean—" He shrugged his shoulders to the sky. "We might have to kill these bastards, but you've got to respect their style."

"Who said anything about killing anyone?" Fabaris turned to Karul, his eyes lighting up.

"It's the last thing any of us want to do." Karul raised his hands. "But surely you'll accept that if we are attacked, we have every right to defend ourselves." He glanced at Carl as if for support. Carl felt more inclined toward Fabaris' position.

"Quite so." Fabaris stood down. "But let's be more eager to find the Archive than to slay whatever stands in our way."

"Which is exactly why I'm glad you're here," Karul said, grasping his shoulders. Fabaris flinched, but only a little, as he reached up and completed the embrace. "And with the sun already playing hide-and-go-seek with the mountains to the west, maybe we should be thinking about a place to sleep."

"I spied an overhang about a quarter-mile back." Luez motioned with her chin, and when Carl looked back, he wondered how he had missed it. "It should do."

"Very well," said Karul. "Let's get a fire going. Sinnie, with dusk coming soon, isn't there something out here you might shoot?"

?

Carl sat alone by the fire, poking it unnecessarily with a stick. Fabaris had joined Finn in his poses, and Ivlana and Karul were hashing out plans for the next day, while Luez was preparing for her mission. Sinnie returned, holding a small rabbit by the ears. She handed it to Ivlana, who held up the skinny creature and flashed Sinnie a weak smile. Sinnie set down her bow and sat down next to Carl.

"How are you holding up?" Sinnie nudged him with her knee.

"I could stand it if I knew we were getting ready for battle, but this..." Carl shook his head.

"I prefer thinking we might not be. Like, maybe they will invite us into the Archive for tea."

"I wouldn't hate a cup of hot chicory tea right now."

"Gods, that would be lovely. I'll have to get some next time I'm in Wells. Whenever that might be."

"I'd settle for a cup of mushroom tea at this point. I kind of miss it, actually."

Sinnie shuddered. "I'd be more than happy never to drink that again." She gazed into the fire for a long moment. "Although I wouldn't mind sitting with Grisol over a cup. How do you suppose she's doing?"

Carl shook his head, staring at the fire to help push down tears.

"Do you miss her? I mean, I know you miss Ujenn, but..." She touched Carl on the shoulder. "Sorry, not my business, I just—"

"I do." He put his hand over Sinnie's to keep it there. "Not the same as Ujenn, but I do."

Sinnie nodded, squeezing his shoulder, her knee leaning into his. Carl looked away, gripping her hand with his, and covered his leaking eyes with his other hand. He wondered if he'd ever see Castle Maer again. If he'd ever meet his daughter. He smiled a little at the thought. Ujenn had said it was a girl, but she'd played coy when he'd asked if she somehow knew, or if she was just projecting her desires, or his.

Chapter:
Twenty-Five

L uez gave Karul a curt nod, scanned the group with her eyes, then turned her back on their company, their warmth, and the fire. She crouched atop the overhang, waiting for her eyes to adjust, then scanned the ridge above her for a very long time. When she was convinced there was nothing moving, she began her climb. She had studied the ridge as they approached, knew it started steep, then became even steeper before leveling off a little toward the top. It would have been a strenuous climb during the day, but it was positively treacherous at night, with only the cloud-muffled light of a half-moon and a couple of the brighter stars to guide her. She moved as steadily as she could, stopping to watch and rest after each of the tricky bits. She was surprised to find she almost enjoyed the climb; it took her back to the best days of her training, when she was given a mountain to climb or a river to cross solo. No matter how difficult the task, it was always easier, and more pleasurable, for her to do alone. And the dark was comforting; it meant she didn't have to spend much mental energy hiding. It was just her hands and feet and a pile of rock a thousand feet high.

The mountain's quiet was oppressive, and Luez had to take extra care not to move too quickly, lest she unleash a little rockslide that might alert someone to her presence. She kept an eye and ear out, as best she could, for owls, which she thought she had heard the night before. It was only logical that the Bird Maer would use owls at night, since they clearly used the vulture and the crows to spy on the group during the day. She hoped the owls would be focused on the cave and not notice her high on the ridge above them. If the Bird Maer got wind of her presence, they could surprise and surround her, and no amount of skill or cunning would save her. This was their home, and she was a spy. She would be lucky if all they did was kill her.

She focused on the climb to put thoughts of her own demise at bay, and she reached the top of the ridge, or as close as she dared get, well before dawn. Her hands were raw and her legs spent, but she had made it. She scanned the ridge top in the direction of the path they had seen, waiting patiently for any sign of movement, any echo of conversation, but all was still. It was too dark to see much, but if someone was there, she would have noticed. She plotted her way across the ridge, moving as smoothly as she could from rock to mound to shadow. When she got past the top of the ridge, she started looking for shelter, as the sun would be coming up before long. She passed by two potential spots, each with their own flaws, before settling on a crevice beneath a large boulder, facing east toward the valley on the other side of the ridge. The crevice was shielded by rocks on the ridge side and the south side, and a scraggly bush on the north side. The valley side was exposed, but no one down below would be able to see her if she was inside. It was as safe a place as she was going to find, and she rewarded herself with a strip of jerky and a few sips of water as she waited for the sun to crest over the mountains to the east.

As the sky lightened, the Great Tooth loomed above her, its dark base giving way to white as it climbed toward the heavens. She could see now that it actually had two peaks, aligned in such a way that they looked like one from a distance. Across the valley she saw a low ridge running parallel to the one she was on, and a larger ridge farther in the distance, the first and second legs of the star from the map. As the light grew, the valley came into focus, and she could see a dozen or more low wooden structures clustered around an earthen mound at the base of the ridge, nestled in a bend where the ridgeline curved to the northeast. In exactly the spot Fabaris had pointed out on the map. Where the ridge petered out, a line of rock extended across the valley to the eastern ridge. It had to be a wall of some kind, as it was too straight to have been a natural formation.

Luez saw some movement among the wooden structures, and a figure walked toward the mound and disappeared inside it. As she waited for the figure to emerge, she studied the ridgeline, and noticed something peculiar about the shape of the rocks. There were several places where the rocks jutted up in an unusual way. As she looked from one to the next, she discovered they were evenly spaced, and two of them were somewhat rectangular in shape, including one situated near the point where the path leading up from the valley would be. She kept her eyes locked on that spot, and after a few minutes she noticed movement. Two figures appeared atop the rectangular rock and seemed to scan the valley to the west, in the direction Luez and her group had come from. She pulled back inside the crevice to be fully out of their sightline and focused her eyes on the village below, whose details became clearer in the hazy morning light. She counted fifteen similar-sized wooden structures, as well as a pavilion directly in front of the mound. The figure she had seen entering the mound emerged and walked into the pavilion.

A shriek pierced the air, like a hawk's cry, but impossibly loud. Luez froze, uncertain where the sound had come from, and as she watched the valley, a bright reddish-orange shape appeared on the eastern ridge and moved across the valley toward the village at an alarming rate. As it approached, she could see that it moved on four legs, had a long, flared tail, and carried a limp brown shape in its mouth, which she thought might have been a mountain goat. The creature wound its way around the edge of the village, moving more slowly as it approached the mound. It stopped, its fiery coloring flipping to gray in an instant, then disappeared inside. The chills running over Luez's body were not from the cold morning air. She had just seen her first dragon.

She watched the village below for a while, frustrated she wasn't close enough to see better. She saw various figures milling about, smoke from several fires, and a group of tiny white specks moving in and out of one of the buildings and roaming around an enclosed space. She thought they might have been chickens. Two figures headed toward the bottom of the ridge just north of the village, returning a few minutes later, followed by two oddly shaped brownish-gray creatures, about the height of the figures accompanying them. They had long, thin legs, squat bodies, and wide, pointy heads that seemed to float on curved necks; they looked like some kind of oversized bird. A murder of crows, perhaps the same one that had been spying on her group the day before, flew up the ridge heading west, and a vulture wheeled in the sky above.

Though she wanted to keep watching the goings-on in the village, she knew she needed some sleep before her next night's trek. She would have to make her way along the ridge after dark, skirting below the watchtower, and try to catch up with her group to warn them. Assuming the mound was in fact the entrance to the Archive, there was no way they could get to it unseen, and even if they could, there was at least one dragon inside. Not to mention however many Bird Maer lived in a village with fifteen roofs, plus whatever those two huge birds were. Her group was outnumbered, out of their element, and clearly out of their depth. She tried to muddle through some possible scenarios for how they could make the best of the situation, but her brain grew ever foggier. At last she gave in, huddled into a corner of the crevice that was sheltered from the wind, wrapped her body in her blanket as best she could, and passed out.

?

Luez awoke to the sound of soft footsteps, quiet voices, and another noise she couldn't quite identify. She squeezed herself as far into the corner as she could, covered her face, and listened carefully. The voices she heard were speaking some form of Wild Maer, she was sure, but she couldn't understand it. The voices dropped to a whisper and the footsteps stopped, but she heard what sounded like the faint padding of large feet, and a kind of huffing, snuffling noise, which stopped just outside the crevice where she was hiding. The snuffling circled the crevice, and several pairs of footsteps crept closer. She heard the scrabble of rocks and felt the presence of something large in the mouth of the crevice. She gripped her sword hilt but maintained her silent position, trying not to breathe. She heard more scratching sounds at the entrance, followed by louder breathing, like a horse, coming from inside the crevice this time. The air turned a hair warmer, and an acrid smell filled the space.

Something poked her blanket ever so gently, and she whipped out her sword as she threw off the blanket, holding the point out away from her body. Her heart faltered and her arm trembled as she crouched, staring into the round black eyes of a creature shaped like an enormous lizard, many times the size of the rock crawlers in the mine, covered in gray feathers, which flared out around its head. It hissed as it drew its head back, but it neither retreated nor attacked, instead cocking its head to one side, then the other, as if studying her. She could hear several of the Wild Maer shouting from outside the crevice, but all her energy was focused on holding her sword out in front of her and trying to calm the trembling in her arm. The creature reached out a claw, yellow like a giant hawk's, with exaggerated slowness, touched the tip of her sword, then pulled its claw back. Luez fought through the dryness in her mouth to swallow, then carefully sheathed her sword, holding her palms out. The creature's mouth closed in what looked like a smile, and it wriggled backwards out of the crevice, dropping a few huge gray feathers in the process.

Two Maer, dressed in skins covered with small brown feathers, crouched in the entrance, spears in hand. A third Maer, larger and rounder in shape, appeared behind them, similarly attired but with gray feathers, and a few large red and orange ones around their neck. This one carried a staff with a curved loop of wood at the end, like a hook. She spoke some words Luez could not understand and gestured for Luez to come out. Though her voice was firm, Luez detected no immediate threat. She crawled out of the crevice, raising her hands as she stood up. One of the brown feather clad warriors removed her sword and daggers, but made no move to bind her hands.

The sun was low in the sky, hovering over the mountains to the west, imbuing everything with an orange-yellow glow. Luez eyed the dragon, which crouched beside the leader of Bird Maer, nuzzling her legs. Luez tried not to stare, but there was no looking away. The creature was about twenty feet long, including a five-foot tail ending in a puffy wisp of feathers. Its rear legs were longer and thicker than its front legs, and its body was as big around as a moose. Its head was three or four times the size of hers, but the crest of feathers starting just above its eyes made it look much bigger. It was covered in gray feathers from head to tail, but it had no wings, and other than the claws and the feathers, its body was more like a lizard than a bird, though she had never seen a lizard with rows of sharp teeth.

The leader said a few words, and the dragon sprang up, swift and lithe, and sauntered toward the ridge top, the leader at its side. The leader turned back and spoke again, gesturing for Luez to follow, which she did. She wished she had been able to study the languages of the Wild Maer when she was in the South, but the one teacher who knew a few dialects had fallen ill and died while she was in training.

The two warriors behind her spoke very little, keeping their spears pointed toward her but not so close as to feel overly threatening. They walked along the ridgeline until they came to the square rock she had noticed from a distance, which she could now see was the remains of an ancient watchtower. A narrow but well-designed path zigzagged down the ridge toward the village. She tried to steel herself for whatever trials lay ahead. She had trained for interrogation, torture, and all manner of deprivation, but as she descended into the valley of the Bird Maer, it all became so real that, for the first time in her adult life, she was truly afraid.

Chapter:
Twenty-Six

Fawul used her staff to flick a rock at Lolo, who was sniffing at a crevice under a boulder.

"Move along, Fluffy. Night's coming, and not all of us can see in the dark, you know."

Lolo swished her tail a couple of times, her eyes bright, leapt up onto the side of the boulder and sprang off, spinning to land neatly on the path ahead facing Fawul.

"Yes, yes, you're very talented. We're all most impressed." Lolo blinked slowly, bobbed her head, then turned and continued sauntering down the path. Sometimes it almost felt like the beast understood her words, but Fawul knew she was only responding to her tone. Lolo was smart enough that sometimes it was hard to tell the difference.

Fawul let Lolo walk ahead while she fell back with the warriors, mostly to get a better look at the spy. She was lean and fit, with hard eyes and harder muscles. She wore fine leather clothes that looked to be of human make, with some kind of built-in armor, and her sword must have come from the humans as well. She had kept remarkably cool when faced with Lolo; as far as Fawul could tell, she hadn't even pissed herself, which almost always happened when strangers came face to face with a dragon for the first time. Fawul had been worried sick that the spy might try to use her sword on Lolo, which wouldn't have ended well for her, but she carried herself like she knew how to fight, so she might have managed to hurt Lolo. Fortunately, she had not resisted, cried out, or begged for help. Fawul took a liking to her, despite the fact that she was a spy for the Old Maer.

Fawul wondered what Tcheen would do with the spy. Death seemed a logical penalty, but not before they had extracted whatever information they could. There was no way the spy could be allowed to return to her group, especially now that she had seen their enclave. But Ayal had been talking up the idea that this group's arrival might herald the Opening, and though Tcheen didn't seem entirely convinced, they had shown great curiosity about the group, asking Freni for details about each of the members, their clothes, how they walked, their apparent hierarchy. Freni looked exhausted in recent days after communing with the birds for most of his waking hours, but he was always eager to show his value, and he hadn't had a better opportunity in a long time.

Two guards stood outside Tcheen's cabin when they arrived near dark. Fawul bowed to the guards, who gave a slight bow in response. Fawul scratched Lolo's neck and gave her a bit of jerky, then slapped her on the rump. Lolo grabbed the end of Fawul's staff in her mouth, shook it a couple of times, then let go, bounding off toward the Mound, where a chorus of squawks and low roars greeted her.

Fawul had her warriors bind the spy's hands as they approached Tcheen's door. She told her warriors to stay, so there were four guarding the spy outside the cabin. One of the guards opened the door, and Fawul stepped in. Tcheen stood consulting with Ayal, who as usual was doing all the talking, more than half of it with his hands.

"This must be it, it must be! Never before have we seen—"

Tcheen silenced Ayal by raising their hand, and Ayal turned and craned his neck to look through the doorway.

"We have the spy," Fawul said, giving a half-bow to Tcheen, who nodded, gesturing for her to bring the spy in.

"Thank you." Tcheen looked from Fawul to Ayal. "You may go now." Ayal raised his eyebrows, side-eyeing the spy as he passed her on his way out the door. Fawul bowed, giving the spy what she hoped was a comforting look as she exited. The guards closed the door, and Fawul stood with Ayal and the four warriors in the growing cold.

"I should be in there!" Ayal whined. "There are things, things I could learn! Just think of it, a real-life Old Maer spy!" He rubbed his hands together, cupped them, and blew into them. "I should be in there!"

"Well, you're not." Fawul arched backward in a stretch. "And neither am I, thank gods. If you want to make yourself useful you could go get Digar. Tcheen will send for him momentarily." Ayal waved her off, and Fawul leaned against the side of the cabin, suddenly drained. She had been on her feet all day, marching up and down the mountain, following that fool of a dragon as it sniffed in every marmot hole on the entire ridge before finding the spy.

"Well, it looks like we won't have to wait," Ayal said as Digar strode into the torchlight, looking impressive in his black-feathered cloak.

Digar stopped, leaning on his spear to catch his breath, the hair on his face matted to his cheeks with sweat. He must have run all the way from the north wall when he saw them return with the spy. He eyed the cabin and hit Fawul with a hard glance.

Fawul laughed as she pushed herself off the cabin wall. "Yes, Tcheen is in there alone with the spy. So I get to wait out here in the cold, with my aching feet and my body covered in dust, instead of slipping into a hot bath, which I surely have earned, thank you very much. It was I, after all, who captured the spy."

Digar did an exaggerated bow, and they stood, a crowd of seven now, waiting outside Tcheen's cabin, straining to listen to what was happening inside. All Fawul could hear were muffled voices, speaking in a language she did not understand.

"That's Old Maer. I'd bet my life on it." Ayal clenched his fist, then ran his fingers through his braids several times. "They never said, but there were a couple of times, there was a catch in their voice, and I could tell, I could tell. They lived among the Old Maer, for a time at least. Mark my words."

The haze of clouds dissipated, allowing the stars and the waxing moon to light the village. A child's laughter could be heard from a nearby cabin, possibly from tickling; it was hard to be sure. Fawul smiled as she heard Lolo and Kiki wrestling inside the Mound. She could almost see Lolo pinning Kiki's fuzzy white head to the ground with her claws, and she heard Kiki's mad squawks as he tried to break free of his sister's grip. And inside Tcheen's cabin, barely audible snippets of an incomprehensible language slipped through the windows like steam vanishing into the night. Fawul had started to nod off, leaning against the wall of the cabin, when the door opened and the spy stepped out, looking as calm as if she'd just had a nice cup of tea with an old friend. Fawul nodded to Digar, who shifted his spear in his hands and pointed toward the Mound. They hadn't had a prisoner in quite a while, but Tcheen liked to keep them in with the dragons to stew a bit before the real interrogation started. Fawul followed Digar and the spy, with two warriors flanking them, to the Mound's entrance. Digar gave Fawul a nod, and she half-bowed to him and the soldiers, gave the spy a quick glance, then made her way toward the bath.

Fawul put her torch in the sconce and laid her cloak across the rack, careful to avoid loosening any feathers, then walked down the two steps into the bath, which was hot enough to take her breath away. Whatever ancient Maer had built it had done a fine job; the bottom and sides were smooth, and the seats were just the right height for Fawul to immerse herself up to her neck. She settled in as the bath soothed her skin, relaxed her muscles, and warmed her down to the bones. She closed her eyes and lost herself in the whiffs of sulphur and the music of water trickling out of the tub, down the sluice and into the channel below, dripping and splashing in the echoey darkness. Other than her occasional solo forays with the dragons, the bath was the only place Fawul could be alone with her thoughts, and here she didn't have to worry about anything but setting her mind right.

The much-anticipated arrival of the human and Old Maer group had set the village on edge for the past week, and the nervous energy was exhausting. Only the children seemed immune to it; in fact, they rather enjoyed it, if the intensity of their stick-fighting campaigns was any indication. The older children had organized an elaborate game out in the east marsh, with rival groups staking out territory, ambushing each other, and sending out raiding parties. It had been Tcheen's idea, to get the children out of everyone's hair while they prepared, though for what, no one really knew. The approaching group wasn't large enough to pose a serious threat to a village with thirty able-bodied fighters, not to mention two mages, four dragons, two hatchet birds, and countless hawks, crows, and eagles. But that didn't stop Digar from running nonstop drills, and the warriors' rhythmic grunts and shouts could be heard from dawn to dusk.

What intrigued Fawul the most, other than the fact the humans and Old Maer were traveling together, was Freni's insistence these humans were from the north, based on something he had seen through the eyes of the birds. He never said how he knew what humans from the north would look like, but he spoke with mysterious conviction. Everyone knew the Old Maer had deep connections to the South, as evidenced by the spy's clothing and weapons, but as far as anyone knew, they had had no contact with the north. Clearly their knowledge of the Old Maer was lacking.

Fawul sighed as she saw the approaching torchlight and heard Freni's footsteps. She had been in the bath for quite a while, and he had surely been working every bit as hard as she, though his work in-

volved his mind rather than his body. Seven straight days of spying
with the vultures, owls, and crows had left him looking haggard, and
he had needed to be carried to the bath the day before, after he in-
habited the Ghost. Not that anyone thought the group would be dis-
suaded by a huge gray crow, no matter how creepy, but its supernat-
ural perception had allowed them to identify one of the humans as a
mage. It had also told them another of the humans carried a sword of
the ancients, the kind that were only found buried with the *Ka-lar*,
or so the legends told. Whoever had defeated a *Ka-lar* could pose a
real threat to her dragons.

"Well done today," Freni said as he shed his clothes and slipped
into the bath across from her. He shivered, closed his eyes, and
smiled. "You're the toast of the valley."

"Lolo did most of the work. Besides, you haven't done so badly
yourself of late." Fawul poked his foot with her toe. He was a little
scrawny for her taste, but he would do in a pinch. Had, in fact, on
several occasions, when need and opportunity had conspired. But
sex was not allowed in the bath, for obvious reasons, and besides, she
was way too tired to do anything this night but collapse against a big
snoring pile of feathers. But it was fun to tease him, watch him get all
flustered trying to figure out if she was messing with him.

"Big day tomorrow, don't you think?" she asked, rubbing his foot
with hers.

"For you, definitely," he said, pulling his foot back without opening his eyes. "I know Tcheen is going to want to put on a show for
our guests, and we all know what that means."

Fawul chuckled. Tcheen liked to have Bobo put on his fiery coat
to impress and intimidate enemies, though it had been a long time
since anyone had dared attack the village.

"I don't imagine you'll be sleeping through the encounter. We always need our little feathered lookouts, and I bet Tcheen sends out
the hatchet birds too."

"Everyone gets to play." Freni sank to the bottom of his chin, his scraggly face poking above the surface like a bird's nest.

"Well I'll let you melt by yourself now. We both need the rest." Fawul wiped most of the water off her body with the old wolfskin, put her robe back on, and padded out, leaving Freni to his soak.

She extinguished her torch in the sand bowl outside the bath cave, since the skies provided enough light to see. When she got to the Mound, the two guards who had been standing outside Tcheen's cabin now stood on either side of the entrance. They exchanged half-bows, and she walked between the two stone slabs, past the pantry room, and into the first chamber, where Bobo was sprawled out, half-asleep. His slitted eyes pointed toward the alcove on the right, where the spy sat against the wall, staring at the creature. Fawul scratched Bobo's neck for a moment, and he leaned into her, giving a rumbly sigh.

"Good night." Fawul gave the spy a little wave as she patted Bobo on the nose. Whether she understood the words or not, the spy blinked in acknowledgment, then closed her eyes. Fawul tiptoed past Maomao, who occupied the passage just beyond the first alcove, facing the spy. Maomao was in her first phase of snoring, gentle and rhythmic; it wasn't until later in the night that she would begin to sound like a demon rising through the rock. Maomao's legs kicked a few times as if she were running in her sleep, and Fawul waited until they stopped before squeezing past. She could just see the white of Kiki's fuzzy feathers heaped against Maomao's rump, and as temptingly soft as Kiki's feathers were, Fawul knew better than to snuggle up to a sleeping toddler with claws like daggers. She felt her way to the dark heap of feathers that was Lolo, stroking her neck a few times before snuggling into her belly. Lolo shifted with a sleepy groan, then wrapped one claw across Fawul's body, her nails curled in so she wouldn't scratch her by accident. Lolo's belly was like a furnace, and Fawul sank down into sleep without thought, worry, or dream.

?

"Wake up." Fawul heard the word as if from a distance, then again, accompanied by a gentle toe to the ribs. Tcheen stood over her, resplendent in their white-feathered cloak and white face paint, matching their pale dragonbone staff. "We have two hours, and there is much to do."

"They are..." Fawul rubbed her eyes and sat up, one hand resting on Lolo's ribs.

Tcheen nodded. "Two hours, at the north gate."

Chapter:
Twenty-Seven

Tcheen made their way through the narrow space of the Mound, giving the dragons a wide berth. As much as they loved the power the dragons gave the tribe, Tcheen had never managed to trust them completely. Mostly because they couldn't tell how smart the creatures really were. Tcheen could tell they understood some of what went on, but it was impossible to know just how much. It was conceivable the dragons were just as smart as the Maer, though on occasion they did things only a stupid animal would do. But then again, so did some of the villagers, so it wasn't fair to hold that against them. It was the uncertainty that gave Tcheen pause; were the dragons dangerous because they weren't smart enough, or because they were too smart?

The morning air grew heavy as the cloud cover returned, overspreading the valley and masking the Tooth in a wooly blanket. If they were to meet the Old Maer and their human companions, it could well be in a steady snowfall, which was fine with Tcheen. They had always thought Bobo's fiery red coat looked magnificent against a snowy backdrop. They needed to present a front that was so powerful and so dazzling it took the intruders' breath away, and any thought of resistance with it. A murder of crows, a couple of hatchet birds, a flaming red dragon, and a dozen warriors ought to do it, they

thought, especially with themself and Digar as centerpieces, in com-
plementary black and white.

The spy, who'd called herself Luez, had said the group had not
come to fight, though it appeared all the members except one were
highly skilled in combat. In addition to the spy, the group had one
who appeared to be a scholar, as well as three warriors, including a
human carrying a *Ka-lar* sword. The other two humans seemed to be
an archer and a mage, whose exact powers were unknown. The spy
and her companions had dispatched a group of five *grosti* without
taking a single casualty, which was enough to give Tcheen pause. Two
grosti had entered the village through the marsh several years before,
killed four warriors, and made off with two of the bodies, depriving
them of their last rites. It had taken a week to hunt them down in
their cave to the east, and even with Bobo and Maomao on their side,
they had lost two more warriors in the battle. If the group came for a
fight, it would be a fierce one, and though the outcome would hardly
be in doubt, victory could come at too high a cost.

The spy had kept silent about the real reason for the group's arrival, saying she did not have the authority to reveal that information. Perhaps it could be extracted through torture, but Tcheen was
not inclined to torture someone who had done no direct harm to
their people. All the spy had said was that her group had come to
prevent great bloodshed, and that if Tcheen wanted further information they would have to talk to Karul, the group's leader. Freni
had seen this Karul up close through the Ghost's eyes. Freni said the
leader was tall and strong, with a fierce look and a proud bearing. He
carried a spear of the Ancients but wore no armor, and he was followed everywhere by a stout female who carried a sword, and who
had faced off against several *grosti* by herself and still lived. Karul was
clearly the leader, though in their encounter with the Deer Maer he
had deferred to another, who had managed to speak their language.
Freni guessed he was a scholar, since he also seemed to have read their

sign at the base of the low saddle. This scholar was the one Tcheen was the most eager to speak with.

Ayal had argued that the group's arrival heralded the Opening, when the Mound's deepest secrets would finally be revealed. Tcheen did not put much stock in prophecies and myths, but they could not dismiss the idea out of hand. Twenty years after ousting the valley's previous occupants, a tough but disorganized group of Boar Maer, Tcheen's tribe still did not know why the Mound was built, or when, or by whom. The surviving Boar Maer, who had integrated into their tribe, had told and retold the myth of the Opening, which they had heard from the occupants before them. It seemed this valley had been home to many tribes over the years, which was no surprise, as it was protected, defensible, and had a hot spring, a priceless commodity in the cold mountain winters. But the north wall had not been built by any Maer in recent memory. Though it had been shored up several times, at its base it was hundreds of years old at least, if not thousands. The remnants of towers and walls along the west ridge must have dated from the same forgotten era, from the time when the Mound was built.

Perhaps the group, which should now be cresting the low saddle of the ridge just north of the wall, had some knowledge of the ancient society that once flourished here, building fortresses, walls, and elaborate baths. Maybe they could provide some answers to the many questions surrounding the Mound, if they didn't force Tcheen to kill them first. The feather on the water clock told Tcheen the group needed to be assembled at the north wall in an hour's time, so they dispatched warriors to remind Fawul, Freni, and Izul to get their beasts ready. Digar would have his troops in place by now, so all that remained was to wake Ayal. Tcheen returned to their cabin, waved away the two warriors standing guard, and opened the door with a gentle push.

Ayal lay sprawled in an impossible position, his limbs and braids splayed about as if they had exploded from his body. Tcheen leaned onto the bed behind him, sliding their hand between his legs and squeezing as they took his ear between their teeth. His back arched and he gave a little cry, which they snuffed out by clamping a hand over his mouth, squeezing him harder as they kissed and milked his ear. He grew hard and he breathed in deeply through his nose as he pressed his body into Tcheen's. His eyes slid back to meet theirs, and they held his gaze, neither of them flinching, until at last they released their grip and gave him a shove that sent him tumbling to the floor.

"Gods' bones be cracked and sucked dry!" Ayal whined, one hand on his crotch and the other on his ear. "I was awake, I was awake! I was just...thinking!"

"Dress while you think," Tcheen said, lifting Ayal's robe off the floor with their toe and tossing it to him. "We're headed to the wall to meet them." They heard running footsteps and opened the door to see Sulee, whose sinewy arms seemed longer than her legs.

"They have crested the low saddle." Sulee's eyes burned bright. She was one of the twelve warriors Digar had chosen to meet the group by the north wall, and pride positively steamed off her body.

"We are on our way." Tcheen held Sulee's eyes from straying inside the doorway. She was a little nosy for a warrior, but that didn't have to be a bad thing. And she spoke Southish, which might well come in handy. "Go now." Sulee nodded, turned, and sped off through the village.

Tcheen peeled two boiled eggs while Ayal went off to the latrine. When Ayal returned, they tossed him one. He ate it greedily, flecks of white and yellow clinging to his beard. Tcheen put one hand on the back of his head and wiped the crumbs off his face with their thumb, holding onto his chin for a moment before letting him go.

"I'm ready," he said as he finished straightening the colorful feathers on his cloak.

"What were you thinking?" they asked him.

"What? I—oh, well, I was thinking, I was thinking about their scholar, and how he was able to communicate with the Deer Maer. I've never heard of an Old Maer who can speak the tongues of the Free Maer."

"The languages are not so far apart." Tcheen thought of the time they had spent in the South training with the Old Maer, passing as one of their own, among the humans at any rate. Though Tcheen had never told him, Ayal would have overheard them speaking to the spy, would have figured out they could speak the Old Maer's language, though he would not know how rusty they were.

"Perhaps when this is all over, I can begin to learn their language." Ayal tiptoed up to straighten a feather on Tcheen's cloak. "Assuming you don't get overwhelmed by the moment and decide to kill them all."

Tcheen gave him a hard look, which he withstood bravely. He would pay for his insolence tonight, and his eyes showed he knew it. Wanted it. Needed it.

"It is time." Tcheen walked out the door and headed toward the Mound. As they walked through the village, they saw the older children and the parents on child duty shepherding the younger ones into the Mound, where the two guards joined a phalanx of warriors standing with spears and javelins at the ready. On the north edge of the village, a dozen of the warriors had formed a line, evenly spaced, and a handful of others lurked around the periphery of the village, on the off chance the group's arrival was a diversion from some unseen foes. Lolo had been sent to sniff the edges of the valley, and a pair of guards stood watch on the high ridge. Tcheen was satisfied with the security plan, but their stomach churned as they led Ayal toward the wall. He was uncharacteristically silent, his face thoughtful, his steps measured. Tcheen put a gentle hand on the back of his neck, and he laid his hand on top of theirs and flashed a weak smile. The group's arrival might prove to be the biggest moment in all of their lives, and the mood of the group gathered inside the wall was tense. The hatchet birds stood by Freni, shifting from one leg to the other, their heads bobbing nervously. Even Bobo sat still in a hump of gray feathers, his eyes fixed on the tiny figures descending the last bit of the low saddle.

Tcheen nodded to Sulee, who stood by the flame at the gate. She heaped dried grass upon it and it burst into life, so bright Tcheen had to shield their eyes for a moment. Several warriors added kindling and a few medium-sized logs, and before long the fire blazed hot and proud. Tiny snowflakes fluttered down as they watched the group emerge onto the valley floor. The Old Maer and their human companions would be at the gate in less than half an hour. Tcheen stood up tall, and everyone present drifted toward them, all eyes locked on theirs.

"We go forth today to greet an unknown force." Tcheen paused, making eye contact with each one of them. "We know not who they are, nor why they come. We know they come with strength, for they have defeated a group of five *grosti*. We know they come with cunning, for their spy would have escaped our notice if not for the owls. Though their numbers be few, we must not underestimate them." Only the crackle of the fire broke the silence.

"We must present a show of force, with the hope we will not need to use it. Freni will send the crows into the air, and the hatchet birds will approach from both sides, but keep their distance." Tcheen gave Freni a sharp look, and he nodded. "Digar and I will walk in front, with the warriors in a line a few steps behind us." Digar gripped his spear and bowed. "Bobo will sit on the wall, opposite the fire, ready to pounce at a moment's notice." Izul nodded his assent, closing his eyes for a moment, and Bobo's feathers suddenly flipped from gray to fiery orange. "Ayal, you will walk behind me and Digar. I want your take, but only once we know it's safe."

"No argument from me, none at all." Ayal looked like he was ready to puke up his egg.

Tcheen made eye contact with each of the warriors. "Be ready. Project strength. Remain calm." The group parted as Tcheen strode toward the gate, Digar falling in at their side. Sulee and another warrior swung the gate open and the group walked out into the field, whose brown and yellow grasses were now flecked with white from the flurries. Tcheen wished for a steadier snowfall, as it would complete the aesthetic, but it was better than rain. Everyone got into position as the group approached from the north, seeming to move in baby steps.

When at last the interlopers got close enough, Tcheen signaled to Freni, and the hatchet birds strode out on either side of the approaching group. Tcheen and Digar took ten steps forward, then stood, spears in hand. The other group stopped, and only two of them walked forth. One was tall and broad and carried a spear with what looked like a bronze tip, and the other, who would have seemed tall next to anyone else, carried a staff and wore his facial hair in tiny braids. An ornate cloak made of various furs rounded out his look, which Tcheen found pleasing, if a bit primitive. The first would be Karul, their leader, and the other the scholar. They stopped about five paces away, and the scholar bowed, in the Free Maer style, his form awkward but his gesture essentially correct. The leader held his head high, his proud expression just short of defiant. It was so quiet Tcheen could hear the snowflakes landing on the dead winter grass.

Chapter:
Twenty-Eight

Fabaris walked alongside Karul, who took tempered strides to come to within ten feet of the apparent leader, a tall, rangy Maer with an elaborate white feather cloak and matching white face paint. They carried a smooth, white spear made of a single seamless length of what looked like bone, but it was too long to be the bone of any creature he'd ever seen. Next to the leader was a warrior, a squat mound of hairy muscles cloaked in black feathers, with black face paint and a wooden spear with an enormous tooth as its point. A dozen warriors flanked them, with brown feathers adorning their cloaks. A smaller Maer stood behind them with braids that moved as if alive. His robe was decked out with a dazzling array of colorful feathers, and he craned his head over the black-clad one to get a look at Fabaris and Karul.

"Do you think the leader is male or female?" Karul whispered to Fabaris.

"Does it matter?" Fabaris whispered back, and Karul grunted in response. In truth, Fabaris could not tell; it seemed the Bird Maer had freer gender expression than the Old Maer.

Two enormous birds like oversized turkeys bracketed Fabaris' group on either side, with long, strong legs and wide, powerful-looking beaks. The birds strutted to and fro, their necks bobbing but their fierce eyes locked on Fabaris and his companions. Atop the wall perched a wondrous creature, like a great lizard covered in bright orangish-red feathers, which flared out above its eyes like a crown of flame. Several more Maer stood at the gate, including two who did not look like warriors, cloaked in gray feathers interspersed with bursts of orange the color of the dragon.

Karul held up his hands in peace, but did not bow as Fabaris had instructed. Fabaris worried Karul would get them all killed, but Karul was stubborn, and that wasn't going to change. The leader bowed back to Fabaris, then fixed Karul with a long, cold stare, which Karul returned, with some heat. Fabaris held out one hand as if to hold Karul back, then took a slow step forward, pulling Stuock's rock out of his pocket.

"We come in peace," he tried to say in what few words of Free Maer he could muster.

"You are goodly armed for these who come in peace," the leader responded in choppy Old Maer.

"The mountains are a dangerous place," Karul said, stepping forward and lowering his hands. "One must be prepared to defend oneself."

"If you come in peace, also you may leave in peace," the white-feathered leader said, gesturing to the path back toward the low saddle.

"We come in peace, but for the peace we seek we may need your help." Fabaris held out the rock between his thumb and middle finger so its shape would be plainly seen. White Feathers took the rock, turning it over in their fingers, then handed it back to Colorful Feathers behind them, who studied it from all angles and whispered in their dialect, too low and fast for Fabaris to understand.

"Where did you get this rock?" White Feathers asked in a stern voice.

"That is a longer story, which might best be told in a less...public environment."

White Feathers turned to consult with Colorful Feathers, and again Fabaris could not make out what they said, but he thought he heard the word 'two.'

"I am Tcheen. What names are you told?"

Karul shot Fabaris a puzzled glance.

"I am Fabaris, and this is Karul. Our leader."

"Very well. Karul and Fabaris, you may come on. The rest will stay here, and you may to leave your weapons with them."

Once Karul had given his spear and knife to Ivlana, they followed Tcheen, who walked beside Colorful Feathers, with Black Feathers behind them, emanating silent menace. As they passed through the gate, Colorful Feathers turned and gave Fabaris a nod and Karul a glance, then turned to catch up with Tcheen, who walked with long, powerful strides. They walked in silence for about half a mile until they came to the edge of a village made up of a dozen or more wooden structures. A line of warriors with brown feathers on their cloaks stood evenly spaced before them, parting to let the group through. They walked on a path that led between several of the wooden structures, which were solid-looking cabins with thatched roofs and wooden windows and doors, all of them closed. They passed by a large pavilion, which had a number of stumps arranged as if for an audience. As they passed it, Fabaris looked to his right and stopped, his mouth dropping open. A low earthen mound sat nestled against the bottom of the ridge, with a large rock atop it in the precise shape of the one Stuock had gifted them.

Karul jerked Fabaris' arm, and he stumbled as he started walking again. Karul's expression was one of wonder mixed with a stern warning to keep his mouth shut. Fabaris blinked his assent. They must not give away any more information than was strictly necessary. At last they reached a cabin, a bit larger than the rest, and Tcheen opened the door and gestured for them to enter. Inside was a sleeping area to the left, and to the right a large rough table with simple carved chairs arranged around it. Tcheen took a seat in the largest chair, while Colorful Feathers pushed open several shutters, bringing light into the cabin, and cold air along with it. Black feathers stood in the doorway as Tcheen indicated the chairs with a sweep of their hand. Tcheen said something to Colorful Feathers, who nodded and hurried out the door.

"Ayal will bring us tea," Tcheen said, then sat silent, staring at the rock, which they turned over and over in their fingers. Fabaris kept expecting Tcheen to continue, but they said nothing, playing with the rock for a while before finally laying it in the middle of the table. Tcheen looked at Karul for quite a while, their facial expression unchanged, then shifted their gaze to Fabaris, who felt powerless as he never had before. Tcheen's gaze was so intense, so unwavering, it felt like Fabaris' skin was being peeled away layer by layer, revealing his soul and all his thoughts. He exhaled audibly when he heard footsteps, and Ayal entered with a steaming pitcher and four wooden cups. He poured the reddish-brown tea, raising the pitcher high above the table as he poured, creating bubbles in the cups, as Fabaris had seen some do in the South. Tcheen blew on their tea and took a sip, then set down their cup, pointed to the rock, and said, "Tell."

Karul shot Fabaris a glance that said he should speak. Karul was only too happy to make proclamations and speeches, but diplomacy had never been his strong suit. Fabaris cleared his throat and took a sip of his tea, which was fruity and slightly bitter, not altogether unpleasant.

"First of all, we thank you for your hospitality," he began, hoping for a positive reaction from Tcheen, or any kind of reaction, but he got none. "We apologize for the unexpected nature of our visit, and we realize how our arrival must appear to you."

"Enough little talk. Tell of the stone."

"Yes, well, this stone was made, and given to us by..." Fabaris looked to Karul for help, but Karul looked as flustered as Fabaris felt.

"By a mage, one with certain...powers, beyond what mere knowledge can provide—"

"We know of mages." Tcheen turned and rattled off a stream of words in their dialect to Ayal, who nodded with bright eyes. "Continue."

"This mage was gifted with a secret, from his master, who received the secret from his master, and so on, down through the ages. The secret was given only in thought, with strict instructions that it never be manifest except in the most extraordinary circumstances."

Tcheen's brow furrowed. "I do not understand. Say again, with easier words."

"The mage was given the shape of the stone in his mind, but told never to make the stone unless it was very important."

Tcheen grunted, translating for Ayal, who looked ready to jump out of his seat with excitement. Ayal responded, and of their back and forth Fabaris caught only bits and pieces: the word why, and perhaps something about opening.

"Why do the Old Maer believe the Mound is important?" Tcheen's eyes were hard and cold.

Fabaris closed his eyes, pressing his hands together. He remembered the tales of the Old Maer from his childhood, how the Free Maer saw them as villains, murderers, thieves, and evil sorcerers.

"We believe the Mound is an ancient tomb of our people, not just the...Old Maer, but the Free Maer as well." Tcheen's eyes darted to Ayal's as Fabaris said the words Free Maer. "Of those who came before there were Free Maer and Old Maer. Of the time when Maer were strong, and united, a time with great knowledge, and art, the very height of Maer civilization." He stopped, as Tcheen's brow furrowed again. "We believe that those who built this Mound were the ancestors of all Maer, and that beneath the Mound lies a great treasure, what we call the Archive, a collection of ancient writings, thousands upon thousands of scrolls, maps, books..."

Tcheen stopped him with a raised finger, then listened as Ayal went on at great length, something about writing, and story, and again the word *open,* or so Fabaris thought. Their dialect was quite distinct from what he had grown up with, and much harder to understand than the Deer Maer's, which had been challenging enough. Ayal waved his arms as he spoke, and his braids danced about his shoulders. Tcheen put up their hand to stop Ayal, then turned back to Fabaris and Karul, their expression softening just a hair.

"We have a story, of that Ayal knows more than me, of a thing called the Opening. It is said that someday will come ones from far away which will open the Mound, and what is found beneath will make a great change for all the world."

"I think our stories tell of the same thing," Fabaris said. "There is something underneath this burial mound, more than just bones."

"That may be." Tcheen's eyes pierced Fabaris' skull. "But maybe they are just stories. Maybe there is great treasure under the Mound, and you come to steal it."

"How could we steal anything from you?" Karul sounded almost angry. "You have many warriors, you have those huge birds, whatever they are. And you have a dragon."

"We have four," Tcheen said, "but one of these is just a baby. They live in the Mound."

"Well then you need not worry." Karul's tone softened. "We are not here to take anything from you. We are here to work with you, to—" He was interrupted by the sound of hurried footsteps and heavy breathing.

"Freni," Tcheen said, looking up as a slight Maer in a gray and red feathered cloak slipped past Black Feathers. The newcomer was one of the two who had been at the gate, standing back from all the warriors. Freni did a quick half-bow, eyeing Fabaris and Karul, then stepped forward, speaking between gasps for air, something about many Maer. Fabaris was starting to figure out the accent, but most of the words were still foreign to him. Tcheen asked a question, which sounded like *How many?* Fabaris could not understand the response, but from the tone it was clear that it was a lot.

"I will think of what you say." Tcheen stood up, draining the last of their tea. "You go now. Come back at dawn. There is a cave, in you can sleep. Digar will show you."

"And what of our friend?" Karul locked eyes with Tcheen. "She is..."

"We captured your spy. She is alive, for now. Go, we will speak on this tomorrow."

Fabaris bowed, and Karul followed suit this time. It appeared he had finally met his match.

Chapter:
Twenty-Nine

Karul stayed locked in his thoughts as he and Fabaris followed Digar's black-feathered mass back through the village. He was perplexed about whether Tcheen was male or female, but he liked the way they ran the place, in complete control, with a robust military presence balanced by a sense of panache. Even the animals were used in a way that was not only strategic but beautiful. Each caste had its own uniform—brown feathers for the warriors, gray with red and orange feathers on the shoulders for the mages and the dragon handler, and of course Tcheen, resplendent in white, and Digar, the very picture of dark menace, with the colorful scholar rounding out the crew like a jester in tales of old. Karul longed for a day when Castle Maer could boast of such stability that they could worry about the color of their clothing. Clearly these Maer were not as wild as he had assumed, and certainly freer than anyone would have imagined.

Karul and Fabaris followed Digar's silent lead as they crossed the half-mile of open field between the village and the wall. Karul did not envy Tcheen's job defending such a wide-open space. The ridges on both sides of the valley provided natural boundaries, but there was just too much ground to cover, too many sides to protect in case of an attack. There was a row of trees to the east, cypress by the look of it, which suggested wetlands of some kind. Perhaps there was a marsh below the east ridge, a natural barrier against an army, but one that could easily be infiltrated by a small group of highly trained fighters. The Tooth rising to the south at least was an area they wouldn't have to worry much about, but the wall to the north was too low to do much good, and too long to patrol effectively. Then again, they had their spy birds, their dragons, and those giant killer turkeys, so maybe they weren't in such a bad position after all.

Karul and Fabaris passed through the gate, veering to the right to stay as far away as possible from the dragon, which eyed them with considerable interest. As before, a dozen warriors stood at attention, watching them as they rejoined their companions, who formed an impromptu half-circle to greet them. Fabaris looked to Karul, his eyes hopeful of a chance to speak, but Karul shot him down with a glance, motioning for the group to come closer.

"Luez is alive," he said to the expectant faces around him. "Or so they say, and I have no particular reason to doubt them. We told them of the Archive, of our errand. Or rather, Fabaris did, with my blessing. They say they have a story called the Opening, when strangers will come to open the mound and make a...a...change to the world, or something. Tcheen seems to be the only one who speaks our language, and not very well."

"They are trying to decide if we are the strangers from their story." Fabaris looked up at Karul apologetically, and Karul blinked for him to continue. "I believe they think we are, and I think they will work with us, given time. But...something they said, or rather something I thought I might have understood, suggested there is another group, a group of many Maer, headed this way."

Karul gave a start. "Kind of you to let me know so soon," he grumbled.

"I did not wish to say it aloud, in case anyone besides Tcheen speaks our language. Plus, I wasn't sure I even understood it right."

"And why would a large group of Maer be heading this way?" Ivlana asked.

Karul and Fabaris exchanged glances. "The High Council may have caught wind of our adventure," Karul said, the words bitter in his mouth. If they felt he had betrayed them by coming here on his own, which in a way he had, there would be no mercy for him.

"More likely it is the *Sabrit*." Fabaris stroked his chin braids. "They might have sniffed out our plans through magical means. They would have sent the *Shoza*. They're...the elite forces who guard the mages," Fabaris explained to the humans. "They are highly trained, like Luez, and they travel with mages among them. Terrible foes. Stealthy. Cunning. Merciless." His hand fell to his side as the smile drained from his face.

"We should watch the marsh," Carl said, eyeing the eastern edge of the valley, barely visible amidst the flurries. "A group like that *Shoza* you mentioned, they'll come in through there. With, probably, some warriors coming down over the ridge, either at the high crossing up there, or the low saddle..." Karul nodded, putting a hand on Carl's shoulder. He was glad of his decision to bring Carl along. He glanced back at the low crossing, no more than ten minutes' walk from where they stood.

"Under cover of night, if I were them." Karul eyed the ridge, rotating to the marsh, just visible past the line of trees from this angle, and the village behind them.

"Speaking of cover," Sinnie said, "and I'm not saying I don't like this snowy field, because I do, I really do, it's just—"

Karul tried to shoot her down with a hard glance, but he smiled in spite of himself. "They have offered us shelter, and here, I believe, are our guides."

Two of the warriors approached, carrying bundles of wood. One of them carried a torch.

"*Do you speak Southish?*" one of them asked, a female whose eyes radiated intelligence.

"*Some of us.*" Fabaris looked to Karul, who shook his head. He could understand a little, but he couldn't say much.

"*There is a...*" Karul missed some of what she said, but heard "*big rock there.*" She pointed with what seemed like an unusually long arm. "*We will take you.*"

Karul nodded. "*Thank you,*" he managed.

"*You are Karul?*" she asked, sounding a little nervous through her boldness.

Karul couldn't help but smile. "*Yes. You?*"

"*I am Sulee.*" She maintained eye contact, a hint of a smile twisting one side of her mouth. "*Follow me.*" She shouldered the wood with ease, turned, and walked through the group, which parted to let her pass.

She led them to an opening in the base of the ridge between the wall and the low saddle where they had come down. Karul had not noticed it before, being distracted by the dragon, among other things. Its entrance was covered by two large wooden frames intertwined with brush, which were obvious up close but hard to spot from a distance. Sulee lowered her bundle of wood and pushed it into Karul's chest, her eyes sparkling with a smile that did not show on her lips. She pulled aside the screens to reveal a squared-out space that might once have been a cave but had been substantially worked at some point in the distant past. There were four Maer-sized piles of straw, with body-shaped indentations, and a fire circle in the center, just like in the cave they had slept in on the ridge far to the east.

"*Tcheen will...before night.*" Sulee spoke directly to Fabaris, who nodded.

"*Many thanks...*" Karul lost most of what Fabaris said, but it didn't matter.

"*Thank you, Sulee,*" Karul said, bowing to her in the way Fabaris had taught him.

Sulee covered her mouth as she laughed, her eyes staying with his. "*You are most welcome.*" She bowed back, turned, and nearly skipped out of the cave.

"She's an odd one." Ivlana frowned as she watched the space where Sulee had left. "A bit...forward, for a low-ranking warrior."

"Someone with a presence like that will rise in the ranks soon enough, if she has the skills to back it up." Karul's mind grasped at the image of Sulee's eyes laughing at him, but it faded into the falling snow. "At any rate, at least we have shelter, and fire."

"Shouldn't we wait for nightfall?" Carl said, eyeing the wood. Karul sighed. Two bundles would barely keep a small fire going from now until the next morning, but Karul's toes were in desperate need of a defrosting.

"I suppose you're right." Karul unslung his bag and lowered himself to one of the straw piles, pulling his blanket out of his bag. "I think we're safe here. I for one am going to catch a little rest. There's no telling what this day will hold, let alone the next."

?

Sulee returned near nightfall, her eyes more serious this time. "*Tcheen wants to see you. All of you. Right now.*" Karul began to lay down his spear, but Sulee shook her head. "*You may keep your weapons. Tcheen has...*" Karul missed the rest, but he picked up his spear with a feeling of relief.

"Tcheen has decided we are allies," Fabaris said.

"I expect they will need us against the group that is approaching." Karul's stomach churned. If the *Shoza* were coming, Tcheen and their Bird Maer were going to need all the help they could get. And it still might not be enough.

As they followed her back through the gate, the dragon was no longer there, and only four warriors stood watch outside. Muted sounds of talking and laughter filtered through the spaces between the cabins. A pair of older children carried two large water gourds on a long pole, stopping to stare at the group as they passed. Karul felt a pang as he pictured the same scenario playing out in Castle Maer. He never thought he would miss the sounds and sights of daily life, of children and adults going about their business. Even the sound of a baby's cry echoing from one of the cabins gave him a warm feeling in his chest.

They were led to the pavilion, where a fire and numerous torches gave a welcoming light. Tcheen stood talking to Ayal, and something in their body language suggested they were a couple, though Karul still couldn't figure out if Tcheen was male or female. Ayal was male, but that didn't necessarily mean anything; there was no way to know what the sexual customs of the Bird Maer were. Karul shook his head. Maybe Fabaris was right. Maybe it didn't matter.

The two mages wearing gray and red feathers, Freni and the tall one whose name he had not learned, stood conversing nearby. Digar lurked in the shadows near Tcheen, taking a step forward as the group entered the pavilion. He gestured for them to sit on a row of stumps that faced the leaders, who took their places in carved chairs, while Tcheen and Digar flanked the small fire between the group and the rest of the leaders. Tcheen said something to Sulee, who nodded and sped off in the direction of the mound.

"Welcome," Tcheen said in Maer, spreading their white-feathered arms. "We have decided to help you to make the peace you say you look for. Exchange for this first, if you will help us defend the village from the group that approach from the south." They paused, fixing each member of the group with a penetrating stare.

Karul stood, attempting to mimic their bow. "We thank you for your welcome, and we accept your offer. We will help defend your village, and the mound, from those who come."

Tcheen nodded, their face unmoving. "We hope you have some knowledge of who must be in this group. Freni will tell of what he sees through the vulture, and I will explain."

Freni, a short, pot-bellied male with a nervous smile, stepped forward and began speaking in their language. Karul looked to Fabaris, who squinted as he listened, nodding along, then shaking his head.

Tcheen turned to the group. "He says there are twenty-six, four who may be mage or scholar, the others warriors. They come three days forward."

Karul nodded to Fabaris, who stood and bowed. "We believe they are from the *Shoza*, those who guard the *Sabrit*, our council of mages. The *Shoza* are stealthy, highly trained, the deadliest of all Maer. If the *Shoza* are approaching, they come to find what is buried beneath the mound, what we call the Archive. They believe there is a scroll there they can use to command the *Ka-lar*." Karul touched Fabaris on the shoulder, keeping his hand there as Tcheen translated. They had decided to be open with Tcheen, and he hoped it was not a miscalculation.

"Do you believe this scroll is to find under the Mound?" Tcheen's eyes were fixed on Fabaris.

"We do," Fabaris said. "This is why we have come, to enter the Archive and make sure the scroll does not fall into the wrong hands. We fear that if the *Shoza* find the scroll, the *Sabrit* may use the *Ka-lar* to attack the humans, who would retaliate, and the resulting war could send the human armies deep into the mountains, even here."

Tcheen furrowed their brow. "Say again, with less words."

Karul stifled a laugh as Fabaris smiled and tried again. "If the *Shoza* find the scroll, they will start a war with the humans. The humans will come to kill all Maer."

"The humans will come with swords and metal armor, like what Carl wears." Karul gestured to Carl, who stood up, turning around to show his armor. "And they have very powerful mages, more powerful than ours, I fear."

Tcheen puffed up. "Do they have dragons? Do they have hatchet birds?"

Carl cleared his throat. "They do not, but you cannot hope to defeat them."

Tcheen's face registered surprise. "You speak as a Maer."

"I am human, but I claim the Maer as my tribe." Karul's heart warmed to hear Carl say it. "What Fabaris and Karul say is the truth. The humans have too many soldiers, too many weapons, too many mages. If they come, we will not survive."

Tcheen spoke to their council in their language, and there was some animated discussion among them before Tcheen turned back to the group.

"I do not know what of you speak, but at these times, we need the other. Let us prepare together to face the *Shoza*, and after we will look for your Archive."

Chapter: Thirty

Sinnie accepted the cup from Ayal, who Fabaris had said was a scholar. He spoke with great animation, seeming to repeat words and phrases at times, and he touched Fabaris' arm a lot when he spoke, in Southish. Karul, Carl, and Ivlana stood with Tcheen and Digar around a stone table with what looked like an engraved map of the valley, pointing and gesturing, talking strategy. She tuned them out, which wasn't hard, given that the Maer language still required effort for her, and turned to Finn, who was leaning in to speak to Ayal in Southish, which she could not understand at all, and Finn paid her little mind.

She noticed Tcheen look up, gesturing for someone to approach, and when she turned around, she saw Sulee leading Luez across the space between the mound and the pavilion. Sinnie almost knocked over her stump as she ran over to hug Luez, who shrank from her touch at first, but finally accepted her embrace and wrapped her arms around Sinnie's neck.

"Gods, you stink like chicken shit!" Sinnie held Luez at arm's length. "What is that smell?"

"Dragons," Luez said, gently slipping from Sinnie's grasp. "You get used to it after a while." The rest of the group crowded around, and Luez waved them back. "I'm fine. They treated me well, and no one tried to hurt me." Fabaris and Ivlana moved toward her, and she put her hands up in defense, then lowered them slowly. "Listen, I'm fine. And I hear we're planning for a visit from the *Shoza*. We have no time to waste." Her tone gave Sinnie chills; if Luez was afraid of the *Shoza*, Sinnie had every reason to be terrified. Luez deflected their questions until they finally filled her in on what they had learned. After a moment, Tcheen waved Luez over, and she went to them, bowed, and took her place with Karul and the others around the map. Tcheen spoke, pointing to various places on the stone, and Karul nodded, speaking back with animation.

Sinnie turned away; she didn't have the stomach to think about the battle to come. She never understood how the warrior types could stand there talking about mass violence, multiple deaths on both sides, and the endangering of children, not to mention dragons. As much as they terrified her, she found herself longing to get a closer look at them.

"Hello," said a voice in Maer, with an odd accent. Sulee stood beside her, giving a slight bow.

"Hi, Sulee. I'm Sinnie, we never really met. I—" She stopped as Sulee waved her hand in front of her own face.

"I...no...speak good Old Maer."

"And I don't speak Bird Maer, or Southish." Sinnie shrugged her shoulders, and Sulee gave her an odd smile.

"Sinnie," Sulee said. "Nice to..."

"Nice to meet you." Sinnie took Sulee by the shoulders, and Sulee giggled as she put her hands on Sinnie's shoulders. Sinnie recalled seeing the Bird Maer bowing to each other, but the shoulder clasp was obviously not part of their tradition.

"*Hello, Sulee,*" Finn said in Southish, touching Sinnie on the back as he wedged himself into the conversation. "*I...*" Sinnie had no idea what he was saying, but Sulee smiled and rattled back at him. He laughed and took her by the shoulders.

"She says she never imagined humans from the north would be so friendly. She heard we were all bloodthirsty killers."

"Gods, right, I keep forgetting. I guess she's been to the South though?"

Finn turned and spoke with Sulee, and she nodded vigorously and spoke back at him. They talked for a bit, and Finn turned back to Sinnie.

"She was in training in the South for a little while, she didn't say exactly what but I'm betting it's the same kind of thing Luez studied. You know, how to be a stone-cold assassin and the like."

"A lot of Maer seem to do training in the South. I guess it's not as barbaric as everyone says it is."

"Well, remember what we thought about the Maer before we met them?"

Sinnie sipped the sour berry wine as Finn spoke to Sulee in Southish. Ayal soon sidled over to join in their conversation, then Fabaris, and Sinnie slipped away, not sure where to direct her attention. Half the group was talking to Ayal in Southish, and everyone else was huddled over the stone map, plotting strategy, which she had no taste for, in Maer or any other language.

She walked to the back of the pavilion, or the front, she wasn't sure, to get a better look at the mound. Once she stepped outside the lights of the pavilion, she could see two warriors in brown feathered cloaks flanking the mound's rectangular opening, half-lit by a torch on a sconce in the doorway. Beyond the lit rectangle of the entrance it was hard to see inside, but she could make out several large shapes, as well as a smaller one, white against the gray of the others. The dragons. The white shape, which must have been a baby, bobbed up and down, then made its way up onto one of the bigger ones, which shifted beneath it. Sinnie took another step closer, and one of the warriors at the entrance put his hand up toward her, his face stern. She gave him a little bow, then returned to the pavilion, draining the rest of her wine and puckering her lips.

"It...good?" Sulee gestured toward her cup.

"I've had worse," Sinnie said. "I mean, yes, it's good," she added when Sulee frowned.

"It's good," Sulee repeated, her accent sounding pretty solid to Sinnie's ears. "Yes." She took a sip and smiled. "I've had worse."

Sinnie giggled, pretending to take a sip of her empty cup, but Sulee was not fooled. She grabbed Sinnie by the wrist, led her to the pitcher, and poured them both another round. They drank, communicating as much in facial expression as in words, until the warriors, the scholars, and the mages had had their fun, and Karul turned to gather everyone for a trip back to their shelter. Everyone said good night, in Maer, Bird Maer, or Southish, and Sulee and Digar escorted them out of the pavilion and into the night. The snow had stopped, but an icy wind had taken its place, and it took them a while to get a fire lit and build it up enough to heat the shelter. Ivlana let Sinnie snuggle with her, and Karul and Carl's low voices merged with the wind and the sound of Ivlana's breathing, forming a raft of quiet sound to send her floating off across the depths of sleep.

?

When she awoke, it was light out. She stretched and stepped to the mouth of the shelter, where Karul and Luez were talking in low tones. Carl wobbled toward them from the frosty field, holding his head. He pushed past them and collapsed against the wall, his face contorted in pain, the copper ring clutched tightly in his right hand.

"Did she speak to you? What did she say?" Karul stood over Carl, who waved him back with the ring hand while holding his head with the other.

"She said the *Shoza* are moving toward the valley, and Stuock is coming to join us." Carl's voice was a croak, and when he looked up,

Sinnie saw that both of his eyes had burst blood vessels, giving him a demonic look.

"Has it been seven days already?" Sinnie asked, counting on her fingers; she thought it had only been four or five.

Carl shook his head, took a deep breath, and accepted the water Finn offered. "No, but I've been trying every morning at dawn, just in case. She said it would take her seven days to get back to full strength, but if something were important, I figured she might reach out sooner."

"We need to get word to Tcheen right away," Luez said. "Otherwise they might think Stuock is part of the *Shoza*." She looked to Karul, who nodded, and she left.

"Did she...did she say anything else?" Sinnie asked, sitting down next to Carl and putting a blanket around his shoulders, which were soaked with sweat.

He shook his head, fixing Sinnie with blood-streaked eyes. "That was it. She just said 'The *Shoza* are moving on the Archive, and Stuock is coming to help you.' I bet it took everything she had just to send that."

Sinnie squeezed him tight, her cheek against his wet, matted hair. He smelled salty and acrid, like someone who had just done some great physical feat. His breath was fast and ragged, but it slowed down after a while, and she sat with him as he took a catnap on her shoulder. Finn sat leaning against a wall with Fabaris. Their hands were interlocked and their eyes were closed, their faces serene but not sleeping. Karul and Ivlana busied themselves sharpening their weapons, rolling up their blankets, and pacing around incessantly. Luez returned, nodded to Karul, and hunched against a wall, closing her eyes. No one dared speak. After a while, Carl awoke, looked at Sinnie with a bewildered expression, then shook his head and gave a weak smile.

"Thanks." He pulled away, pushing against the wall to stand up, rejecting the hand Sinnie offered him. "Anybody got something to eat? I'm starving all of a sudden."

"There's a little bit of jerky left." Karul handed him a rough stick, and Carl tore at it with his teeth like a wild beast.

"I was hoping maybe breakfast was included in our accommodations," Finn said. "With any luck, that's why Sulee's coming back."

"She might have more than one reason for visiting us." Luez side-eyed Karul, a smile in her voice.

"Yes, let's joke about who's hot for whom on the eve of the most important battle of our time." Karul braced himself with one arm on the top of the doorway and leaned halfway out.

"Let's not get ahead of ourselves." Fabaris opened his eyes and stood up. "We might be able to talk sense to the *Shoza*, broker some kind of deal."

"I thought you were supposed to be our scholar, our fountain of knowledge." Karul swiveled his head toward Fabaris, his voice rising with irritation. "Tell me, in all the songs and scrolls and tales you know, of a time when the *Shoza* did anything other than kill whatever stood in their way."

"The *Shoza* are not mentioned in any of the scrolls I am aware of. It's kind of the point of their existence. But that doesn't mean we can't try."

"You can try." Karul turned to look outside again, squinting at the sun cresting over the east ridge. "The rest of us will prepare for battle."

Karul stepped back inside as Sulee entered, carrying a large steaming bowl. She said some words in Southish, and Karul laughed and answered her in a halting fashion. Evidently his Southish wasn't very good. He bowed to her, then took the long spoon from the bowl and raised something lumpy and drippy to his lips. He cocked his head sideways, his mouth twisting into an odd shape, then smiled and said a few more words. She bowed to him, then did a half-bow to the rest of the cave and disappeared.

Fabaris looked to Karul, who had taken another spoonful of the stew.

"Mountain goat." Karul smacked his lips. "And turnips, I think. Ivlana, is there any of that salt left?"

?

Sulee returned a couple of hours after breakfast and led them to the village. The sun had chased away the clouds, and it warmed the left side of Sinnie's face as she walked. When they reached the pavilion, she saw Tcheen consulting with Luez and the two mages, whose names she couldn't recall. One was short, pot-bellied, and smiling, the other tall, thin, and dour.

Tcheen turned to the group. "Freni has sent a hawk, and has seen your mage, Stuock, with some other, in a valley two days far. The time is not enough."

"Stuock is fit for his age, but he is not young," Finn said. "It might take him longer."

"His power, is it worth?"

"Yes, he has the power of...destroying things with his mind. He can break rock from thirty feet away. He can crush your skull without touching you. His power is greater than mine."

"And what can you do?"

Finn looked down, embarrassed, but Karul cleared his throat loudly, and Finn spoke. "I can make my body hard like rock, I can jump great...very far, and I can heal, with time. And I learned some of what Stuock knows, but only a small part."

"So it is worth." Tcheen turned to the mages, speaking in a low voice in their language.

Karul stepped forward. "I'm sure it would be worth it to have Stuock here, but I don't see how—"

Tcheen stopped Karul with an icy glance. "Our mages have a plan." They turned to Sinnie, looking her up and down, and she wanted to slink back behind the others and hide. "You, fast runner, what is your name?"

"Sinnie," she peeped.

"You know riding of horse?"

"Yes, I'm not the best, but I can ride. Do you have a horse?"

Tcheen shook their head. "Better. We have dragon."

Sinnie felt faint, and she grabbed hold of Ivlana for support. "You want me to...ride a dragon?" She had been eager to get a closer look at the dragons last night, but now her skin was crawling from the idea.

"Izul can control dragon, from far." The tall mage nodded. "Fawul can show you how. Only Bobo can take riding."

"Okay, but—"

"You know this Stuock, yes?" Sinnie nodded, frozen in Tcheen's gaze. "And you speak his language. Only here I speak Old Maer, and four speak Southish. None of these can be spared."

"Well when you put it like that, I—"

"We will get you food. You leave now."

Sinnie nodded, breathing in deeply to steady her nerves.

"You will find him by night. He will ride Bobo here. You run back."

Sinnie looked at Finn, who mouthed 'dragon,' giving her a thumb's up. She glanced at Carl and the rest, seeing them only in a blur, then followed Sulee off toward the mound, Finn running to catch up.

"I've got to see this." Finn link arms with her as they walked, his eyes sparkling in the torchlight. His enthusiasm lifted her just out of reach of the flames of despair licking at her heels, but it didn't stop her heart from beating twice for every step she took.

Finn walked with her to the mound entrance, then stood outside as Sinnie followed Fawul inside. Fawul had insisted she come to meet the dragons in the mound; apparently it would help convince Bobo to accept her. Though they did not speak the same language, Fawul's calm demeanor and kind smile reassured Sinnie. Fawul gestured toward an alcove in the second chamber, and Sinnie stepped inside. Fawul called to Bobo, speaking to him like one would a dog or a cat, repeating his name and making clicking sounds with her mouth. It was hard to take a dragon named Bobo seriously, but when she heard the deep huff of his breathing and his dark shape filled the doorway, Sinnie's breath stuck in her chest. The head emerged, the size of a wine barrel, covered in gray feathers, which stuck up behind Bobo's head like a fan. Two huge yellow-clawed feet followed, and the rest of him flowed out into the chamber, his body curling against the walls as his head turned toward Sinnie. He was close to twenty feet long, his feathers tight against his lithe body, which ended in a long, swishing tail, with an oval flare of smaller feathers at the tip. His hind legs were thicker than a person's, twice the size of the front legs, which jutted out, birdlike.

Bobo fixed Sinnie with deep, round eyes, and Fawul held out her hand in front of his face, touching the space just above his toothy mouth. She muttered some words, and the creature blinked and stepped toward Sinnie, rubbing his snout on her leg as she stood petrified. Fawul made a gesture like petting, and Sinnie closed her eyes, opened them, and put a timid hand on the spot Fawul had just touched. The dragon closed his eyes and leaned into her touch, and Sinnie ran her hand up between his eyes, around his crest, and scratched his neck like one would a cat. Bobo made a noise not unlike purring.

Fawul tugged on a leather strap, part of a rudimentary bridle and reins. Sinnie wasn't sure she would be able to manage it, but Bobo kneeled before her, and she slung her leg over his shoulders, where a fur had been attached in lieu of a saddle. Fawul patted Sinnie on the arm and said a few words in their dialect, with an encouraging tone in her voice. Sinnie dismounted, and Fawul took Bobo's reins and led the beast out of the mound. Sinnie followed, Bobo's tail flicking against her legs as she walked.

The tall mage joined them outside, bowing to Sinnie, then to Finn. Fawul spoke to the mage, who translated into Southish for Finn, who nodded, then turned to Sinnie, his eyes bright with excitement.

"They say Izul, the dragon mage, will be keeping an eye out, and Bobo knows the way. All you need to do is hold on and enjoy the ride."

Sinnie's cheeks were flushed and her breathing uneven, but she couldn't peel the smile from her face.

"I'll see you on the other side." She blinked at Finn and mounted the kneeling dragon once again. She fell against Bobo's neck as he raised up from his kneel, turning his head around to look at her. There was something reassuring in his calm eyes, or at least she told herself there was. She straightened up, patted Bobo on the neck, and he turned and paced away from the mound, Sinnie swaying on his back. His back was narrower than a horse's, and without a saddle it was a little uncomfortable, but she quickly forgot her discomfort as she looked out over Bobo's feathered crest, then turned to see his tail whipping back and forth with each step. She rode as if in a dream, Bobo's body moving as smoothly as a snake around the switchbacks.

When they reached the top, she pulled back gently on the reins, and Bobo stopped and turned toward the valley. His head twitched, and the feathers on his crest flicked from gray to fiery orange in an instant. Sinnie looked down at the small crowd standing outside the mound. One of them was jumping up and down and waving at her like an idiot. Finn. She smiled and raised her arm, giving him two wide waves, then pulled on the reins, and Bobo turned and began sauntering down the switchback on the other side.

Chapter:
Thirty-One

Finn put down his arm, which was tired from waving, and turned to Sulee, who stood next to him, staring up at the ridge top.

"All these years I've wanted to ride Bobo, and Sinnie gets to ride two days after she's met him. It isn't fair." Sulee eyed the departing pair with a rueful smile, then turned to Finn, her eyes lingering on his face, his hands, his tattoos. "Sorry, I didn't mean to stare. It's just..."

"I get it," he said, touching her shoulder for a moment. "It took me a while to get used to all the...little differences."

"Yeah. When I was studying in the South, I saw humans obviously, but they kept us mostly separate. Anyway, Tcheen wants me to show your group around the east marsh. They plan to have you cover that front when the...what did you call them?"

"The *Shoza*." Finn felt a chill just saying it.

"Right. When the *Shoza* come. You think your friends are ready?"

"I'm sure everyone's dying for a chance to move. We've been marching for weeks, and all of a sudden we're spending half our time in a cave. A very nice cave, don't get me wrong, but it's been a little weird."

"Well I doubt it's going to get any less weird. Hopefully a little walking will do us all good."

Sulee led the group through the village, across the field to the strip of trees on the edge of the east marsh, a ten-minute walk. Fabaris had stayed behind to talk to Ayal, and Sinnie was off on her adventure, but everyone else was there. Finn and Luez were the only ones besides Sulee who spoke Southish, so they translated for Karul, Carl, and Ivlana.

The tree line was only about ten yards wide, with stumps and obvious chopping stations here and there. It would make a good hiding place to watch for anyone coming across the marsh, which was the mission they had been tasked with.

"We will have two guards in the old watchtower up there." Sulee pointed to a bump on the eastern ridge, similar to the one atop the high ridge to the west. "They will blow their horn if they see anything. Freni will also have some birds in the air, though between this and the west ridge, he will have his hands full, so we will all need to keep an eye out."

Luez translated for the rest of the group, and there was much silent nodding.

"The water in the marsh comes from the base of the ridge over there?" Luez pointed to where the east ridge grew taller before becoming one with the Great Tooth.

"Yes, there are several streams and springs. The southern part of the marsh is the wettest and hardest to cross, so it seems likely if they come over the east ridge it will be in this area."

Luez kept staring at the southern end. "The *Shoza* will know we would expect them here, so they might head over the higher part of the ridge there, make their way across the mountainside above the streams, and come down along this tree line."

"That part of the mountain is not fit for goats." Sulee stroked her beard. "It can be crossed, but it's dangerous, and exposed. I guess if these *Shoza* are experienced climbers they might—"

"They are, and they could." Luez spoke with such quiet force that Sulee left her mouth open for a moment. "With your permission, I'd like to scout that area out, just to be on the safe side."

"Sure, of course." Sulee gave Luez a crooked smile. Finn couldn't tell if it was one of respect or annoyance. "Tcheen said you all will be running the show over here, and my role is to support you. Which is weird, because they never give up control to anyone. But maybe not so weird, since you obviously know what you're doing."

"I don't." Finn raised his hand a little, hoping to lighten the mood. "In case anyone's..." He lowered his eyes at the dead stares he got in return. Only Ivlana seemed a little amused, though she wouldn't have understood what he'd said. "Right, I'll just...I'll just translate," which he did.

"Luez is right," Karul said. "She has the same training as the *Shoza*, or better. She will know, once she gets on the mountain, whether they could cross there."

Carl nodded. "Sulee can show us where it's safe to walk through the marsh. We don't want to sink knee-deep in mud with swords and arrows flying."

Finn translated for Sulee, who nodded.

"Right. Luez, do your thing and I'll show them around."

Luez gave Sulee a half-smile. Finn was pretty sure he'd never seen Luez have a non-serious interaction before this voyage, and now he'd seen her both hug and smile. It was all he could do not to run over and test his luck by giving her a hug. Luez turned and trotted off, disappearing into the tree line.

Sulee showed them the main paths, which she said the children used for their war games. There were footprints everywhere, makeshift log bridges over standing water, and little stick forts here and there among the scrubby bushes, which had lost all their leaves and wouldn't be much good for cover. They heard cries and shouts of play from a group of children hurling sticks at each other across a reedy stretch of water.

"We should get the children to show us around," Ivlana said. "I bet they know this area better than anyone."

Sulee nodded when she heard Finn's translation, then called out a name, Gora. A tall girl with shorn hair came running, stepping right and left to avoid puddles. She stopped five feet away from Sulee and gave a deep bow. As Sulee spoke, the girl eyed the group nervously, especially Finn and Carl. Finn couldn't imagine what it must have been like for the children, seeing humans for the first time. It had been hard enough for him seeing the Maer at first, even as an adult. Gora looked down as Finn smiled at her, but soon turned her gaze back up to him for a moment before snapping back to look at Sulee and speaking a few words, one of them sounding like the Maer word for 'yes.'

"She will show us around. But first I—" Sulee stopped as two boys came running from another direction, calling out with some urgency. She turned to Gora, who shrugged. The boys arrived, huffing as they bowed to Sulee, then stood gaping at Finn and Carl for a moment. Sulee cleared her throat, and they turned back to her and began speaking over each other, repeating the same words several times, possibly something about feet, Finn thought. Sulee asked them a question, using some of the same words, and they nodded, repeating themselves and babbling on until Sulee held up her hand to stop them.

"They say they've seen footprints on the eastern edge of the marsh, footprints with sandals, and not the kind we wear."

"They can show us?" Karul asked once he heard Finn's translation.

"Yes. Let me get the others cleared out." Sulee spoke to Gora, fast and serious. Gora nodded and spun off, dodging her way between puddles to the stick-throwing children. When she spoke to them, they quickly turned and wove their way through the marsh and trees and sped back toward the village like a flock of birds. Gora rejoined the group, and the two boys led the way, with Sulee and Gora following them, and the rest of the group behind. The boys pointed this way and that as they made their way through the pools and trickles and tufts of dry grass. Finn got his boots wet a couple of times before finding his footing, and Carl, Karul, and Ivlana marched behind, their footsteps loud and squishy.

They crossed a stream by hopping over a set of stumps spaced nicely apart, but the ground on the other side was sopping moss over thick mud. Finn pushed out a little energy to soften his footfalls, so he didn't get any wetter, but Karul, Carl, and Ivlana made little effort to avoid the muck. As they neared the ridge, the wet spots grew rarer, and they walked on easily identifiable paths of trodden grass. One of the boys called out, and both ran ahead with Gora, searching the ground until they found the tracks. They pointed and beckoned Sulee, who joined them. Carl and Karul butted around Finn to get a look, and Finn was happy enough to step aside; he'd never been much good with tracks. They all stood staring at the ground for a long moment, then turned to each other, their faces grim and silent.

"Scouts," Karul said after a while.

"How did they make it past the birds undetected?" Sulee's face was a snarl of incredulity. "And why did Bobo not smell them? He was off hunting this way not two days ago."

Karul studied the ridge as Finn translated. "Could a mage make them invisible to a bird's eye or a dragon's nose?"

Finn nodded. "Sure. There are mages who specialize in light, shadow, illusion, the senses, and the like. So I guess the *Shoza* have one of those." His heart sank as he translated for Sulee. He had heard stories of illusion mages and the trouble they could cause, and he had seen firsthand what Theo could do with light and shadow, even as a mage in training. His heart gave a twinge as he thought of Theo's face, his bright eyes, his crooked little smile.

"Well at least now we know what to expect." Carl's face was calm, as if he'd faced scores of mages in his time. Finn wished he'd occasionally freak out a little bit, but it seemed panic was not in Carl's nature.

"We have to go tell Tcheen." Sulee gazed out across the ridge, then over to the foot of the Great Tooth, where Luez would have begun climbing by now. Finn didn't bother to translate, as the name alone made the meaning clear.

"I'll stay and wait for Luez," Ivlana said. Karul nodded, putting a hand on her shoulder. Finn doubted Karul noticed the look Ivlana gave him as he did so. She tried to hide it, but she was clearly smitten with him. It must have killed her to see how Karul looked at Sulee.

They followed Sulee back to the village, where they found Fabaris and Ayal talking and drinking tea in the pavilion next to a warm fire, as if a band of assassins and mages weren't bearing down on them like thunderclouds sweeping across a plain.

Chapter:
Thirty-Two

F abaris listened as Sulee spoke to Ayal, unable to make out anything except the words 'foot,' 'Tcheen' and possibly 'marsh.' The sound and rhythm of the Bird Maer's language were becoming more familiar, and there were a lot of words in common with Old Maer and what little he remembered of the language from his childhood, but they just spoke too fast. He hoped to get a chance to study it more once this was all over. If he even survived.

Karul pulled Fabaris aside and explained that they had found footprints in the marsh that could not have belonged to the Bird Maer, so the assumption was that the *Shoza*'s scouts had arrived before the main force they had been tracking. Sulee beckoned Karul and the others to follow her to Tcheen's cabin, leaving Fabaris and Ayal alone again in the pavilion. Ayal watched them go but continued sipping his tea, making no move to follow them.

"I don't know about you, but I plan to be in the Mound with Maomao and the children when this all goes down. Do you fight?"

"Not very well." Fabaris moved his shoulder, wincing at the pain, which was muted by Finn's healing hands but not entirely gone. "I tried to step in when my group was attacked by the *grosti*, and I was almost killed for my trouble. I certainly wouldn't be of any use at the moment."

"Well I was hoping to have a little more time, just a little more, but things seem to be moving faster than expected. I guess I should go ahead and show you inside the Mound now, before things get too far out of hand." Ayal's head twitched and turned periodically as he spoke, like a sparrow.

"I thought you would never ask." Fabaris stood up, eyeing the Mound's rectangular opening and the peculiarly shaped rock perched on top.

"Tcheen hasn't given me the go-ahead yet, but I think it's past time. If they don't like it, they can take it out of my hide. Come." Ayal popped up, his braids flying as he turned and walked toward the Mound.

The guards took a half-step to either side, bowing to Ayal as he entered. Fabaris stood looking at the stone around the entrance, hoping for some kind of inscription or symbol, but either there was none or it had been erased by time. An earthy scent with acrid undertones wafted through the entrance as Fabaris stepped inside. He stood in a rectangular chamber, with another opening leading deeper into the mound. There was a torch just inside the entrance, and another further in. The chamber had open spaces on either side containing various earthenware containers. A low, cajoling voice carried from further into the mound. Ayal put out a hand to stop Fabaris, who wasn't moving anyway.

"Fawul is talking to Maomao, telling her to keep Kiki under wraps. I think she's getting ready to take them for a little walk."

"I'm guessing Maomao is the mother and Kiki is the baby?"

"Yes. Kiki tends to get a little excited, and Maomao can be a bit protective, just a bit. That's why Fawul is here; she knows how to keep them calm."

"I know...Bobo, is it? The red one? Went with Sinnie to retrieve Stuock, but the other one?"

Ayal nodded. "Lolo is doing a run around the ridges, just as a precaution. Which seems like an extra good idea now that we know about the spies. Come in here, I think they're getting ready to move, and we need to get out of the way."

Fabaris followed Ayal into a second chamber, this one with three smaller niches set into the walls on either side. Several of them appeared to have furs on the floor, though it was hard to see, as there was no torch in the room. A large gray hump filled much of the opening leading further into the mound, and squeaks and a low growl echoed out. Ayal gestured for Fabaris to go into one of the niches, then stood in front of Fabaris and called out. Fabaris couldn't understand what Ayal said, but he thought the response might have included the word 'ready.' The gray shape shifted to the side, and Fawul appeared in the opening, smiling. She strode forward, followed by a fluffy white creature that looked like an elongated chicken, the size of a mastiff, with a splay of white fuzz framing its bulky head. It stopped, one claw in the air, sniffing, then turned and bounded toward Ayal, who crouched in a semi-defensive posture, laughing as the creature jumped up on him and nuzzled his ear, squawking and whining like a puppy.

"Don't worry, she's just a playful thing." Kiki eyed Fabaris over Ayal's shoulder, sniffing the air in his direction, then tumbled over backwards as Fawul hooked it with her staff, yelling something equal parts good-natured and stern.

Fabaris pushed his back flat against the wall of the alcove as Maomao's dark shape filled the doorway, blocking out the light. Her body was bigger than a horse, but she moved with the lightness of a cat. Her head turned toward them for a moment, her shining black eyes fixing on Fabaris as she huffed out through her nose. A warm blast of breath hit him, smelling of carrion and bile, and his knees grew weak as she kept her eyes on him for a few moments before turning and flowing forward, her long flared tail swishing behind her as she moved out of the room.

"They're really something up close, aren't they?" Ayal moved out of the alcove, and Fabaris followed, watching the dragons exit the Mound. "I remember when I was a kid, Maomao, we called her Didi back then, we did, wasn't much bigger than Kiki is now."

"Where will they go on their walk?"

"Kiki likes to climb, so they'll probably go straight up the ridge, then maybe down to the south marsh so she can splash around a bit. Fawul will keep them inside the valley, with the *Shoza* on the prowl."

"Does Fawul sleep in here?"

Ayal nodded. "And Izul sometimes. And when it gets cold, really cold, anyone with a sick child stays in the first chamber. Though no one really trusts Kiki around the little ones, for good reason. She's not malicious, but she can be a bit rough." He beckoned Fabaris into the next room, which was wide open, like the first, with hay covering the floor. The musky, acrid scent was overpowering.

"Bobo and Lolo usually sleep in here, and Kiki and Maomao in the last chamber." He led Fabaris through the doorway into a larger room, with alcoves along the side walls, and a great square block of stone in the center of the back wall, about four feet on each side. On it lay an assortment of small objects: statuettes, colored stones, teeth the length of daggers, and what looked like the scales of an enormous snake.

"This reminds me of the burial cave of the Deer Maer we encountered on the way." Fabaris moved closer to the block, his eyes drawn to the scales and teeth. The teeth were far bigger than those in the mouths of the dragons in the valley.

"Go ahead, you can touch them. They were here before our tribe moved in, long before, from scale dragons, we think, which as far as I know are extinct."

Fabaris picked up a tooth, touching the tip to his finger. It was impressively sharp, and he tried to picture the size of the creature it had come from. The scales were as big as his palms, strong and light like turtle shell. He replaced the items on the stone and stepped back to examine it. It had no markings on it, but it was darker than the surrounding stone, almost black.

"One assumes the Opening you speak of involves this block of stone?"

Ayal nodded, running his hand along the edge of the block. "It goes deeper underground than above, much deeper. We did a test dig to see how deep it went, but we had to stop for fear of causing structural damage to the Mound. I can't imagine how it would be opened, short of battering it for days or weeks with large rocks. The legend suggests some kind of magic would be involved, but we know of no mage with this kind of power."

"Stuock may. According to Finn, Stuock has the ability to make and break rock, though on this scale, I don't know." Fabaris picked up the torch that guttered in a sconce near the entrance, scanning the walls for markings, but again there were none, aside from what must have been dragon claw marks.

"I hope he has the ability to break more than rock," Ayal said. "It sounds like we are going to need all the help we can get to fend off these *Shoza*. At any rate, Tcheen has decreed we will take no action regarding the Mound until after..." Ayal trailed off, staring down the long hall to the daylight outside the Mound.

"Your tribe seems strong. You have dragons, you have hatchet birds, and you have the service of my friends, who are an impressive fighting force."

"I know, but I have had dreams, dreams of fire, dreams of death." Ayal's whole body shook, like an extended shiver, and he leaned back against the block.

"Are your dreams often prophetic?"

Ayal shook his head and emitted a single barking laugh. "Dreams are just the mind doing math on the past and the future. My mind is very good at math though."

"Well hopefully your calculations will prove inaccurate in this case."

?

Fabaris and Finn were invited to eat in Sulee's cabin, which she shared with another female and two males, along with four children, two of them almost teenagers and two younger. Fabaris could not determine whose children they were, as the adults seemed to share responsibility for parenting them. He also could not tell which of the adults were paired up, or if they even had individual partners. They ate squash and bean soup with crunchy bits of some kind of crawfish here and there, the shells of which had to be picked out and tossed into a communal waste bowl. It was lively to the point of being chaotic, which surprised Fabaris, given the battle that was bearing down on the village.

Since Sulee was the only one who could communicate with them, there was a lot of hand-waving, repetition, and laughter when she was too engaged in another conversation to translate. Fabaris managed to spit out a few words the others could understand, and he picked up more and more of their conversation, though he could not keep up with what seemed to be the funniest jokes. The adults tried hard to avoid ogling Finn, but the kids made no pretense, peeking at him from their benches along the wall. He obliged them by making little faces and winking, especially at the little ones, who would giggle and hide behind each other before popping back up for more. Fabaris had kept himself from thinking of what the future might hold for him and Finn, but seeing how good he was with the children made his heart flutter and his stomach ache.

When dinner was over and it was time to leave, they taught the adults the Old Maer shoulder clasp, and bowed back as the children bowed goodbye. Sulee led them back through the village, which had grown quiet, beyond the wall to their shelter, giving them a taper to restart their fire.

"Luez said to tell you the others might be up late planning strategy with Tcheen, so you shouldn't wait up for them." The smile in Sulee's eyes burst forth onto her lips as she turned and ran back through the gathering dark toward the village.

Fabaris rebuilt the fire while Finn pulled the screens over the entrance. When Fabaris turned away from the flames, Finn stood facing him in all his hairless glory, his clothes in a heap on the floor. Fabaris stepped to him, running his hands over Finn's bare chest and shoulders as they kissed long and slow. Finn let out little moans as Fabaris grabbed his hips and began kissing his chest and stomach, his hands making his way through the only area of Finn's body with as much hair as his. He teased Finn until his squirming reached a fevered pitch, then Fabaris stood up, and Finn turned around, lowering himself down to a crouch on the straw. Fabaris knelt down behind him, spit into his hand, and rubbed it over himself and Finn, who breathed in deeply as Fabaris edged into him. Fabaris forgot all about his injured shoulder as they moved together with sudden urgency, and when they were done, they lay cuddling for a while before going at it again, more slowly this time, as the fire burned low and the cold air from outside chased them under covers. They fell into a sleep so deep Fabaris hardly noticed when the others came in, though he did feel the fire's heat and hear its crackle, interspersed with the whispers of his companions.

Chapter:
Thirty-Three

C arl sat just outside the shelter in the morning chill with the copper ring on his head, his thoughts fixed on Ujenn. He pictured her eyes, imagined the glowing clarity when she would put her hands on his face and touch her hairy forehead to his. But the ring was cold on his head, the ground frozen beneath him, the air biting at his nose, ears, and fingertips. In his mind was only silence. He'd known there was little chance of hearing from her again so soon, but with the *Shoza* less than two days away, he had to try. He put the ring back in his pouch and stood up, his knees popping, and looked out across the frosty plains to the dark ridge and the gray sky ahead.

"No luck?" Karul stood leaning against the shelter's entrance. Carl shook his head, and Karul put his hands on Carl's shoulders, touching foreheads with him. "You will see her again, Carl. I will fight by your side and make sure of that."

Carl squeezed Karul's shoulders, then let go. "Your words to the gods' hearts."

"Want to warm up a bit with that slow-ass *Ka-lar* sword of yours?" Karul picked up the sword, which Carl had leaned against a rock just outside the shelter, and tossed it to him, hilt first.

Carl grinned, swinging the sword a few times to get his blood flowing. "I'll take it easy on you, so you don't get too worn out for the big event."

Karul's eyes narrowed, and he took several steps to the side, his spear held at an angle in front of him. "Do your worst, skin man."

They danced, thrust, parried, and swung until Carl had worked up a good sweat. Karul was taller and stronger, but he was still relatively inexperienced fighting against a swordsman, so Carl got the best of him more often than not. But Carl knew if Karul's temper were up, if they were playing for keeps, it would be a different fight, one he was not so sure he would win. This was comforting, knowing that battle loomed on the horizon.

After consulting with Tcheen and Sulee over breakfast, they spent the morning running through scenarios in the marsh. Neither the birds nor the dragon had picked up a hint of the scouts, but the children had been kept away from the marsh as a precaution. Tcheen had several of their trackers scouring the south marsh, in case the *Shoza* had been scouting there as well, though the steep mountainside above made it an unlikely point of entry. The east marsh offered little cover, as most of the shrubs had lost their leaves, but they made sure to check every stick fort, evergreen, and stand of grass just to be sure. Their plan was to have Sinnie shooting from among the trees, with Finn backing her up. Luez would hide in the southern end of the east marsh, while Karul, Ivlana, Sulee, and Carl would patrol the forest edge. Freni, the bird mage, would send sparrows if help was needed at the wall, or crows if at the Mound. Bobo would be stationed near the Mound, with Lolo at the wall, but the dragon mage, Izul, could send them wherever they were needed. Maomao and Kiki would stay in the Mound to guard the noncombatants, in case the rest of their defenses failed. Sulee had given each member of the group a whistle for signaling, one note if they spotted someone, many notes if battle was imminent.

It was ten minutes' run to the wall, or the portion near the western ridge at any rate, where they thought the *Shoza* most likely to cross, and half that time to reach the Mound. That meant if they needed help, they would have to wait a while for reinforcements. And if the *Shoza* were anything like Luez, there would be no time, only death, swift and sure, for anyone caught with their guard down.

They went over the main paths of the marsh several times, noting potential hiding spots. They considered destroying the stick forts, but decided they might use them for cover if the *Shoza* were spotted coming down the east ridge and they had time to set up. Carl wondered how many of the *Shoza* would have Luez's level of training; surely there would be regular warriors as well, and they would not be as stealthy, though if magic were involved, all bets would be off.

The smell of roasting meat reached them around noon, and Sulee told them, with Finn interpreting, that the feast would start at midafternoon. Carl wondered at the wisdom of having a large gathering with such a force bearing down on the valley, but they needed to fortify their bodies and souls, and Tcheen would surely have ample lookouts posted.

The atmosphere in the village was equal parts tense and festive, with armed warriors posted on the outskirts, while children chased each other and played hide and seek between the cabins. Two mountain goats were roasting on a huge fire inside the pavilion, and several large pots simmered there as well. Berry wine was served, though everyone seemed to be drinking in moderation. The Bird Maer were plenty friendly, but as Carl did not speak their language he communicated mostly in smiles and raised cups, which suited him fine anyway. He hoped Sinnie made it back in time for the feast. Back in Brocland, she would decorate the chapel with flowers whenever there was a holiday or festival, no matter how minor.

There were no flowers to be had in winter, but the pavilion had been adorned with holly branches, puffy winter grasses, and strings of multicolored feathers. A group of older Maer stood together, singing a song that was by turns upbeat and melancholy, and many heads watched them, nodding with the beat of the drum played by a white-haired female sitting on a stump.

"Cheers." Finn sat down on a stump next to Carl and raised his cup.

Carl touched it with his, nodding. "I suppose you'll be breaking your regime for the feast."

"Oh gods yes. The rule doesn't apply on holidays anyway. And did you smell that goat? The Bird Maer surely know how to roast a beast."

A boy of about eight approached with a tray of eggs, hesitating a few feet away from them.

"Come," Carl said in Maer, hoping his smile would convey the meaning. The boy stepped to them, said something in his language, and bowed as they took the eggs.

Finn shook the egg, making a face. "They're raw."

"I think that's the point." Carl cracked the egg as he had seen another one of the attendants do, slurped it down, and dropped the shell in a bowl in the center of the boy's tray.

"Well then bottoms up I guess." Finn cracked his egg, making a mess as it slid into his mouth. "Thank you," he said to the boy, giving a little bow with his head as he dropped the shell in the bowl. The boy gave a quiet smile, then continued to a group of Bird Maer listening with smiles to a story told by an older male who was missing several front teeth.

"You'd hardly think the village was about to be attacked. I quite like their way of preparing for battle." Finn eyed the western ridge. "I hope Sinnie makes it back in time. She would love this."

"I was thinking the same thing. If we could get hold of Freni, maybe he could give us an update."

"I bet he has his hands full. Wait, isn't that..." Finn pointed to the top of the ridge, where a dark shape stood, flashing flame color for a long moment before returning to gray and descending.

"Is there anyone riding it?" Carl looked up, but he couldn't see very well at such a distance.

"I think so." Finn squinted, then smiled. "I believe that's Stuock, which would make sense if everything went according to plan."

"That would put Sinnie running back as we speak, with Stuock's guard."

"I feel sorry for anyone trying to keep up with her. I tried to go on one of those runs of hers, and I had to give up less than halfway through. And I thought I was in shape from all my routines!"

Tcheen summoned Finn, Freni, and Izul to greet Stuock and Bobo as they arrived at the Mound. Carl approached, but stood at a distance, along with Ayal and Fabaris, as the dragon moved to the edge of the Mound and kneeled. Stuock was shorter than Carl had imagined, and he dismounted with an unexpected spring in his step. He looked to be about sixty, though it was hard to tell with the Maer, but he moved as if he were a decade or two younger. Stuock stood gaping at the stone atop the Mound, jumping up and down, pointing and hugging Finn. Finn returned the embrace, then turned Stuock by the shoulders toward the group and introduced him in Southish, which Freni then translated into their language.

Tcheen stepped forward, towering over Stuock. "Tell us what you know about the *Shoza* who move to us." Carl took a few steps closer to hear better.

"You speak our language?" Stuock's bewildered expression straightened up as Tcheen continued to stare. "Yes, well, from what I have heard, I have a few friends on the *Sabrit*, you know, and on the High Council—"

"Tell." Tcheen held out their arm, not without a hint of menace.

"All right, there are said to be eight of the *Shoza*'s elite guard, the best of the best, plus at least twenty highly trained warriors, as well as three mages: one who controls fire, another wind, the third shadow."

"Two dozen warriors and three mages?" Tcheen sounded incredulous. "They think they can take our village with this number?"

"Do not underestimate the power of their mages." Finn spoke more forcefully than Carl would have, but Tcheen did not react.

"Nor of the elite guard," Stuock added. "One of them is worth five of their regular warriors, and even they are far better trained than most."

Tcheen stood silent for a moment, staring at Stuock, who shrank a little from their gaze. "And what do you bring for us, besides news? Have you no mage skills to add?"

Stuock gave a hearty nod. "I do, and I will, but Finn is every bit as powerful as I, perhaps more so."

Tcheen looked down at Finn, then back at Stuock. "We have mage of bird, mage of dragon." They pointed out Freni and Izul as they spoke. "The dragons fight, the birds spy, and we have fighting birds also."

"Well, we're going to need everything we've got, I'm afraid." Stuock glanced over at the pavilion, a hungry look in his eye.

"You, eat, drink." Tcheen pointed to the pavilion. "We will talk more after."

?

Carl sat sipping his wine, watching the rest of the group eat. Fabaris came over, took Stuock by the shoulders, and spoke to him for some time. Finn interrupted them by bringing a plate with several eggs, a pile of nuts, and a cup of berry wine. The three of them sat conversing in Maer, switching to Southish as Ayal sidled over and joined the conversation. Carl's attention drifted, and he turned to study the western ridge, but saw nothing. He turned back to watch the festivities, which distracted him for the moment. Ivlana was drinking with Karul, telling what looked to be a war story, complete with wine-sloshing gestures and overly loud exclamations.

Luez appeared next to Carl and gave him a grim smile. "Not one for parties either, I see."

"Never have been." Carl took a careful sip. Even in the service he was known as the quiet one; though he did his share of drinking, it tended to make him withdraw into himself. "It's good to see smiles and laughter though."

"If I read the body language correctly, Ivlana is making her final play for Karul's affections."

"It looks like he may finally be receptive." Carl noticed Karul laughing more than usual, throwing his arm over Ivlana's shoulder as he took a drink.

"It's been a long time coming. I just hope she doesn't get her feelings hurt when this is all over and he pretends like it never happened."

Carl raised his eyebrows at Luez, who was not normally one to gossip. "We have a saying in Islish: *It is better to have loved and lost—*"

"Than stay at home and lose anyway. We have that one too."

"Yours is more poetic than ours, but the sentiment is the same."

"And there they go." Luez elbowed Carl, and they watched as Ivlana walked out of the pavilion, her eyes turning to Karul, who drained the last of his cup, glancing briefly at the two of them, his eyes sparkling with mischief, before trotting after her. Carl closed his eyes, imagining a copper-colored cord reaching out across the mountains to Ujenn, alone in her bed in Castle Maer. Or perhaps she was lying with Grisol, their bodies interlocked, their hair matted together with sweat. He wondered if he would ever feel Ujenn's touch again, feel her look deep into his eyes, probing his mind, pouring into him like quicksilver. He thought of his unborn child growing in Grisol's taut belly. Would she look like Grisol, or like him, or maybe somehow like Ujenn? Would she be Maer, or human, or something in between? As he watched Ivlana and Karul's shadows disappear into the darkness, he felt a chilling certainty that he would never find out.

Chapter: Thirty-Four

I vlana let Karul beat her to the shelter entrance so she could watch his thick legs and ass power across the wet grass, stumbling occasionally with the wine in his system. She closed the distance at the end, tackling him as soon as he moved the screens aside. They tumbled onto the straw-covered floor, and she managed to end up sitting on top of him, both of them laughing in between gasps for air. She slid her hands up his chest and over his broad shoulders, finally wrapping them playfully around his neck as she slid her body down. She clenched her legs around his, pressing herself against him, feeling him stiffen beneath her. She hiked up her tunic and smothered his mouth with hers as she tore his clothes from his body. She reached down and held him firm as she raised her hips and lowered herself slowly onto his tip, holding in place for a moment as she watched his desperation grow. His eyes widened and his smile followed as she sank all the way down and started moving, her hands holding loosely around his neck. They wound up quickly, and before she knew what was happening, she was shuddering over him, their bodies pressing into each other with the fury of warriors locked in mortal combat. He let go with his body before he released her gaze, then closed his eyes and held her in stillness as the throbbing subsided.

He started to speak, but she clamped her hand over his mouth, stood up, and adjusted her tunic. He lay there, staring at her, his eyes shining in the shelter's dark. She turned, smiled at him over her shoulder, and stepped out into the cold, misty rain, crossing the field with bold strides.

?

The guards opened the gate for her without a word, though she was sure she saw smiles on their faces. Luez gave her a knowing smirk and handed her a cup as she returned to the pavilion. Ivlana hid her smile behind a gulp of wine and stood watching as several Maer removed a mountain goat carcass from the fire and went to work with large bone knives. Karul returned, holding out her sword and belt, which she had left in the shelter. His face was straight, but his eyes told another story, one she hoped to hear when the fighting was done. She nodded as she took the sword and reattached the belt. She had no illusions about some great romance. She had seen the spark between Karul and Sulee, and she knew she was not his type, but none of that mattered. She was giddy with more than just wine as she was led, along with the rest of her group, to the row of stumps nearest the fire pit. Tcheen stood, with Ayal off to the side, and silence descended as everyone found their seats.

Tcheen began to speak, in slow, dramatic tones, not unlike the ones Karul had used as they had set off on their adventure. Though she couldn't understand the words, she fell under Tcheen's spell, her eyes locked on their white-painted face. They gestured at the mound, at Ivlana's group, making a deep bow as they did so, then pointed toward the Great Tooth, building up to what sounded like battle talk, which Ivlana didn't need a translator to understand. If Castle Maer were about to be attacked by an elite group of Wild Maer, complete with every stripe of mage under the sun, she would be listening to Karul make this speech. Fabaris would be at his side in place of Ayal, who stepped forward as Tcheen finished on a thundering note that seemed to echo off the ridges, the wall, and even the Great Tooth itself.

Ayal stood before the silent group, his head cocking to look at each face individually before he spoke. His speech had a different rhythm than Tcheen's; his words seemed to loop back on themselves, repeating almost like a refrain in one of Fabaris' longstories, not quite poetry but more than mere prose. Most of the warriors in Castle Maer avoided Nightsong, but Ivlana had always found it soothing, meditative. Ayal's voice had the same effect on her, though she did not understand the words. Any thought she might have had that the Wild Maer, or the Free Maer, were somehow different, more primitive, than anyone else, vanished into the mist. Ayal moved the audience for just long enough, then let Tcheen make a less somber announcement, which Ivlana could puzzle out easily enough: Dinner was about to be served.

"Looks like I got here just in time." Sinnie landed heavily on a stump, sucking down a waterskin between deep breaths.

Finn jumped up and dragged her off her seat in a hug, speaking to her in Islish, their faces close together, their smiles mirroring each other. Carl stood up and pulled her away from Finn, held her tight, then released her and said something low and earnest sounding. Ivlana leaned toward Sinnie, hoping to get one of her famous hugs, but Sinnie turned away as a tray of meat was brought around, followed by another tray laden with bowls of stew. Though her mouth was full of food, Sinnie never stopped smiling. After she had destroyed a meaty shank and used her fingers to wipe the last of the stew from her bowl, she sat back down, her wide eyes soaking up the scene.

"I'm glad to see you back," Ivlana said, laying her hand on Sinnie's arm. "We were worried you would miss the festivities."

"Are you kidding me? I ran extra fast just to get back to this. Stuock's guard is probably still collapsed at the top of the ridge, but I wasn't going to wait for him any longer. What did I miss?"

"Nothing much. Just some battle planning. Oh, and we found footprints in the marsh, so we know their scouts have come ahead of the group."

Sinnie's face fell, and she nodded, her smile fading but not entirely gone. "Do we...do we know how far out the *Shoza* are?"

"Last I heard, they should be here by tomorrow night, or thereabouts."

"I guess that means tonight is our last chance to sleep for a while then. Gods, I'm so exhausted. I don't know if I can wait until dark."

"Well let me know whenever you're ready. I got a little cold last night without you."

Sinnie smiled and touched Ivlana's knee, then turned to watch a group of children who were doing some kind of circle dance where Tcheen and Ayal had been standing. They were accompanied by a flute, played passably by one of the older girls, the one who had taken them to see the tracks in the marsh. Everyone clapped as they finished and took a bow. Only Tcheen remained unmoved by the gaiety; they stood, arms crossed, surveying the gathering as one would study a river before fishing. Ayal joined the children for a frenetic dance, his feathers flowing and rippling like a rainbow reflected in choppy water. Karul stood talking with Luez, and when he caught Ivlana's glance, his eyes flashed at her. She turned away to hide her smile and saw Sinnie watching her, grinning. Ivlana couldn't tell if Sinnie had figured out what had happened between her and Karul, or if she was just having a really good time. Perhaps a touch of both.

When dusk came, they had eaten, drunk, and talked themselves into a cheery, quiet state. Tcheen put down their cup and strode over, with Ayal trailing in their wake.

"Join me in the baths," they said, hardly slowing down. Ayal flashed an apologetic smile and followed Tcheen to an entrance not far from the mound, which Ivlana had noticed, but hadn't known what was inside.

?

Tcheen cleaned the nails on one hand by scraping them with the nails on the other, held them up in the torchlight, dunked them, and went to work again. They did not look up until the whole group had laid their clothes on the wooden racks and slid into the scalding water. Only Sinnie showed any modesty, which was understandable, given the expanse of pale skin that covered her from face to toes, except for patches of hair under her arms and around her sex. Finn and Carl at least had enough hair on bodies not to look completely ridiculous; they were both well-built, even attractive in their own way. But neither had the height or shoulders or blinding hot gaze of Karul, who studiously avoided eye contact with her.

"You like our baths." Tcheen was not asking.

"Very much so." Karul sank down to his chin. "In fact, the first thing I'm going to do when we get back is have one built. We have a hot spring, though it's not more than a trickle. Still, we will figure something out."

"You will not regret. In winter, it saves us."

"It's no wonder this valley has been occupied by so many different groups. It's a near perfect setup."

Tcheen stared at Karul. "Speak plain."

Karul flashed a genuine smile, as if to show he was not intimidated, though he clearly was. They all were.

"Your valley is perfect."

Tcheen nodded, surveying the group. They seemed to look longest at the humans before turning back to Karul.

"Tell me more of your war. The one you try to stop."

Karul ran his hand down from his nose to his chin, then turned to Fabaris, as Ivlana had known he would. Karul was at his best leading the plans for an imminent attack, and the farther the situation got away from that, the more he liked to have others do the work.

Fabaris sat up straight, twirling his chin braids furiously for a moment before extending one arm toward the center of the pool.

"Over a thousand years ago, men and Maer lived in peace, two separate but equal civilizations. We know not why, but a war began between the two peoples. It was long, it was bloody, and it was devastating to all. Men had gained the upper hand, but had not the strength to keep it. A Great Treaty was signed, a promise of peace. A hope for the future."

Ivlana sat, transfixed as Fabaris detailed the history of the Great Betrayal, the retreat into the mountains, and the journey to the Place Below. He even sang a verse, one about them burying their songs and deeds where the ancestors dwell. His face was reverent, serene.

"Enough history. Tell of the war."

Fabaris snapped out of his reverie. "Right. There are those in the *Sabrit*, our council of mages, who seek in the Archive the secret to awaken, and control, the *Ka-lar*."

Ayal, who had been staring up at the ceiling, turned to Tcheen, his braids slapping his own cheek, and said something in their language. Tcheen nodded.

"You have faced *Ka-lar*," they said to Carl. "Tell."

Carl closed his eyes for a long moment, a pained frown on his face. "The *Ka-lar's* tomb near my home village had been disturbed by members of Karul's tribe. Maybe they thought it would do their bidding; we do not know. It stalked and killed Maer and human alike, so we went off to face it. We were told bronze was needed to destroy it. I had its sword, which had been taken from it before it awakened, and we had its dagger as well, which we had melted and forged into arrowheads for Sinnie's bow. Finn, Sinnie, and I entered the tomb." Carl paused, staring down at the water. He had left out the part where he and his friends had killed Roubay and the others, and the two Maer children. Those parts Ivlana knew, but she had never heard the story of the *Ka-lar*. She sat up straight, her eyes fixed on Carl, along with everyone else's.

"It had the strength of many Maer, and a cruelty, a cunning, greater than anything I have ever known. We fought with sword, with arrow, with magic. I wounded it, but it bit me in the neck, nearly to death. Finn held it at bay while Sinnie finished it off with her bronze-tipped arrows. I don't know if the bronze from the Ka-lar's weapons had magical properties or if the metal itself hurt the creature, but in the end it was destroyed, after a fierce battle. Only through the wisdom of the scholar from my village, and through Finn's magic, was I healed. And even after, I was not myself." He looked down at his hands, then back up at Tcheen. "My body was healed, but my mind took much longer."

Tcheen stared at Carl in silence for a time. "There are *Ka-lar* tombs near here, two that we find. We do not enter. How many there are, do you think?"

Fabaris cleared his throat. "There would be hundreds, we think, spread out throughout the Silver Hills, as we call these mountains. It is believed there is an ancient spell in the Archive, beneath the mound, that would allow its caster to awaken them and control them. The *Sabrit* are looking for this spell, and if they find it, they would use it, and the *Ka-lar*, to start a war with the humans."

"A war we could never win," Karul said. "Their numbers are too great, their weapons, their armor, their magic—they would defeat us, at great cost no doubt, but they would prevail, and they would proceed to scour the mountains for every Maer, male, female, and child, and they would wipe us from the earth."

Tcheen nodded, speaking low to Ayal for a while. Ayal's eyebrows raised, then his face lowered into a deep frown.

Tcheen fixed Karul with a long stare. "After this battle, we will help."

The silence that followed was broken only by the gurgle and drip of water, the sputtering of torches, and after a while, the sound of hurried footsteps. Sulee ran into the cave, firing a burst of speech at Tcheen and Ayal. Everyone looked to Tcheen, who nodded at Sulee, then turned back to the group.

"The...night birds have been taken, or killed. The *Shoza* are not seen. We must prepare." They stood up, water flowing down their muscles and curves, their breasts dangling as they leaned over to pick up what looked like a wolfskin and rubbed it over their body.

"The mages say from the distance, they cannot come before the morning, probably the next, but more than such we do not know. Go. Sleep. Be ready at dawn."

Chapter:
Thirty-Five

Tcheen sent Sulee to inform the adults they would be moving the children into the Mound at first light. Freni had estimated the *Shoza* wouldn't arrive until dark even if they moved through the night, but with the owls' disappearance, there was no way to be sure. Freni said the pair of owls that had been following the *Shoza* that night had suddenly stopped responding, and he feared they had been killed. Perhaps the vultures would be able to give news in the morning. In the meantime, everyone needed to get some sleep, as there was no guarantee when they would be able to close their eyes again.

Ayal remained uncharacteristically silent as he followed Tcheen, his face drawn with worry. They stopped, took his chin in their hand, and gave him a soft kiss, then walked straight for their cabin, sending the guards posted outside away to a safe distance. When the door was closed and a taper lit, Tcheen gestured for Ayal to remove his robe, watching as he stood, eyes down, awaiting their command. They hadn't decided what exactly they were going to do to him this evening, but they felt something like pity at his plight. He would be useless in the coming fight, stuck in the mound with Kiki, Maomao, and the children as the sounds of battle raged outside.

Tcheen stepped to him, running their fingers over his shoulders, neck, and face, jerking his chin up so he stayed with their gaze. Any thought they had of taking it easy on him vanished as they saw the hunger in his eyes. They put their hands on his chest and shoved him onto the bed with the full force of both hands, and he let out a cry of surprise as he landed. Tcheen grabbed his feet and jerked him toward them, grabbing him between the legs and squeezing as he squirmed and whined. His eyes begged for more, and since it could be the last time, they would make sure it was not something he would soon forget. They let go of him, dropped their clothes, and straddled his chest, pinning his arms beneath their knees.

"Tomorrow I go forth to satisfy the gods of war. Tonight, I am the god who must be satisfied."

Ayal nodded, his eyes bright and wet, as Tcheen gripped his hair in their hands and moved their body forward.

?

Tcheen awoke to the sound of Ayal's light snore, and they rolled their leg over him, caressing his face and beard as he yawned and turned to face them. Tcheen traced their fingers over his cheek, behind his ear, over his forehead, and down his nose, stopping on his lips, which parted to kiss their fingertips. They lay cuddling for a while, foreheads pressed together, as the faint light of a gray dawn peeked through the gaps between the shutter and the frame. Tcheen wished the two of them could stay in this moment forever, enveloped in each other's warmth, ignoring the call of death that bore down upon the village. They clung to Ayal a bit longer, until they heard Digar's footsteps approaching the cabin. They pressed their lips against Ayal's, touched him on the back of the neck, then gently untangled their body from his and rose to greet the bloody day.

The morning passed as in a dream, moments flowing together like raindrops merging on rock and dragging each other in rivulets down to the ground. Orders were given, positions laid, strategies outlined, but it all felt unreal. Tcheen had shepherded their tribe through several attacks, and they had come to think of their valley as impregnable, their people indomitable, their future inevitable. But the events of the past few days had changed everything. The coming of the Old Maer and their human companions might herald the Opening, but so might the arrival of the *Shoza*. Only in that case, it might be the opening to a future far darker than anyone imagined, one they might not be around to see.

The sky was a featureless blanket of pale gray, with no sign of sun, rain, or snow. The vulture they had sent out to spy on the *Shoza* had vanished just as the owls before them, and Freni had argued against sending out the crows, for fear the same might happen to them. Tcheen had agreed, reluctantly, preferring to save Freni's strength for the battle ahead. They had stationed Freni at the wall with the hatchet birds, along with Lolo, Digar, and half of the warriors, since that was the easiest place for a force to cross. The other half remained with Tcheen by the path leading down from the west ridge, along with Stuock, whose magic of destruction they hoped could counteract that of the *Shoza*'s mages. Sulee was with the Old Maer and the humans in the east marsh, and a handful of scouts patrolled the south marsh just in case. Both the east and west ridges had a pair of guards posted atop them, so if they spotted the *Shoza,* their horns would sound. All that could be prepared had been done, and there was nothing left to do but to wait.

They waited through the day and into the night, their eyes and bodies weary from the nervous tension. The clouds finally dissipated after midnight, allowing the stars and a bulging quarter moon to provide an eerie light. The warriors stood, silent, staring at the ridge, toward the wall, toward the south, everywhere except at each other. No sound and no breeze disturbed the chilly dark, and the night seemed to stretch on into an eternity vaster than the heavens themselves. About an hour before dawn, one of the warriors ran over to Tcheen, pointing to the ridge above, his eyes wide with dread.

At first, it looked like a cloud sat atop the ridge, obscuring the remains of the ancient watchtower. But as Tcheen stared at the cloud, it began spreading down the ridge, flowing along the path. There was no horn from the ridge top, no shouting, just the mass of fog rolling down toward the valley. Tcheen sent one of the warriors to the wall and signaled the javelineers hiding on either side of the path to be ready. Izul approached, his eyebrows lifted.

"Send Bobo halfway up the ridge," Tcheen commanded. "If they are coming down, I want him to attack from the rear just before they get to the bottom." Izul nodded. "Has Lolo sensed anything at the wall?"

"Not since last check. Wait." Izul closed his eyes, a thick vein standing out on his forehead. When he opened them again, his face radiated fear. "Many Maer are coming down the low pass. A huge mass of Maer, I know not how many, but it feels like an army. Lolo is very afraid."

"Impossible!" Tcheen punched their palm, blood boiling in their ears. "The vultures would have noticed a group of that size days ago."

"They were said to have a mage who controls shadow." Izul rubbed his ears, which he always claimed helped him think. "They might have managed to hide the group, though if they possess such power..."

"If they have that many warriors, we are doomed. It must be some trickery."

"Perhaps they can create an illusion of things that are not real. Or make what is real seem different. Making ten look like a hundred, for instance."

"Yes, that must be it. Have Lolo creep up and sniff it out."

"I will. Her smell and hearing should help her discern their true number. Unless they can control other senses too."

"Make it so." Tcheen eyed the fog, now a third of the way down the ridge, about as far as it would be if it were covering a group walking. It would be some time before it reached the bottom. Tcheen gripped their dragonbone spear, closing their eyes to feel its power.

It had been some time since they had called on it, but they felt the energy, the subtle vibration when they squeezed the engravings just below its tip.

Footsteps beat across the village, and a warrior stopped, gasping, and bowed to Tcheen. "A great number...coming down the low saddle. A hundred or more." The warrior nearly collapsed to the ground, his chest heaving from the run.

"It is a mage trick." Tcheen motioned for someone to give him water. "They are fewer. They mean to distract us. You will stay and fight here." Tcheen pointed to one of the other warriors. "You, run to the wall and tell them to hold the line." The warrior nodded and took off at a sprint. Tcheen turned to the one who was still catching his breath. "Sit for a moment, then be ready to charge."

Tcheen scanned the path leading up the ridge, and they had to look carefully to spot the javelineers, who hid among the rocks on the third bend from the bottom. Bobo was nowhere to be seen, which was no surprise, given his stealth and coloring, but Tcheen knew he was just above the javelineers. Tcheen was surrounded by stout and well-trained warriors, but they would have given anything to have Digar at their side as they charged up to meet the intruders. As it was, they had resigned themselves to staying below, as there were three possible fronts to the battle, and they needed to be prepared for the unexpected. They sent eight warriors to defend the second bend, another four at the first, with Tcheen, Stuock, Izul, and a half-dozen warriors waiting at the base of the path.

"Stuock, stay with Izul. Destroy anyone who tries to approach him."

Stuock nodded, eyeing Izul and the fog, which kept rolling, overspreading more than half of the hill, creeping toward the fifth bend.

"Lolo reports there are some, but not many." Izul shook his head, blinking hard.

"What in the gods' shit does that mean?"

"I don't know," Izul moaned. "Dragons don't count like we do, but it means there aren't a hundred, but some...if I had to guess, not more than a dozen?"

"Plus a mage or two." Tcheen ground their teeth. The fog had passed the fourth bend. "Ready," they hissed, gripping their staff.

A single whistle note sounded from the east marsh. The enemy had been spotted. A shout rang out from the third bend above, now inside the fog. The javelineers had struck. Other cries followed, cries of surprise, fierce yells, agonizing screams. Lolo's piercing shriek echoed along the ridge from beyond the wall. The enemy was attacking on all fronts.

Out of the thinning fog burst a huge flying mass, soaring above Tcheen's head and onto the pavilion, where a dark figure dropped, and another soared off to the east. The figure on the roof stood, barked a word, and a tiny spit of fire shot forth from their hand, racing toward Tcheen's group. Tcheen shouted as they leapt out of the way, and fire exploded all around, singeing the hairs on their legs as screams erupted from the spot of the explosion. Tcheen rolled over and raised to their knee, seeing four of their warriors engulfed in flames, only one of them rolling far enough to put themselves out. Stuock pulled Izul away from the fire and helped bat out the flames on his cloak. Another shout, and another spit of flame seared through the air from atop the pavilion, and one of the cabins was engulfed in roaring flame. The figure on the pavilion hunched over, as if gasping for breath, then stood up again and began pressing their hands together.

Tcheen gripped the runes on their spear, attuned themself to its vibration, and held on as the spear took off, soaring toward the pavilion. Tcheen softened their grip as they approached, landing a little sooner and more roughly than intended, and as they tumbled to their feet they were hit full in the chest by a blast of fire that sent raging streaks of pain up their neck and face, though their dragonskin vest had protected their vitals. They staggered, but kept their feet, raising the spear overhead and bringing it down on the mage, whose face glistened with sweat, eyes full of the knowledge of what was to come as the spear burst through their chest and their eyes went blank. They slid lifeless down the spear's shaft, and Tcheen yanked out the spear and rolled onto their back, touching the wet burns on their face, clawing the air around them in search for some gesture or position that would soothe the searing pain.

They looked back at the melee on the ridge, dimly visible in the light of the burning cabin. The fog was lifting, and spears and swords clanged and clattered in the flame-lit darkness, biting into flesh, pulling screams and souls from bodies. A wave of javelins peppered the middle of the enemy ranks, dropping one and staggering several others. Near the rear, one of the *Shoza's* bodies was jerked sideways, then flipped, hovering in the air for a moment before dropping, limp, to the ground. Bobo's gray feathers were nearly invisible in this light, but his screech was deafening, sending several more of the Shoza tumbling to the ground. He pounced on the fallen ones, and more screaming ensued.

Tcheen looked toward the wall, but it was too dark to see anything other than the flame above the gate. They turned toward the east and saw the figure flying toward the marsh. It had to be the wind mage, since the fire mage was dead and the shadow mage seemed to be with the group at the wall. Tcheen gripped their spear again, faced the figure diminishing to the east, and let out a throat-burning scream as they shot out into space, ripping through the air toward the treeline.

Chapter: Thirty-Six

Sinnie watched as the figure flew toward her, silhouetted against the flames in the village. Another figure, flying faster and more erratically, sped after, closing the distance between them in seconds.

"I've got someone coming this way," Sinnie called to Finn over her shoulder. "You keep an eye out on the marsh. I've got this." She pulled back an arrow and trained it on the flying figure, but they were moving too fast for her to see who it was, or to get a reliable shot. As the lead figure neared the treeline, they slowed and turned to face their pursuer, drifting ever more slowly backward toward the trees. Sinnie could just make out a dark flowing robe on a slight frame. She hesitated, unsure who or what she would be shooting at. The figure came to a stop in mid-air and held out their arms toward the second one, who was hurtling toward them at unbelievable speed, a blaze of white streaking through the sky. Tcheen—it could only be them—suddenly took a nose-dive, spiraling down and bouncing off the ground, their spear twirling through the air and landing some distance away from their motionless body.

Sinnie released her arrow, and the robed figure jerked and plummeted toward the earth, slowing just in time to land. They crouched over with the arrow stuck in their back, heaving for breath. They stood slowly, their dark eyes locked on Sinnie, and stretched one arm above their head, balling their hand into a fist, which crackled with blue sparks. Sinnie fumbled for an arrow but it slipped back into the quiver, and before she could draw another, she saw Ivlana's low, round shape barreling out of the forest, heading straight for the mage. The mage swiveled, threw their fist toward Ivlana, and let forth a three-forked bolt of blueish lightning, which lit up Ivlana's body. She froze, arched her back, and slumped to the ground, where she lay still as a stone.

Sinnie screamed as she fired another arrow at the mage, but her scream threw off her aim, and the arrow vanished into the darkness. The mage crouched, breathing heavily, then stood up just as Sinnie steadied herself for another shot, which found its mark. The mage dropped to the ground, twitched twice, and stopped moving. Sinnie sprinted over, pulled her long knife, and plunged it into the mage's unmoving chest once, twice, three times, her eyes nearly blinded with tears and rage. Karul came running from the forest and knelt by Ivlana, holding his trembling hands above her face. Sparks flew as he touched her forehead, and he tumbled backwards and let out a shout that began as pain and surprise before turning into an otherworldly howl. He turned toward Sinnie, his face streaked with tears, then stalked back to the forest, his chin jutting forward almost as far as his spear.

Sinnie leapt to her feet and spun around as she heard grunting and shuffling from the treeline where Finn had stood. She sheathed her bloody knife, unshouldered her bow, and nocked an arrow as she ran toward the sound of the scuffle. Finn stood facing two crouched figures, dark silhouettes against the gray pre-dawn light. The figures took turns jabbing at him with their swords, despite his futile attempts to block with his staff. He didn't seem to be bleeding, so he must have had his force shell up, but he was wincing in pain and breathing hard. Sinnie loosed a wild shot as she neared the edge of the treeline. Her arrow thunked into a tree, distracting the two for a moment. Finn dove to the ground next to one of them and held out his staff sideways, and the one closest to him suddenly flew back into the other as if lifted by a gust of wind, sending them both tumbling to the ground. Sinnie put an arrow into one before they could stand, and was about to fire another round when Finn rushed in, swinging his staff overhead.

His staff struck one of the prone figures with a horrid thud, and they collapsed to the ground, while the other rolled out of the way, breaking off the arrow in their leg and springing up in an unexpected direction that made Sinnie's next shot miss. Shouts and clangs sounded from the treeline in the direction Karul had moved, but Sinnie stayed focused on the figure, who closed on her in the blink of an eye. She stumbled as she tried to back up enough for a shot, falling onto her back as the figure's sword flashed overhead. She rolled out of the way as the sword struck the ground, then scrambled to her feet as the sword flashed again, hitting her right in the chest and pinning her to a tree. Her breath failed her and her vision blurred as the sword swirled around for another strike, then flew off with a clang. She slumped to the ground, gasping for air, and watched helplessly as the figure spun away from her, ducking under Finn's staff and tackling him.

Her breath returned in a painful instant, and her hands moved to where the sword had struck her, but there was no blood, only pain. The *Ka-lar* armor had stopped the blade from penetrating, but her heart was beating out of sync, and every breath was an ordeal. She heard shuffling and shouting as Finn and the *Shoza* rolled on the ground. Silver flashed, and Finn let out a shriek. Sinnie inched her way up to standing, using the tree for support, and as she leaned down to pick up her bow, the pain almost made her pass out. She steadied herself against the tree and caught her breath as Finn kicked free of the *Shoza* and stood up, a circle of blood now visible on his tunic. The *Shoza* darted in with their knife, and Finn held out his fist and let out a great shout. The *Shoza* went flying backwards, slamming against a tree and tumbling to the ground, rolling slowly to their side. Sinnie pulled back her bow, gritting her teeth against the pain, and fired an arrow into the *Shoza*, who stopped moving.

Karul's roar was unmistakable, and Sinnie drew another arrow, her breath coming more steadily now, but still too shallow for her to move. Finn put a hand on her shoulder, his face streaked with sweat and blood.

"I'm fine," she said, looking down at the growing red spot on his stomach. "You're—"

"I'll live. Can you—"

Sinnie shook her head. "Go. I'll catch up."

Finn darted off, and she heard Karul's howl of pain, metal singing against metal, more shouts, grunts, and blows. Footsteps approached through the forest from the south, and she drew back her bow, her arm shaking as she tracked the sound. A figure appeared, running in a crouch, and pulled up as they saw her.

"It's me," Luez whispered, moving closer.

"What about Sulee?" Sinnie's voice trembled. Luez looked down and shook her head.

Sinnie bit her lip and pointed with her chin where Finn had run, and Luez disappeared into the trees. Sinnie closed her eyes and tried to block out the sounds of battle all around her: shouts and screams from the village, the clangs and grunts of a heated fight in the treeline just north of her, the screech of a dragon in the distance. She pictured Finn doing his poses in the bailey of Castle Maer, his eyes closed, his arms extended, his breathing steady and slow. She forced her breath to go deeper, pulling the pain out of her a little bit with each exhalation, and she felt her legs steadying, her heartbeat slowing, her mind settling. She opened her eyes, and her vision cleared; the first hint of light grew over the east ridge, and she pushed away from the tree, took three deep breaths, and moved along the edge of the treeline toward the sound of fighting, which had died down for a moment but now began again, a little farther away.

She crept closer, her legs not yet ready to run, passing the bodies of two fallen *Shoza*. They were Maer, she could see that clearly now, wearing fine leather armor with metal plates sewn in, just like Luez. Steel swords lay on the ground next to them, and they had daggers in their belts and boots. She heard a cry that sounded like Carl, and she forced her legs to move faster, running out of the treeline cover on the marsh side. Ahead she saw Karul slumped against a tree, his breathing heavy, a body at his feet, while Finn and Carl faced off against two *Shoza*, one of them moving as if injured.

She raised her bow for a shot, but Finn was blocking her line of sight, so she crept closer and was about to release her arrow when something punched into her side, knocking her off balance. An arrow was stuck in her mail, and she spun toward the marsh, scanning for movement. She saw nothing but shadow, and she took cover behind a tree as another arrow whizzed by her head. Her side stung from the arrow, but it had not penetrated. She saw movement behind a scrub bush, and she trained her sights on the center of the bush, her arms on fire with the effort of holding the bow drawn.

The bush quivered, and she fired. A shout rang out from behind the scrub, and a figure stood up and fired back, the arrow sinking into a tree next to her. She drew an arrow and fired again, but the figure had disappeared by the time her arrow arrived. She heard Carl scream, and she turned to see him drop his sword and clutch at his neck, his shield raised against the sword blow of another of the *Shoza*. Finn leapt to tackle the attacker, and the other ran toward him but stopped cold as Luez appeared out of nowhere and plunged her sword into their back. Sinnie turned back toward the bush and saw a dark shape moving in an erratic pattern toward her with unbelievable speed. Her arrow missed, and the *Shoza* was upon her, their sword scraping against the tree inches from her head. She dropped her bow and pulled out her long knife as she ducked behind another tree, but the *Shoza* anticipated her move. The sword flashed down so fast she could hardly see it, then stopped in mid-air as a streak of white flew in over her shoulder and pierced the *Shoza's* chest with a horrifying crunch. The *Shoza* fell backward onto the ground, with Tcheen's long white spear jutting up out of their chest, swaying as the body heaved, then went still.

Tcheen planted their foot on the *Shoza's* chest and yanked out the spear, their eyes locked on Sinnie's. The hair had been burned off their face and neck, leaving only black and red skin, and the white feathers of their cloak were singed brown and black around the edges. A scream pierced the air, subsiding into a gurgle, and a sudden quiet rang in Sinnie's ears. She turned and saw Luez pulling her sword out of a motionless *Shoza*, and Carl laying on the ground, his hand on his throat, with Finn kneeling over him. Luez ran over to Karul, who slumped against the tree, his hand pressing into his side. Without a word, Tcheen turned and limped toward the two fallen *Shoza* who lay motionless on the ground, jabbing their spear into each of them, then leaned against the spear, their breath raspy and shallow.

Sinnie dropped her knife and ran to Carl. Finn's hand was pressed over Carl's, with blood flowing between his fingers. Finn moved Carl's limp hand out of the way and pressed both of his hands onto Carl's neck. Finn's eyes closed and the veins on his forehead and neck stood out with exertion, sweat trickling down his trembling face. Carl looked up into Sinnie's eyes as his hand patted the pouch at his side. His lips moved, but no sound came out. His fingers fumbled at the pouch, and Sinnie knelt, clasped his hand, and reached into the pouch. Her fingers found the copper ring, and Carl blinked as she pushed back his mail coif and placed the ring on his head. He gave a weak smile, then closed his eyes, his face falling, troubled, his eyes squinting hard with concentration. Sinnie held on tight to his hand, her eyes blurred by tears, her heart crushed by a black shadow growing inside her.

Chapter: Thirty-Seven

Ujenn felt the faintest pull when she called out for Carl across the unknowable distance. Her heart swelled up but was bound in by the silence following his feeble response. *Is everyone safe?* Her jaw and fists clenched as she scanned the void for some sign of Carl, but the emptiness engulfed her, chilled her to the marrow. *Are you coming back soon?* Her spine went hollow as the copper cord linking her and Carl thinned and snapped.

Ujenn lay back on the bed, crossed her arms over her chest, and stared at the thatched ceiling above her. Grisol's face appeared, her eyes wet and questioning, and Ujenn shook her head. Grisol's tears fell onto her face as she slumped over Ujenn, and they lay in silence, neither of them having the strength to even wrap an arm around the other. The Castle was waking up, but the sounds of low talking, babies crying, and fires being started were like tuneless music echoing in a well. Ujenn sank into the darkness, let it swallow her, her heartbeat slowing like water dripping from an almost empty jug.

Chapter:
Thirty-Eight

F inn used his fingers to close Carl's vacant eyes, shuddering with the finality of the gesture. Sinnie knelt by Carl, her hands touching his face, her eyes red and brimming. She turned to Finn, closed her eyes, and wrapped herself around him, her face hot and slick with tears. He closed his eyes and held her tight for a long time. After a while her sobs became silent heaves, and the sound of Karul's raspy breathing pulled Finn back to the present. He squeezed Sinnie's shoulders, touched her forehead with his, and went to Karul. Luez was pressing the blood-soaked edge of her cloak against his stomach. Finn's eyes were heavy and his head throbbed as he knelt next to Karul, whose eyes were open but distant. He put one hand on Karul's neck, feeling his pulse, which was slow but steady. Luez moved her hands and cloak aside as Finn slid his hands under Karul's tunic and pressed them down on the wound.

His head spun and his chest burned, but he locked onto Karul's energy and poured everything he had into it. Luez steadied him as he tipped to the side, and he held on, finding the silver thread inside himself and linking it to Karul's unsteady life force, doing what he had been unable to do for Carl. As his own energy waned, he felt Karul's becoming steadier, still weak but no longer fading. He held on for a few moments longer, then collapsed into Luez, who lowered him to the ground, rolling up her cloak to put under his head.

"He will live," Finn said before letting himself slip away into the darkness.

?

As Finn drifted into consciousness, he was greeted first by a throbbing headache, then a sharp pain in his side, and finally a weakness in his limbs that left him unable to move from the mat of straw where he lay. From the low stone ceilings and the smell, like a henhouse where some of the chickens had died, he surmised he was in the Mound, in a kind of alcove. Distant torchlight cast uneven shadows across the walls and ceiling, which he studied as he lay trying to gather his strength, but there was none to gather. He felt utterly drained, as from a long illness, and so he lay, and stared, and tried to steer his thoughts away from the terrible events he had witnessed. But try as he might, he could not avoid the creeping memory of Carl's empty eyes, the pallor of his skin, the slick of blood on his face and neck. Carl had died, and Finn had been unable to save him.

He lay chewing on that thought for some time until one of the Bird Maer checked on him, smiling when she saw he was awake. She said something in her language, but Finn could only reply in Maer, "Get Sinnie." She nodded as she examined his side, lifting something wet and slimy off the wound. She grimaced and replaced it with great care. She lifted his eyelids and looked in each one, put a finger on his neck, and held it for some time, her head bobbing ever so slightly, as if counting. When she had finished looking him over, she said something that sounded comforting, then turned away. Another of the Bird Maer, a teenager, came by with a cup of water and helped Finn sit up to drink it. The pain in his side took his breath away, but he steeled himself against it and drank the cup dry, sip by tiny sip, then lay back down, with the youth's help. He faded away as his eyes closed, and when he opened them again, Sinnie stood over him, smiling as though holding back tears. Daylight filtered in from somewhere, so he knew he must have slept.

"They said you're going to be okay. You just have to rest." Her fingers interlaced with his, her grip waking his hand up.

Finn nodded. "How's...everyone else?"

Sinnie put her fingers over her mouth, looking down, then back up. "Ivlana's dead. Killed by the air mage. And Karul took a serious sword wound, but he's going to be okay. Thanks to you. I wish I could have...if I'd only focused a little bit more, I—"

Finn gripped her fingers hard. "I know. I keep seeing it over and over in my head, what I could have done differently." He raised himself up on his elbows a little, wincing with the pain. "But then I think of what would have happened if I hadn't been there. It would have been worse. And you, if you hadn't been there, would I have survived? If we hadn't been there, the *Shoza* would have streamed through the village and turned the tide of the battle. If it hadn't been for you, and me, and Carl, and all the rest—the battle might have been lost."

Sinnie wiped away tears as her head gave a little shake. "I don't like this journey anymore. I want to go back, I want to take it all back."

"Go back, where, to Brocland? Marry some nice boy, spend your days chasing after children and sheep?"

Sinnie sniffed, smiling a little. "It doesn't sound half bad, actually."

"But then you never would have gotten to ride a dragon."

Sinnie squeezed Finn's hand, and he fell back on the bed, a grim smile on his lips, his temples clenching as he tried to hold back tears his eyes were too dry to release.

?

The Bird Maer burned the dead in the remains of their cornfield, where the ashes could feed next year's crop. Eighteen piles of straw and wood, eighteen bodies laid out naked under the frozen sun. Ivlana and Carl's bodies joined Sulee, Freni, and a dozen warriors, along with Bobo and one of the hatchet birds, in a final assembly, with the whole village standing in a semicircle around them. The other hatchet bird bobbed and squawked as it circled the body of its companion, and it took Fawul some time to corral it with her whip and hook. The dragons huddled together as the fires were set, Lolo leaning against Maomao, who kept Kiki caged in with her front legs.

Karul wept like a broken man. After the battle, after Carl's death, he had pledged his life and all his future works to Finn and Sinnie, his eyes desperate for forgiveness, which was not theirs to give. But when he turned toward the funeral biers, Finn was sure it was Ivlana's that his eyes stayed with as the flames billowed around her, fanned by the breeze, her smoke mingling with the others as it drifted across the valley.

Finn didn't understand Ayal's words, but he was moved by the speech, the sounds of which echoed in his mind as he watched the flames where Carl's body lay. Sinnie held his hand, her head on his shoulder, and it was the first time Finn could remember when neither of them had anything to say.

Their fallen received far better treatment than the bodies of the *Shoza*. Those were dragged to the top of the low ridge to feed the vultures, with the hopes of attracting a few new recruits, since the air mage had killed the ones Freni had been working with.

The skulls of the fallen heroes were placed on a makeshift memorial deep inside the Mound. Finn briefly wondered which was Carl, and which Ivlana. There was no telling the human from the Maer skulls lined against the wall. Finn had not been beyond the entry alcoves when he was recuperating, and he was awed by the scale of the place, the weight of the stone, the heavy darkness. The memorial was in a large chamber in the farthest part of the Mound, off to the side, with words painted on the wall above in the flowing script of the Bird Maer, which Finn could now recognize, though he couldn't read a word. In the center of the chamber was a huge block of dark stone with several large teeth, scales the size of saucers, and assorted figurines and other tokens laid out atop it. Ayal told him, in Southish, that the teeth were from a scale dragon, and that they had been there long before the Dragon Maer had arrived.

Finn laughed for the first time since before the battle. Ayal cocked his head at him.

"Sorry, it's just...we've been calling you the Bird Maer all this time. But Dragon makes more sense."

"Freni would have been pleased to hear that, most pleased."

"Are there scale dragons in these parts?"

Ayal shook his head, the beads on his braids clacking. "No one in living memory has seen one. They are thought to be extinct, gone forever."

"Sinnie's father said he saw one, many years ago. A baby, he thought."

Ayal's eyes lit up. "I shall tell this to Izul. He will be very keen to hear of it."

"And the inscription over the...skulls, what does it say?"

Ayal pointed to the top line of the text, moving his finger along in the air as he read. "Here lie the remains of those who fell defending the Mound from the bloody *Shoza*. They gave their lives for the Opening. Let their names ring out through the valley and up to the tip of the Great Tooth, so that the ancestors may hear the calls and be pleased. And this here is a list of their names."

"And the...the Opening, as Fabaris explained it to me, you think...it involves this block of stone?"

Ayal nodded. "We dug around it, when we first came, we dug and dug, but even at a Maer's height of depth the stone continued underground. So we decided to leave it in place, in the hope that someone would come who would know what to do. Perhaps you?"

"Maybe Stuock could. I don't know how much help I'd be." Finn ran his hand along the top of the block, down its sides to the ground.

He had mostly recovered from the energy drain he had used to restore Karul, but with Stuock he had only worked at breaking small rocks, no bigger than his head. Even at full strength, he didn't see how he could do anything to such a mass of stone.

"I have faith." Ayal's face remained twisted in a sly smile. "Tcheen does not quite believe, but the stories are too old not to have a grain of truth. If it is not you, it will be someone who comes after, maybe not in my lifetime, but they will come. They will come." He bowed to Fabaris, who entered the room and bowed back at him.

"A most fitting place for the fallen." Fabaris stood staring at the skulls for a time, then at the text above it. His fingers moved through the air following the lines, stopping periodically as he mouthed silent words. "A memorial to those who died for the Opening." He looked over his shoulder at Ayal, pointing to a word.

Ayal nodded. "Yes, that's it. You can read our writing but not speak our language?"

"I can make out some words. It is not so different from the language of the ancient texts, which I can read, given time and space. But if the Archive is in fact to be found beneath us, there will be much opportunity for me to learn."

"And what is it you hope to find, deep beneath the rock?"

Fabaris' eyebrows raised, his eyes grew distant, and he sighed. "Everything."

Finn's heart lurched as he saw the expression on Fabaris' face. If they managed to unearth the Archive from beneath this block of stone, there was no way Fabaris would ever leave it.

Chapter:
Thirty-Nine

F abaris took a hard look at the stone block, which they had convinced themselves covered the entrance to the Archive. It might be possible to excavate it manually, but it would be a staggering undertaking, and they were short on hands after the battle. And if they did decide to move all that earth, they might undermine the integrity of the Mound itself, as the stone was close to a wall. The plan was to have Stuock and Finn try and break the rock with their magic, though no one had any idea if that would be any safer, or if it was even possible.

Fabaris turned and put a hand on Finn's cheek. "You're looking well."

"I am. I feel almost like myself again. I've managed to heal my stab wound, more or less." He pulled up his tunic. The scar was closed, still a bit red, but better than it had been the night before. "I gave Karul another boost this morning. That took it out of me a little, but I'm on the right path."

"I noticed you've started doing your poses again."

"I had no choice. Once I stopped moping, I saw it was the only way to get myself back."

Fabaris leaned in and gave Finn a light kiss. "I didn't want to say anything, but you were acting a little sorry for yourself. But you had every right to, and now—" He ran his hand through the air from

Finn's head to his feet. "I hope you'll save a little of your energy for tonight." It had been since before the battle, two weeks at least, and Fabaris was in serious need of release.

"You're the one who needs to save his strength for tonight." Finn's eyes twinkled as his hand brushed against Fabaris' thigh, moving up.

Fabaris swatted it away with a smile and opened his mouth to speak when Digar limped in, looking none too well. He held up one finger to Ayal, and then to Fabaris and Finn, who exchanged a puzzled glance.

"One day," Ayal said in Southish. He bowed to Digar, who gave a faint bow to the group, then turned and shuffled out. Ayal turned to Finn. "Tcheen wants you to start work tomorrow. Are you up to it?" He looked Finn up and down and nodded when Finn said yes. "Very well then, very well. They are preparing another feast for the occasion. Lolo has been on a tear with the mountain goats these past few days, working off her grief. If she keeps up like this they're going to go extinct. We're going to have to make quite a batch of jerky. It's a good problem to have, a good one."

?

Despite his earlier bravado, Finn was gentle with Fabaris that night, and patient, so patient. Finn pushed him to the edge and held him there, the two of them trapped in an ever-growing bubble of passion that stretched farther than Fabaris had thought possible. When at last it burst, Fabaris saw comets streaking across his mind with tails in every color of the rainbow, soaring between swollen moons and never-ending clouds of stars. When their bodies finally pulled apart, a sense of oneness enveloped them like a cocoon, protecting them from the frigid darkness.

?

Tcheen stood with their arms crossed, Digar looking grumpy and fierce at their side, as Finn and Stuock conferred. Fabaris stood by Ayal, who for once had no words to repeat. Fabaris closed his eyes as he searched his memory for the lines to songs he had set aside for further study. There had to be something of use in those ancient rhymes, but for the moment it eluded him. He was snapped back to the present by a deep 'crack' from the stone, which he felt through his feet as much as he heard it. Finn and Stuock stood back from their work, sweat streaking down their faces, which Finn had to wipe away with his sleeve, given the lack of hair on his forehead. The square rock had a jagged fissure in its surface, running halfway down to the ground. Dust and shards of rock littered the floor around it. A loud huffing blew in through the door, and Fabaris skittered back when he saw Maomao poking her enormous head in, her mouth open in an odd way, as if she were smelling through it.

An arm looped over Maomao's neck, and Fawul's body squeezed through to block the entrance. Fawul spoke some words of badgering encouragement, and Maomao withdrew. "Sorry," Fawul said, one of the words in their dialect Fabaris understood without having to think about it.

Finn and Stuock set at the rock again, each with one hand on the stone and the others clasped together. Another 'crack' crumbled the remaining portion of the rock above ground and sent puffs of dust shooting out from the ceiling. Finn and Stuock slid down to sit against the wall, their faces drawn with exhaustion. Ayal walked over to inspect the damage, moving chunks of rock and sweeping the remaining dust to the side with his foot. Fabaris brought water to Finn, who drank greedily, spilling some down his tunic. Stuock sat holding his head, breathing audibly. After a while they stood up, conferred for a moment, and walked toward Tcheen.

Stuock spoke. "We will try again later, after some food and some fresh air." Tcheen nodded, their face almost softening for a moment, then murmured to Ayal, who bowed and hurried away. Fabaris was intrigued by their relationship; they were clearly lovers, and peers in a sense, but Ayal showed a deference to Tcheen that felt deeper than mere obedience to a strong leader. And Tcheen's body language always seemed protective of Ayal. At first Fabaris thought it was just the way of the Bird Maer, or the Dragon Maer, as they apparently called themselves. But after observing the group at large, he found the Dragon Maer to be, on the whole, no different from any Maer he had met. This relationship was unique in the village, perhaps in all the world. But wasn't that the way of love?

Fabaris followed Finn and Stuock out to the pavilion, where several goats hung over great fires, one of them low for roasting, the other suspended a little higher over a smoky fire that was constantly being fed with brush. Karul joined them, still moving with difficulty, but his grimace was more smile than pain at this point.

"Progress?"

Fabaris nodded, stroking his chin braids. "They have removed the top portion, though as you can see it has taken its toll. They have done their spell twice, and I would be surprised if they had more than one left in them today."

"I wish there was something I could do. I feel so...useless."

"At the risk of lecturing you, I should think the best thing you could do would be to rest up and heal."

"Bah! I've rested enough, and the healing will come. I'm going to take a little walk, over by the marsh. Build up my strength, for the journey home." Karul stared off toward the treeline. "I won't be long."

Fabaris touched him on the shoulder. He had seen the little shrine Karul had set up where Ivlana fell, an arrangement of pine and holly branches in the shape of a body. Karul had never said anything, but Fabaris sensed that he mourned for more than just his lieutenant and bodyguard.

When they had filled up on roasted mountain goat and stewed carrots, they returned to the Mound, where Finn and Stuock readied themselves for their next attempt. Finn led Stuock through some of his poses, and Stuock smiled as he tried to imitate Finn's body positioning. Stuock had to be about sixty years old, but he moved like a man closer to Fabaris' age. Tcheen watched them intently, with something like curiosity in their eyes.

After some stretching and meditation, the two mages returned to the rubble, kneeling on the floor to put their hands on the rock. The floor trembled in sync with the shaking of Finn and Stuock's bodies, and Fabaris' heart jumped when the wall behind them was rent with a jagged crack from floor to ceiling as the ground beneath Finn and Stuock bucked, then collapsed, and the two of them slipped away in a roar of rock and dust.

Fabaris ran to the edge of the hole, which was twice the width of the stone. The hole extended under the back wall, half of which slumped as dirt and rock showered down from a new crack in the ceiling. The sounds of coughing and groaning filtered up from the darkness below.

"Torch!" Fabaris cried. "Torch!"

Ayal came running, torch in hand, and lay flat against the ground next to Fabaris, holding the flame down into the hole. Finn and Stuock lay on a mound of rock, sand, and dirt. Stuock grasped his leg, his face contorted in pain, and Finn rolled onto his back, blinking at the dust. He sat up, gave Fabaris a faint wave, and turned to Stuock, who grunted in pain, but in the dim torchlight it looked like he was smiling.

?

They lowered themselves down on a knotted rope, and with the aid of their torches they examined the room, a circle some thirty feet wide and domed at the top, minus the gaping hole where the rock had been. Set in one wall was an enormous metal door, shining orange-gold, with runes and images covering it from top to bottom. In front of the door stood a statue of the same burnished orange metal, the color of the speaking rod back at Castle Maer, which Fabaris knew to be bronze. The statue was as tall as two Maer, and stood in the center of a semicircle of floor inlaid with arcane designs that shone as brightly as the door and the statue. Fabaris and Finn helped Stuock down from the pile of rubble, and Ayal knelt by him, examining his leg.

Stuock's shin was broken, but the bone wasn't sticking out. With a wad of soma leaves from Ayal in his cheek, he slumped contentedly against a wall and closed his eyes. Finn sat down heavily next to Stuock and breathed out a long breath. He looked up at Fabaris with a soft smile.

"You go check out the big shiny stuff. I'll be right here if you need me." He waved in the direction of the statue, then turned to speak to Stuock in Southish. "I'll help you heal in a little bit, once this incredible headache subsides." Stuock softened his eyes and leaned his head against the wall.

"I'm fine. And what is a little pain when faced with such..." Stuock's hand made a slow circle in the direction of the statue and the door. "I'm not sure if I really believed it existed."

"We don't know what exists, not yet." Fabaris couldn't stop the grin that kept reasserting itself on his face. "But I bet it'll be worth every step of the journey."

Fabaris joined Ayal, who was crouched by the bronze runes inlaid in the floor, his mouth moving silently. The runes were very similar to the Ancient Maer cylinder scrolls he had seen, which would usually take him days to puzzle out.

"Yes, here it is! Look! It says, Archive!" Ayal pointed to a group of letters laced together with flowing lines and dots. Fabaris stared at the word, pushing his mind to see letters, patterns, anything, but he could not make it out. "And look here, it says..." Ayal ran his fingers in the air over the words before and after. "Something about the shape of...the soul, and light—" As his fingers brushed against the bronze letters, light flashed from the statue, and a fiery orange bolt shot out at Ayal, sending him tumbling and skidding backwards along the floor, coming to rest in a heap against the far wall.

"Ayal!" Tcheen's scream echoed through the chamber as they dropped their spear and ran to Ayal's motionless body. "Ayal!" Tcheen's voice was high and distressed as they took Ayal's head in their hands and spoke, urged, pleaded—Fabaris couldn't understand the words, but the meaning was clear. Ayal's eyelids fluttered open and his eyes, wide and unseeing, moved in circles around the room before settling on Tcheen's. He opened his mouth and let out a groan, clutching Tcheen's arm with both hands.

"Water!" Tcheen cried in a hoarse voice. Karul hurried over with a waterskin, and Tcheen let a few drops fall into Ayal's mouth. Ayal sputtered, shook his head, and blinked several times, his eyes narrowing, focusing, staring into Tcheen's. Tcheen cooed and murmured to Ayal, who nodded, giving a weak smile as he loosened his grip on Tcheen's arm, his fingers kneading rather than squeezing. After a few moments he sat up, with Tcheen's help, and drained half the waterskin. Tcheen kissed him on the forehead, holding his face in their hands. Ayal said something, and Tcheen grabbed him under the arms and lifted him to his feet. He stood, wobbly, leaning on Tcheen.

He looked over at Fabaris. "Don't touch the runes. Don't touch." He gave a little giggle, letting go of Tcheen to stand on his own, his arms wide for balance.

Fabaris nodded as his heartbeat slowly returned to normal. "Well now we know what not to do." He looked up at the statue, whose face was eyeless, featureless, and still it felt like it was watching them.

Chapter:
Forty

Ayal walked back to the runes once his balance returned, but the high-pitched whine in his ears showed no sign of letting up. He knelt a few inches farther back than before and brought his eyes back to the runes. The fog in his brain made it harder to read, but he fought through it, squinting and rubbing his temples as he stared at the words he had been reading before he was zapped. *The shape of the soul,* he was pretty sure about that part, and the word *light,* but the words in between and on either side eluded him. It was amazing how similar the writing was to their own, though Fabaris' puzzlement showed it was farther from the Old Maer dialect. Fabaris had waxed poetic about his pet theory that all human and Maer languages were derived from one source, and that Maer and humans were no different beneath the skin. Ayal was inclined to agree, especially after the time he had spent with Fabaris and his friends, but it made him question which Maer were really the Old ones. Perhaps the Dragon Maer were the Old Maer, and the Old Maer were in fact a more recent offshoot, spliced from the trunk after the Great Mistake.

"What's this?" Fabaris pointed to an indentation in the floor at the very edge of the bronze inlay. It was the size of a walnut and irregularly shaped, like a mix of a hexagon and a pentagon. As Fabaris held his torch close to it, they could see that it was black inside, not gray like the surrounding stone, and the odd shape was a three-dimensional one. The inner edge of the hole was touching the outer rim of the inlay, a thin band of bronze running in a semicircle surrounding the runes from wall to curving wall.

"I have no idea." Ayal leaned over and looked at it from all angles, but there was nothing more to be seen. He turned his eyes back to the runes, trying to calm the throbbing in his skull so he could focus.

"The shape of the soul," Fabaris murmured, his eyes growing distant, his lips moving. After a moment, he snapped his fingers, a broad smile growing on his face. He stood up and walked over to Tcheen, who stood with crossed arms and an impatient furrow to their brow. He spoke to Tcheen in Old Maer, something about a rock, then asked a question. Tcheen pulled out the rock Fabaris had given him when they first arrived and held it out to Fabaris, who turned it slowly in his hand in front of the torch.

"Don't you see?" He handed the rock to Ayal, who studied it, puzzled. It was a rather unexceptional rock, except for the fact that its shape was exactly the same as the one atop the Mound. Ayal's face warmed and the hair on his neck stood up.

"Yes, it's the same shape, the very same!" He rushed over, holding the rock next to the hole in the floor, careful not to touch the bronze. He turned it over and around until he found the right angle. It was precisely the same shape, but it was just a little too big to fit in the hole. He handed it back to Fabaris, who repeated the process, then sat back on his knees, holding the rock in his hand.

Fabaris squinted, staring off into space. His face relaxed for a moment, then tensed with focus. He began reciting something in Old Maer, solemn, rhythmic, dark. He raised his finger slowly as he spoke, then pointed it energetically as he finished a line, which he then translated into Southish.

"The soul shines like the setting sun; know its shape, and the door to all wisdom shall open." Fabaris looked to Ayal, as if for approval. "It's from an ancient poem I learned in study."

"It's a nice bit of poetry, but I'm not sure how it helps us. Unless..." Ayal turned back to the runes, whose meaning suddenly became clear. "The shape of the soul stops the light." He twisted his mouth as a sour taste came into it; there was something off about the line.

"What light do you think it's referencing? What do—" Fabaris stopped when Ayal put up his hand. He needed quiet to study the words again. After a few moments more he saw it. What he was reading was not the beginning of a sentence; it continued from the words before it. He stared at the words for a while longer, and the word "use" popped out at him.

"Use the shape of the soul to stop the light." That rang true to him, but it still didn't explain about the light.

"Maybe that means if you put something in that hole, something of the right shape, it will stop the statue from shooting lightning at you?"

Ayal threw up his hands. "Your guess is as good as mine, I'm afraid." His teeth felt hollow as he remembered the feeling of the jolt the statue had given him. He wasn't going to touch anything to do with the runes.

"But how would we make something of just the right size? Do you have any sculptors in your village?"

Ayal bobbled his head. "We have a few carvers of wood, and some who dabble in stone, but this would have to be perfect. I don't know if we have anyone that good."

"You happen to be in the presence of the one who made the rock in the first place." Finn inclined his head toward Stuock, who smiled.

"I wonder if it matters what the shape is made of." Fabaris toyed with his chin braids, and Ayal found himself fingering his own braids. "The soul shines like the setting sun. Why the setting sun? Why not the sunrise, or just the sun?"

"The setting sun is orange. What shines and is orange? What?"

They both looked up at the bronze statue, gleaming golden orange in the torchlight.

?

Ayal watched as Finn laid his hands on Stuock's leg, closed his eyes, and remained still for a long time. Stuock's face contorted and his toes curled, but he had refused Ayal's offer of another wad of soma, saying it would dull his mind to the point he wouldn't be able to work his magic. After a while Stuock's face relaxed, and everyone sat, resting or talking quietly, as Finn worked.

Tcheen sat next to Ayal, put their hands on his shoulders, and began massaging, their powerful fingers sinking deep into the muscles, releasing all tension. "Are you sure you're okay? When I saw you lying there, I..."

Ayal leaned back into Tcheen and closed his eyes. "I'm fine, just fine, now." He reached back and put his hands on Tcheen's muscular legs. They flinched, and he moved his hands away from the burned parts of their upper thighs, settling on their knees. They had such a powerful body and mind, capable of such extremes of violence and tenderness. If something had happened to them during the battle, Ayal would have been utterly lost.

Food was lowered, and after everyone had eaten, Finn helped Stuock stand on his good leg, shouldering him over to the edge of the runic inlay and helping him sit close enough to study the hole. He called for a piece of wood, but no one had any on them. Tcheen offered their spear, and Stuock balked. He spoke to Tcheen in Old Maer for a moment. Tcheen nodded, holding out the spear again. Stuock turned to Ayal, speaking in Southish.

"I think the spear would work, but there are no guarantees. From what I see, as long as you don't touch the bronze with flesh or metal, the statue should not be activated. It makes sense, magically, but who knows? Then again, the staff is magical, is it not?" He repeated the words in Old Maer, and Tcheen nodded. Stuock turned back to

Ayal. "I don't know what that would do. It could be better or worse. I am not an expert in this type of magic. I doubt if any living Maer is."

"He wishes to touch the hole with my spear, to see if the statue shoots him." Tcheen's face was inscrutable, even to Ayal, who shrugged.

Tcheen motioned for everyone to clear away as they positioned their spear tip near the divot. Ayal wanted to tell them no, but Tcheen's face had hardened, and experience had told Ayal there was no way to deter them when they got like this. So he backed up, along with everyone else, held his breath, and watched as Tcheen stuck the tip of their spear into the hole. Nothing happened, but when they lifted the spear, a thin shaft of white light shot up from the hole. Tcheen jumped back, but other than the light, there was no sign of any reaction. They put the spear tip in again, and when they removed it there were two thin rays of light, bright enough to show on the ceiling above. Tcheen looked back at Ayal and motioned him over.

Ayal knelt to examine the divot. The black interior now had two irregular holes in it, where the light was coming out, as if the black were a coating that had been scraped away by the spear tip. He looked up at the tip, which had bits of black dust on it, like charcoal.

"Do it again, but this time rotate the spear, see if you can scrape more of the black coating off."

Tcheen looked at their spear tip, tested its sharpness with their fingers, then nodded and lowered the tip into the hole again, rotating it. More and more light came pouring out of, and Ayal waved Tcheen off. Wherever the spear tip had scraped, a pure white light burst forth, almost too bright to look at.

"We need sharp sticks, like a...like a small wooden knife, a tong, something a little pointy. I will go." Ayal started to stand but Tcheen pushed him back down, shaking their head and handing him the spear.

"I will go. You stay here and think." Tcheen climbed the pile of rubble and powered their way up the rope and out of the hole, returning a few minutes later with a collection of wooden utensils and sharp sticks. Ayal gave Fabaris a sheepish look, and Fabaris smiled, took the sticks, and scraped the rest of the soot away. The shaft of light from the hole lit the ceiling thirty feet above.

"Now all we need is a piece of bronze big enough to make the shape." Stuock looked around at the blank faces around him.

Finn's face lit up after a moment. "Sinnie has arrowheads made from a *Ka-lar* dagger. They should be enough." He huffed his way up the rope, and when he returned, Sinnie was with him. She laid out six arrows, popped their heads off one by one, and laid them on the floor next to Stuock, who stopped her after four.

"That should be enough. Finn, I might need some help with this."

Finn nodded, the fatigue evident in his face, and sat down cross-legged next to Stuock. They held hands while Stuock closed his other hand around the four arrowheads, looking from the blaring white of the hole to his hand. He closed his eyes, and his hand and head began to tremble. He let out a groan through gritted teeth, which grew louder between rough breaths until at last he sighed, let go of Finn, and opened his hand. He held out a gleaming chunk of bronze that looked to be the exact size and shape of the hole.

"Shining like the sunset." Fabaris held the shape up to Ayal, then to the others. Ayal nodded, watching intently as Fabaris leaned over, rotated it until it was in the correct orientation, and carefully fitted it into the hole.

Chapter:
Forty-One

F abaris lifted his hand as the bronze shape blocked the light completely, and a low hum vibrated the floor beneath him. He stood up and took a step back, his mouth dropping open as the statue moved with a high-pitched squeal of metal. It turned away from them, its limbs moving with remarkable fluidity, took two booming steps toward the door, then stopped. It took the door handle in its enormous hand and pulled, and the door came free with a screech, then swung open. The statue moved its back toward the door, let its arms hang to its sides, then stopped moving. Silence returned to the room, and not a single breath could be heard. Fabaris took the torch from Ayal, inhaled deeply, and took a step onto the runes, then another, until he stood in the massive doorway, the torchlight showing a long, wide chamber filled with shelves, tables, chairs, and pedestals. His breath caught in his throat as tears flowed down his cheeks. Ayal appeared beside him and touched him on the shoulder.

"The Archive," Fabaris whispered.

"The Opening," Ayal murmured.

?

Just inside the door was a table with four brass lamps the likes of which none of them had ever seen. There was no reservoir for fuel and no wick, only a pyramid-shaped top that could be rotated, but not removed. When they twisted the top, a dot on the top lined up with a similar dot on the lamp, and bright white light poured out of the opening, like the light from the hole in the floor outside, penetrating far into the darkness. There was a second set of double dots on the tops, and the lamps shed a circle of light when they were lined up. Two of the lamps did not seem to work, but by shining the light from one of the others into them, Fabaris could see a kind of dull, translucent crystal inside.

"I've never seen anything like it." Ayal's tone was reverent, amazed.

"Nor have I, but I've read of something like this." Stuock studied one of the broken lamps, closed his eyes for a second, and pulled the top off without effort. "It's called sunstone, or that's how it's translated in Southish. It's *brightstone* in Maer."

"*Brightstone*." Ayal repeated the word several times in Old Maer. "It is magical?"

"No, not as far as I've read. It occurs deep underground in certain places, and it shines when exposed to air. For many years, apparently, before it runs out."

"That would explain the soot coating the divot." Finn put his hand on Fabaris' shoulder, and Fabaris covered it with his own.

"We have the light. What shall we find?" Ayal's eyes glimmered as he gestured toward the seemingly endless collection before them. Fabaris slipped away from Finn's touch and followed Ayal farther into the Archive.

?

The chamber was lined with stone shelves, four long rows on either side of the room, with a series of stone tables, chairs, pedestals, and what looked like statues or sculptures farther in. The shelves were lined with bronze cylinders, each resting on neatly indented stone cradles, one on each end of the cylinders. Small brass plaques engraved with the same elaborate script as the runes were inlaid in the shelves in front of each cylinder, with larger plaques at the end of each row. The plaques and cylinders showed no corrosion, like the runes and the statue outside. There must have been some kind of ancient magic at work.

"Maps, I think, yes, maps." Ayal pointed to the plaque at the end of a row. Fabaris looked down the row, twisting the lid on the lamp to illuminate the distance. Several spots had missing cylinders, perhaps the very ones given to Karul, and to the other seed castle to the east.

"Songs, or poems, I'm not sure which." Ayal stood puzzling over the next plaque, shaking his head. Fabaris stared at the script, but the shapes refused to come together into anything comprehensible. Ayal pointed to another one. "This one's history, for sure. See this character here?" Fabaris examined the script, and he could make out letters that spelled something vaguely familiar from his studies. They walked along the ends of the other five rows, which Ayal read out loud: sacred texts, law, philosophy, nature, and the last one, which Fabaris could plainly see, *Sabra*. Magic. That word hadn't changed at all.

In the center of the chamber, between the two sets of four rows, were several dozen pedestals, each with its own cylinder and plaque. There were also sculptures and statues of all kinds, from lifelike Maer-sized statues with exquisite detail to abstract shapes and designs, including a particularly compelling Shape of the Soul, made of shining brass, the size of Fabaris' head. Four stone tables were spaced evenly along the center aisle, with perfectly even grids of lines and squares carved into their smooth surfaces.

"For making the imprints," Fabaris murmured. Ayal's head swiveled toward him, his eyes curious. "The cylinders were rolled over animal skin to make copies. I imagine the lines helped them measure and align the skins so the imprints would be straight."

"Have you seen such things before?"

"Yes, we have the cylinders for several maps at Castle Maer, and a couple of poems. I could recite them by heart, but I do not understand all of the words."

"I would like very much for you to recite one for me someday, very much."

"It would be my pleasure. I will recite them for anyone who wishes to hear. My favorite is called the Ballad of the Place Below. I know that one in Ancient Maer as well as in the modern translation. It's the story of how the Maer survived underground after the Great Betrayal."

"After the war with the humans, long ago?" Ayal waved his hands in a circle.

"Precisely."

"Funny. In our stories it is called the Great Mistake."

Fabaris gave a start; he had heard that phrase once before, and had been sworn to secrecy never to repeat it, on pain of death. "Tell me of these stories."

"It's a cautionary tale, about how the Maer long ago went to war with the humans, and when things went badly, they signed a treaty, which stopped the hostilities. But the Reckless King decided to go back on the treaty and attack the humans. And things went south from there, all the way south."

Fabaris stared at the gleaming mass of the Shape of the Soul, his head spinning with the possibilities. "Great Betrayal or Great Mistake, if a treaty was ever made with the humans, it would be here. This, as much as the *Ka-lar* scroll, is why we came. Perhaps it would be in history? What would be the word for *Treaty* in ancient Maer?"

Ayal smiled, stepped over to one of the tables, and wrote with his finger in the dust. "This is our word for it; it would likely be similar, most likely."

Fabaris studied the word for a moment, committing it to memory, then nodded. "Very well, I think I can find it if it looks anything like that. I'll take a look in the history shelves, see if anything jumps out at me."

"Yes, and I'll look on all the pedestals first, then come join you." He put both hands on Fabaris' shoulders, his eyes shining with glee. "This is the greatest thing that has ever happened to me, your coming to us. The greatest, by far."

"I can say the very same about our meeting you. Now let's get to work."

?

Fabaris found several plaques with the word *treaty* on them, but none of them stood out as different from the others. He made a mental note of their locations and went to find Ayal. On his way he saw Finn helping Stuock hobble around the magic shelves. Stuock was grinning like a child getting first pick at the banquet table, and Finn wore a sullen frown.

"I bet you wish you'd worked harder on your ancient script lessons in study, eh?" Stuock ran his finger across the words of a plaque, shaking his head. "It's been far too long for me. This...will take a while."

"More than a while. A lifetime." Fabaris briefly met Finn's gaze, looking down again as he saw the expression on Finn's face. Finn must have already guessed what was just now dawning on Fabaris. There was no way he was leaving this place. Castle Maer would have to find a new scholar, for his place was here in the Archive. He did not dare to ask himself if Finn would stay here with him. "But for now, there's the small matter of the Great Treaty to find, if it's here, which—"

He paused as he saw Ayal waving him over, his body wiggling like a nervous puppy. Fabaris bowed his excuses, avoiding Finn's eyes, and hurried over to where Ayal was standing. Before him stood a pedestal, with a line of brass around the edges and several words inlaid in brass.

"The Great Treaty." Ayal ran his fingers across the words, and Fabaris' face went numb as the words became clear. In the center of the pedestal were two stone cradles, but no cylinder.

Chapter:
Forty-Two

Finn helped Stuock over to where Ayal and Fabaris stood, slack-jawed, in front of a pedestal that was empty except for two stone cradles. Finn stretched and rotated his shoulder as Stuock let go of him and hopped over to the pedestal, running his finger over the brass plaque.

"This writing is damnably familiar, yet it eludes me." Stuock shook his head. "Agreement? Accord?"

"This is, or was, the Great Treaty." Fabaris touched each word as he said it, but Finn couldn't make heads or tails of the letters. "It would seem someone saw fit to take it with them before they sealed the place up."

"So it's out there somewhere? But in whose hands? Is it lost, or is someone keeping it secret?" Stuock's voice rose as he spoke.

"If I knew that, I—I guess we wouldn't be here. Or perhaps we would, since we still need to look for the—" Fabaris paused, exchanging an odd glance with Stuock, then turning to Ayal. "Sorry, the *Ka-lar* scroll, the one that allows one to wake the *Ka-lar* and, presumably, control it."

"This is what the *Shoza* came looking for, yes?" Ayal asked, his head cocked almost sideways.

"So we believe." Stuock grabbed Finn's shoulder and leaned on him again. For such a little guy, he was quite heavy. "I received word they were making their move, against the Great Council's wishes, or at least behind their backs, a kind of power grab. Most of the mages would be opposed, but in the *Sabrit*, the most powerful do as they wish."

"And this scroll, did you find it?" Ayal's braids clacked as his head swiveled from Fabaris to Stuock.

Stuock shook his head. "I have only scratched the surface of the *sabra* section, but nothing yet. I will need time, and of course your help, and your dragon mage as well, anyone who can be trained to read this script. I need to rest and heal before I can help make a full inventory, but if it was once here, it should still be."

"We could all use some rest." Fabaris offered his shoulder, and Stuock shuffled onto it. "We should go above and let everyone know what we found. And perhaps have a bite to eat?"

Finn gave a sigh of relief. Between breaking the rock, stabilizing Stuock's leg, and acting as a human crutch for over an hour, he was exhausted, hungry, and not a little cranky. He knew perfectly well why, but he wasn't about to admit it to anyone, let alone himself. So he played it cool as they made their way out of the Archive, helping Tcheen and Karul lift Stuock out of the round chamber on a makeshift rope harness. They emerged from the Mound in darkness and ate their fill of still-warm goat, then Finn made for the shelter on his own, though he and Fabaris had been offered one of the cabins. Many of the adults in the village had died during the battle, and the households had been rearranged to provide the best child to adult ratio, though the strain was evident on everyone. Fabaris joined Finn as he was sound asleep, sliding under the blanket and giving him a boost of needed warmth.

?

The next day at breakfast, Karul announced his intention to return to Castle Maer in two days' time. Luez said she would join him, and Sinnie glanced at Finn, her eyes hopeful. Finn looked to Fabaris, who flashed a weak smile and turned away, then squeezed Finn's hand and stood up.

"I request permission to stay." He bowed slightly toward Karul. "There is work to be done here, and I would trust this work to no one else. Ayal and I will tend to the Archive, and Stuock will stay on for a time, to study the magical holdings. Tcheen has already given their consent."

"You don't need my permission, old friend." Karul stood, his face soft, and grasped Fabaris firmly by the shoulders. "But you will be sorely missed back at the castle." He touched Fabaris' forehead with his own, and everyone stopped moving, chewing, breathing. Finn felt his heart slow to a crawl, then stop.

Fabaris sat down next to Finn, wrapping him in his arms, his tear-streaked face pressed against Finn's. "I know I can't ask you to stay, but if you would—"

Finn held him tight. "This is your place, not mine." He let his tears flow, barely noticing as the others slunk away. "I'm not sure where my place is anymore, but it's not here."

They said no more as they sat, their faces glued together, their breath mingling in the closed space formed by their interlocking bodies.

?

The entire village was assembled to see them off, decked out in all their feathery splendor. They formed two lines, and Karul walked between them, touching the outstretched hands on either side as he passed. Luez followed, also touching hands, then Sinnie, with Finn bringing up the rear. He left a little space between himself and Sinnie, in memory of Carl. When they got to the head of the line, Tcheen, Izul, and Ayal stood waiting for them, along with Fabaris, resplendent in a colorful feathered cloak like the one Ayal wore. Each of the leaders clasped shoulders with them, and Fabaris gave each of them a bracing hug. After he hugged Finn, Fabaris held him at arm's length for a moment, then leaned in to give him a long, soft kiss. Their lips stuck together for a moment in the cold before they separated, locking their teary eyes one last time, then Finn turned and followed Sinnie, dragging his leaden heart up the high pass.

?

The weather on their return trip varied between chilly and frigid, with bouts of snow and sleet slowing their progress on several occasions. They spent an entire day holed up in a cave as a blizzard howled outside, and Finn was more than glad to have Sinnie's body heat to keep him warm, though it did not help the chill growing in his heart. The worst was the slog through the mud and slush as several warmer days melted the snow just enough to turn the ground into a morass of half-frozen muck. Finn discovered, much to everyone's delight, that he could channel his energy through his hands to warm their feet at day's end, which made him terribly hungry and tired. Sinnie saw him suffering and shared part of her jerky with him, which he accepted, his ascetic regime be damned.

At Karul's suggestion, they stopped and laid offerings at the Deer Maer's burial cave, small figurines he had been carving by firelight along the way. It was hard to tell, but Finn thought one of them was supposed to be Carl, and the other Ivlana. As they squatted by the cave, talking in low voices, a figure approached from across the valley, perhaps the same shaman who had greeted them before. Karul trudged through the crunchy snow to meet him, and the two exchanged greetings, though not many words; Finn doubted if either of them could understand the other, but their gestures of friendship were clear.

When Castle Maer at last came into view, Karul let out a 'whoop' that echoed off the hills. Sinnie hugged Finn, then danced over to hug Luez, and even Karul.

"Gods, I've never been so glad to see anything in my entire life." Sinnie's smile went from her eyes to her feet, and she turned to Finn, squinting in the morning sun, a stray lock of hair blowing over her eyes.

He smiled back at her, but his heart did not leap at the sight of the castle. All he saw was a ruined fortress full of Maer he hardly knew. Without Fabaris, without Carl, the place would feel empty.

"It will be nice to have some hot food for a change. I don't know how much longer my stomach could take this diet of jerky and nuts." He tried to sound chipper, but his words rang flat.

Sinnie touched his arm, looking up into his eyes with understanding. "You miss Fabaris. I do too. And Ivlana. And Carl. Especially Carl."

They looked back up at Castle Maer, neither of them speaking for a moment. Karul was talking loudly and making oversized gestures to Luez, who was smiling, really smiling. Finn was happy for them, and he was glad their adventure was coming to an end, but there was an emptiness in his gut that went deeper than hunger.

Sinnie grabbed his arm and walked close to his side. "So what are you thinking, after we get back and rested? Are we Brocland bound?" They had talked of many things on the return journey, but they seemed to have had an unspoken agreement not to discuss the future during their trip. Sinnie flashed a quiet smile as they started walking faster to keep up with Karul and Luez, now that the end was in sight.

"I guess so." Finn squeezed her arm. "Our parents will be glad to know we're still alive. And Elder Gummache will expect a full report. Gerald Leavitt too, I should think."

"Yes, for sure. He owes me a fat bag of denri, which I will split with you, of course."

Finn waved her off. "I still don't know what to do with what we earned before."

"Well once we're back in civilization, I'm sure it will go fast. You're getting it whether you want it or not."

"Fine. What are you going to tell Leavitt? I mean, I'm sure he's on the level, but what if he's not? You don't want to say anything that could—Ow!" Finn jumped as Sinnie punched him in the arm.

"I'm not an idiot. I'll talk to Karul and Ujenn, and I'll only tell him what they want me to." She put her hand to her mouth, nibbling on her nails. "They're probably going to be pissed. Karul gave Carl the business when he found out about Carl's deal with Leavitt."

"Given what you went through for them, I bet they'll be understanding."

"Well, they'll just have to deal. Honestly, that's not what I'm most worried about."

"What then?" Finn's voice rose, softening.

"Ujenn's face. When we tell her about Carl."

"I bet she already knows. What with those copper rings and all."

?

Ujenn stood just inside the gates, with what looked like the entire population of Castle Maer standing in a semicircle around the edge of the bailey. The place was ablaze with torchlight, and the smell of roasted goat and mushrooms was thick in the air. Ujenn held the bronze-tipped rod out to Karul, who shook his head and kneeled before her. Finn could not hear what he said, but Ujenn closed her eyes and nodded, gesturing for him to stand. He moved to the side, next to Luez, and Ujenn summoned Finn and Sinnie with her chin.

Finn's legs felt wobbly as he approached. Ujenn's eyes were somber, heavy with fatigue.

"Carl is dead," she said, her voice firm. "I would have you show me how."

Sinnie looked to Finn, her eyes wet and pleading. He touched her shoulder and stepped forward, handing Ujenn the copper ring Carl had used to communicate with her.

"He fell protecting me, and Karul. The *Shoza* had attacked us just before dawn, and there were so many of them, we—"

"I said show, not tell. Follow me. In a moment." She turned to the silent ring of Maer gathered in the bailey. She held up the rod and spoke, her voice ringing loud and clear against the castle walls.

"We mourn the loss of Ivlana and Carl, who gave their lives to protect our heritage. Fabaris has chosen to remain with the Archive, to unlock and preserve its secrets, which will help us reclaim our place in the world. We have lost much, yes, but we have gained far more. We will have a lifetime to grieve the dead, but tonight, we celebrate the return of our brothers and sisters. At sundown, we feast!" Her voice rose, and the Maer cheered, their voices lifting and echoing to the mountaintop. Ujenn shot Finn and Sinnie a grim glance, and they followed her through the bailey and into the keep.

?

Ujenn's room was lit with several tapers smelling of mint and other herbs. Grisol sat on the bed next to Ujenn, touching her back, as Ujenn drank from a wooden bowl, then held it out to Finn. It was foul, bitter, and biting, but he choked it down. Ujenn rubbed oil on Finn's temples, then on her own. His head grew light, his arms heavy, and he felt as if he were somehow removed from his own mind, but still aware of it. Ujenn pulled his hands up and placed his fingers on her temples, and she put her fingers on his. His eyes closed, and he felt himself falling backwards, not in space but in time, their journey back from the Archive flashing before his eyes. He saw the Deer Maer, the driving snow, the high pass, a series of faces: Tcheen, Ayal, Digar, Fabaris, and many others. He saw the Archive, the bronze statue, the breaking of the rock, the funeral, the blur of his recovery. He was plunged back into the battle, from the beginning now: the *Shoza* jabbing him with their swords, the screams, the blows, him tumbling on the ground. He saw Carl, deflecting one sword as another came in over his shield and hit him in the neck. He saw Tcheen's face as they wrenched their spear out of the fallen *Shoza*, and then Carl, laying on the frozen ground, Finn's hands over his neck, Carl reaching for the copper ring. Carl closed his eyes as Sinnie placed the ring on his head, his face pained, but a smile fluttered over his lips for a brief moment before everything went black.

Ujenn dropped her hands to Finn's shoulders and pressed her head against his chest, her body heaving with silent sobs. Grisol kept her hand on Ujenn's back, looking up at Finn and Sinnie, her eyes wet, her expression fierce and tender at the same time.

Chapter:
Forty-Three

Ujenn took Sasha from Grisol's arms, touching noses with her. Sasha's face lit up and she kicked her chubby legs in the air. Grisol sighed and blinked her a smile.

"What do you think, warrior? She is a sturdy little thing." Ujenn touched Sasha's hairless nose with her finger. Thankfully she at least had hair on her cheeks and chin, and her little beard was coming in nicely, but the odd patches of skin around her eyes and nose had taken some getting used to. "But, with a little guidance, I think we can push her toward scholarship. With Dunil at her side she'll be trilingual in no time."

"What makes you think she won't be a mage like you?"

"I don't think it works that way, but..." Ujenn pressed her lips against Sasha's warm forehead, thinking of Carl. "Carl told me that he had the gift when he was young, but it disappeared when he became an adult." She held Sasha at arms' length, which was no easy feat, little chunk that she was. "So who knows."

"Mmm." Grisol closed her eyes, laying her head back and touching Ujenn's knee with her fingertips.

Sasha's eyes opened and closed as Ujenn swayed her gently back and forth, staying closed for a little longer each time, until at last they remained shut, and she started making that little farty snore she had. Ujenn crept over to the fur-lined basket, still swaying her. She lowered her in, then picked up the basket and continued the sway until she was sure Sasha was out.

She slid under the blanket, snuggling up to Grisol, who was doing a poor job pretending to be asleep. Ujenn could almost hear Grisol smile as she ran her hands over her body, a little curvier now than before, which was more than okay. After a moment Grisol rolled over to face Ujenn, her eyes hungry, and pulled her in for a kiss with sudden, unbridled urgency. Ujenn sank into her embrace and they wasted no time, working each other up and pushing, pushing until they collapsed in a sweaty heap, moments before the baby began to cry, yanking them from their ephemeral bliss.

?

Ujenn walked into the bailey, a cup of hot tea in her hand, before the autumn sun had chased away the tendrils of mist. Jundum knelt in the garden, checking the tender fall greens just poking through the rich soil. He smiled up at her as she broke off a stem of seedweed for the pigeons. The guards at the front gate saluted her, and she gave them a faint wave as she made her way to the roost, in no particular hurry. Once the castle came alive there would be few such quiet moments, and she relished each slow step up the stairs, the strain on her muscles, the cooing of the pigeons, the chill breeze that increased as she approached the battlements. She tossed a meager handful of seeds to the birds, who fell upon the little pile in a frenzy. Stromus spread his wings and boxed the others out until he had had his fill, then backed up and let them have the rest. She poked her finger through the cage, and he pecked it ever so gently. She slid open the door while the others were occupied, and he hopped up on her arm, nodding his black head three times before looking up at her, cocking his head this way and that.

Ujenn retrieved the note from her pocket and attached it to his leg, which he stretched out to make the job easier. She held him out to the east, pointing off down Valleys Road.

"You are Brocland bound, my sweet. Brocland." He ruffled his neck feathers and gave her a double 'coo,' then flapped off to the east, his wings squeaking fast and strong. He knew the way, having made it back when she sent him in a little cage with Finn and Sinnie when they left, but she always worried his old habit of flying west toward Stuock would take over. He flew straight and true, off toward the land of the humans, toward Sinnie, who had promised to wait until the fall equinox before heading to the Isle to meet with Gerald Leavitt.

Ujenn trusted Sinnie, despite the fact that she had kept her pact with Leavitt secret until her return from the Archive. She wasn't deceitful by nature, and she had proven her loyalty. As long as she didn't tell Leavitt any more than they had agreed, there would be no harm done. And Sinnie's relationship with Leavitt all but guaranteed he would trust the message received. As for Leavitt, she still had some doubts about him, but if Sinnie trusted him, Ujenn had little choice. She only hoped the Realm's rulers did not have designs on Castle Maer or the lands beyond.

As she returned to the bailey, Goi came running up to her.

"Ujenn, can I go down to help with the farm? I could run back for seeds, or if there's a problem, I could—"

"I believe you have Islish lessons this morning, don't you?"

"Yes, but—"

"No buts. Your studies come first. You can run down and help out in the afternoon."

Goi nodded, his face sullen. "Yes ma'am."

Ujenn put her hand under his chin. "You are very important to us. We will need your legs in the times to come. But we will also need your brain, and your tongue. If you can't speak Islish, you will be stuck in Castle Maer for your entire life, and you will never see Brocland or the lands beyond."

He smiled, turned, and ran off back toward the keep, passing Grisol on the way. Grisol had Sasha in a sling across her chest, her bow slung over her shoulder.

"I'm going to take her with me down to the farm. Pulua can help me look after her. I don't think there will be any trouble."

Ujenn nodded and smiled. "Be safe." She kissed Sasha on the top of her fuzzy head and gave Grisol a peck on the lips. The sun had crested the east wall, warming her face. She closed her eyes and inhaled through her nose, savoring the smells carried on the breeze. The heady floral scent of the wood hyacinths mixed with the odor of damp earth and oniongrass crushed underfoot. Winter would be upon them in a few months, but the farm was thriving, and they would not go hungry. There would be ups and downs, births and deaths, but it felt at long last like Castle Maer was more than just a dream. It was a home, a rock on which to build a life, a story, one that might someday be worthy of being preserved in the Archive.

Acknowledgements

This book is the result of the work of many people, and I could never have done it without them. I would like to thank:

My wife Sarah, who gave valuable critiques and endless support.

My longtime critique partner Beth Blaufuss, whose many careful suggestions helped keep me on the right path.

My faithful beta reader, cheerleader, fellow writer, and father-in-law, Tom Zaniello.

My friend Robert Rigby, and my Twitter buddy Louise Willingham, both of whom provided invaluable sensitivity insight.

My publishers, editors, and writing gurus, Jessica Moon and Mandy Russell of Shadow Spark Publishing, who helped temper the uneven edges of the manuscript. I especially want to thank Jess and Chad Moon for the amazing work they did on the cover, and Mandy for going the extra mile helping me edit and re-edit the scenes of intimacy.

My sensitivity reader, Arina Nabais, whose insightful questions and suggestions helped me understand my characters and my story better. The revisions I made based on her input make this a book I am proud to put out into the world, and wherever I have faltered in my representation, I pledge to own my mistakes and keep learning.

My mapmaker Cass Merry, whom I rather shabbily neglected to mention in the acknowledgments for Hollow Road, and whose patience and attention to detail never cease to impress me.

As always, I want to thank the brilliant, glittering hordes of the #amwriting and #amwritingfantasy Twitter communities for their constant support and inspiration.

And most importantly you, the reader. I thank you for sharing your time with me, and I hope you will join me on our next adventure very soon.

Also by Dan Fitzgerald

The Maer Cycle
Hollow Road
The Archive

About the Author

Dan Fitzgerald is a fantasy writer living in the Capitol Hill neighborhood of Washington, DC with his wife, twin boys, and two cats. When he is not writing, he might be gardening, doing yoga, cooking, or listening to French music. His debut novel Hollow Road, book one of the Maer Cycle Trilogy, came out in September 2020. The Archive is book two of the trilogy, and book three, The Place Below, is scheduled for release in March 2021.

Find out more about Dan and his books at www.danfitzwrites.com, or look him up on Twitter or Instagram, under the name danfitzwrites.